AMERICA'S MOST ACCLAIMED ROMANCE

BRENDA JOYCE

"For scorching sensuality and raw passion, Brenda Joyce is unrivaled."

—Romantic Times

CONNIE BROCKWAY

"Connie Brockway delivers!"

—New York Times bestselling author Tami Hoag

CAIT LOGAN

"Ms. Logan is one of the most popular writers in the genre."

—Romantic Times

STEPHANIE MITTMAN

"Ms. Mittman might very well be the standard against which all future Americana romance is judged."

—Affaire de Coeur

Outlaw Love

Outlaw Love

Brenda Joyce

Connie Brockway

Cait Logan

Stephanie Mittman

A DELL BOOK

Published by
Dell Publishing
a division of
Bantam Doubleday Dell Publishing Group, Inc.
1540 Broadway
New York, New York 10036

ISBN 0-440-22280-X

Printed in the United States of America

Published simultaneously in Canada

September 1997

10 9 8 7 6 5 4 3 2 1

OPM

Sundown

❧

Brenda Joyce

1

The day began just the same as always. Dawn had hardly crept over the just-awakening town of Aurora when the first cock began to crow. Emily pulled the quilt higher over her head, cocooned in an illusionary warmth because outside, she knew, it was bitterly cold. Winters came early to western Wyoming, right on the heels of bluebells and summertime.

Emily tried very hard to remain deeply asleep, in spite of all the chores awaiting her and the schoolhouse she had to open. She did not want to wake up. Not yet. Because if she did, she would remember something she did not want to recall. But the cock crowed louder. Insistently, shrilly. The fog of sleep began to lift itself from Emily's consciousness.

Emily felt it then, the vast piercing arrow of grief. *Mama.* She closed her eyes as wet heat burned her lids. It was nine months now since the funeral. Would she ever feel the way she had before her mother's death? Would she ever hear that darned cock and want to wake up? Would she ever be happy again?

From across the hall there was a loud *thump*.

Gritting her teeth, Emily threw the covers off and immediately began to shake from the cold. At least Papa was home. She hadn't heard him come in last night, even though she'd managed to wait up until well past midnight. Usually he made enough noise to wake the dead.

Emily's grief came rushing back full force. She could hardly choke down the lump of anguish rising up from her chest. She shut off her thoughts. Shivering, Emily rushed into her homespun drawers, chemise, and petticoat, choosing a well-worn blue flannel dress from the hook beside the bed. She splashed frigid water on her face from the pitcher on the bureau. As she braided her long, honey-colored hair, she avoided the looking glass on the wall. Generally speaking, she was pretty enough, although no beauty. A bit on the plain side, Emily's features were as small and even as could be, her hair neither blond nor brown but somewhere in between. Now, however, her eyes were ringed with terrible dark circles, and Emily was aware that these last few months she had aged, appearing far older than her years. She had also lost weight; most of her gowns were too big for her now. Henry Cooper had stopped courting her six months ago, and Emily, although hurt at the time, couldn't really blame him. Her grief had turned her homely, and what man wanted to take a woman who couldn't smile or laugh on a twilight buggy ride?

Emily thought that she looked like an old woman. She had turned nineteen last week.

Emily bent to retrieve her boots, then rushed from the small room she called her own. Strangely, there were no snores coming from her father's room just across the hall, and his door was ajar. Emily tried to ignore her despondency. Papa's drinking had begun way before his wife's death. Emily couldn't remember an evening when he hadn't come home even just a little bit drunk, if not thoroughly soused. Mama had always ignored his intoxication. Although it hurt Emily to see him stagger in the front door, hardly able to see or talk, she had chosen to ignore his behavior too, no matter how hard it was to do. But his drinking was getting worse. He was coming home later, neglecting the farm more. Emily had a schoolful of children to teach five days a week during most of the year. She could hardly manage the farm by herself.

Emily shoved aside the small flame of anger burning in her breast. Papa was a good man, and one day he would come to his senses and give up the bottle; Emily was certain of it. She hurried down the stairs. Her teeth chattering as she worked, Emily quickly lit the cooking fire and stoked it.

Using water drawn from the well the night before, Emily set the kettle to boiling. Throwing a thick wool coat on, she hurried outside. The tabby who'd just birthed a half dozen kittens came strolling out of the barn as Emily fetched the pail of corn for the hens and the rooster. As she scattered the meal around the chicken house, she collected a dozen eggs, trying not to worry about her father or think about her mother. Emily could hear Tess lowing in the barn, waiting to be milked.

Within ten minutes Emily had taken care of the

cow, grained down their spotted mare, and even fed the tabby. On her way back to the house she paused in the smokehouse to take a side of bacon down. Moments later she had the bacon on, the grits simmering, and was cracking the eggs into a bowl. The aroma of fresh, hot coffee began to fill up the kitchen.

She was warm now and hung up her brown coat. She glanced worriedly toward the stairs.

It was getting harder and harder to wake Papa up in the mornings. A glance at the pendulum clock ticking loudly in the parlor told her that it was six fifteen. She had to be at school in exactly one hour and fifteen minutes. Fortunately, Betsy Green would ring the school bell and start the class if Emily was late. Betsy was thirteen, exceptionally bright, and Emily knew that she guessed the reason why Emily was late so often these days.

She sighed and started for the stairs. Maybe she and Papa could have a frank talk. They had no extra money, but they needed help on the farm, even if it was only one of the boys from school for an hour or so every afternoon. Of course, if her father would give up the bottle they wouldn't need any extra help until the spring planting, and that was five months away.

Emily hesitated at the foot of the stairs. The bacon was nearly done. She was almost afraid to go up, but that made no sense, none at all.

She turned back toward the kitchen and removed the bacon from the fire, setting the pan down on the scarred wooden counter. She set the bacon out to drip. Then she turned back and started slowly up the stairs, her pulse racing a bit. She listened for the sound of her father's heavy snoring as she went up, but heard absolutely nothing.

Emily became worried. Lifting her skirts, she ran up the last few steps.

She shoved open the plank bedroom door. The bed was empty—and it was covered with blood. Emily screamed.

And then she saw him. Not Papa. A stranger. A man with midnight-black hair, lying prone on the floor, where he had fallen right out of her father's bed. His shirt, once pale blue, was not just gray with dust and dirt—it was dark brick-red. Right to his waist. Blood had already begun to stain the sheepskin lining of his leather vest.

Emily blinked and looked again. The man had long legs sheathed in buckskin pants, and slung low on *both* hips was a pair of evil-looking revolvers.

Her gaze flew upward as her heart seemed to stop. The man's complexion was dark, but somehow his skin was starkly, oddly white beneath its olive coloring.

Emily's back was against the doorjamb. *Dear Lord.* The stranger appeared to be dead. For a long moment she just stared, frozen with disbelief, her heart racing.

Then Emily regained her senses. She rushed to the stranger and knelt beside him, parting his bloody shirt. She laid her ear against his chest, holding her own breath. She had been certain he was dead, so when she realized that his heartbeat was steady and distinct, she jumped to her feet, backing away.

Emily gulped a lungful of air, realizing that she had to act, and quickly. She rushed downstairs, returning with scissors, a pan of hot water, thick clean

cloths, and a bottle of her father's whiskey. Now, as
she knelt beside the stranger, she noticed that his
chest was rising and falling, not unevenly, but slowly
and rhythmically, as if he were sleeping.

She swallowed. He was hardly sleeping, but now
she looked at his face and realized that, in spite of the
short growth of whiskers on his jaw, he was a young
man, perhaps only a few years older than she. For
just a moment she noticed his mouth, which was
full, and his nose, which was arrow-straight and set
between achingly high cheekbones.

Emily removed the vest carefully and used the
scissors to cut his shirt off. Her hand was trembling,
but she could not seem to control it. He did not stir.
A piece of the fabric was stuck to his wound, and she
used the hot water to loosen and remove it. As she
did she tried very hard to ignore his broad, bare chest
and washboard-flat abdomen. She had never seen
any man half-naked before, especially not one with
the face of an archangel and the physique of Hercu-
les.

Her thoughts were indecent, so Emily pushed
them away, increasing her concentration. The moment the piece of linen came free, the wound began
to bleed again. Emily used a wad of clean cloth to
stop the bleeding, an image of Doc Drummond appearing in her head. As soon as she had stopped the
bleeding and bandaged the wound, she would have
to go fetch him . . . wouldn't she? Of course she
would!

Of its own volition her gaze fell to the man's hips.
To the two sinister Colt revolvers holstered there.
She should get the sheriff too.

When the bleeding had stopped, Emily removed

the now-red rag and lifted up his shoulder. Kneeling, she peered beneath him at his back and was rewarded by the sight of a small, clean exit wound. She released him and uncorked the whiskey. She did not hesitate, pouring the alcohol over the wound.

He cursed explosively. Before Emily could react, his hand was on her wrist and he had jerked her down to the floor and underneath him. His body covering hers was big and hard, and the ice-cold barrel of one of his revolvers was pressed firmly against her temple.

"Don't move," he said, his mouth against her cheek. His hot breath feathered her ear. "Move and you're dead," he said.

2

Emily was so terrified that she forgot to breathe.

He cursed, using the *F* word, which she had heard Billy Martin utter several times and had reprimanded him thoroughly for. But this man was not eleven years old. He was closer to thirty and, in spite of his wound, incredibly strong. Emily began to shiver. Her teeth chattered loudly. She was pinned to the floor like a goose about to be trussed up for Christmas dinner.

"Jeeesus," he growled, rolling off her abruptly. But Emily was not free. He sat up, still gripping her wrist so roughly that Emily knew it would soon turn black and blue. She looked up into a pair of blazing amber eyes. Still lying on her back, Emily did not dare move. Especially as he continued to point the gun right at her face.

His expression changed. His startling eyes widened, losing their raw fury, and then he glanced around the room. "Jesus," he said again. His gaze returned to her, moving over her from head to toe and then back up again. Emily's fear increased. Her heart lurched with dread.

Sweat trickled down his temple. His glance moved to the hole in his own chest. He stared at the wound. Emily stared at the gun.

He suddenly seemed to realize their predicament. His sharp, intense eyes returned to Emily, then to the pile of bandages not far from her shoulder. His eyes narrowed. "Hand me that bottle."

Although she was more frightened than she had ever been in her entire life, Emily said hoarsely, "I can't."

His burning eyes jerked to hers. Incredulous.

She licked her lips. "You're breaking my wrist."

He released her immediately. And he moved the gun slightly so that it pointed down, somewhere in the vicinity of Emily's knees.

"Are you going to shoot me?" Emily heard herself ask in a croaking tone of voice.

"No."

Their gazes collided. His eyes still burned. He was, Emily realized, far more than an outlaw—he was a desperado. For desperation was clearly etched upon his chiseled black countenance. "May I sit up?"

His nod was abrupt.

Emily began to breathe again, although now she was perspiring profusely. Slowly she sat up. She noticed that his wound had not started bleeding again. Not that she cared.

Afraid to stand, Emily crawled on all fours and retrieved the bottle. As she turned, she caught him staring at her. Her cheeks flamed.

His expression was impossible to read. His eyes had become singularly hard. "Bring it here," he said.

Emily did as he asked, still on all fours. Although he snatched the bottle from her, his gaze never wavered from her face. And his gun realigned itself, now pointing in the vicinity of Emily's chest. He lifted the bottle and tossed back what had to be a glassful. Whiskey streamed down his chin and ran down his chest.

Emily watched a rivulet race down his tightly indented abdomen to the waistband of his breeches, where it disappeared.

She lifted her eyes and saw him watching her. The corners of his mouth seemed to lift slightly, but not in a particularly friendly fashion. He held up the bottle. "I'll share."

Emily shook her head. "I don't drink."

His gaze, somewhat warm now, slid over her. "I'll bet you don't."

Emily lifted her chin. Had he just insulted her?

This time he slashed a cold smile at her. A smile that did not reach his golden eyes. Cougar eyes, Emily realized. He reminded her of a dangerous mountain lion, made her feel as if he were stalking her, intent on mauling her to death. Emily swallowed. "Mister," she whispered, "I'm going to be late. I have to get to school."

He smiled, without mirth. "Like hell. You're too old to go to school."

Trying to sound dignified and trying not to be hurt, Emily said, "I'm the teacher."

His eyes narrowed. A silence passed, and then he said, "Bet all the boys fancy you, now, don't they?"

Emily backed away on her rear end, amazed by his

statement, her bosom heaving. She felt the flush on her cheeks. "Are you making fun of me?"

"No." He drank from the bottle again, lifting the revolver as he did so, aiming it at her head. When he set the whiskey down, he said, "I didn't tell you that you could go."

Emily became motionless. She was sweating buckets, her underclothes were wet, and even her flannel dress was starting to stick to her like a second skin. "What do you want?"

"I want you to help me." His gaze met hers. He used the revolver to gesture at the bandages.

"And afterward?" Emily whispered.

"We'll see," he said. His golden eyes held hers.

And for one long moment Emily was mesmerized, unable to look away. When she did, Emily clenched her fists and stared at the rag rug she sat on. It hit her hard then. She was in the clutches of a madman, a dangerous outlaw, one with a gun he wasn't afraid to use—a gun he had undoubtedly used before. What if he didn't let her go after she had bandaged him up? The thought was so horrible that Emily shoved it aside.

She looked at the gun in his hand, then at the empty holster on his right thigh. Her gaze moved immediately to the sister gun tied to his other thigh. And in the course of her perusal she noticed that his buckskin pants gloved him quite indecently.

She flushed, ripping her gaze away to anywhere but there, where she certainly had no right looking. Flustered, dry-mouthed, even light-headed, her gaze lifted, only to collide with his. He cursed very softly, a wave of guttural sound that rolled over Emily in warm, sensuous waves.

"You seem to know what to do, so do it," he said harshly.

Very cautiously now, her hands shaking, Emily cut strips of cloth and laid them out, refusing to even glance at him. One thought drummed through her head. How could she possibly bandage him? She was going to have to wind the strips fully around his chest and back. Which meant that she would have to put her arms around him—she was going to have to touch him. Emily was certain that she would faint if she touched him that way. She wished that she hadn't cut off his shirt.

"Hurry up," he growled.

"I'm going as fast as I can," Emily retorted sharply. Then she realized how tart she had been, and her glance jerked to his dark face. He was scowling—and drinking more whiskey.

Emily prayed that he would pass out.

"You ready?" he queried, waving the gun at her.

She inhaled, for courage. "Maybe you should put that gun away."

He smiled. "I don't think so." Using the gun, he waved her toward him.

Perspiration pooled between her breasts. Emily sidled over to him, bandages in hand. She refused to meet his eyes again and, instead, stared at his hard chest. Another rivulet of whiskey was meandering down one thick slab of muscle, past one erect, copper-colored nipple. I will not faint, Emily told herself very firmly.

She knelt beside him, holding up a strip of linen; then, boldly, she pressed it against his chest.

He tensed, grunting.

Emily looked up and saw the pain in his eyes.

"I'm sorry," she whispered. She was acutely aware of the fact that not even an inch separated their bodies and that he felt hard and warm and vitally male beneath her fingertips, even through the bandage she held in place.

"Hurry it up."

Emily nodded, flushed, winding the strip around his back. As she did so her breast brushed his arm. She prayed he hadn't noticed, her own body laced with new tension and nervousness. As she knotted the linen she kept her eyes downcast. Her pulse raced alarmingly.

When she was almost finished he shifted, and his upper arm brushed her breast again. Emily jerked away, shocked by the rush of sensation contact with him had caused. Henry Cooper's kisses had never affected her in such a way. Of course, those had been chaste little pecks on the corners of her mouth. And Emily had the horrible suspicion that The Outlaw bumped into her on purpose. Which made him reprehensible as well as dangerous.

Of its own volition, her gaze skidded to his. He was unsmiling, staring at her.

Emily was paralyzed.

"Thank you," he said roughly.

Emily realized he had put the gun down. But before she could assimilate this, the front door slammed. "Papa," she gasped.

The exclamation wasn't even out of her mouth when he had seized her arm and dragged her up against his body. "Is this his room?" he demanded.

Emily nodded, incapable of speech. The barrel of his revolver was pressing into her shoulder.

"Strip the bed," he said. "Now."

Emily rushed to obey. She tore the bloodstained sheets and quilt off, fighting down her terror. When she was finished he gestured her out of the room, the bundle still in her arms. Emily started to protest.

He grabbed her shoulder and kicked open the door to her bedroom. Then he pushed her forward, inside.

Emily's eyes widened.

"It's just the two of you, right?" he asked, low.

"Y-yes," Emily managed.

He nudged the door closed with the toe of one dusty black boot. "He ever come into your room?"

Emily was becoming dazed. "Papa?" she squeaked.

"Yeah. Your daddy."

She shook her head, beginning to tremble.

"You listen to me and you listen good," he said. "I need a place to heal up, and this is it. Do you understand?"

Emily did not blink. Her heart sank like a boulder. "Yes."

"Good." He was savage. "Now, I'm a mean son-uvabitch. You understand that?"

She nodded, wetting her lips.

"I'm wanted in three states. For killing three men. You got that?" he demanded.

Emily, on the verge of tears, nodded. "Yes," she whispered.

"I can kill again, in the blink of an eye. I've got nothing to lose." His brilliant amber eyes bored into hers.

Emily nodded, a tear finally spilling down her cheek.

"You go downstairs and do whatever it is you have

to do. But you don't say a word to your pappy about me or he's dead. And you don't say a word to anyone else either, 'cause the result will be the same. If anyone comes here looking for me, your daddy is dead. And maybe you too. Is that clear?"

Emily choked down a sob.

"And forget about school. Not today. Today you're staying home—where I can watch you."

Emily was shaking violently, hugging herself, tears falling now of their own accord. "I have to make Papa breakfast."

"You go do that." His gaze was hard. "Just remember what I told you and we'll get on just fine." He stared.

Emily nodded.

Using the gun, he gestured for her to go.

Emily waited one instant, and then she fled.

3

Outside her bedroom door Emily paused to wipe her eyes. She fought for courage and calm. But how could she find her equilibrium when an outlaw was holed up inside her bedroom—and intent on staying there? *Dear, dear Lord.* He had threatened to kill both her and her father. Emily swallowed hard.

"Em!"

Emily hurried down the stairs. She pasted a smile on her face. "Good morning, Papa." She suddenly realized that her father hadn't come home last night. "Papa." Her tone changed. "Where did you sleep last night?"

Gus Anderson turned away from the door where he'd hung up his coat, his movements slow, exaggerated. His eyes were red. He was a husky man who looked every one of his fifty years. "Fell asleep in town." He looked away, sheepish. "Sorry, Em."

Oh, Papa, Emily thought, wanting to cry. She moved forward, trying hard not to think about the outlaw upstairs. "Come, sit. Let me fix you breakfast."

Her father heaved himself into a chair. "You're such a good girl, Em. What would I do without you?"

Emily began cracking eggs into the frying pan, her back to her father. Tears slipped down her cheeks. She imagined that the outlaw was listening to their every word. She was trapped, frightened, but she was also angry. "You don't have to worry, Papa. I'm not going anywhere."

"One day you'll marry and move out," Gus grunted.

The aroma of the frying eggs soon filled the kitchen, and Emily poured her father a mug of coffee. When she handed it to him she was smiling. She forced extreme cheerfulness into her tone. "I don't think so, Pa. What man would want an old maid like me? And what would my children do?"

"You're hardly an old maid, Em. And the good folk of Aurora can find another teacher, though not one like you." Gus sipped the coffee, then choked. "Em! You're gonna be late for school today!"

Emily slid the eggs onto a plate, added five strips of bacon, and set the plate down in front of her father. She quickly sliced a hunk of cornbread and threw it in the frying pan, heating it in the sizzling bacon fat. "I don't feel well today, Papa," she said as she forked the bread onto her father's plate. "I'm not going to school today." An image of the dark outlaw filled up her mind. As did the eleven freshly scrubbed faces of her pupils.

Her father paused in the act of lifting a forkful of

eggs to his mouth. He turned and stared. "You *never* miss school. That school is your *life*."

Emily flushed. "I had a fever this morning. Look at me. I'm soaked to the skin."

Her father regarded her closely as Emily plucked at her damp flannel dress. "Then you'd better go lie down."

Emily's heart leapt. "I was changing your bed. Let me finish up here in the kitchen, do your room, and then I'll rest a spell." Oh, Lord, she thought frantically. Was she going to have to spend the day in her room pretending to be ill—while keeping company with the outlaw? How would she endure it? How would she survive?

It flitted through Emily's head that if she was exceedingly brave—and terribly clever—she might get the jump on him. Instantly Emily dismissed the notion. What was she going to do? Barrel upstairs with her daddy's possum rifle? Or worse, try to take him on with a kitchen knife? She'd wind up dead, for sure. Even wounded he was incredibly strong. Emily didn't think she would ever forget the hot, hard strength of his body when he had pinned her to the floor.

"You want me to go down to the school and dismiss the class?" Gus asked.

Emily turned away from her father so he wouldn't see all the blood draining from her face. She did not want to be alone with the outlaw. But she had no choice. "I guess so," she said hoarsely.

"You know, you don't sound good. Maybe I should get Doc Drummond too." Her father began shoveling the food down.

"No!" Emily forced her voice down. "I think the

worst is over. Just dismiss the school. I'll be fine if I rest up today."

Gus shoved his plate aside, sighing. "All right. If you say so, Em." He stood. "You should know. Like your ma, you are." He smiled at her. "Sensible and always right."

Hugging herself as a chill entered her heart that matched her thoroughly chilled body, Emily walked him to the door. "Thanks, Pa."

He planted a kiss on her cheek. "Now go lie down."

Emily nodded.

Raphael felt the hammers banging inside his head as he stood at the bedroom door, which he had cracked open to listen to the conversation taking place downstairs in the kitchen. Accompanying the hammers was a burning pain that seemed to go arrow-straight through his chest and back. His tongue was thick, his mouth dry. He was in bad shape, but he'd been in worse shape plenty of times and had always survived. Nine lives, a gypsy woman had once said. So far, he figured, he'd used up about ten of them.

He'd chosen the Andersons' because the old man was a drunk, the girl a spinster. For a while he'd be safe.

It all came back to him then: riding like a bat out of hell, knowing old Harrison wanted to kill him— with good reason—his horse breaking his leg, and that gut-wrenching moment when Raphael had had to put the barrel of his Colt up against Sarge's head. Even now he felt a stabbing of grief as he thought about his dead mount. He'd bartered two pack ponies and a mustang for the big gray from a Sioux warrior a half dozen years ago, and never had he regretted it. Sarge had been one of the best horses he'd ever had. Bighearted, which was what counted. And Raphael should know, considering his father had raised the finest horseflesh in the East, and maybe still did.

Harrison was not going to look for him here. When Raphael had put Sarge out of misery he'd had minutes to decide what to do, where to go. On foot, bleeding badly, and being pursued, he'd immediately decided on the Anderson farm. In the past month that he'd been working on the Harrison ranch, he'd done his homework, knew all about everyone who was a resident in Pitkin County. And he'd been only a half mile from their farm too. Luck, it seemed, was with him once again.

Raphael figured he needed a day or two to recover, and then he'd have to slip into town. In the meantime, the girl could take care of him. Guilt slid over him then. He didn't like scaring her, but he'd had no choice. Not when Harrison and his allies meant business—and their aim was to swing him from a tall tree at the end of a rope.

Of course, little Emily Anderson was a lot tougher than she looked. She ran the school like a middle-aged matriarch, just the way she ran her home, yet all the children loved her. Now he saw why. Clearly she did not have a mean bone in her small body. And running the farm almost single-handedly was no simple task. Raphael was well aware of the fact that her life had been especially difficult these past two years, as her mother wasted away with consumption. Indeed, the entire town was extremely

fond of Emily Anderson. He'd heard her name mentioned numerous times, even at the whorehouse.
Despite the recent loss of her mother and her father's
drinking, no one seemed to feel sorry for her. Even
the working girls liked and admired her.

Raphael moved slowly toward the bed. He sat
down hard, the strong smell of fresh coffee and sizzling bacon seeming to follow him. His stomach
groaned. Which was a good sign.

Then the steps creaked as she came up them. His
entire body tensed. He did not move.

He heard her enter her father's room. A few moments later he heard her snapping sheets. She was
making up the bed he'd bloodied so thoroughly.

He listened to her tidying up, until compulsion
made him stand. Stifling a groan, he walked to the
door, opening it soundlessly. Emily's bedroom faced
west and thus was dimly lit, but her father's faced
east. The door to his bedroom was open, the curtains pulled aside, the windows cast wide. Sunlight
flooded the room and hall. For one moment
Raphael could take his fill, knowing she was entirely
unaware of his presence.

Curiosity made him stare at her face through half-
closed eyes. She was not his type of woman, of
course—he preferred fleshy, flashy ladies of the
night—but his heart seemed to lurch at the sight of
her. She had cared for him, even if at gunpoint, and
any fool could see that she was as pretty as she was
good. Although she was small, her body was intrigu-
ing, pleasingly curved in all the right places. The
kind of body that would fit just about any man real
good. He couldn't help but wonder what her age
was. She looked all of fifteen. He knew she was close

to twenty. She'd even called herself an old maid. For some odd reason her self-disparaging remark had made him angry then, just as remembering it made him angry now.

She turned to leave the room. It was at that moment that she saw the saddlebags he'd carried with him after leaving Sarge dead on the trail. He had dropped them beside the bed. Raphael remained motionless, regarding her intently. She hesitated, and he could feel her mind working, feel her fighting her ethics. She finally bent. Raphael did not smile, but watched her place the bags on the bed and quickly open them. Her hands were shaking. She gasped.

He almost smiled then. Curiosity could kill the cat. But not in this case.

And because he knew what his saddlebags contained—a few necessary items and several thousand dollars in freshly minted greenbacks—he turned away silently, moving back to her bed.

A moment later she appeared in the bedroom doorway, her face pale, her eyes accusing. Raphael lay on the bed, but he met her gaze calmly. She stared.

He wondered why she was so upset. He'd already confessed to being a cold-blooded killer. So what did it matter if he was also a thief? Unless she hadn't believed him in the first instance.

Their eyes held.

"I'm hungry," he finally said.

She came to life. "You must be feeling better." She marched forward and tossed the saddlebags onto the bed, beside his hip. "I found these in Papa's room."

He kept his face expressionless. "They're mine. Thanks."

"I'll fetch breakfast," she said abruptly. She flew from the room.

Raphael leaned back against her pillow, which smelled strongly of woman and lavender bathwater. Something seemed to stir below his belt. He was disgusted with himself.

A few minutes later she came upstairs carrying a tray that contained enough food to feed four men. Raphael hid a smile as she approached and placed the tray on the bed beside his saddlebags. She thought him an outlaw, a killer, and a thief, but she wasn't going to let him starve. He held her gaze. "Smells real good."

She nodded, a slight tinge of pink appearing on her cheekbones. "Do you need help?"

He didn't. But he couldn't seem to get the words out.

Her jaw tight, she reached behind him. Raphael did not breathe as she pushed a second pillow behind the first, then slid her arm beneath him. He could not tear his gaze away from her face, which momentarily was inches from his. Her color higher now, she grunted and propped him upright.

Then she plopped the tray on his lap. "I'm sure you can handle a knife and fork by yourself," she said tartly.

He couldn't help it. "I don't know. I'm a lefty. My left hand is useless with this wound."

She toyed with her apron.

His stomach chose that moment to growl loudly again. He wondered if she would figure out his game. Any man who wore two guns could use two hands.

Pursing her mouth, Emily came and sat down beside him. Raphael couldn't help wondering what he was doing, playing games with her, a spinsterish virgin. But he didn't come into contact with a woman like this very often. No good woman had ever catered to him, and he was enjoying every moment of their interaction.

She stabbed the eggs. Guilt won and he caught her wrist. "I can do it."

She froze. "It's all right. I—"

Hoofbeats sounded outside.

Raphael was on his feet, gun in hand—his right hand—and at the window overlooking the front yard before Emily or any human being could blink. She cried out, her tone accusing. He ignored her, peering outside from behind the muslin drapes.

"It's just Papa," she said, standing, hands fisted and on her hips. "You're not badly hurt!"

"It's not your daddy. Different horse, younger, stronger," he said. His pulse accelerated as he recognized Lloyd Harrison astride his buckskin gelding.

"You can see all that?" Emily asked, amazement written all over her face.

He wheeled, his heart pounding now. He reached her in a stride and seized her arm, hard. "Go downstairs. You haven't seen anyone or anything unusual. I'm going to be listening to your every word."

She nodded, her eyes wide, frightened, and glued to his face.

"Just remember," he said, shaking her once. "Harrison is no match for me. And you don't want his blood all over your conscience."

"I understand," she croaked.

"Good." He released her as Harrison pounded on the front door. "Go and greet him, and while you're at it, put a smile on your face."

Emily left, tripping in her distress and haste.

4

Wiping her hands on her blue apron, Emily ran to the front door. Her heart was beating so hard that she felt light-headed and dizzy.

At the door she paused, trying to compose herself, or at least her features. But she was scared. She had an image of blood all over her kitchen floor.

"Gus! Gus Anderson! You home?"

Emily opened the door, recognizing Lloyd Harrison's voice. Harrison owned a ranch half the size of Pitkin County, and he was Aurora's most important and wealthy citizen. In fact, he was the authority the townsfolk of Aurora turned to in times of crisis, self-appointed though he was.

Emily had little doubt that the outlaw she was hiding was the reason for Harrison's visit. She opened the door, managing to smile. "Good morning, Mr. Harrison. What brings you way out here?"

Harrison didn't dismount. As usual, he was riding one of the finest pieces of horseflesh Emily had ever seen, a big, deep-chested buckskin. Emily walked across the porch, laying her palm on the gelding's dark, soft muzzle. Her own piebald mare was four-teen years old this year. Her hand was shaking quite visibly.

"Mornin', Miss Emily. Sorry to be disturbin' you folks." His expression was grim. "Your father around?"

Emily scratched the horse's chin, reminding her-self to breathe. "Papa went to the school. I had a touch of fever this morning, so I decided to stay home. He should be back very soon." As soon as the words were out she wanted to kick herself, hard. She didn't want Harrison lingering and waiting for Gus to return.

"Goddarnit," Harrison exploded.

Emily was too distraught to protest his use of the Lord's name.

"Sorry, Miss Em, but I got a scoundrel to catch. You ain't seen a Texian around these parts? One bleedin' like a stuck pig? One as dark as sin and just as dangerous?"

Emily's heart sank. She thought about the out-law's saddlebags, chock full of greenbacks. Had the outlaw stolen the money from Harrison? What kind of fool was he? Her gaze darted to her left. Just above her left shoulder was her bedroom window. She knew he stood there listening to their every word. And he was hardly a fool.

"Course not," she said. "I haven't seen hide nor hair of anyone, much less a dark Texian bleeding like a stuck pig." She was perspiring heavily again. After this encounter was over she would have to bathe. But how, exactly, could she accomplish that with

the darned outlaw hiding in her room? And did this
make her an accomplice to his crimes? Did this make
her a thief—a murderer?

Suddenly Harrison shifted. "There he is," he
grunted in satisfaction.

Emily stiffened. For one instant she thought Harrison had seen the outlaw standing at her bedroom
window. And then she realized her mistake.

Their old paint mare trotted into the yard with
her father on its back. Harrison waved at him. Relief
came and went, leaving dismay in its wake. Her tension spiraled. She hid her shaking hands in the pockets of her apron. Darn that outlaw! Why couldn't he
have barged into someone else's home to hide?

"Howdy, Lloyd. Good to see you," Gus said as he
pulled up beside the rancher. "Come on inside and
set a spell. Em makes the best breakfast this side of
the Sweetwater."

"Can't." Harrison's tone was flat. "I was just telling your daughter that I'm tracking a man. He's
wounded too, maybe real bad. I know he's close by.
Found his horse with a busted leg just a mile down
the road. The sonuvabitch is smart—oh, 'scuse me,
Miss Emily. He must've used that Injun trick to dust
his trail clean, cause neither me nor the sheriff could
find a single footprint, blast his hide. But there was
blood all over the saddle. I knew I'd got him too.
He's dangerous, Gus. You make sure to keep a sharp
lookout, 'specially with a fine little lady like your
daughter here."

"I ain't seen no one, Lloyd, 'cept the kids at Emily's school."

Emily kept her hands jammed in her pockets. Her

heart was pounding with explosive force. "Beg pardon, Mr. Harrison, but what *did* this man do?"

Harrison turned a piercing gray stare upon her. "He stole from me, that's what he did, Miss Emily. I took him on, gave him work, paid him, and fed him. Took him right under my roof, I did, for an entire month, and he was so smooth he had me likin' him, he did. And Veronica too. We had him up to the house a half dozen times for supper. But you know what? I thought something was wrong, deep in my belly, I did. Now I'm sure he's one of them boys in the Whiskey Peak gang. Maybe even the leader. When I catch him, I swear, I'll string him up myself." Harrison grunted.

Emily shivered, stepping away from the buckskin. The Whiskey Peak gang had been rustling Pitkin County cattle for over two years now, and no one had been able to bust them up. What kind of man, she wondered, accepted employment and hospitality, then stole from his employer and host? Emily said dryly, "Mr. Harrison, a man is innocent until proven guilty. Surely you would not take the law into your own hands?"

"Don't you go preaching at me!" Harrison shouted.

Emily jumped.

Harrison recovered his temper, but his eyes were hard. He tipped his hat. "Now, Miss Emily. Why don't you skedaddle on inside and let me have a private word with your pappy?" His smile was superficial.

Emily nodded, forcing her own smile, knowing the rancher was not one to be disobeyed. She left the two men outside, but as she closed the front door she

listened hard to their muted voices. Harrison was
doing most of the talking, and unfortunately Emily
could not decipher a single word he said. Somewhat
guiltily, Emily went to the window and glanced out
to see the rancher talking and gesturing very fervently. She watched her father glance quickly toward
the house. Emily jumped away from the window,
certain that he had seen her.

What else had the outlaw done? Emily had a distinct feeling that it was worse than robbing Harrison
blind and stealing a few head of cattle—and that was
bad enough.

She wondered if he'd killed someone else, someone in Aurora, someone she knew—and the thought
made her sick.

Emily avoided her bedroom all that day.

Fortunately her father spent the afternoon fixing
the south fence, so he hadn't witnessed the fact that
she was as healthy as a horse. Emily had done every
house chore she could think of, then made up a half
dozen more.

She had laundered her father's bloodstained
sheets, beat the parlor rugs, and set a potted roast to
simmering. She had even washed the outlaw's sheepskin vest, removing the bloodstains. All day long she
worried about the upcoming night. Where was she
going to sleep?

Certainly not in her bedroom with a man who
was not her husband, a man who was not just a
stranger but a self-confessed murderer and a thief.

Her heart felt as if it were wedged in her throat.
Emily had never been so nervous. As she and her
father sat down to supper, all she could think about

was the dilemma facing her. She hadn't eaten a thing all day, but her nerves were stretched so tight that she could not get more than a forkful of beef down now. Emily got up to clear the table.

"You still sick, Em? You're awfully white," Gus said, lighting up his pipe.

Emily pumped water into the sink. "I'm a bit under the weather," she said, not exactly lying.

Her father stood, scraping back his chair. "I'm going out for a while."

Emily froze.

"I promise not to be too late."

Emily's heart raced with alarming speed. "Papa . . ." She couldn't think of a thing to say. But she did not want to be home alone with that outlaw, dear Lord, no. "Papa, what about the killer outlaw in these parts? The one Harrison was hunting."

"He must be long gone by now. Besides, the man's a rustler, nothing more."

"How do you know?" Emily asked fearfully.

Gus patted her back, then shrugged on his woolen coat. "Harrison didn't say anything about this Raphael Caldwell doin' nothin' more than stealing some money and his stock. Course, that's bad enough, and one day he'll swing for sure." At the door Gus paused, giving Emily a long look. "No one said he's a killer. Em, you *always* champion the underdogs. How come you're judging a man you never met?"

Emily shrugged, smiling stiffly. "Guess Harrison just scared me," she said softly.

"Don't you worry none. Now, get to bed so you won't disappoint your children tomorrow."

Emily nodded. Gus left. The front door slammed hard behind him, and a moment later Emily heard the piebald's hoofbeats cantering out of the yard. Slowly Emily turned and faced the stairs.

Raphael smiled at her.

Emily's heart seemed to skip an entire handful of beats.

He came down the stairs. Emily suddenly flushed. He had donned the spare shirt she had seen in his saddlebags, a red plaid, but he had not bothered to button it. Emily was faced with an expanse of his hard, slabbed chest and flat, indented abdomen. The dark hair dusting his chest arrowed right down his torso, disappearing into the waistband of his buckskin pants. The outlaw was wearing his guns.

"Wh-what do you want?" Emily whispered, dragging her eyes upward to his dark, chiseled face.

"I haven't eaten since this morning." His golden gaze was piercing. "If you don't mind, Miss Emily?"

For one more minute Emily stared, and he stared back, almost defiantly. Then he said softly, "You did just fine today, Miss Emily."

As if it were her cue, Emily rushed across the kitchen to the stove, circling around him as she did so, while he sat down in her father's chair. Breathing hard, she ladled the potted roast, some carrots, parsnips, and onions onto a plate, adding a hunk of white bread. She stole a glance at him as she worked and caught him studying her. Emily almost dropped the plate. He averted his eyes.

She set the plate in front of him. "Coffee?"

"Please." He began to eat, fast, like someone famished.

Emily moved the coffee in its tin pot onto the fire

to heat it. She stole another glance at him. It was warm in the small kitchen, and she was acutely aware of the fact that they were together and alone. Why did her father have to go out, tonight of all nights? Emily despaired.

Emily handed him a mug of hot coffee. Her hands were shaking. As soon as she set the mug down he caught her wrist. Emily cried out. Their gazes locked.

"I'm not going to hurt you," he said quietly. "You don't have to be so afraid."

"I'm not afraid," she said, lying.

He smiled suddenly. A real smile, an amused one, one that lit up his eyes. Emily was incapable of movement. He still gripped her wrist. But gently.

"I'm not going to hurt you," he repeated firmly. "I just need another day or two to recover my strength."

Slowly Emily nodded.

He studied her, finally releasing her. Emily backed away until her rump hit the counter. She swallowed and managed to ask, "What about tonight?"

He resumed eating. "What about tonight?"

His tone was very casual, unconcerned. Emily watched him eat. His profile was actually perfect. "We can't sleep together in my bedroom," Emily said very hoarsely.

He laid his knife and fork down and stared at her. "We can and we will."

Emily inhaled.

"I already said I won't hurt you." His jaw was flexed. Suddenly he was on his feet. And he was six feet tall, towering over Emily. His presence seemed to fill up the entire room. "You can even take the bed." His tone was sarcastic. "I'll sleep on the floor."

Emily wanted to protest. But she couldn't form the words.

He seemed angry. He gestured at the sink. "Finish the dishes. I'll wait."

She could not believe what was happening. "The barn. Why don't you sleep there?"

"Because I trust you about as much as you trust me," he said flatly.

5

As if he was afraid she might bolt and run, he held her elbow firmly as they went upstairs.

Emily's breathing was shallow. She was filled with disbelief and dread.

They entered her bedroom. Emily jerked when he shut the bedroom door behind them. Her eyes wide, she watched him set the kerosene light down and cross the room, taking one of the pillows off the bed. He tossed it on the floor.

She hugged herself, unmoving.

He crossed the room, taking the throw from her single wooden chair. Not looking at her, he lay down on the rag rug on the floor, pulling the wool throw up to his shoulders. Emily stared.

His eyes were closed. "Would you close the light, please?"

Emily did not answer. She walked around to the far side of her bed and climbed up on it. With her back to him, she took off her boots, but not her

stockings, and certainly not anything else. As she settled under the covers she realized that her bed
smelled of horses and leather and whiskey and man.

As she reached for the lantern her gaze settled on
his face. If anyone ever found out about this she was
ruined.

His lashes did not even flutter. Emily couldn't
help but stare. His eyebrows were thick, slashing. His
cheekbones were high and prominent. His nose was
aristocratic and straight. And his mouth was slightly
parted. There was a cleft on his chin.

He might be an outlaw and a killer, but he was a
very attractive man. In fact, Emily had never seen
such a striking man before. Just gazing at him made
her heart flutter.

Surely he was not already sleeping. Emily knew
she was not going to sleep one wink that entire
night, not with him lying half an arm's length away
from her. But before she could lift the dome off the
lantern and blow out the wick, his eyes opened and
he stared directly up at her.

Emily blushed. There was something very com-
pelling about the intensity in his amber eyes.

"If you want company, all you have to do is say
so," he said in a very soft, sensuous drawl.

Emily gasped when she understood his meaning.
"No! I most certainly do not want *company*!"

Giving her a look that seemed to smolder, he
turned onto his side with a grunt of pain, putting his
back to her. "Then turn out the light and think
about something else."

"I don't know what you mean," Emily said, this
time dousing the light. Her tone sounded high and
oddly breathless to her own ears. And the image of

his dark, intriguingly sculpted face remained there in her mind. She kept seeing those brilliant golden eyes, that full, mobile mouth. Emily curled up around the pillow.

What, she wondered, would it be like to be kissed by such a dark, dangerous man?

And she was shocked at herself. Ladies did not entertain such thoughts. Not ever. Emily screwed her eyes closed. But she failed to find sleep—just as she failed to turn off her treacherous thoughts.

Emily hardly slept that night. And the first thing she saw when she awoke was a pair of brilliant amber eyes, trained directly upon her. Raphael sat in her bedroom's single chair, staring at her—apparently watching her while she slept.

Fortunately the covers were up to Emily's chin. She stared back at him, wide-eyed, flushing.

"Good morning," he said.

"It is hardly a good morning," Emily said breathlessly. "How long have you been watching me?"

Instead of denying it he said, "About an hour."

Emily threw off the covers and slid from the bed, only to realize her predicament. She had to wash and change her clothes. There were no ifs, ands, or buts about it. "You're going to have to give me some privacy."

He stood, and if the movement hurt him he gave no sign. Not answering her, he walked over to the window, putting his back to her.

Emily comprehended then that he was not going to leave her room. "My father is still asleep, passed out cold, I am sure. Go downstairs!"

"Just do what you have to do and hurry it up."

He did not face her. His shoulders seemed impossibly broad—and very rigid. "I've seen plenty of naked women before. And even if I were tempted, you're not exactly my type."

His words struck Emily with brutal force. She should not be hurt that he found her plain and unappealing. She should be relieved. But tears seemed to burn behind her eyelids.

Emily, her hands shaking, began to undo the buttons down the front of her dress. Suddenly she stopped. She could not disrobe with him in the same room; she could not.

He cursed, spun around so quickly that she was startled, and strode past her and out of the room. Except for the creak of her door as it opened, he did not make a sound. Emily wondered where he was going to hide. Meanwhile, she could hear her father snoring from across the hall. Somewhat bitterly she wished her father were up and about to discover the outlaw's presence on their farm. But then, of course, Caldwell would kill them both—or would he?

Very rapidly, Emily stripped, bathed with the cold water left in the pitcher on her washstand, and dressed in a gingham dress. She hurried downstairs, then halted, stunned. A fire was flaming in the hearth, and he'd set a kettle to boiling.

Bewildered, Emily glanced around, but Raphael was not present. She slipped on her duffel coat and went outside to do her morning chores. He fell into step beside her as she crossed the yard. To her surprise he took the pail of grain from her hand. He was wearing one of her father's ponchos.

"What are you doing?" Emily asked, pushing open the door to the chicken coop.

"You're running late." He scattered the corn as the clucking chickens and the rooster flocked wildly around them. "Go milk the cow. I'll meet you in the barn."

Emily did not move. "I don't understand."

He squinted at her. "You work too hard."

"I still don't understand."

He had finished, and he shoved open the henhouse door for them both. "Haven't you ever heard of repaying someone's hospitality?"

Emily knew she was staring at his dark, handsome, impassive face. She thought about how he had repaid Lloyd Harrison. "You're an outlaw."

"Maybe I had a sister once."

There was something tragic underlying his words. "What happened?" Emily heard herself say.

His smile was brief and brittle. "I said maybe. Let's go. Or we'll be late." He poked her shoulder blade.

Emily entered the barn, then whirled, realizing what he had just said. "*We'll* be late?"

He nodded, gesturing at Tess, who was regarding Emily with soft brown expectant eyes.

"What do you mean, *we*?" Emily cried in panic.

"I'm going to school with you," Raphael said flatly.

"You're coming to school!" Emily gasped.

His smile did not reach his eyes. "That's right."

"I don't understand," Emily cried.

"It's simple. I'm not ready to leave the lair, and I don't really trust you."

"But . . . the children."

"Tell them I'm your cousin. Just got into town. From Rock Springs."

"I don't have a cousin," Emily said through stiff lips.

He smiled, a flash of white teeth. "Now you do. Let's go. You'll be late." His hand cupped her elbow. "I'll grain the mare."

The school bell pealed. Emily kept tugging on the rope, acutely aware of the man standing behind her. The sun was high now, and bright, warming up the late-autumn day. Laughing, chattering children filled up the school yard. "Mornin', ma'am," was a repeated chorus as the children hurried past Emily. Each and every child, from the youngest, six-year-old Terrence, to the oldest, fifteen-year-old Randy, eyed Raphael with curiosity as they entered the single-room schoolhouse.

Emily counted ten students, which meant that she was missing someone. Out of breath from all the bell-pulling, she shoved strands of hair back into her bonnet. She refused to meet Raphael's eyes, but knew he followed her as she walked into the school. Didn't he worry about the children talking about him? Or did he plan on leaving town before it could matter?

Emily had already stoked the potbellied iron stove, but the classroom was hardly warm. As Emily moved to the front of the class, she was aware of Raphael slouching into a seat far too small for him in the very back. Ten heads swiveled to regard him. "Good morning, class," Emily said, assuming her schoolteacher's tone. It was at once firm and enthusiastic.

Ten faces turned back. "Mornin', ma'am."

Emily kept her gaze trained on her students, but she couldn't help seeing Raphael out of the corner of her eye. If he left tomorrow, she would be glad. "We have a visitor today. My cousin from Rock Springs. He's staying with me and my father for a while, a *short* while, and being as he is an educator himself"—Emily smiled as her eyes met Raphael's cool golden ones—"he wished to accompany me to school today. Where is Jesse Arnold?"

"Jess had to stay home. Her mama's ill," Betsy Green said soberly.

"I hope it's not serious?" Emily asked with instant concern.

"She can't keep down her food," Betsy replied.

Someone snickered. Fifteen-year-old red-haired Randy Willis. "Got something cookin' in the oven again, I'll bet."

Twelve-year-old Webster joined him in another round of coarse laughter.

Emily stared. Their laughter died. Randy shifted in his chair; Webster dropped his eyes to the desk in front of him. "That was crude and uncalled for," Emily said quietly. "Perhaps, Randy, you might like to take a walk outside to think about what it might be like if someone said something unkind about you—behind your back."

"I'm sorry, ma'am," Randy said, looking up. "But I heard it's true."

"Whether it's true or not, until Liza Arnold makes a public statement it is crude and uncalled for to make comments about such a sensitive topic."

Randy hung his head.

"Now," Emily said, realizing that Raphael was no longer slouched but regarding her very intently. She flushed. "Our first lesson today is geography." She wet her lips. How was she going to teach when he kept staring at her? A little devil appeared inside of Emily's head. One with a pitchfork, prodding her on. Emily looked right at Raphael. "And being as we have such an unusual visitor today, perhaps he might like to lead today's lesson?" She smiled warmly. "We are studying the eastern coast of this country."

Raphael just stared.

Ten heads turned to regard their visitor.

"Miss Emily, ma'am," Raphael said, apparently unflustered, "I wouldn't presume to take over your classroom when clearly you are doing such a fine, outstanding job. Besides, it's my brother who's the educator. You got us all mixed up."

The children tittered. Emily knew she was red-faced again. "Your twin brother?"

"My exact twin."

"Very well, it seems I have made a mistake, but that's what happens when family stays apart so many years."

"Guess so." Suddenly he rose to his feet. "But I think I'll see if I can fix that banging shutter."

Emily started in surprise.

He fixed the loose shutter, using tools left in the shed outside, and also repaired the tree swing, which had been coming off its hinges for some time now. Although Emily saw that he favored his left arm, clearly he was well on the mend. When Emily dismissed the class for their midmorning break, he remained inside, patching up a particularly drafty window. As the children played tag and hide-and-go-seek, the steady sound of his hammer could be heard through their squeals and laughter.

Emily watched the children, nibbling on a piece of cornbread she had taken to school that morning. All that day she had been agonizingly aware of his presence at school, and now, listening to the banging hammer, she couldn't stop herself from wondering about him. He was a killer. He had said so. But he didn't act like a killer, now, did he? What killer patched up a drafty, rickety schoolhouse?

Emily wondered if he had lied. But if so, why? The answer was easy—in order to scare her so she wouldn't reveal his whereabouts to Harrison or anyone else. Which brought Emily back to some incontrovertible facts: He'd barged uninvited into her home, badly wounded, being pursued by one of Aurora's most outstanding citizens, and he'd threatened her and her father quite succinctly. He had, in fact, taken the Andersons hostage. And he had thousands of dollars in his saddlebags. He was, surely, a thief. And Harrison was convinced that he was a member—or even the leader—of the Whiskey Peak gang.

There was no other explanation for his behavior. For if he were innocent of wrongdoing he would go to the sheriff, not hide out in her home. But why would a rustler go to work for one of his victims?

"Miss Emily?"

Betsy's soft voice jerked Emily right out of her thoughts. She smiled, patting the wooden bench beside her hip. Betsy sat down. "Are you feeling better today? We were all real worried about you when you didn't come to school yesterday."

"I'm much better, thank you."

Betsy hesitated.

"What is it?" Emily asked.

Betsy looked at Emily, and then her gaze wandered to the schoolhouse's front door. The sound of hammering had ceased, Emily realized. And then Raphael appeared on the front step, his red flannel shirt unbuttoned and tucked loosely into his pants. He held the hammer in his right hand.

"Is something wrong?" Betsy asked.

Emily's heart lurched. She faced Betsy and managed a smile, no easy task. Betsy's gaze seemed inclined toward the dark, handsome outlaw. "Whyever do you ask?"

Betsy shrugged. "I don't know. You just seem nervous today, upset even, or scared. It's him, isn't it?" Betsy nodded at Raphael, who leaned a hip up against one of the posts supporting the porch's overhang and was now languidly lighting up a cheroot. He glanced at them without lifting his head.

"Of course not," Emily lied. And the two women stared at Raphael.

He suddenly ground out his smoke, tossing it aside. He strode toward them, his strides long, leisurely. Emily felt Betsy stiffen. She found herself thinking about how long and strong his legs were—how feline his movements.

"He reminds me of a mountain lion," Betsy whispered mirroring Emily's thoughts exactly. "Not in a rush, all golden and lazy, but ready to pounce—at any moment."

Emily's jaw tightened. "You exaggerate, dear," she said.

And Betsy said, "I didn't even know you had any kin, much less in Rock Springs."

Emily failed to reply.

$$6$$

Veronica Richards restlessly paced the large space of her father's wood-paneled study, trodding upon numerous Indian rugs. Her strides were long and lithe and unhampered because she was clad in a split riding skirt, her habitual attire. Her raven-black hair was pulled tightly back into a long, thick braid, accentuating her breathtaking beauty. Her flawless oval face was dominated by a pair of emerald-green eyes and a pair of full red lips. But Veronica was scowling. Worry was etched all over her face. Her fists were tightly clenched.

Her father had taken off after Raphael two days ago. He had not yet returned. Had he caught him? Was Raphael even now in jail? Veronica could not imagine her father failing at anything; he was a "winner" and proud of it. Hadn't he carved out of the implacable Wyoming wilderness—practically with his own two bare hands—this huge ranch, losing two wives and a son in the process? Veronica's mother, although still alive, had abandoned them a half dozen years ago, returning to Boston to live with her kin.

No, Daddy would win—he always did—especially in this instance, when he was so damned furious.

Veronica wondered if he guessed the truth, or some of it. That made her pause, staring out the study window at the strip of deserted road that appeared so suddenly out of the fir-clad hills. She did not see her father cantering toward the house.

Veronica could not understand his being so angry over the theft of cash, even if it was a considerable sum. She knew Lloyd. There was another cause for his anger—could it have something to do with her?

Veronica's hands unclenched. A three-carat diamond glinted on the fourth finger of her left hand, above a platinum wedding band. It was a year and a half now since she'd been widowed. Her husband, the stupid fool, had gotten himself killed by rustlers. But she hadn't married Billy for his intellect; she'd married him because he was the son of a neighboring rancher, and pleasantly handsome to boot. And because Lloyd had demanded it.

Veronica was still angry about his death. She was young and beautiful, while the nights were long and lonely. The eligible men in Aurora were as witless as Billy had been, and the only beau she'd consider was Henry Cooper, who was so moonstruck it was pathetic. Instantly Raphael's dark, devastating image came to her mind. She inhaled, hard. She was so angry. He hadn't been moonstruck at all.

"How was school today, Em?" Gus asked.

They were eating supper, reheated potted roast

from the day before. As usual, Gus's appetite was poor. But Emily, for the first time in a long time, was famished. She had cleaned her plate.

"Fine," Emily lied, her gaze straying to the window and outside. When she and Raphael had returned to the farm, Gus was in the house, so Raphael had slipped into the barn through the back doors, giving Emily a long, warning look. There had also been a challenge there.

By now, she mused, he must trust her somewhat. She had lied to protect him, making her an accomplice to his crimes. If she hadn't revealed his presence to her father or anyone else by this time, surely he knew she would not do so. Besides, he was well enough to leave. Wasn't he?

That notion disturbed Emily, although she could not fathom why.

"Heard Liza Arnold's in the family way again," Gus said, pushing his chipped plate aside.

"Poor Liza," Emily whispered. This would be her seventh child. Why didn't her husband leave her alone? As much as Emily loved children, no woman could decently rear more than four or five or even six. Emily had always wanted four. But she was almost too old now, and when Henry Cooper had jilted her she'd had to face reality. At her age, with her plain looks, she would probably remain a spinster.

Suddenly Emily wondered if the outlaw had a wife and children. Instantly she dismissed the idea as absurd. Again, she stared out the window at the barn shrouded in the starlit Wyoming dusk.

But it really wasn't absurd. He might be an outlaw at present, but he hadn't been born an outlaw, and

he had a good, decent streak in him—Emily had
seen it that day. He had a family—he'd mentioned a
sister. It was more than likely that a good-looking
man of his age also had a wife.

Abruptly Emily stood, carrying the plates to the
sink. She did not want to think about the kind of
woman the outlaw would take to wife, but one of his
remarks was forever engraved in her mind: He'd seen
plenty of naked women before, and Emily wasn't his
type.

Emily told herself that she did not care. Not at all.
In fact, she was darned glad she wasn't his kind of
woman. Otherwise, she'd have to worry about him
making all kinds of improper advances that night.

Gus went into the parlor to smoke. Emily cleaned
up the kitchen, waiting for Gus to leave. She was
almost finished scouring the last frying pan when she
heard him scrape back his rocker and walk across the
creaky parlor floor.

"Em?" He entered the kitchen. "Goin' out for a
while."

Emily nodded, not meeting his eyes, her heart
lurching hard. Very studiously she kept scrubbing the
pan while he donned his jacket and left the house.
But her pulse was racing now. Raphael was out in
the barn, and they would be alone again on the
farm. She heard her father's horse trotting out of the
yard.

She thought about the outlaw sleeping on the
floor of her bedroom, just inches from her bed.

She thought about him fixing the shutter at the
school, and the swing.

She thought about his high, high cheekbones, his
long black eyelashes, his very sensual mouth.

What is wrong with you! Emily scolded herself.

Emily had set aside the last portion of roast, potatoes, and cherry pie. She'd left everything covered with a dishrag on the counter behind a bag of cornmeal so Gus wouldn't notice. Now Emily fixed up a tray, refusing to dwell on her behavior or thoughts, thinking only about the fact that it was decent to feed the outlaw. Especially after all he'd done at the school that day.

Using her hip, she shoved open the front door and crossed the yard, carefully carrying the tray. She'd forgotten her coat, so she began to shiver before she reached the barn. As she stepped inside, the tabby appeared, wrapping itself around her ankles. There was a small kerosene lamp on, and Emily saw him before she'd even shaken the tabby off her feet.

He had the light set up on two bales of hay. A small mirror was hanging from a nail on a post. He was shirtless, clad only in his buckskin pants and his dusty boots—and the linen bandage, of course. He was shaving.

Emily knew he had to have heard her enter. But he gave no sign, concentrating on scraping the days-old growth of beard off his face. Emily faltered.

The tendons in his back flexed as he moved. The muscles in his right arm bulged as he lifted his hand. There was something very disconcerting about watching a man like him half-undressed in the midst of performing such an intimate act. Emily found it difficult to breathe properly. Only a wife should be witness to this kind of circumstance.

Yet she failed to avert her eyes.

He cursed. "Damn it!" He wiped a speck of

blood off his chin, turning. There was a strange glow in his gaze. "I'm not doing a very good job here."

Emily recovered her wits and her tongue. "Of course you're not. How can you see in this gloom?"

"Can't stand a beard," he said, facing her fully now.

Emily didn't know where to look. She wanted to avoid direct eye contact, but she didn't want to look at his naked torso, because his swarthy skin was stretched taut over his very flat abdomen, and there was something mesmerizing about the indented lines of muscle there. Looking lower was even worse. She finally, reluctantly, met his gaze. "I brought you supper. Can't that wait until morning?"

"It itches. Next thing you know, I'll have lice." He stared. "I may not be an upstanding citizen, but I do believe in cleanliness." He held up the razor. "Can't do a good job with my right hand." His gaze narrowed. "Want to help?"

Emily knew he could do a decent job with his right hand; she'd seen him using it that day. "I beg your pardon?"

"Would you help me get rid of this beard, Miss Emily . . . ma'am?"

His tone, she decided, was mocking. Yet somehow it was belligerent, challenging. Then Emily decided she was imagining things. His arm had to hurt him after the way he'd used it at the school. "I think you can wait until the morning," Emily heard herself say. She walked over to him, still oddly breathless, and placed the tray on the stacked bales beside the kerosene lamp. She was careful not to allow even her skirts to come into contact with him. But she felt his eyes upon her.

"Scared?"

Emily jerked, meeting his gaze.

"Are you scared?" he asked, his tone flat.

"Of course not. If you haven't killed me by now, it's unlikely you'll kill me at all."

He smiled slowly. "Yeah. Real unlikely."

Emily decided that it was hot in the barn. She realized that she was hugging herself. And that he was holding the razor out to her.

"Very well," Emily snapped. She took the razor. "You'll have to sit. You're too tall."

"Think I don't know how small you are?"

Emily looked into his eyes, wondering what he meant exactly. There was something behind his words. He sat down on the bales, gave her a feline smile, and turned his cheek toward her. Emily stared at his perfect profile.

"Well?" he asked softly, glancing very briefly at her.

Emily flushed because he'd caught her ogling him, and she lifted the razor. Only to realize that her hand was shaking.

Quickly Emily dropped her hand. But he'd seen. He turned, his gaze intense.

"It's cold," Emily lied, avoiding his eyes. "I'm shivering and—"

"You're shaking."

Her gaze flew to his. When she spoke, her tone was strangled. "This isn't a good idea."

It was a moment before he replied. "Yeah, it's a real bad idea."

Emily was ready to flee. But before she could take a single step, he caught her wrist. His grasp felt like a manacle. "You have a beau?"

"What?" Emily gasped.

"You have a beau? A sweetheart?" His eyes bored into hers.

Emily tried to jerk her wrist free and failed. Panting, she said, "That's none of your concern!"

"So there's no one."

"I . . . I did have a beau. Henry Cooper. But it didn't last."

"He ever kiss you?" Raphael asked.

Emily stared at him in shock.

Slowly, not releasing her, he stood. "Guess that's answer enough."

Emily's heart was beating so hard she felt faint. Surely he was not intending what she thought he was!

A long moment passed. Raphael did not move. Emily's skirts actually covered his boots.

Then he said, "May I kiss you, Miss Emily?"

Emily's eyes widened. He was *asking* her?

His jaw flexed. "If you say no, I'll walk away. That's a promise."

Emily opened her mouth to reply—to say no—and failed to utter a sound. Images danced through her head, of this man embracing her, kissing her . . . *dear Lord*. "Yes," she whispered.

His eyes softened, then something flared there, hot and bright. He reeled Emily in. As his hands slipped to her waist, holding her loosely now, Emily's breasts brushed his bandaged chest. She found it distinctly difficult to breathe. She was acutely aware of his hands on her hips, of his chest against hers, and she was even aware of their legs touching, his thighs hard and warm. Raphael bent his head.

Emily did not move, allowing him to feather her mouth again and again with his lips.

And Emily would have never dreamed in a million years that the outlaw could be so gentle. That a kiss could cause so many fluttering sensations, affecting so much of her body. His mouth continued to brush hers, perhaps a dozen times, and Emily finally sighed. Her body was melting, hot and molten, delicious yet coiled up tight, and her fists were uncurling, her fingers spreading over his bare shoulders. Emily wanted to dig her nails into his muscular arms, but didn't dare. Then Raphael made a sound, the kind of sound Emily had never heard before but recognized now as something both sexual and male. Her own excitement and wonder increased. Her body was feverish and filled with yearning.

Suddenly his grip tightened on her waist. His tongue flicked over the barely parted seam of her lips.

Someone moaned. Emily realized, dazed, that it was herself.

And suddenly she was in his embrace. Every inch of her body was crushed against his. His mouth was on hers, and it was no longer gentle, but greedy and devouring. Emily felt his tongue enter her and fill her, and at the same time she felt his maleness pressed up, rock-hard, against her hip.

Emily knew she should stop him. But she told herself, just a little bit more. . . .

Raphael suddenly gripped her upper arms, hurtfully, and pushed her away. Emily was so surprised that she stumbled. "You had better go," he said.

Emily did not fall. She clung to the stacked bales

of hay for support, met his smoldering eyes. She could not seem to think.

"I'll sleep in the barn tonight," he said.

Emily could not sleep. She sat on the edge of her bed, clad in her flannel nightgown, fingering the lace at the edge of one cuff. She replayed the kiss in her mind.

Emily hugged herself. Just thinking about the kiss and the outlaw was making her as feverish as when she had been in his arms. What was happening to her?

And why had he kissed her in the first place? He'd said he didn't like her. Clearly, Emily decided, he had lied.

Emily stood and walked barefoot across her bedroom to the window. She did not notice the cold. She pulled apart the plain muslin curtains and stared out into the starry night. A half-moon beamed back at her from above the shadowy barn. It occurred to Emily that if the outlaw was thinking about her, too, and he looked toward the house, he would clearly see her silhouetted against her brightly lit bedroom. Of course, he wasn't thinking about her.

But what was he thinking about?

Emily knew her thoughts had become dangerous. He was an outlaw, a fugitive. He was not the kind of man any respectable lady should think about—especially not the way Emily was thinking about him. And he was almost healed. He could leave the farm, and Aurora, anytime now. In fact, in the morning he might even be gone.

Reluctantly, Emily turned and left the window

and climbed into bed. But it was a long time before she found sleep.

Gus's snores filled up the corridor as Emily raced past his room. She'd slept only a few hours the night before, waking up well before dawn, thinking about the outlaw, his kiss, and his departure. She hurried downstairs, whipping on her long duffel coat. She was so agitated that she forgot to make a fire and set the kettle to boil.

Emily dashed across the yard. It was only when she reached the barn that she paused, filling her lungs with frigid air. The morning was dark and overcast, promising snow.

Emily pushed open the barn doors as quietly as she could. Quickly she stepped inside, out of the cold, into the barn's musky warmth.

Relief swept her. He was still there.

Stretched out on his back, a blanket up to his chin, Raphael stared at her out of golden eyes. Emily began to blush. Whatever was wrong with her, rushing to the barn this way?

Slowly, he threw off the blanket and sat up, flexing his torso. As he stood, glancing at her from under his lashes, he reminded Emily of the mountain lion she and Betsy had discussed the day before. "Good morning," he said. "Something wrong, Miss Emily?"

Emily felt her color increasing. "I thought you might be gone," she heard herself say.

He smiled. "Without a proper good-bye?"

Their eyes locked. Emily thought about another feverish kiss. "How is your wound?"

"Better." His stare remained steady, relentless.

He was going to leave. Emily knew it, could feel it. He certainly had no reason to stay. Emily tried to imagine life without the outlaw, and failed. Before, her day had been dreary, routine. In two days he had changed everything. "When are you leaving?"

His glanced dropped. He bent and picked up the blanket, folding it. "I thought I might cut you some more wood down at school today." His gaze suddenly lifted, piercing hers and leaving her breathless. "The woodpile's awfully low."

Emily stared. He could leave, but he wasn't. He was staying, at least for another day. In spite of the danger involved. "That would be fine," she whispered.

Realizing that she had joined him in a conspiracy of silence and lies.

The door to the sheriff's office burst open. Maclaine, heavyset and white-haired, was bent over his desk. The office was a small room with windows looking out on Main Street. There was another desk for his deputy and a cabinet for files. Maclaine jerked as Lloyd Harrison stormed in.

"Goddamnit, winter's comin' early this year," Harrison said loudly as the door banged shut behind him.

Maclaine sat back in his chair, his weight making it creak in protest. "Howdy, Lloyd. Any luck?"

"No luck, and I want to know why the hell you're sitting here and not outside doin' what you should be doin' to protect the citizens of this town from an outlaw like Raphael Caldwell."

Maclaine stood. "We covered half the territory yesterday. No sign of him. He's gone to ground, Lloyd, but we both know he'll come out, sooner than later, and that's when we'll nab him."

Harrison gave Maclaine a dark look and strode over to the door that led to the two jail cells behind the front office. It was ajar and he glanced past it, saw no one present. "Where's Ken?"

"My deputy's doin' his rounds." Maclaine heaved himself to his feet. "We can talk, no spies here, but there isn't much to talk about."

Harrison paced over to Maclaine's desk, the two men facing each other over its cluttered width. "Listen, Judd, we got big trouble and you know it. We got to find him before he does any real harm. Find him and make a little accident happen. A fatal one."

"You don't need to panic. He's wounded and, like I said, hiding. We both know he hasn't left these parts. Too much is at stake. We'll find him, but he's smart, Lloyd, real smart. We won't find him until he comes out of his lair."

Harrison scowled. "Might be a week or two. I can't sleep, not with that bastard on the loose."

"Maybe. But I do have a plan."

"Really?" Harrison was sarcastic. "Pray tell."

Maclaine's pale-blue eyes were steady. "He's gonna come out for a purpose, and he's only one man. We got one telegraph in this town. And that's in the railroad depot."

Harrison jabbed the air with his finger. "You watch that damn depot twenty-four hours a day."

"Already am." Maclaine smiled, smug. Then he saw that Harrison was still frowning. "Now what's wrong?"

"I got the strongest feeling he's right under our nose," Lloyd muttered. "Goddamnit!"

★ ★ ★

"G'night, ma'am," seven-year-old Theodore Green cried, his hand in his sister's. School was over for the day.

"Good night, Miss Emily," Betsy said, her cheeks a bright pink. Her gaze slid to Raphael, who stood just behind Emily, then dropped to the ground. "Mr. Anderson."

Raphael smiled, tipping his hat. Betsy hurried away, practically dragging her little brother with her.

Silence fell over the school yard. A few flakes of snow were drifting down, and one landed on the tip of Emily's nose. She was very aware of Raphael's presence. He seemed to emit a physicality that had a magnetic pull upon her. And upon Betsy as well.

"We better hurry, before the storm hits," he said, his eyes moving over her.

"I'm going into town." Emily met his topaz gaze. "I want to call on Liza Arnold. She might need something. Her boys run wild half the time. Perhaps I can help."

Raphael stared at her without replying.

"She's expectin'," Emily murmured, knowing that she blushed. But the real issue was whether he would trust her.

"I know," Raphael said. He squinted at her. "Then you'd better hurry. You can ride home with Gus."

"I intend to," Emily replied, something swelling inside her heart. How odd it was—it almost felt as if they were a couple, with him telling her how to get home.

"I'll see you at the farm," Raphael said. "Anything you want me to do before you get home?"

Emily shook her head. "I won't be long. I'll have

plenty of time to fry us up some pork for supper tonight." Her breath seemed to lodge in her throat. *Us*. There was no *us*.

The corners of his mouth lifted. "You are one helluva cook, Miss Emily." His eyes danced. "The way to a man's heart, they say."

Absurdly, Emily was pleased. She looked away, reminding herself that she did not care to please him, or find his heart. "Good-bye."

He did not reply, starting toward the farm with his long, lazy stride. Emily watched him for a moment, then turned, hurrying down the road that led to town. It was a brief ten-minute walk. The road was rutted, and muddy and frozen in places. She kept thinking about how the issue of her going unescorted into town and his returning to the farm alone had never come up. He trusted her. He knew she wasn't going to turn him in. Emily's heart seemed to dance a bit—even though she chastised herself sternly for her feelings.

Liza Arnold was delighted to see Emily. Blond and plump and twice Emily's age, she gave Emily a warm hug. "It's so sweet of you to come calling, Emily, with you so busy and all."

Emily entered the woman's front parlor, which was cozy and cheerful. Color was in evidence everywhere, the draperies yellow and sprigged with green leaves, the wallpaper red floral, the couches green damask. "How are you feeling, Liza?"

"Good enough, considering." Liza herself wore a purple wool shawl.

"Jesse didn't come to school again today." There was no rebuke in Emily's tone.

"If only I had another daughter," Liza said earnestly. "She'll come to school tomorrow, Emily, I swear it, but I can't keep up my home when I'm feeling as poorly as I did yesterday. Today I'm much better though."

"I understand," Emily said. "Is there anything that you need? Anything I can do to help?"

"I haven't been able to get down to the mercantile for a special Christmas order I placed," Liza said thoughtfully.

"I'd be glad to go and fetch your order."

Liza beamed. "That is so good of you, dear. But before you go, how about a cup of coffee? Don't you want to sit and chat?" Liza beamed.

"I do, but I can't," Emily said, thinking of the conversation she'd just had with Raphael. "I have to start supper when I get home."

Liza's face fell. "Well, did you hear that Harrison lost one of his vaqueros to that Whiskey Peak gang?"

"No," Emily said slowly, Raphael's image forming in her mind, "I didn't. Are you certain that he was killed by that gang?"

"It's what Lloyd says," Liza said grimly. "And he should know. That poor vaquero, Pete Benson, was shot right in the back of the head."

Emily felt ill. She spoke her thoughts aloud. "Murder is a far more serious offense than cattle theft." But even as Emily spoke she recalled Raphael's confession that he was wanted in three states for murder. *No.* It was an instant protest inside of her head. *No.* He was a thief, maybe a rustler, but not a murderer. It was impossible.

"I'd say," Liza said. "By the way, have you heard the latest news, that a dangerous outlaw is on the loose? Lloyd Harrison is furious, swears he's gonna

hang him up by his toes himself, he is. He stole every
single penny Harrison had in his safe. I say he should
be strung up, Emily, before he steals again. A man
works hard for his share in this life, we all do. I don't
want him busting into my home and taking my valuables!"

And it was a fact. Emily had seen the proof; she
had seen those damning saddlebags filled with greenbacks. "I have to go," Emily said, far too abruptly.
Her cheeks burned. What would Liza say if she
knew that Emily had been hiding the outlaw on her
farm? In the barn? In her *bedroom*? What would she
think if she knew that the outlaw had kissed Emily—
not chastely—and that Emily still dreamed about it?

And Emily was afraid. It had already occurred to
her that one of the children might mention that she
had a cousin visiting—and that someone might make
the connection to Raphael. Before, she had assumed
that by then he would be gone and it wouldn't matter. But he hadn't left. He'd gone to school with her
twice. How could he take such a risk? Why would
he take such a risk? Emily didn't know what to
think.

And wasn't she one of Aurora's most upstanding
citizens? She had been born and raised in Pitkin
County. She'd taught the school ever since she was
fifteen. No one would ever question her, or even
dream that she might lie through her teeth and har-
bor a fugitive—a fugitive who was a self-confessed
murderer. Would they?

Before Emily departed she gripped Liza's hand.
"Liza, when was Pete Benson killed?" She had to
know.

"Last week, I believe," Liza said, staring closely at Emily. "Why do you ask?"

Emily mumbled some inane reply. Last week she hadn't met Raphael. Last week he had not been holed up on her farm. She did not know where he had been or what he had been doing last week.

A few minutes later Emily was hurrying down Main Street. Guilt now shrouded her like a cloak, and with it came a sneaking suspicion that she had lost her mind. What if she was seeing in Raphael what she wanted to see? *What if he had killed that vaquero?*

And then Emily recognized the buckskin tied up in front of the mercantile. Her heart sank. She did not want to bump into Lloyd Harrison, not even in passing. But she had to pick up Liza's special order as she had promised.

Pasting a smile on her face—certain that the whole world could see her guilt and would soon discover her secret—Emily marched up the steps to the boardwalk and entered the store. Bells jingled above her head, announcing her entrance. Emily glanced around and saw Harrison standing at the counter, speaking with the mercantile's proprietor, Jacob Goldberg. There were no other customers present.

And there was not going to be any avoiding him, Emily realized in dismay. Sucking up her courage, she walked up to the counter. "Good day, Mr. Goldberg. Good day, Mr. Harrison."

Harrison grunted, concentrating on the pipe he was smoking, although Jacob smiled warmly at her. "What can I do for you today, Miss Emily?" He spoke with a strong German accent.

Stammering slightly, Emily explained that she had come to pick up a special order for Liza Arnold. Jacob brightened, turned away, and disappeared into the back room. Emily stared at a jar of penny candies, fidgeting. She fingered a display of lace doilies.

"How's Gus?" Harrison asked.

Emily met his gaze for a split second. "Just fine, thank you."

Harrison puffed away. "Hear you got a cousin visiting from Rock Springs."

Emily froze. Dread filled every pore of her body, every fiber of her being. The mercantile seemed to lack air. She was about to be revealed.

"It's nice when family comes visiting," Harrison said, turning away.

Emily's knees buckled. She gripped the counter hard as Jacob came out from the back room, a paper-wrapped parcel in his hands. "Here you are, Miss Emily."

Emily couldn't even get a "thank you" out.

"Daddy!" A young woman's high-pitched voice filled the store. "I have to talk to you!"

Emily glimpsed Veronica Richards hurrying into the shop. Veronica was a year older than Emily and had been widowed last year. She was raven-haired and ivory-skinned and unquestionably lovely. Emily had admired her striking beauty for as long as she could remember. Now, however, Veronica appeared to be on the verge of tears.

Emily was too distraught herself to wonder what was wrong, an uncharacteristic reaction for her. Although Veronica had never been Emily's friend, Emily did not hold her self-absorption, occasional

aloofness, and vanity against her. Emily was certain that if she'd been blessed with such looks she'd have been a tad selfish and vain as well.

"What are you doing in town, Veronica?" Harrison seemed perturbed. "Why aren't you home? A storm's coming. I hope you were escorted!"

"Daddy, I have to talk to you!" Veronica ran toward her father, wearing a split riding skirt and a sheepskin coat. "You left the ranch two days ago, before I could get a word out." She pouted.

"You know I have to find that damn thief. I want what's mine. I want back every single penny he stole. And I want him locked up in jail, where he belongs."

"You have to find him," Veronica said harshly. Her eyes blazed. "I thought by now you'd have found him and locked him up!"

Harrison patted his daughter's hand. "We'll find him and do more than lock him up. Don't you worry, honey." He smiled at his daughter. "Your loyalty makes me very happy, Veronica."

Veronica smiled at her father through a sheen of tears.

Watching her, Emily had a bad feeling. She recalled Harrison mentioning that Raphael had actually dined with him and his daughter—that the rancher had taken Raphael in under his roof. Veronica was so very beautiful, as different from Emily as night from day, and she was widowed now, and Raphael was a striking man.

"You want to do some shopping?" Harrison asked his daughter, who was sniffling into an exquisite handkerchief.

She shrugged.

"I'll be over at the jail," Harrison said. He nodded at Goldberg. " 'Day, Jacob."

Harrison left. Emily stood alone with Veronica at the counter. She said softly, "Veronica, what's wrong? You seem very upset."

Tears spilled down Veronica's cheeks. "I am upset!"

Emily could barely breathe. Her heart raced. "Because of the outlaw?"

Veronica jerked, and the two women's gazes met. "Did you see him? When he was working for us? Sometimes he came to town."

Emily wet her lips. "No. I've . . . never met him."

Veronica dabbed at her eyes. "I hate him. The bastard!"

Emily froze. Then her pulse resumed its beat, but painfully. "He didn't . . ." She was sick, dread-filled.

"He did more than steal Daddy's money," Veronica said bitterly. "He did more than sup with us and sit with us and smoke on the porch. He courted me, he did, every single day, with sweet words and sweeter promises, making me fall in love with him—taking advantage of a widow in her grief and loneliness!"

Emily felt all the blood draining from her face. She stared. And thought she might die.

"I hope he hangs," Veronica cried. "It's what he deserves!"

8

Emily rushed blindly out of the mercantile and down the steps of the boardwalk. The snow was falling harder now, and it was bitterly cold out. Icy, frigid air assailed her as she half-ran down Main Street, stumbling on the ruts left by the last cattle drive.

It wasn't until she passed Liza Arnold's house that she realized she had forgotten her parcel. Emily could not turn around and go back. The stabbing pain in her breast prevented her from doing that.

She should have known. She should have guessed. She wasn't his type to begin with. Veronica Richards was his type of woman.

How the knowledge hurt.

Emily glimpsed the apple orchard where she'd played as a child. Her steps slowed. In another few minutes she'd be at the farm. She had forgotten to look for Gus in town, and it was too late now. And the scoundrel outlaw was at the farm, probably inside her home—blast his very hide.

How could he have toyed with her in such a reprehensible manner? How could she have been such a fool? Clearly he did not possess the least bit of conscience, and she should have realized that from the very start when he had barged into her home, taking both her and her father hostage.

Emily reminded herself now that he was a killer, a thief, and entirely without remorse. She refused to think about his odd behavior at school that day.

And if it hadn't been so cold out Emily would have paused in the yard to debate going inside. But she was freezing, and she had a supper to start, and there were no other alternatives. Gritting her chattering teeth, she pushed open the front door. The warmth of the kitchen immediately cocooned her. A crackling fire danced in the hearth.

He had also stoked up the stove. Emily refused to be grateful. She was merely relieved that he was not present. She turned and hung her coat up, shaking off the snow first, feeling very grim indeed. She no longer wanted his help, not in any shape or form. She wanted him gone, the sooner the better. It flashed through her mind that she could turn him in.

She marched into the larder for onions and potatoes and set to work slicing, dicing, and peeling. Never had she concentrated so hard. Tears seemed to burn her eyes.

She was a good citizen. She *had* to turn him in.

Emily stopped slicing. She wiped her eyes with one balled-up fist. If only he hadn't been so helpful at school. If only he hadn't kissed her.

The front door opened and closed. Emily stiffened, listening for Gus's heavy footsteps. She heard nothing. Her heart accelerated wildly.

"You walked home," he drawled, almost in her ear.

Emily whirled, only to find him less than a handspan away. He was holding a side of pork, which he'd clearly gotten from the meat house. "Yes, I did," she said frostily. Imagining Veronica in his embrace.

He set the slab of meat down, then slowly met her eyes. "Where's Gus?"

Emily gave him her back and whacked off a chunk of lard. She slammed it into the frying pan and set it on the stove. She watched it melt then begin to sizzle.

"He coming home?" Raphael asked.

"I assume so," she said, not turning. She scooped up the onions and potatoes and tossed them into the pan. She stirred the contents far more vigorously than necessary. She wished she were stirring up pieces of his hide instead.

"Something happen in town?" he asked her back.

"What could possibly happen in a small town like Aurora? Except for a dangerous killer-thief running loose and taking innocent citizens hostage?"

He was silent.

Emily knew she'd wounded him, and a quick sideways glance over her shoulder confirmed it. But she refused to feel bad. He deserved far worse than mere verbal insults.

Emily moved past him without touching him in order to retrieve a jar of salt. When she returned from the pantry he had his hip against the counter, blocking her way. She halted.

He stared.

Emily swallowed. She had to know. "Did you kill Pete Benson last week?"

His eyes widened. He did not speak.

And Emily was ashamed. "I'm sorry—"

"Course I did," he suddenly drawled. "How could you even think otherwise?"

His eyes were gold, but ice cold. Emily knew— she *knew*—he hadn't killed the vaquero. This man wasn't a killer. A thief and outlaw, yes, but not a cold-blooded killer.

"What else is bothering you, Emily?" he asked in a hard, mocking tone.

She dared to move past him. Her hip against his— she facing forward, him facing the kitchen—she salted the pork. Hating his sudden familiar use of her name. She was furious with him for using her, for preferring Veronica to her, but she wasn't going to turn him in. He did not deserve hanging, and she knew Aurora well enough to know that he would not be given a fair trial.

"Well, Emily? Clearly you are upset. With me. And I don't think it has much to do with a dead cowboy."

She jerked, meeting his eyes. The words rolled off her tongue without her quite knowing how. "Maybe you should ask Veronica Richards that."

His answer was silence. Once again, surprise filled his eyes.

Emily whirled away, staring down at the pork, her cheeks flushed, dismayed with herself. Now he would think her jealous—and he would be right.

"Look at me."

Emily obeyed.

His golden gaze was steady, boring into hers. "She a friend of yours?"

"No,"

"I didn't think so." He jammed his hands into the pockets of his buckskin pants, a gesture Emily had never seen him use before. "Isn't a man innocent until proven guilty?"

Emily would not relent. "Don't you throw my words back at me, twisting up their meaning!"

"So now they're twisted up? Meaningless? So now you judge me and hang me all at the same time?" His eyes flashed dangerously. "Where's the judge? Where's the jury? Who appointed you to those positions?"

Emily backed up until her buttocks hit the stove. His anger hit her like a bucket of ice water. But the stove was hot and she jumped away, feeling cornered, trapped. Her kitchen had never been so small, so airless.

"You believe Veronica, of course. Because I'm a killer and a thief." His jaw was flexed.

"Self-confessed!"

He stared. A long moment passed, during which his unrelenting gaze made Emily very uncomfortable—made her even feel that she was in the wrong, which was absurd. He was a thief—she'd seen the saddlebags—and that made him conscienceless, a liar. At least.

"You're awfully naive, *Miss* Emily. You don't know diddly about life." He turned and crossed the room, his strides longer than usual and very hard.

"What does that mean?" Emily cried.

He paused at the door, slowly facing her. "It means exactly as I said."

"My mother was sick for two years—I watched her die a little bit more each day before my very eyes," Emily said with a sob. "My father's been a drunk for as long as I can remember. My beau jilted me in my greatest time of need. I work this farm, practically alone, and teach a schoolful of children too. How dare you tell me I'm naive! I know more about life than a rat like you ever will!"

"You're naive, gullible, and too damn trusting," he said flatly, after a pause.

Emily wiped her eyes, which were tearing shamelessly. "Yes, I am too trusting."

He ignored the jibe. "Every man and every woman in this life has got secrets and dreams." He stared coldly. "Including Missus Veronica Richards. Lies, *Miss* Emily. Whatever she said—and I can imagine just what she said—is all a pack of lies."

"She said you seduced her," Emily heard herself accuse.

He laughed without mirth. "I never touched the 'lady,' not that I wasn't invited to."

Emily's mouth dropped open.

He wheeled on one booted heel and left the house. The front door slammed behind him. And that next morning he was gone.

He didn't have the heart to take the old paint mare, leaving the Andersons without a horse. So he walked. He'd steal a mount in town.

It was still snowing, heavily, which was fine with him because the snow covered his tracks. He huddled in Gus's poncho, his hat pulled down low. For some damn reason he couldn't stop the aching in his gut. It seemed to reach the vicinity of his chest.

For the hundredth time he told himself that he did not care what prissy Emily Anderson thought about him. He'd come to Aurora for a reason; he had a job to do. And wasn't the first rule of life not to get involved with anyone? He'd learned that as a small half-breed boy, knocked around by his father and ridiculed by his stepmother. He'd run away from Dillon, Texas, at the age of twelve. He'd never looked back, except for that one single time when he'd called on his half sister to see how his only childhood ally had grown up. That reunion had been poignant—and brief. Margaret's husband had not looked kindly on the appearance of her half-breed half brother in their lives.

Raphael gritted his teeth, not against the cold. He hated memories; they always hurt. If he could survive the surgery he'd cut out his own heart, maybe even his own soul. How easy his life would then be.

Emily Anderson thought the worst. He just could not believe it.

She had seemed like an angel, rescuing him from pain and anguish, tending to him as if she cared, trusting him with the children. *Damn her.*

He was glad he'd seen the truth—that she was no different from anyone else. And damn his own heart for crying out bitterly in protest, even now.

The snow was falling harder. Raphael regretted not having a horse. Squinting, he could just make out the Green home with its white picket fence, marking the beginning of Main Street. Raphael's pulse accelerated. Mooning about a spinster woman was not a good idea. Not when he had at least two very sincere enemies in the neighborhood: Lloyd Harrison and Sheriff Maclaine.

Then, grimly, he added another name to the short list: Veronica Richards, who was out for, at least, his blood.

Raphael cut through the Greens' backyard. It was just dawn, but smoke was already curling out of the brick chimney of their house. He could not have chosen a better time to come to town, other than the dark of night. Visibility was bad, making it perfect for him.

Keeping in the shadows of the just-awakening households and then the shuttered shops, Raphael hurried down Main Street. It was a broad, rutted dirt thoroughfare, with short boardwalks on either side. A few of the stores were brick-fronted, but most were wood-sided like the residential homes. Aurora was a very typical small Western town. Raphael had passed through hundreds like it these past dozen years. Nothing new here.

Emily's image flitted through his mind.

He paused behind the corner of the livery. He heard horses snickering inside the barn and decided this was where he'd find a mount. Just across the street was his goal: the railroad depot, with its swinging, faded sign. At this early hour he knew it was closed. Two doors down was the Aurora jail.

Raphael saw no movement across the street. Maclaine, he knew, would be at home with his wife and two children. His deputy was eighteen, as innocent as a lamb, and probably asleep.

Looking every which way, he decided the coast was clear and darted into the open. Running hard, he crossed the wide, empty street. The snow made the going slippery, but he kept his balance and quickly entered the alley.

Panting a bit, his breath forming vapor in the cold air, he skirted around behind the depot. He did not hesitate. Raising one gloved hand, he broke the windowpane on the back door. He did not smile as he stuck his hand inside and lifted the bolt. Child's play. He opened the door, stepped inside, and shut it.

He paused in the dark, taking off his gloves, warming his hands, searching the office with his eyes. Behind the clerk's counter was the telegraph.

Raphael crossed the room and paused, thinking, then began to hammer out a brief, succinct message. I HAVE THE EVIDENCE, AND I NEED HELP.

His goal achieved, Raphael started thinking about Emily again. Surely she would not hold school today. The school was two miles out of town, and in a blizzard no one would be able to make it home. He realized that he was worrying. Yet she was not his affair.

"Hey, you!" someone shouted from behind.

And Raphael whirled to look down the barrel of a Colt .45.

2

Raphael was frozen. He could not believe his goddamn luck. But at least he'd gotten the wire out.

"Hands up!" the deputy shouted.

Raphael did not want to kill, or even wound, this green boy. He could easily take him out. Ken Sanders did not even have his beard yet, and his hand, pointing the Colt, was shaking ever so slightly. Slowly, Raphael raised both palms. "Take it easy," he drawled.

Sanders jerked his head toward the back door. "Move! And don't try anything or I'll shoot off your head!"

"Don't want that," Raphael said easily. He moved slowly across the office toward the flushed deputy. Sanders backed up when Raphael was within reach. Raphael smiled at him.

"Out!" Sanders barked.

Raphael walked past Sanders to exit the depot. As he did so he could hear Sanders panting.

Sanders came up behind him on the street outside, which remained deserted. Suddenly Raphael stumbled. Sanders's forward motion caused him to crash into Raphael, even though he realized what was happening at the last moment and tried to halt himself. Too late. Raphael reached behind him and jerked hard on the younger man's ankle. A second later Sanders was on the ground, flat on his back, and his own Colt was pointing directly between his eyes.

"Sorry," Raphael said, straddling him and holding the gun easily.

"You bastard," Sanders cried. And then his eyes widened, moving past Raphael—just as Raphael felt something cold and hard press brutally into the back of his head.

"Drop it," Maclaine said.

Maclaine was not afraid. He shoved Raphael across the street, causing him to stumble repeatedly. He did not avoid poking Raphael's wound frequently with the barrel of his gun. Raphael was no longer complacent. He did not have a single doubt that he wouldn't remain alive for very long in Maclaine's jail. Help would arrive, but undoubtedly far too late, when he was six feet underground.

"You're a cool one, you are," Maclaine sneered as Ken Sanders opened the jailhouse door for them. He shoved him hard again and Raphael moved forward, grunting. Maclaine had probably opened up the exit wound in his back. Raphael thought he could feel moisture there.

"If I were you, Maclaine," Raphael said, as the deputy unlocked the iron-barred door to one of the two cells, "I'd think real carefully about my future.

Something happens to me, and my friends are gonna be real mad."

Maclaine pushed him into the cell. "You shut up! You're a murderer, a thief, and a rustler. I think we can safely say the hanging'll be at high noon. Whole town will turn out, that's my guess." He smiled coldly. "We ain't had a hanging in Aurora in years."

Raphael looked at him. "Being as there's no point in protesting my innocence, on all three counts, I won't waste my breath."

"Where's Harrison's money?"

"Don't know nothing about it," Raphael said.

The gun whipped out, so quickly that, even though Raphael had known it would come to this, he could not move aside. It struck him high up across the face. Blood gushed down his cheek from the outside corner of his left eye.

Ken Sanders gasped, turning white.

Maclaine ignored him. "Where you been hidin' these past few days?" he asked.

"Up in the hills." Raphael managed to smile. No easy task, with blood pouring down his face and his left eye hurting like hell.

Maclaine struck him with the gun again. This time Raphael was prepared and he ducked, so the barrel only grazed his shoulder. Sanders cried out.

"You need some new *cojones,* boy," Maclaine snarled at the deputy. "This one's a killer, remember? Well, Caldwell, guess you buried the loot somewhere and we'll never know. But guess what? It don't matter." He smiled, but it was more of a sneer.

Raphael did not reply, thinking about the wire. Maclaine's smile increased, and as if he'd read

Raphael's mind he said, "We cut that wire three days ago."

Raphael turned white.

Emily had one thought, one she could not chase from her mind as she walked the two miles to school: He was gone. As soon as she had begun her morning chores, she had dashed outside, already knowing the truth. Emily had stood in the open doorway of the barn staring at its empty interior for many, many moments. He had left. Without even a good-bye.

And she cared. She shouldn't, dear Lord—he was amoral, he preferred Veronica, he had used her—but she cared. She just knew he wasn't a killer, and maybe he'd had a reason to steal. Harrison was an awfully abrasive man.

Emily wiped her eyes with the sleeve of her coat. Ahead, the small, whitewashed schoolhouse beckoned, its pitched rooftop framed by pines. A group of children played in the front yard. Emily was usually the first to arrive. Today she was late. She had performed her chores like a sleepwalker, very dazed and strangely grief-stricken.

She would never see him again.

"Miss Emily! Miss Emily!"

Emily paused in the yard, blinking at Theodore Green, who was running toward her. She hoped there were no traces of tears on her face. "Good morning, Theodore." She pasted a smile on her lips. "Can you help me stoke up the stove?"

The freckle-faced boy was panting, his breath puffing in the icy air. "They got him, Miss Emily! They got him this morning, they did!"

Randy came forward, all slouched over, hands

jammed in his dungarees pockets, but his eyes were bright. "Caught him breaking into the depot, they did. It was a trap. Maclaine knew he'd try to use the telegraph. Whole town's talkin' about it."

Emily's world had stopped. And with it her heart and lungs, or so it seemed. Then she shoved the veil of shock aside. "The . . . outlaw?"

"Caldwell. Yeah." Randy smiled happily at her.

Five other children were grouped around them now, their voices raised in excitement as they began discussing the astonishing news.

Emily could hardly assimilate what she had heard. Her heart resumed beating, but she was filled with anguish. The air in her lungs seemed to choke her. Dear Lord. What would happen now?

"Miss Emily? Are you all right?" Betsy asked with concern. "You are white as a sheet."

School. She had a schoolful of children to teach. Emily swallowed, smiled. "Randy, ring the bell, please. Everyone, inside."

Randy walked over to the bell to obey, and it began to peal across the countryside. The children trooped into the school. But Emily did not move.

It finally hit her.

They had caught him, he was in jail, and maybe his life was at stake. And Emily did not want him to die.

"Hello, Miss Emily." Ken Sanders had opened the jailhouse door at her knock. He smiled at her.

Emily managed to smile back. She clutched the wicker basket she carried more tightly. "May I come in?"

Ken's eyes widened as he finally noticed the basket, and then he flushed. "Please." He stepped aside.

Emily moved into the front office of the jailhouse. The door to the back room where the two jail cells were located was wide open. But Emily glimpsed only Raphael's boots, for he was lying down on a cot, the rest of his body hidden from her view.

Ken shut the front door. "You sure look pretty today, Miss Emily."

Emily jerked, realizing that the deputy was blushing. "Thank you," she said. Out of the corner of her eye she saw the boots disappear from the end of the bed. Then she noticed that Ken was regarding the basket she held.

"I'm sure no one's thought to bring the prisoner his dinner," Emily said with a firm smile.

Ken's eyes widened in surprise. "You brought Caldwell dinner?" he exclaimed.

Emily had the odd feeling that he had thought the dinner was for himself. "Mr. Sanders, all men need sustenance, and more importantly all men should be treated with decency and kindness. Yes, I brought Ra—Mr. Caldwell his dinner."

The deputy had recovered. Before Emily knew what he was doing he had taken the basket out of her hand. "You sure are kind, Miss Emily, kind and good, like everyone says. Henry Cooper is a fool." He was blushing again. Emily could not believe her ears. Then Ken added, "I guess he does deserve a last meal."

"A last meal!" Emily cried.

"Just a figure of speech."

Emily stared at the deputy. "I do hope that law

and order will prevail in Aurora, and not hysteria and a distorted need for vengeance."

"Sure," he mumbled.

Emily watched him set the basket on his desk. She despaired. How could she visit Raphael if she did not bring him his dinner?

Ken faced her. "You want something else?"

Emily tried to think of an excuse to stay, or visit Raphael, and failed. Numbly, she shook her head, glancing toward the jail cell. And she cried out.

Raphael stood gripping the bars, in full view now. And his left eye was swollen and turning black and blue. Dried blood marked his cheek. Without another thought Emily dashed past the deputy and into the back room. "What has happened here?" she cried. But up close it was even worse. Raphael had been hit brutally. He regarded her impassively. Emily felt close to tears.

Ken raced up behind her. "Miss Emily, you shouldn't be in there!"

Furious, Emily whirled. "Who did this?" she demanded.

Ken was pale. "He . . . uh . . . fell."

Emily knew a lie when she heard one. She turned to face Raphael. "How badly are you hurt?"

His gaze flickered over her. "I'll live. Until the hanging."

Emily gripped the bars. "There won't be a hanging!" Their gazes held. Emily saw the resignation written in his eyes. Terror assailed her. "This is America!"

"This is Aurora," Raphael returned, far too calmly.

"Miss Emily, you can't talk to the prisoner," Ken said from behind, with real dismay.

Emily turned. "I insist upon seeing the prisoner. I want to tend his wound."

"You can't!" Ken was aghast.

"I can and I will."

"I'll have to check with Maclaine."

"You'll do no such thing." Emily assumed her best schoolteacher's voice, one stern and filled with warning. "This man deserves medical treatment. Unlock the door, Mr. Sanders."

"Miss Emily . . ." Ken hesitated.

"Unlock the door," Emily commanded.

Sighing, he reached for the keys on his belt and unlocked the door. Immediately Emily shoved her way inside. "Now, bring me hot water, alcohol, and a fresh, clean cloth."

"I can't leave you here alone with him!" Ken cried.

"Oh, please," Emily snapped. "This man is hurt. And one only has to look at him to know that he is not a killer."

But Ken would not budge. He glanced anxiously toward the front office, as if waiting for reinforcements. "I cannot leave you alone, inside, with him."

Emily decided to ignore him. She reached up and gently touched the lower edge of Raphael's jaw. "Let me look."

"Take your fill," he said carelessly.

It was an ugly cut, and Emily was sick just looking at it. "I'm afraid this will scar without stitches."

Raphael shrugged. But he turned his head so their eyes could meet. "Won't be my first scar, Emily," he said very softly.

"But . . . it's a shame," she returned, her voice as low.

Something seemed to fill up the space between them. Raphael asked, "Did you mean what you said?"

"Yes." Emily did not have to ask him what he was referring to. "I know you did not kill that vaquero, or those other three men."

The corners of his mouth turned up ever so slightly. A warm light appeared in eyes. And Emily's heart turned over.

It was then that Emily became aware of a commotion outside the barred window to his cell. *Ping! Ping!* The sound of objects hitting the bars was accompanied by youthful male snickering. Somebody was throwing stones at Raphael from outside the building.

"Forget it," Raphael said softly. "It's just a couple of kids."

And then Emily heard two voices that she recognized, voices belonging to Randy and Webster. She froze.

"Yeah," Raphael said, understanding in his eyes.

"Oh, dear Lord," Emily whispered, stricken. Realizing with brutal clarity that it was only a matter of time until one of the children identified him as her cousin from Rock Springs and she was found out.

10

"Stay away from that window," Emily said breathlessly. But she was frightened. What would she do, what would she say, when the entire town accused her of being an accomplice to this man's crimes?

"I already have," Raphael said.

Emily whirled at his oddly somber tone. She saw compassion—and pity—in his eyes.

"Maybe you should 'fess up now, claiming a real soft, tender heart." He spoke so low that Ken Sanders could not have heard him.

It struck Emily that he was worried about her—when he was the one in dire circumstance. "I'll be fine." She would, she decided, tell the truth when the time came. She did not believe in dishonesty.

From behind they heard a door open and slam shut, followed by Maclaine's baritone. "What the hell is going on in here?" he demanded.

Emily gave Raphael a last look as she moved away

from him, wondering if she would ever see him
again—if she would ever be close enough to even
touch him again. His amber eyes remained steady
upon her. It almost appeared that he mirrored her
sentiments exactly, but Emily knew she was seeing
what she wanted to see.

"Miss Emily Anderson!" Maclaine shouted.
"Good Gawd!" He was genuinely shocked. Then he
turned on Sanders, who was literally cowering. "You
let her in there? You lost your marbles?"

Emily watched Maclaine open the door, and then
he jerked her out of the cell. She shrugged free as the
door banged closed. She watched him lock it, feeling
very much like crying. Her heart seemed to be
breaking. Raphael remained standing in the center
of his cell, carefully observant through the iron bars.

"What in Gawd's name possessed you, Miss Emily? Your father ought to take a strap to your hide."

Emily wet her lips. "Sheriff Maclaine, I demand
to know what happened to Mr. Caldwell."

Maclaine's watery blue eyes widened. "Beg your
pardon?"

"Who beat him up?" She stared coldly.

Maclaine's posture changed. His hands went to his
hips. His chest puffed out. "Now, see here, little girl,
you seem to be making an accusation, one I do not
like. Why don't you go back home and tend to your
daddy? Ain't it about time to get his supper on?"

Emily sucked up her courage. "Do not take that
condescending tone with me, Sheriff. I asked a simple question. I would appreciate a simple answer."

It was a moment before Maclaine could respond.
"He fell." His eyes had narrowed.

"When is the circuit judge due in town?" Emily asked, praying it would be soon.

"Not for another two weeks, if he's on time." Maclaine crossed his arms. "What does the judge have to do with the prisoner?"

"Surely he will be tried, and fairly," Emily said.

Maclaine laughed. "You sure are something, Miss Emily. Now I see why Henry Cooper went and jilted you. Good day. Give my best to your pa."

But Emily did not move. Maclaine's condescension and brutality infuriated her, and his lack of respect for the law terrified her. She darted a glance at Raphael. He had come up to the bars, which he gripped, and his expression was strained.

"Maybe I had better wire the federal marshal myself," Emily said.

Raphael's eyes widened. Maclaine's eyes bulged. "Now, you listen here, girlie! You get home where you belong, and keep your nose out of my business!" He marched forward until he towered over Emily. "Do you understand me?" he roared. His breath smelled sour, of tobacco and whiskey and bad teeth.

Emily swallowed, backing up, until her rear end hit the door. "I believe you have made yourself very clear," she said huskily. Her gaze met Raphael's again. I'm sorry, she thought, so sorry.

And he was upset. Distress was written all over his handsome face. "Go home," he said, low but distinct. "Do as Maclaine says."

Maclaine jerked, regarding Raphael briefly, then grabbed Emily's arm. He dragged her over to Ken. "Get her outta here. And no one—I repeat, no one—visits the prisoner!"

Emily was propelled forward. Dismay filled her. But she was angry. "Let me go, Mr. Sanders."

In the front office the red-faced deputy released her arm. "I apologize, Miss Emily." He hung his head.

"For your behavior—or his?" Emily snapped.

He grimaced, but before he could reply, the front door opened. Emily's eyes widened as Veronica Richards ran into the room. "Sheriff! Oh, God, Sheriff!" Tears were pouring down her face. "Sheriff!" she screamed as Maclaine came hurrying out of the back room.

"Veronica, honey, what is it?" Maclaine rushed to her.

Veronica collapsed in his arms, sobbing and incoherent.

Emily watched her, a distinct sense of dread creeping over her.

And past the weeping woman and the sheriff, she glimpsed Raphael standing in his cell, his expression grim.

Emily walked over to Veronica, laying a hand upon her back. "Veronica? It's me, Emily Anderson. What's wrong? What has happened?"

Veronica turned away from the sheriff to look at Emily, but as she did so she saw Raphael. She screamed. "Him! I know it was him!" Her face was contorted with fury, and it made her spectacularly ugly.

Maclaine caught her before she could run into the back room. "What's happened? Veronica, tell us what's happened." He shook her hard.

She blinked, meeting Maclaine's eyes. "Daddy!"

she choked. "I found him this morning . . . in bed . . . dead!"

Emily stared. And glanced toward the stranger in their midst.

"Oh, Gawd, no!" Maclaine cried as Veronica again collapsed against his chest.

Emily hugged herself. "Did he die in his sleep, Veronica?" But she already knew the answer.

Veronica shoved herself free of the sheriff. "No," she cried bitterly. "Oh, no. He was murdered while he slept—shot point-blank, right in the head."

Emily stood on the boardwalk outside the jail, watching as two cowboys from Harrison's ranch halted their mounts in front of the hitching rail. A pack horse trailed behind them, a large, oilskin-covered body hanging over its back.

Emily was not the town's only observer. Except for Veronica, who had collapsed in a chair inside the jail, every single resident of the town seemed to have gathered on the boardwalk. People were talking, some voices hushed with fear and shock, others raised in fear and anger. Emily hugged herself.

"Emily."

Emily turned and saw her father striding un-steadily toward her. She did not smile at him as he came and put his arm around her. He reeked of alcohol. "I just heard. God-awful. Can't believe it."

It wasn't Raphael. Emily would remain loyal to her belief that he wasn't a killer. Surely she was too sensible and intelligent a woman to be fooled by a man merely because he was good-looking and he had kissed her once, unforgettably.

But Emily was sick, frightened, uneasy. She slid

her arm around her father as Maclaine walked over to the body and uncovered it. Emily averted her eyes. She wanted to remember Lloyd Harrison as he had been in life, in spite of his faults, because she'd heard what a bullet to the head could do at close range. She heard people gasp. Someone began to weep.

"He's been dead awhile," Maclaine announced. "Veronica says she found him at eight this morning. My guess is he got it in the middle of the night."

Emily couldn't help wondering where Raphael had been last night. She didn't have a clue as to when he'd left the farm. She felt sicker than she had before.

Someone came up on her other side. "This is so terrible."

Emily flinched, meeting Betsy Green's blue eyes. And all she could think about was that Raphael was in the jail directly behind them. She licked her lips. "Yes, it is."

Betsy found and gripped her hand. "There's a murderer loose among us. I'm scared."

"Don't be," Emily said. "Whoever did this had a reason. No one wants to hurt you."

"I hope you're right."

Suddenly the jailhouse door opened. Emily shifted and saw Veronica as she staggered out. She was wobbling like a drunk. Instantly Emily raced to her and put her arm around her. Veronica leaned heavily upon her, making Emily think that she would keel right over without support.

"Veronica, let me take you across the street to the hotel. You need to lie down."

"No. I don't want to lie down. I want justice!" Veronica's voice rose to a shout.

Heads turned her way. Murmurs of agreement sounded. Emily stiffened. Maclaine raised up his hands. "Folks, folks, I want everyone to be calm. We got nothing to worry about! The killer's locked up, behind bars, and there ain't goin' to be any more murders here in Aurora!"

A few men cheered.

"I say we string him up now!" someone shouted.

Emily was still appalled that Maclaine would speak as if Raphael's guilt were a proven fact, but now she froze, her gaze shooting to the speaker. George Smith's chubby, almost cherubic face had changed beyond recognition.

"Hear! hear!" someone cried.

"String him up!" a woman shouted hoarsely.

"Sheriff Maclaine!" Emily strode down the two steps of the boardwalk to face the sheriff. "We do not know that Raphael Caldwell is guilty!"

"We know. Ain't no other possible suspect," Maclaine said with open exasperation.

Emily looked from the sheriff to the crowd. She saw the faces of everyone she'd grown up with— men, women, and children, many of whom she liked, loved, respected, and admired—but they all appeared to be strangers now, monstrous strangers, thirsty for a man's blood. Emily was stricken.

"Go get him!" the barber, Swenson, shouted. "Hey, Sheriff, what are we waiting for?"

The crowd roared in agreement.

Suddenly Maclaine nodded. The sheriff and the two cowboys from the ranch strode past Emily and into the jail. A moment later they reappeared, with

Raphael held roughly between them. Emily met his gaze. Although his jaw was flexed, she saw that he was afraid.

And she was terrified.

"We'll take him out to Oak Meadow," Maclaine decided.

The crowd cheered.

Suddenly Emily felt someone jerking on her coat sleeve. She turned and met Betsy's wide, stunned eyes.

"I don't understand," Betsy whispered, her gaze going from Emily to Raphael. "Your cousin?"

"He's not my cousin. I lied," Emily whispered back, her heart pounding like a drum.

"I still don't understand," Betsy cried.

And Emily heard a child shout, "Hey, that's Miss Emily's cousin from Rock Springs!" But it was unclear if anyone else heard him, because the entire crowd was animated, talking, cheering, jeering at once. The throng had turned into a mob.

Emily looked at Raphael. He gave her a smile that would melt the most frozen of hearts. I love him, she thought helplessly.

"Let's go." Maclaine pushed him forward and down the steps of the boardwalk.

Emily acted. "No!" she screamed, flying after the sheriff and Raphael, racing around them to block their progress. "No!"

"Get outta the way, Miss Emily," Maclaine said dangerously.

Emily almost thought he might strike her to force her aside. Apparently Raphael thought so too, because he stiffened, his eyes glowing dangerously. Emily lifted her chin. "No."

Maclaine started to speak, but Emily cut him off. "No! Raphael Caldwell is innocent, and I know it for a fact!" she cried loudly.

The townsfolk grew silent. Tension rippled through the crowd, and with it, expectancy.

"What the hell are you doin'?" Maclaine demanded.

"Raphael could not have killed Harrison last night," Emily said. She felt her cheeks beginning to burn.

"How do you know?"

Emily shot a brief glance at Raphael, who was as still as a statue, and then at her father, who was suddenly alert, and at Betsy, who was mesmerized. "I know." She licked her lips, gulped air, and raised her voice another octave. "I know, because last night he was with me, all night long."

"What?" Maclaine said, his face paling.

"How clear do I have to be?" Emily cried, avoiding Raphael's eyes. "He spent all of last night with me—in my bedroom—in my bed."

11

Emily's words were greeted with absolute silence.

Emily's heart had never pounded more swiftly or harder. She was light-headed. Weak-kneed. Everyone gathered around the jail was staring at her in disbelief and shock. Including her father. But Emily had to turn her gaze slowly to Raphael.

He was staring. As fully surprised as everyone else.

Maclaine recovered first, speaking over the sudden murmuring of the crowd. "Do you realize what you've just said, Miss Emily?"

Emily nodded. "It's true," she said, her voice low.

Gus stumbled forward. "Can't be true!" he cried, aghast.

"I'm sorry, Papa," Emily whispered.

Gus regarded her as if he did not know her.

"I think she's lying!" Veronica's shrill voice pierced through Emily's barely discernible words. "She's lying!"

"Why would Miss Emily lie?" someone asked—it

was Liza Arnold, her face drawn into lines of pity and concern.

"Because she's always been jealous of me," Veronica flared. "Always, ever since we were children."

"I'm not lying," Emily said, taken aback by Veronica's vehemence. "And I'm not jealous of you or anyone else, Veronica. Raphael spent all of last night with me."

"Raphael?" Veronica asked mockingly.

The entire town was staring, at Emily, Veronica, and Raphael. His face had become completely expressionless. Veronica remained furious. It crossed Emily's mind as she looked from Raphael to Veronica that the widow had strong feelings for the outlaw too—and that she was the one who was jealous. How ironic it was.

"All the more reason to string him up," Maclaine spat, "if he ruined Miss Emily."

Emily inhaled, stunned.

"Miss Emily is lying," someone said. It was a young male voice, which Emily recognized. She turned to regard fifteen-year-old Randy Willis.

He stared at her with open accusation. The freckles stood out on his pale face.

"What are you sayin', boy?" Maclaine asked.

Randy faced the sheriff. "She brought him to school with her yesterday and the day before. Said he was her cousin from Rock Springs." His gaze shifted to Emily, filled with bitter hurt. "You lied to us."

"Dear Lord!" a woman gasped. "She brought an outlaw to the school!"

Emily wanted to explain to Randy and the other children, but what could she say? The crowd was growing restless. Everyone was talking up a storm, all at once. "He's not a bad man," Emily tried, but was cut off.

"What is going on here, Miss Emily?" Maclaine demanded. "You lost your mind? Bringing a killer to a schoolful of children?"

"He's not a killer!" Emily cried. "He's never killed anyone!"

"She had no choice." Raphael's words rang out with utter conviction. "I held her hostage and threatened her and her father with their lives."

"No," Emily whispered.

His gaze was diamond-hard. "She had no choice," he repeated, "but to do as I said."

"You rape her too?" Maclaine asked. "Huh?" He gripped Raphael's elbow tightly.

"No," Emily said, answering before Raphael could speak. "No. He did not." She swallowed. "I was willing."

Gus hid his face behind his hands.

Raphael gazed steadily at her, a long moment going by. "Yeah," he finally said. "She was willing."

"Gawddamnit," Maclaine said. "He's still a killer and a thief. Let's go. To Oak Meadow."

"No!" Emily cried. But Maclaine was pushing Raphael forward. Emily whirled, facing her father. "Papa! He's been with me at the farm for three days. He didn't hurt me, and he helped at school. He's not a killer. Please do something!"

Gus's eyes widened. At first he did not move. But he knew his daughter well, and in spite of his stupor he must have sensed the depth of her emotions, for his expression suddenly hardened. "Sheriff! You can't hang a man for something he clearly did not do. If my daughter said he was with her, then he did not murder Lloyd."

Maclaine turned, brows lifted. "Go home, Anderson. Or better yet, go back to the saloon. And your daughter is not to be trusted. She hid an outlaw, a fugitive from justice—and that's a crime too."

Emily turned white.

"Gus Anderson is right," Liza Arnold said, stepping forward. "Emily would never lie; it's not her nature. Caldwell said himself that he forced her to hide him. That man should do right by her. We don't hang men for seducing pretty women." She smiled at Emily. "And Emily has taken care of just about everyone in this town. We shouldn't turn on her now, or blame her for fallin' for the devil himself. Besides, what if he's innocent?"

Emily wanted to hug her. A few murmurs of agreement met Liza's suggestion.

And then Emily realized what Liza actually meant. Her eyes widened. Surely Liza was not referring to marriage! Her gaze flew to Raphael. He seemed stunned as well.

"Now, I don't know about that," Gus said. He put his arm around Emily. "Just because my girl made a mistake . . . She's a good girl and—"

Liza cut him off. "Gus Anderson, your daughter's already nineteen, and if she don't marry soon, she never will. Won't be the first shotgun wedding. Besides, what if she is in the family way?"

Emily could not believe that this conversation was taking place, much less in front of the entire town. She caught Raphael's piercing regard and hung her head. She was beginning to shake. Then she glimpsed Veronica, who was white. Veronica's eyes met Emily's, her face a mask of hatred. Then she turned and stalked back into the jail.

"Now, hold on, folks." Maclaine raised both hands. "We got a murderer on the loose. First Pete Benson, then Lloyd Harrison. If it ain't Caldwell, then who is it?"

No one answered. Men and women shook their heads. But Swenson said, "Guess you better find out soon, yes, Sheriff? Before we've got another murder on our hands."

Hands on his hips, Maclaine faced the crowd. "Then we can kill two birds with one stone. Randy, get the reverend."

Emily lost her ability to breathe. Raphael had turned oddly white. Suddenly Liza had her arm around Emily, and she smiled at her, squeezing once. But Emily felt as if she were in the midst of a dream. Surely she would awaken at any moment!

"I'm here," Reverend Prescott said, stepping forward. His pockmarked face was set gravely. "Sheriff, there is no real need for haste. Perhaps I should speak privately with the parties involved."

"There most certainly is a need for haste," Maclaine said. He pushed Raphael forward until he stood beside Emily. "Marry 'em."

Prescott hesitated.

Gus stepped forward. "Reverend, what if there is a child on the way? I think my daughter's gone and decided her very own future." Gus looked at Emily. "Headstrong," he said. "Just like her ma."

Emily was quaking. She had to protest—either that or wind up wed to a total stranger, an outlaw, a thief. But if she now denied her own words, Raphael would die. Emily did not speak.

"My dear, is this what you want?" Prescott asked gently.

Emily met his gaze. She was terrified. She nodded. She would not, could not, did not dare look at Raphael.

"Step forward."

Suddenly Emily found herself standing side by side with Raphael as the reverend asked Raphael his full name. Her pulse was explosive. Prescott asked the crowd if he could borrow a ring. Liza Arnold promptly produced her wedding band. And Prescott began reciting the words she knew by heart. Emily felt faint.

"Do you, Raphael Caldwell, take this woman, Emily Anderson . . ."

Emily closed her eyes as the reverend's steady baritone washed over her in a calming wave. She heard Raphael murmur, "I do," and she promptly blinked. She still failed to find the courage to look at him.

"Do you, Emily Anderson . . ." Prescott began.

Emily realized she was twisting her hands, and she forced them to be still. "I do," she squeaked.

"You may put the ring on Emily's fourth finger," Prescott said.

Emily's legs were weak. She felt Raphael lift her left hand. She kept her eyes on the ground as he slipped Liza's ring on her finger. She stared at the worn gold band as tears blurred her vision. *Oh, Lord.* What had she done?

"In the eyes of God, I do pronounce you man and wife."

There was a deafening silence in Aurora.

And Emily finally glanced up. To her utter amazement she saw something soft and warm and steady in Raphael's golden gaze. Then Maclaine spoke.

"Okay, boys. Now let's string him up."

12

Murmurs of surprise greeted Maclaine's words.

Emily was in shock. She could not move. Surely Maclaine did not intend to hang Raphael now.

"You heard me," Maclaine barked. "Sanders!"

The deputy grabbed Raphael's arm, beginning to propel him forward. Emily felt as if she were inside a whirlwind—in its very vortex. Her gaze clashed with Raphael's. She recognized the sheer disbelief that she saw there as a mirror image of her own stricken emotions.

How could this be happening?

"Sheriff," Emily cried desperately as Raphael was urged forward. He stumbled, half-turning around to stare at her. "Sheriff!" Emily screamed.

But Maclaine ignored her, rudely brushing by, Harrison's two men on his heels. Emily was frozen. And then Liza Arnold put her bulk smack in front of the sheriff and his men. "Maclaine! This is a wrong, and two wrongs don't make a right."

Someone in the crowd muttered in agreement. Someone else cried, "String him up!"

"Move aside, Missus Arnold," Maclaine said coldly. "We got a killer here, one I mean to hang."

Liza did not move. "You just let Reverend Prescott marry them, you did, and now you want to bury the groom? Have you no heart, Maclaine?"

"Look, Missus Arnold, you're interfering with the law." Maclaine's watery blue eyes narrowed. There was a warning behind his words.

"And I'm interferin' too," Gus said, suddenly stepping forward beside Liza. He no longer seemed very drunk. "You can't do this, Sheriff. My daughter says he's innocent, and Emily don't lie."

Maclaine laughed. "Hate to say this, but your daughter's a liar and a goddamn good one—and don't we all know it? She hid this man at your farm, did she not?"

Gus's face was pale. "She had her reasons."

"Yeah, we all know what they were, now, don't we?" Maclaine's smile was not pleasant. "Let's put it this way—her reasons weren't very ladylike. But then, your daughter's just proved she's not much of a lady, hasn't she?"

Liza gasped. Gus lost all of his color. Emily could not believe what Maclaine had said. Worse, she wanted to die. And everyone in town, it seemed, had fallen silent.

Had a pin dropped, it would have been heard.

Suddenly Raphael's voice cut through the shocked silence. His tone was surprisingly calm for a man about to swing. "Maclaine," he said, "at least let me kiss the bride."

Maclaine gave him a disparaging look. "Ain't you

gotten your fill already, Caldwell? Sanders, boys, let's go."

"I'll come willingly," Raphael interrupted before Ken could move, "if you let me have a proper good-bye." His golden eyes were cool. Suggesting that if his demands were not met he'd fight dangerously, taking a few good men with him when all was said and done.

Emily realized she was hugging herself. Sweat was running down her body in rivulets, and she found it difficult to breathe. Her gaze met Raphael's. She could read nothing there other than a readiness to do battle when the odds were dismally low.

The sheriff folded his arms. He studied Raphael. "Fine. Go ahead," Maclaine said brusquely after a moment.

Raphael was steered toward Emily by Sanders. Emily did not move away. Her eyes widened, her heart raced. This could not possibly be the end for them—it had to be the beginning! Emily realized that she was crying.

He suddenly smiled at her.

"Don't cry," he said in a low voice. His gaze held hers. Something urgent and fine flickered there.

"I can't help it," Emily whispered. "This isn't right. I . . . I can't bear it if you die." She swallowed. "Maybe . . . I'll die too."

Raphael didn't respond, his gaze searching, as if trying to gauge the depth of her feelings, the truth behind her words. Then he turned to Sanders. "You mind? I really don't feel like kissing my wife good-bye with you breathing down my neck."

Ken released his arm, taking a small step backward. Maclaine—and the entire town—continued to watch them carefully. Emily realized that she was trembling. "I can't," she whispered.

Raphael moved closer to Emily. He slid his arm around her waist. Anything tender she had seen in his eyes had disappeared. Suddenly Emily wanted to move away from him, for there was a strange, flat light in his eyes, one that was frightening. But his grip was viselike as he bent toward her. Then his mouth found hers.

An instant later she was pinned against his side, his arm a band of steel around her torso. And he had one hand around her throat. "I'll kill her," he said, his voice ringing out with utter conviction. "Break her neck in two. No one move."

And no one did move, not in that next instant, which seemed to stretch into an eternity. All eyes were riveted on the outlaw and Emily, while Emily was absolutely frozen, refusing to comprehend what Raphael—her husband—had just said. But it struck her cruelly. He was again taking her hostage. But surely he would not hurt her—would he? Surely this was a ruse.

Yet Emily could not even turn her head to look up into his eyes because of the grip he had on her neck.

"Let her go." Maclaine shifted his body slightly. His right hand, at his hip, opened wide. Inches from his gun.

"Get your hands up!" Raphael snapped.

Maclaine's hands went up, open-palmed. "You fool. You'll never get away with this."

"Everyone," Raphael snapped, his grip tightening on Emily's throat. Emily choked. *"Everyone! Hands in the air!"*

Dozens of hands went into the air. As they did, Raphael began dragging Emily with him as he moved toward Maclaine. Emily stumbled, acutely aware now of her small neck in his large, powerful hand. She had no doubt that he could snap it in two if he wanted to.

But he wouldn't. Emily believed that with all of her heart—didn't she? But if so, why was she terrified?

They paused, face to face with Maclaine. Quick as a snake, keeping his grip on her throat, Raphael pulled the sheriff's revolver from his holster, using the arm he'd had around Emily's waist. Then he swung the gun up and out and down—on the back of Maclaine's head. The sheriff collapsed on the ground.

"You killed him!" someone gasped.

Raphael clamped one arm around Emily's waist, simultaneously pressing the barrel of the revolver against her temple. "Unfortunately, Maclaine is hardly dead. But I guarantee he'll have a sore head when he wakes up." His gaze measured the crowd. "I'm taking her with me," he said. "For insurance."

No one spoke. No one moved. Emily finally glimpsed Betsy and Liza standing side by side, as white as a pair of ghosts. She thought she must be whiter than they were. The barrel felt cold and lethal against her skin. Her temples were throbbing, maybe from the pressure of the gun. She held their eyes.

Emily's fear must have shown, because Liza cried, "Let her go! Just let her go! Miss Emily's never harmed anyone! We'll let you ride outta here, mister!"

Raphael's smile was brief and unpleasant. "I'm

not partial to a hole in the back—although that's a sight better than swinging from the end of a rope." He jerked Emily forward. "You fire at me or chase me, and she's dead."

"Don't," Gus cried. "Don't hurt my daughter!"

Emily could not turn her head to meet her father's eyes. She did not dare, not with the barrel of the revolver pressing into her temple. She was afraid he might pull the trigger mistakenly—or not. But she knew Gus was frightened. She heard the anguish in his voice.

Emily realized now that her knees were weak and almost useless, that Raphael was holding her upright. Belatedly, she recognized the cause of her terror: She did not know the man who held her hostage, not at all. She never had.

He pushed her toward the closest horse. Emily wasn't quite sure how he managed it, but suddenly she was astride, and so was he, behind her. And they were galloping out of town.

Miraculously, perhaps, no shots rang out.

They rode like the wind for what seemed a very long time. Raphael did not let the bay gelding slow until they were well into the hills and forging up a shallow creek. In spite of her fear Emily felt sorry for their mount, for the water was freezing—she knew it because her shoes and stockings were soon soaked. But a few minutes later Raphael urged the bay back out of the creek onto the opposite bank. In a small clearing among the firs, he finally halted their lathered, blowing horse.

Emily was numb. She did not move as Raphael slid to the ground. She saw him stroke the bay's neck, but the gesture and the brief, soft words he uttered held no meaning for her. She stared.

He looked up. His gaze was piercing and direct.

Emily felt tears gather in her eyes. She blinked to hold them back.

He drop-reined the bay and moved over to her, holding up his hands.

Emily's grip on the pommel of the saddle tightened.

"C'mon down," he said. "Your legs are probably sore, chafed. You need to get dry too."

Her thighs felt raw. The rough, madcap ride had torn her pantalets in too many places to count. Emily imagined that she would have more than a few blisters. And her toes were numb from the frigid water. But she shook her head negatively.

His expression, which was hard to read, did not change. He settled his palms around her waist. Emily tensed, but to no avail. He pulled her out of the saddle and down to the ground.

For an instant Emily found herself thigh to thigh and bosom to chest with him, half in his embrace. She yanked her arms free of his grasp. But the moment he released her she stumbled and would have fallen if he hadn't caught her.

And Emily *was* in his arms. A place she had dreamed so often of being, stupidly. It was the last place she wanted to be now. She tried to shove free of him, but his mouth tightened, as did his grip.

"Emily."

Tears were again burning her eyes. Emily finally looked up to meet his gaze.

"Don't you know that I would never hurt you?" he said.

Emily's heart skipped. "I . . . I don't know what to think."

"I would never hurt you," he said, low and firm. "Not ever. Not after all that you've done for me."

She looked away, blindly. Oddly enough, she had hoped that he would never hurt her because he cared, not because he owed her. She was hurt. She was ten times a fool.

"Here." He peeled off the bandanna tied around his throat. He wasn't wearing a coat, just the sheepskin vest, and Emily wondered if he was cold. "Use this to dry your legs and feet."

She heard him moving away. Emily wiped her eyes with one frozen fist—she wasn't wearing gloves—and stared after him. He disappeared into the firs.

She realized he was probably taking care of his natural needs, but a number of minutes passed and he did not return. Emily's pulse had returned to normal by now, and with it, her confusion. She truly did not know what to think, what to believe. Her heart was screaming one thing, her mind another. But dutifully she used the bandanna to dry her ankles and feet the best that she could.

Finally Emily was curious. She decided to follow him.

It was easy to find his trail, because he wasn't trying to hide it and he hadn't gone far. He was crouched down behind some boulders where the stand of firs ended. They were high up in the hills. As Emily came up behind him she realized with a start where they were: within a quarter mile of the Harrison ranch!

His arm whipped out and he pulled her down to

her knees beside him. "Don't make noise. Don't stand either."

Emily nodded, her eyes wide. From where they crouched she could see the barns, corrals, bunkhouse, and the ranch house itself. It was the middle of a working day, and they did not see a soul. Only a few horses stood dozing in the paddocks.

"I don't understand," Emily finally whispered. Her nerves were tingling with unease. "Why are we here?"

"I don't expect you to understand." He turned his back to the spread and slid down the rock to sit cross-legged on the ground. Emily watched him draw tobacco from a pouch in his breast pocket, and with it, a small sheet of paper. He deftly rolled the weed, nipped the ends between his teeth, and struck flint on the toe of his boot. Eying her once from under his long, dark lashes, he took a deep, slow draw.

Slowly Emily sat down beside him. "Do you think this is the time and place to rest and smoke?" Her tone was not sarcastic. It trembled.

"You sound worried, like you care." His golden eyes flickered over her.

"Course I don't," she retorted. "Why would I care?"

He took another long, leisurely draw. They both watched spirals of smoke curl into the cold air and finally drift apart and disappear. "Why would you lie," he asked, very casually, "to save my life?"

Emily hugged her knees to her chest, careful to make sure her skirts belled fully about her. Not even the tips of her wet shoes showed. Why had she lied about them spending the night together? "I believe in justice."

He faced her, the movement sudden. His eyes smoked. "You still think me innocent?"

Emily stared, but did not hesitate. "Yes, I do."

He ground out the cheroot and tucked it back in his breast pocket. Suddenly his fingers were tilting up her chin. "You're an amazing woman, Emily. You amaze me."

Emily could not speak. His fingers were warm and strong under her chin, and the feel of him coupled with his proximity and his strikingly handsome face were making her insides do handsprings. It crossed her somewhat-dazed mind that he was going to kiss her again. His eyes were hot and bright. Emily felt liquid, molten.

Instead, he smiled, dropping his hand. "We'll camp here for the night," he said.

13

It didn't make any sense. Emily remained seated against the boulder, watching Raphael rummage through the bay's saddlebags. Why would they spend the night so close to the Harrison ranch—so close to Aurora? Something was afoot. This man was not all that he seemed.

But Emily had no answers, and Raphael wasn't talking. It was late afternoon now, with dusk rapidly approaching. It was far colder than it had been at high noon. Emily huddled in her coat. At least she had a coat. Raphael wore nothing but a flannel shirt and his sheepskin vest. He had to be cold.

He turned, smiling. "Hit the jackpot."

Emily watched him stride toward her, his legs long, sheathed in his buckskin pants. She averted her eyes. He was holding beef jerky in his hands. "Hungry?" he asked.

Emily realized that she was, and she nodded. He squatted beside her, handing her several pieces of the dried beef. "I'm sorry we can't make a fire, because there's coffee in those bags too."

Emily chewed on the jerky. She'd already known that they would not have a fire to warm them that night.

Raphael returned to the saddlebags. He had already untacked the bay, which was nibbling a few winter-dry shoots of grass. He removed the bedroll from the saddle and laid it out on the ground beside Emily. Their gazes met.

Immediately Emily looked away.

"We're going to have to share," he said.

Emily's heart banged wildly against her ribs. Avoiding his eyes, she nodded.

It was dark an hour later, the first evening stars popping out of the blue-black sky. Raphael had spent most of the past hour pacing and rubbing his arms. His breath formed vapor in the cold night air.

Emily had remained enveloped in her coat. But she was acutely aware of the fact that, if she was cold, he was freezing. "Raphael," she said.

He turned, his gaze steady on hers.

"Why don't you get into that bedroll? I'm fine."

"You know what?" He was already striding to her. "I accept the offer." He was on his knees, then sliding onto his back. "You don't trust me?"

Emily looked down at him. At his striking dark face, at his sensual lips. "Of course I trust you," she said somewhat hoarsely. She did not tell him that she did not trust herself.

"I don't mind sharing. In fact, it's a good idea. We'll keep each other warm."

He was right, and Emily knew it. But she could

not imagine spending the night in such proximity to him.

"C'mon," he said, his tone low and silky. "Slide in. Truth to tell, I'm frozen to the bone." He held open the topmost part of the blanket.

That decided it for Emily. She had no wish for him to catch pneumonia and die. Flushing, she moved onto the bedroll, sliding down on her back beside him. She looked up. He remained on one elbow, gazing down at her. This close, she saw just how golden his eyes were.

He gave her a brief smile and slipped down onto his back as well. Neither one of them moved.

Emily stared up at the stars. She was as stiff as a board. In fact, she was so tense that breathing was difficult. And the entire left side of her body—shoulder, arm, hip, and thigh—was pressed against Raphael. He might be cold, but to Emily, he felt warm and strong and male.

Emily dared to look at him. His face was turned toward her and he was staring. "This is hell," he said. His eyes dropped to her mouth.

Emily quickly jerked her gaze up to the stars. "Yes. It's very cold. I . . ."

But suddenly he was looming over her, one arm on each side of her body. "Forget the cold. Why? Why did you lie? Destroy your reputation? Marry me? Why, Emily?"

Emily felt his arm pressing against her breast where it crossed over her body. His breath feathered her face. It was clean and fresh. His scent was raw, musky, utterly masculine. His face was mere inches from hers.

"I didn't want you to die," Emily said helplessly.

"Why?" His eyes were scorching.

Emily shook her head. It was a confession of uncertainty. She was afraid to even answer the question silently to herself.

He dropped to one elbow and then used his left hand to cup her cheek. Emily stopped breathing. His eyes were fierce. "I'm not bad, Emily. I'm here because—" He stopped in midsentence.

"You're here because of what?" Emily whispered.

"Did you lie because you care?" he whispered back. "Just a little, maybe?"

Emily opened her mouth to reply, and shut it. His hand had slid into her hair. It was braided, but loosely after the travail of the day, and she felt it loosening even more. Finally she nodded. "Yes."

His eyes blazed. His hand in her hair, cradling her head, tightened. "Emily. You're my wife."

Emily had stopped breathing. Her pulse rioted. Her eyes were drawn from his incredible eyes to his straight, aristocratic nose, and then to his sensual mouth. He was so beautiful that it hurt just looking at him. "Yes," she said softly.

He bent closer. His chest crushed her breasts through his vest and her coat. His mouth covered hers.

Emily hesitated only a second. Then she threw her arms around his shoulders, clutching him hard. His mouth opened hers. Their tongues met and mated in a timeless dance. Emily strained to get closer to him. His body came down on hers, every inch of it, including his rock-hard maleness. Emily's thighs parted.

He tore his mouth from hers. "Emily," he gasped, his hands under her coat and on her breasts. Her nipples were hard, and as he stroked her Emily cried out. "Emily," he said again.

Suddenly he was removing her coat and Emily did not care. He rained kisses on her face, her mouth, her throat. His hands roamed her breasts, cupping them through her dress. Then his face was there, and he was teasing her nipples through the two layers of gingham and cotton. Emily felt him undoing the dozens of buttons down the back of her dress.

When her dress hung open in the back, he lifted his head, breathing harshly. "Do you want me to stop?"

Emily's eyes widened.

"I want to make love to you, Emily. I've wanted to make love to you from the moment I first laid eyes on you, but then it was different. It wasn't like this." His hand stroked her cheek. "If you tell me to stop, I will."

Emily's heart was bursting with emotions she could not deny or contain. And suddenly she thought that he loved her too. His eyes seemed impossibly tender, even though so hot and bright. "Don't stop, Raphael," she said, reaching up to caress his beard-roughened cheek. "I want you too."

His eyes widened, brightened. And then he was sliding the dress up over her head. Emily was wearing a faded, lace-trimmed chemise beneath it. He stared at her breasts, his jaw hard and flexed. "You're beautiful, Emily," he said roughly. Then a smile flitted across his face. "Inside and out."

Emily was overwhelmed with joy. "Thank you," she said. She cupped the back of his head, startling him, and slowly guided him down to her. He

moaned, nesting his face in her bosom, and then he
was tugging gently on her nipple. Emily cried out.

He became voracious then, suckling her, one
hand stroking over her other breast, then roaming
down her belly, treacherously low. Emily parted her
legs for him with complete trust and total abandon.
He cupped her sex. Began rubbing it gently.

Emily could not stand it. She threaded her fingers
through his hair, teeth clenched.

"God," he said, and then he slid down her body
and buried his face between her legs.

For one instant, as his tongue stroked over her
femininity, Emily was shocked. And then the intense
pleasure began to crest. Emily heard herself moan-
ing, knew she was thrashing, but she could not stop
herself. Her hips were undulating against him. And
suddenly Emily exploded.

Her soft cries rent the night.

When Emily floated back to earth she was cradled
in Raphael's arms. He was panting harshly, almost in
her ear. His muscular thighs kept hers spread wide.
Through his buttersoft buckskins, Emily felt his
long, thick arousal pressing against her sex.

She was dazed, quivering with tension, and the
feel of him was wondrous and exciting all at once.
Emily felt her body tightening.

"Honey," he said. He kissed her briefly. "It's going to hurt."

Emily could not answer. She was too busy exploring the hard muscles and bones of his shoulders and
back beneath his shirt and vest. He moaned against
her neck.

Emily wiggled against him, which caused him to
moan again, more harshly. Her hands found his hips.

She had the most unladylike desire to reach down and grab his buttocks.

"Go ahead," he whispered. He took her wrist and guided her hand where she'd been thinking of placing it.

Emily stroked the high, hard buttock muscle, aware of his body tense and hard against hers. Or was her own body quivering against his? It was hard to tell. The intense pressure was building again. Suddenly Raphael lifted his head and their eyes met.

Emily was almost taken aback by the wild light she saw in his eyes.

He seized her hand and shifted his body slightly. Before Emily realized what he was doing, he had pressed her palm against his stiff manhood. Emily was shocked to find it throbbing.

"God," he said again. His mouth covered hers, opening it, greedy and devouring.

Emily hooked her ankles around the backs of his calves.

His palm slid down between her thighs. He rubbed her, back and forth, and then Emily felt him unbuttoning his pants. His manhood sprang against the heated skin of her inner thigh. It was hot and velvety smooth.

He pressed against her.

Emily's fingers dug into his hips.

He cried out, driving into her. Emily cried out too. But the pain was brief, because the feeling of him inside her was the most pleasurable thing Emily had ever experienced in her life. As he thrust inside her, slowly, Emily rocked against him.

"That's it," he said. "That's it, Em."

And Emily was lost. The sky beyond his head was filled with shooting stars and exploding lights. His own harsh cries joined hers, filling up the Wyoming night.

14

Afterward, he cradled Emily in his arms. Emily buried her face between his shoulder and neck, one of her palms resting on his flat, hard abdomen. She had never dreamed she could feel the way she was now feeling. Complete, but filled with joy. Raphael suddenly pressed a kiss on the top of her head. His fingertips, resting against her throat, moved softly on her skin in a gentle caress.

Emily looked up into his eyes. She smiled, feeling shy. Her love for him seemed to flood over her in waves. She had never known love before, she realized.

He smiled back. "You're so pretty, Em. But I bet you hear that all the time."

"No. Hardly ever. Maybe once from Henry Cooper before he jilted me."

"The men in Aurora are blind." His hand slid over her shoulder. "I liked making love to you, Em."

She blushed. "I liked it too."

His eyes twinkled. "I know you did. I'm surprised they didn't hear you down at the ranch."

Emily punched his belly lightly. "You are not a gentleman."

His expression changed.

She thought about the fact that he was an outlaw—a thief. "I'm sorry," she said quickly, but even as she spoke she knew in her heart that it wasn't true: He wasn't bad, he wasn't a criminal, not of any sort—he *was* a gentleman. Emily had no doubts.

"You're also the kindest person I've ever met," Raphael said, kissing her forehead.

"I believe in you," Emily replied. Her hand found his. She gripped it tightly. "And I know that when you're ready you'll tell me all that needs to be said."

His eyes darkened. Suddenly he bent and his mouth covered hers. Heatedly. It was a long time before their lips parted, and when they did, Emily lay beneath him. "You tired?" he asked huskily.

Emily was acutely aware of the fact that he was aroused again—and that her own body was hot and tight and feeling an urgency she now recognized. "No," she whispered.

He smiled, briefly, then began kissing her again. This time Emily allowed her hands to roam his back with utter abandon. Suddenly he rose up over her, stripping off his vest and shirt. "I want to feel your skin," he said, his eyes hot. "Naked, against me."

Emily sat up and pulled off her chemise. Raphael's eyes went to her bare breasts. Emily felt a little bit uncertain, but her concern for modesty vanished as Raphael's hands went to his buckskins. She watched him slide them down his hips. Her eyes widened. He was beautiful in his virility.

"Have you ever seen a man naked before?" he asked quietly.

Emily shook her head. "I saw a young boy once." She lifted her eyes. It was hard to think. "It wasn't like this."

He grinned. "I'll bet it wasn't. Take off your drawers, Em. Let me see you too."

Emily felt flushed, but she obeyed. When she was stark naked Raphael slid his hand down her shoulder, over her breast, down her waist and hip. He caressed her thigh, knee, and calf. When he lifted his gaze to hers, his eyes were blazing.

Emily opened her arms. He dove into them.

"Why don't you get some sleep?" Raphael asked later. "I know you have to be tired by now." His grin was teasing.

Emily snuggled against him. Although they remained nude, it was toasty warm inside the bedroll. "I don't think I can," Emily replied truthfully. "I'm too happy."

His smile faded. The light in his eyes changed. He did not respond.

And suddenly Emily was uneasy. "What's wrong?"

"Nothing." He forced a smile. But it was a shadow of the real thing.

"No. Something is wrong." And many questions suddenly filled her mind. She did believe in him, completely. But he was a stranger, and he hadn't yet told her anything, not even where he was from. Emily was acutely aware of the mystery still surrounding

this man. What if she was wrong about him? What if
he didn't love her?

But they were now man and wife. Not only were
they married, they had consummated their relationship. What would happen next? He was an outlaw.
He could not stay in Aurora. But he would not think
of leaving her, would he? Emily was prepared to
follow him—until she thought about her father,
who needed her. And Emily's own smile died. She
was afraid.

"Nothing is wrong." His smile was forced. "Emily, I want you to know something. No matter what
happens, I didn't do any of the things I've been accused of doing, and . . ." He hesitated.

Emily clutched herself. "And what?"

"I would never hurt you," he said, whisper-soft.
"Not on purpose anyway."

Emily was not reassured. She was terrified.

"Get some sleep." It was a directive. He was already closing his eyes.

Her bubble of joy had burst. Emily shut her eyes,
worrying about the future—dreading it.

"Emily. Wake up."

Emily heard him as the thick haze of sleep lifted.
His tone was low, urgent. Emily forced her eyelids
open and saw a thousand shining stars. Clearly it was
the middle of the night.

And Raphael knelt over her, fully dressed, his expression grim.

Emily sat up. "What is it?" Not only had he
donned all of his clothing, but behind him the bay
was tacked. He was leaving? Leaving her? Emily refused to believe it.

He stared at her. "I have to go," he finally said. "There's something I have to do."

"What?" Emily was wide awake now, her gaze riveted to his. "What do you have to do? You're not leaving without me, are you?" she cried.

His expression was strained. Nor could Emily read his eyes. "I hope to be back in an hour, maybe less." He paused. "In which case I'll take you home."

"Take me home?" Emily echoed. "And then what?"

For a moment he did not answer. "And then my business here will be done. I'll be on my way."

Emily could not believe her ears. She stared at him, wide-eyed. "You're leaving?"

"I can't stay in Aurora. Emily . . . you know that."

"But what about me? What about us?" Emily whispered, trying to hold the tears back.

He seemed to flinch. "I don't know," he finally said.

"You don't know," Emily repeated, woodenly.

"Emily, you married me to save my life, and I am grateful. I will always be grateful. But surely you don't want a man like me."

"I married you because I love you," Emily cried. Tears streaked her face.

"Oh, God," he said. Suddenly his hands were on her shoulders. He dragged her up against his body. Emily did not feel the cold on her bare flesh. "I don't want to hurt you," he cried. He kissed her, hard.

Emily tried to push him away and succeeded only because he let her. "I'll come with you," she said.

"No. You can't. It's too dangerous."

"What's too dangerous?"

He shook his head, refusing to answer her.

Blindly, Emily turned, groping for her chemise. She pulled it over her head, hurting so badly inside that she thought she might die. "I thought you loved me," she whispered, pulling on her drawers, not looking at him.

He remained silent.

Emily turned to regard him, bitter and accusing. His expression was distraught. "This is all my fault," he finally said, his own tone filled with bitter regret. "I never should have made love to you."

"No, you shouldn't have!" Emily snapped. But immediately she regretted her words. "No, Raphael, I'm glad you made love to me, because I will treasure the moments I spent in your arms for the rest of my life."

He groaned.

Emily turned away to finish dressing. He spoke to her back. "Emily, if I don't come back tonight to take you home, then I want you to stay here until dawn. At daybreak walk on down to the ranch. Someone there will take you back to the farm."

Emily whirled, shrugging on her coat. "But you just said you'd come back! That you would take me home!"

"I plan to. But I might not be able to."

"Why not? What is going on?"

"I may run into some trouble. Hell, Emily, if Maclaine has the chance he'll shoot me in the back, and you know it as well as I do."

Emily swallowed. "I don't know what you're doing, but don't go, Raphael. Please. I don't want you to get hurt—or worse."

He reached out and cupped her cheek. "Damnit. You're making this so goddamn hard."

"Good," Emily retorted. Then, "But not hard enough to dissuade you, right?"

"I have a job to do."

"What job?"

His mouth firmed. "If I could tell you I would. I don't want you getting hurt, Em."

"What do you think you're doing?" Emily cried. "You're the one hurting me, Raphael."

His jaw flexed. Emily saw that his temples throbbed. "I don't want you dead."

Emily gasped.

Suddenly he hauled her forward and kissed her hard again, but briefly. Then he was striding away and leaping onto the bay, which cantered into the woods. Emily watched the firs and the night swallow him up.

She was bereft.

And then she knew what she had to do. She started running. She was going to follow him.

15

Raphael had never felt worse.

How had it come to this? he wondered, as he trotted the bay down the slope. He hadn't meant to fall for Emily Anderson. Yet he had gone to the farm to hide from Maclaine and Harrison, very purposefully. He'd told himself that the Anderson farm was the perfect choice, and it had been, because, as he'd thought, he'd been able to take Emily and her father hostage without any trouble. Yet maybe he'd chosen their farm for another reason. He'd seen her several times in town before the night he was shot. She, of course, had not seen him. He had made sure of that.

Now Raphael recalled watching her scold two children on Main Street for running in front of a dray while chasing a red ball. Even then he'd thought her incredibly pretty, but more important, her kindness and caring had been apparent. She loved those two little boys. Her concern for their safety was touching. After chastising them she had watched with a small, sweet smile as they ran down the boardwalk. Raphael had wondered what it would be like to know such a woman—to have such a woman care for him.

Maybe he'd fallen in love with her then and there, he mused. Or maybe it had happened the very next time he'd seen her, her cheeks flushed with embarrassment as she peeked into the saloon, looking for Gus. He'd felt for her, understanding her predicament. How he'd wanted to shake Gus, wake him up, get him sober. Maybe he'd fallen in love with her bit by bit, each and every time he'd looked at her, heard her, observed her while she hadn't known he was watching.

Did it really matter? He had a job to do. He was in Aurora for a reason. While he hoped to accomplish his mission he did not want Emily hurt—or worse, dead. He had to keep her in the dark for her own sake. And if he survived, then what?

He knew only one life. He understood only subterfuge, danger, and violence. But he was tired, and achingly aware of it. He was tired of hunting and tired of hiding. He was tired of chasing and being chased. He was tired of looking over his shoulder and tired of wondering when he might get a bullet in the back like the vaquero. Pete Benson had been his partner. His death still hurt, and it wasn't the first time Raphael had watched a partner die. One day, Raphael knew with utter certainty, his partner would mourn his—Raphael's—passing.

Emily was the kind of woman to make a man think about hanging up his spurs, laying down his guns. She made a man think about hard, honest work, a homestead, and babies.

Raphael reined in the bay and slid to the ground. His thoughts would get him killed if he wasn't careful. He needed to focus on the task at hand—to get in and out of the ranch in one piece.

Leaving the bay tied to a tree, Raphael began a stealthy approach to the closest corral. It was empty. No livestock to whicker and give him away. Ahead was the bunkhouse. Smoke curled from the stone chimney. Raphael paused, his body pressing against the split rails, and stared through the dark at the ranch house. It was slightly elevated, on a small, gentle hillock of land. Raphael would be out in the open when he ran toward it. And there was a light on in one upstairs window, causing him to curse. Veronica was home, and she was awake.

Still, he had no choice. He darted forward, running easily now past another corral and then into the open stretch between the outbuildings and the ranch house. His strides lengthened. Stars lit up the night, allowing him to see the ground, but also exposing him should anyone be watching. Somewhere up in the hills a wolf howled, the sound lonely and aching.

He reached the veranda and halted, pressing his spine to the gray stone wall of the house, regaining his breath. He tried the front door. It was unlocked, as always.

Not that a lock would have kept him out.

He slipped inside, his eyes adjusting to the darkness. The floors were pine, but covered with rugs. He stepped carefully, making sure not to cause any floorboards to creak and groan. Listening carefully, he cocked his head toward the stairs. As he moved he tried to discern if Veronica was wandering about. He heard nothing and hoped she'd fallen asleep with the light on.

Raphael continued down a corridor and entered Harrison's library. He went straight to the heavy walnut desk. Fortunately it was under a window, and the stars outside cast some light for him to see what he was doing.

He opened the center drawer and rifled through it, removing a sheath of papers. Raphael sat down, struck a flint, and quickly glanced through the correspondence and files. He smiled when he found the letter he was looking for: a reply from the railroad depot manager in Casper. The letter had dates. It was very specific. Harrison was dead, but the rest of the Whiskey Peak gang were not. Harrison couldn't swing for Benson's murder—and Raphael knew Harrison had killed him—but it was still a hanging crime to rustle cows. Raphael folded up the letter, which arranged for the secret transport of the livestock, and stuck it in his breast pocket.

Something crashed in another section of the house, possibly in the front parlor. Raphael heard glass breaking.

He froze. A moment later he was on his feet and at the door. He listened, but heard nothing else. Whoever was there, he—or she—was now silent. And then he saw a light coming down the corridor in his direction.

He whirled, crossing the library in three strides, his goal the window.

"Halt!" Veronica cried from the doorway.

Raphael obeyed. He turned slowly, saw the pistol in her right hand.

"You bastard," she hissed. In her other hand she

held a kerosene lamp. Her face was starkly white, the same color as her nightgown, but ravaged with her grief. Her green eyes were wild, filled with hate and anger.

"I didn't kill him," Raphael said carefully.

"Then who did?" she spat.

"One of his partners, I believe."

"My father didn't have a partner. You're lying!"

"You're a fine one to call the kettle black," Raphael said. "You sure you don't have an ax to grind?"

"Oh, you think I'm jealous? Because you made love to that plain little Emily Anderson?" Veronica hissed. "As if I care!"

Raphael tensed. "You know, Veronica, a man'd have to be blind not to see how beautiful you are—on the outside. And he'd have to be blind not to see how beautiful Emily Anderson is—inside and out."

Veronica's mouth stretched into a grimace. "She is not beautiful! She's plain, homely, a drab spinster, an old maid! Do not dare compare her to me! I'm not jealous. Hardly! I would never accept your advances, not ever! I thank God we weren't together. That I didn't let a murderer—my father's murderer—in my bed!"

"I don't recall ever making an advance to you. Seems to me you're the one who did all the advancing."

"You looked!" she accused.

"As I said, a man'd have to be blind not to notice a beautiful woman—and a fool to accept what you were offering." He kept his tone low, reasonable. "I am not a fool. And I didn't kill your father. Put down the gun, Veronica."

"I hate you!" She began to cry. "You know what? I think I'll kill you anyway. I can get away with it. I'll say you broke in here trying to rape me. . . . No. I'll say you raped me and tried to kill me!"

Raphael was still. Veronica was hysterical, and her temperament was hardly stable to begin with. "We can find your father's murderer, Veronica. Don't you want to do that?"

Veronica raised the gun higher, pointing it at Raphael's forehead. Her hand shook. "No. You did it. Confess. Confess now."

He shook his head. And then he saw something behind Veronica that filled him with disbelief—but he tempered his expression before his shock could show. "I won't confess to a crime I did not commit."

Before Veronica could retort, Emily said, "Raphael is not a killer. Drop the gun. Before I shoot off your head." And she poked the barrel of a rifle into the back of Veronica's head.

Veronica froze.

"I mean it," Emily whispered, ashen. She held the rifle with two hands. Both of which were shaking. Her teeth were also chattering, loudly.

Raphael smiled at Veronica. "Drop the gun, Veronica. Emily doesn't speak lightly about these kinds of things. Not only that, she's all shook up. That rifle just might go off by mistake."

Veronica dropped the pistol.

Raphael strode swiftly across the room and picked it up as Veronica sank to the floor. She moaned, resting her face against her knees. Raphael ignored her. His gaze met Emily's. He saw just how frightened she was. She was far paler than Veronica. She had lowered the rifle, but it was vibrating as if it had an energy of its own. "Is that thing loaded?"

"I don't know," she whispered. "I don't think so. I took it off the gun rack in the front parlor when I saw Veronica coming down the stairs."

"Maybe I'd better take that," he said, tucking the pistol in his pants. Emily handed him the rifle. Raphael cocked it. "Nope. It's empty." His heart was pounding hard. She was so damn brave. "You the one who made enough noise to wake the dead?"

She nodded, wetting her lips. "I knocked over a lamp." She gazed into his eyes. "I followed you."

"I can see that." He searched her blue eyes, wishing he could grab her, hug her, kiss her, and even make love to her all over again. He felt like a cup, one overflowing not with water or wine, but with rich, deep, heady feelings that could only be soul-deep love. "You do know," he said as lightly as he could, "that this is the third time you've saved my life?"

"Yes," Emily whispered. "I am aware of that."

Their eyes held. Hers, he saw, were wet and sheened with tears. "Honey," he whispered, too low for her to hear.

"Who killed Lloyd Harrison?" Emily asked. She was rubbing her palms on her skirts. He imagined that they were damp.

Raphael wet his lips. "I can't answer that."

"Why not? Because it's too dangerous?" Emily asked with bitterness. He remained silent. "Who are you?" Emily cried.

"I'd tell you if I could." He held out his arm. "Let's go. I'm taking you home."

Emily did not move. "And then what? You're still leaving? You're still leaving me?"

"I have to leave, Emily. I have no choice." But I don't want to, he thought, aching to tell her.

"Everyone has a choice," Emily said, crying.

He dropped his hand. "That's too simple."

"Well, I am a very simple woman," Emily said. Her gaze moved over his face. Tears streamed down her cheeks. "Take me with you," she said hoarsely. "Please."

"I can't." And he let his sadness show. "I would if I could, but I can't."

Emily turned away.

16

The next week passed slowly. Emily cried for several days, until she had no tears left to shed.

Gus did his best to comfort her. "Em," he told her, his arm around her, "I shoulda never let you marry him. I'm so sorry, Em."

Emily wasn't able to reply.

"There will be someone else," Gus offered.

"Never." And Emily ran upstairs to her room.

Liza had come to comfort her too, as had Betsy. But Emily had been born and raised in Aurora, and she knew every single one of the town's one hundred fifteen residents, from the Merrits' newborn, who was ten weeks old, to Mr. Petris, who was ninety-nine. No one else came. The few times Emily was in town she realized why: She was a fallen woman now. People went out of their way to avoid her, actually pretending that she did not exist. The town was ashamed to have one such as her in their midst.

Emily was too grief-stricken to care. One day, she knew, she would have to face the ugly reality of scandal and shame, but that day was far away.

It was Sunday, the Lord's day. As Emily dressed for church she was glad she was still too numb to feel, otherwise she might have dreaded facing the entire town for Sunday's sermon. But she didn't care about her neighbors and peers. She needed the Lord now as she'd never needed anyone before. She wanted to pray, and she wanted to ask questions. Mostly she wanted to ask why. *Why, Lord, why have You done this to me?* Emily couldn't recall a time when she had ever hurt anyone. Losing her mother had been horrible enough. Yet the pain and heart-break she was now afflicted with were somehow worse, and it seemed highly unfair, a gross injustice that needed to be rectified immediately. Emily felt, for the first time in her life, that she did not understand God.

Gus hitched the piebald to their buckboard, and together they drove the two miles to church. As they pulled into the winter-bare yard, couples and families in their Sunday best were entering the clapboard structure. Gus braked, looped the reins up tightly, and climbed down, holding up his hand for Emily. Emily paused. Heads were turning her way. Men, women, and children were staring. She glimpsed Ken Sanders, saw the pity on his face. He jerked his gaze away so that their eyes would not meet. Then she spied Maclaine, ruddy-faced, staring coldly at her from behind Ken. Emily ducked her head. Feeling her cheeks begin to burn, Emily allowed her father to help her down from the wagon. She hid her left hand in the pocket of her coat. Her left hand—

and the gold wedding band she'd borrowed from Liza and never returned.

As Emily and Gus crossed the bare yard, their shoes crunching on the icy snow, their neighbors ducked their heads, averted their eyes, and turned away. Emily felt the grief over the loss of Raphael renewing itself. Somehow she could imagine him being with her now. How she needed his strength and power to lean upon. No shoulder could be stronger, broader. But he wasn't there, he would never be there, he was gone, and she still didn't know a thing about him. How was she going to survive? Emily just didn't know.

"Miss Emily," someone whispered, pausing behind her and Gus.

Emily flinched as she turned, then realized it was Betsy. The younger girl's face was covered with concern. At the sight of her compassion, Emily almost burst into tears. The two girls embraced and clung.

"I'm glad you're here," Betsy whispered.

"I would never miss church," Emily replied in the same hushed tone. And briefly they shared a soft, sad smile.

"C'mon, ladies," Gus said.

Then, on the church steps, Emily came face to face with Veronica Richards. Emily froze.

Veronica stood with her hands on her hips, her eyes blazing. "Well! If it isn't Emily Anderson. Or should I say Missus Emily Caldwell?"

Emily felt herself turning a brilliant shade of red. "Good day, Veronica."

"Where's your husband, Missus Caldwell?" Veronica's smile was ugly. "Oh, dear, how could I forget? He abandoned you!"

Emily could not think of a reply. She felt her eyes watering up, and it had everything to do with the truth of Veronica's words.

"You have some nerve!" Veronica cried loudly. Heads turned their way. "This is a God-fearing place. A godly place. A place for *good* people. You have no right coming here!"

Emily didn't even try to reply. Her father suddenly stepped between her and Veronica. "Now hold on, Missus Richards. My daughter's got every right to come to church, or anywhere else, for that matter. She is an upstanding citizen, one who has done more for this town than anyone else. You should follow her example, young lady."

Veronica's eyes widened. So did Emily's. Emily reached for and gripped Gus's hand. She could not remember his being so forceful in years.

Then Veronica's surprise vanished. She sneered. "Oh—I should take up whoring too? No, I don't think so." She whirled and strode into the church.

Emily's pulse pounded painfully. Gus squeezed her hand. "Don't listen to her, Em. She's half the woman you are, and we both know it."

"Thank you, Pa," Emily managed.

Reverend Prescott appeared. He was smiling, but his eyes were filled with compassion. "I couldn't help overhearing. Do come inside, Emily. Please. No one is more welcome in God's house than you."

The service was over, and Emily couldn't wait to get home.

Yet as it was the Sabbath and no one had any chores awaiting them—merely Sunday dinner— most of the congregation remained in the yard, chat-

ting animatedly. Emily stood on the front steps with
Gus, realizing she dreaded passing through the crowd
to reach their buckboard. She felt like a pariah. The
men and women she had known since she was a
child had stared at her throughout the service as if
she were a monster with two heads.

Suddenly someone gasped. A murmur went
through the crowd. Gus said, "Good God!"

Emily jerked, saw Raphael, and her eyes widened.

He was astride a huge black mount and flanked by
two other riders. They were walking their horses
into the yard very slowly, forming a barricade that
would prevent anyone from leaving—unless someone wished to try and ride through the line of horseflesh and men. But Emily didn't think anyone was
going to try, because Raphael and the two men were
all holding guns. And there was something very se-
vere and set about their expressions and their squared
shoulders and stiff spines. These were men who
meant business.

Emily was frozen. Then her heart started beating
wildly. She did not understand, was afraid to understand, but seeing him was the most beautiful sight
she had ever seen in this world.

The three riders fanned out and halted, completely blocking the entrance to the churchyard.
"No one move," Raphael said in a loud, resonant
tone. A voice of authority.

Emily swallowed. She did not understand this.
Not at all. Or did she?

Suddenly Maclaine pushed to the front of the
crowd. "Arrest him!" he shouted. "He's a murderer
and a thief!" His face was starkly white. His pale
blue eyes bulged.

Raphael pointed his revolver calmly at Maclaine's forehead. "You try anything and you're dead." His smile was cold. "My pleasure."

Maclaine froze. He was not only white, but sweat was pouring down his fleshy face in streams.

Raphael shifted his body slightly. He was wearing a heavy overcoat, and it swung open. Emily cried out. Pinned to his vest was a silver star—the kind worn by a United States marshal.

And then she looked at the other men and saw their tin stars. Emily thought she might faint. Gus gripped her arm. "I'll be damned," he whispered. "He's a lawman!"

Murmurs of amazement were rippling through the crowd.

"Judd Maclaine," Raphael said firmly. "You are under arrest for conspiring to murder a U.S. lawman, who most of this town knew as the vaquero Pete Benson. For being one of the leaders of the Whiskey Peak gang. And if we can prove it in a court of law, you'll hang not just for rustling the stock of your neighbors but for the murder of your partner, Lloyd Harrison."

Someone cried out. It was Veronica.

Emily held on hard to Gus as Raphael slid from the horse and approached Maclaine, his spurs jangling. Emily was terrified, could not move. The moment was so explosive that the crowd did not utter a sound or a collective breath. Maclaine remained tensed.

And Maclaine moved. He went for his gun.

Raphael was faster and already had the advantage of the draw. His gun went off loudly. Maclaine was hit in the shoulder, and he fell onto his back, crying out, dropping his own weapon.

Raphael kicked the weapon aside, bent, rolled Maclaine roughly over, and snapped handcuffs on him. All around the pair, people began to talk, shocked and amazed.

Suddenly Veronica was running through the crowd. She paused, wild-eyed, in front of the prone, bleeding sheriff and the U.S. marshal. "Is it true? Did he kill my father?"

"I believe so," Raphael said calmly. "They were partners and they had a falling out. The issue was, of course, money."

Veronica stared. "My father had nothing to do with that gang of rustlers!"

He eyed her. "I have proof, Veronica. Proof. He and Maclaine were stealing cattle and shipping them through a spur out of Casper."

She cried out, soblike, pressing a fist to her mouth, then turned and ran through the crowd. A moment later she was in her small buckboard, urging the mare to a wild gallop. The wagon careened between the two other lawmen and out of the church-yard.

Raphael ignored her. He stared across the crowd. His gaze finally met Emily's.

Emily wiped the tears streaming down her face. "Raphael."

He began walking to her. People moved out of his way.

Emily went to him, unaware of commanding her feet to move. "You should have told me," she said huskily.

"I wanted to." With bare fingertips he removed

the tears from her face. "I wanted to, badly. But I was afraid that if you knew the truth Maclaine would silence you the way he and Harrison silenced Benson, the way he wanted to silence me."

Emily nodded, crying all over again.

"Don't cry," he whispered. "It hurts me when you cry."

Emily nodded, and burst into sobs.

Raphael opened up his arms and took her into his embrace. He held her hard, her cheek against his chest. Emily felt one of the points of his tin star pressing into her face. She laughed while she cried. He wasn't a thief or a murderer. He was a lawman. A United States marshal.

"Emily," he whispered.

Emily looked up into incredibly soft, gentle golden eyes.

"I didn't take those vows lightly," he said.

"Neither did I," she whispered, hope winging in her breast.

"Will you honor me by remaining with me as my wife?"

Emily reached up to cradle his striking face. "Oh, yes," she said. "Oh, yes, Raphael, I love you so that I would follow you anywhere."

He bent and kissed her. It began chastely, but quickly became hot and greedy. Someone chuckled, and then the crowd around them was applauding. Emily was only vaguely aware of the fact that they were onstage. Their mouths parted. They smiled into each other's eyes.

He stroked the hair at her nape, under her bonnet. "What if I told you that I'm taking off my badge?

Laying down my spurs?" he asked. "Hanging up my guns?"

Emily did not move. She could hardly breathe. Finally she whispered, "That would make me very happy."

"You make me happy," he said. "Being with you, Em, it's like coming home."

Emily closed her eyes, ready to weep again. With joy.

"What would you say," he asked huskily, the sound of tears thick in his voice, "if I said I wanted to take up farming?"

Emily looked up. "I would say," she said, as hoarsely, "that's a fine idea."

They smiled, their eyes meeting, and kissed again.

While Betsy blushed and Liza beamed and Gus whooped and threw his Sunday hat into the air.

Heaven With a Gun

❦

Connie Brockway

1

Texas, 1883

Jim Coyne balanced his chair on its back legs and hooked his ankles over the top of the hitching rail outside the Cattleman's Saloon. It was as good a place as any to keep an eye out for "news." Although after four weeks Jim had concluded that "news"—as Jim knew it—was about as likely to show up in Far Enough, Texas, as Queen Victoria.

A week ago the first of the cattle drives had started drifting north on their way to the market. The huge herds passed on either side of town, a river of beef parting to flow past an island of human habitation. Instead of dumping fish on the town's shores, this particular river had the unfortunate tendency to dump teenage cowboys on Far Enough's shores. After weeks on the range the boys were always surly, always ready for trouble, and always looking to establish their manhood. In other words, they were just like testy adolescents anywhere, which meant that though entirely dislikable, they were not—much to Jim's annoyance—desperadoes.

Depressed, Jim squinted up at the sky. Blue. Endless, vacant expanses of bright blue rolling off in every direction. Even after nearly a month here, he still hadn't gotten used to so much unfilled sky. It was eerie. Like the canvas of a landscape artist with only one color on his palette.

Jim tipped his hat over his eyes to shade his face and stared disconsolately down the street. On either side of the main thoroughfare, second-story false fronts tipped toward each other, arcing over the street like tipsy neighbors nodding hello. The low horizon should have held some charm for someone used to measuring buildings in hundreds of feet. Should have, but didn't.

In New York, brownstones and steel filled the sky with something to look at. Evenings there were illuminated by sulfurous gaslight, not silver moonlight, and the stink of river sewage, not cows, scented the air.

God, he missed it.

"You don't look too happy, Mr. Coyne."

Jim had almost forgotten his companion, the local newspaper's twenty-year-old editor, a lad with a fearsome case of hero worship and the unlikely name of Mortimer James. It sometimes seemed to Jim that the Wild West was populated solely by children and broken-down relics. At thirty-six, Jim feared he was quickly joining the brotherhood of the latter.

"I'm gonna die here, Mort. You'll find me tomorrow, slack-jawed and vacant-eyed, just sitting here. You'll knock me over and you'll hear this odd sound—like a pea rattling around in a soup kettle, and you'll know my brain simply dried up overnight, having atrophied like any unused limb."

Mort grinned and slapped a folded copy of what Jim assumed was the latest issue of the *Far Enough Guardian* against his thigh. "Ah, Mr. Coyne. It isn't that bad. You've already been here a month. Eleven more and you'll be back in New York."

"Eleven. Jesus. I hope this isn't supposed to be a pep talk, Mort."

"Make the best of the situation, Mr. Coyne. You told me the story comes first, that a reporter makes sacrifices for his craft."

"Yeah, and I stand by my words," Jim said. "But you gotta be alive to write the damn story, and much more of this town and I'm going to die of boredom."

"You really hate it that much?" Mort asked, his voice roughening.

Jim shook his head, giving up. He just couldn't hurt the kid's feelings. "It's not *here* I hate so much, Mort. It's *being* here. I'm a political reporter. I report political events, not how many cows pass through town on a given day."

"Steers," Mort corrected.

"Whatever. The point is, I don't belong here. I belong in New York, wading through the graft of Tammany Hall." His mouth curved with tender nostalgia.

"I have a friend who works for the *New York Daily* and telegraphs me stuff," Mort began, and Jim closed his eyes. He'd heard this before. It appeared young Mort had compiled a veritable dossier on his life. "I asked about that sewage scandal, and he said if you hadn't insisted your paper print your story without hard evidence to back it up, you'd still be in New York."

Jim snorted. "I wrote the truth."

As any self-respecting newsman would, Mort ignored this piece of nonsense. "He also said you used real suspect methods of getting your information. Like blackmail."

Jim shrugged. He hadn't blackmailed anyone. *Intimated* consequences, perhaps, but then, the people he'd been intimating things to weren't exactly pure as the driven snow.

"You've got a reputation for being one of the most unapologetic, single-minded, ruthless reporters ever to hit the streets. My friend says *that's* what got you in trouble."

Mort's eyes, Jim noted, were gleaming with adulation. The kid was all right.

"Nah," Jim said, unhooking his ankles and coming down on the front legs of his chair with a bang. "The reason I'm here is simple, Mort. This is what happens to dumb-ass crusading reporters who piss off their publisher by getting said publisher's paper sued for libel. They get a trumped-up assignment as 'field correspondent' and a one-way ticket to purgatory on the Union Pacific. Or, considering the heat, maybe it's hell."

"Having trouble with the heat, Jim?" a voice boomed as a meaty paw smacked Jim between the shoulder blades.

Had to be Vance Calhoun, the local bank president. He was the only man in town who took every opportunity to cow other men, even under the pretense of bonhomie. Jim knew a lot of politicians in

New York who clapped backs just like Vance—and a lot of police captains. He rubbed his jaw in memory.

"You on your way in?" Vance jerked his big, florid face toward the saloon doors. "Let me buy you a drink." He glanced at Mort. "I'll even buy you a sarsaparilla, boy." He sauntered through the doors without bothering to wait for an answer. Who wouldn't want to share bar space with the town's richest citizen?

"What a horse's ass," Mort said, red-faced.

"Yup. But a rich ass. And an ass with the only private stash of honest-to-God whiskey behind the bar counter." Jim glanced up at the sky and considered his options. A drink with Vance—albeit a free drink—or more staring at all that blue nothing. It was a toss-up.

The doors to the saloon suddenly banged open. A kid no more than fifteen years old, acne-scarred and skinny as a Seven Dials whore—and dripping with blood—stumbled out. He pitched into the hitching rail and somersaulted over it, landing in a crumpled heap.

A pair of bandanna-sporting boys followed him out, bootheels aggressively drilling the raised plank walk as they stalked toward the stairs at the end of the promenade.

"We ain't done with you yet!" one of them shouted at the limp figure. Jim didn't like the odds and he didn't like the look in the red-shot eyes of the truculent-looking boys bearing down on the skinny kid. The kid moaned. Blood dribbled down his chin. Jim swore under his breath.

The boys were nearly to him. With a sense of weary resignation he stood up and stepped in front of them, blocking their way. He was a relatively large man, broad in the shoulders. He made a good block. The duo stumbled to a stop.

"He looks sorry," Jim said.

"You say somethin', old man?" the boy nearest Jim asked. Jim winced at the unfair appellation. Thirty-six wasn't *that* old.

The boy snickered. He was so blond his hair looked white, and Jim would have bet money he'd yet to make his first acquaintance with a razor. Which only meant he would be itching to prove his manliness in other ways. Like stomping unconscious boys—or "old men"—into bloody messes.

"Your friend down there looks like he's sorry for whatever he's done," Jim explained patiently, pointing at the kid who had begun a slow crawl across the rut-riven street.

"Not half as sorry as he's gonna be." The other boy shouldered his way in front of his pal. He was short, plug-shaped, and grimy. "And what the hell business is it of yours anyway?"

"Lookee these duds, will ya, Tom?" The blonde flicked the edge of Jim's coat with a grubby forefinger.

"Where the hell did you come from, greenhorn?" Tom asked disparagingly. "Though a feller your age ain't so much green as moldy."

The blonde broke into uproarious laughter and Jim smiled weakly. A wit.

"Man comes from New York, Tommy," Mort supplied helpfully, peeling a splinter off the rail and popping it into his mouth.

"I told you not to call me 'Tommy,' you pencil-necked grebe," the squat boy said. Mort raised his hands in surrender and Tommy-Boy returned his attention to Jim. "New York, huh?" He stepped closer. "Well, Mr. New York"—he reached up both hands—"you better learn to mind your own business"—he placed both hands on Jim's shoulders—"if you're thinking to live long in these parts." He shoved.

Jim didn't budge. The boy scowled, broke into a pathetically sly grin, and scrunched down, telegraphing his intention way ahead of the act of sending a round, windmilling blow at Jim's head. Jim ducked it with a lazy bend of his head.

Cowboys, he thought pityingly, had no idea of how a real brawl went. On a Saturday night in the Bowery, they'd last five minutes. Ten, tops.

Straightening, Jim caught Tommy's arm on its return flight and spun him around, shoving him heavily into the saloon's exterior wall. The boy's breath came out in an audible—and rancid—*whoosh,* and Jim stepped back, hoping that would be the end of it. He'd no desire to bruise any knuckles or loosen any teeth. Particularly his own. He *was* getting old, and Tommy looked like the type who, once encouraged, would have the tenacity and brains of a punch-drunk pit dog.

"You better watch it, mister!" The blonde's hands curled into fists at his side, but his eyes betrayed hesitation and he didn't come any farther. "You don't wanna mess with us. You'll end up like . . . like . . ."

"Like?" Mort prompted innocently, rolling the wood splinter to the corner of his mouth.

Jim looked around. The kid in the street had vanished.

"Where the hell'd he go?" The blonde demanded, hanging over the edge of the rail. "Mister,
you got a powerful lot of hurt comin'—"

"You boys better come back inside and have a
drink," a feminine voice advised as plump breasts
cushioned up against Jim's arms on either side.

The boys' eyes glazed over. In a split second their
aggression cartwheeled into pure adolescent lust as
Merry and Terry, the Carmichael twins, postured
within arm's reach. No bigger than circus ponies,
and covered in just about the same amount of stained
satin and limp feathers, they were pretty and plump,
like bread dough on the rise, all fragrant and moist.
Right now their eyes—most times as empty as a politician's promise—were hinting things no boy had
the right to expect and very few men ever got.

"Go on," Merry purred. "Don't disappoint me.
I'll be right in and . . . we'll get acquainted."

"Skedaddle, boys." The pair hesitated.

"You can keep my seat warm," Terry encouraged
huskily. They just about tripped over each other in
their hurry to comply.

"Thanks," Jim said, dividing his smile between
the women. "I don't know why you came to my
rescue, but I appreciate it."

Merry patted his arm. Terry snorted in amusement. "You're a big, fine-looking man, Mr.
Coyne," Merry said—at least, Jim thought it was
Merry. He never had figured out which was which.
"And I knows you're a fancy journalist and have
smarts that make Terry's there look like a cracker
barrel next to a feast, but you don't know jack about
some things, do y'all?"

"No, ma'am," he agreed earnestly.

"You poor man, you must not have any women-folk in your family," Terry said.

Though he didn't contradict her—his beloved stepmother had made it clear that you never contradict a woman—Jim actually had six females in his family. That was the problem.

His mother had died when he was three. A dozen years later his father had remarried a widow with five girls of her own. From the first moment they'd surrounded him with soft smiles, giggles, and shining clean looks, Jim had adored each and every one of them. From the littlest girl child, who'd used him to launch a lifelong career of lash-batting success, to the oldest, whom he seemed to exasperate with no more than a word, his stepsisters had taught him one thing: Women were enigmas.

"You wanna visit me a little later, sugar?" Merry suggested coyly.

"Sorry, ma'am," he said. He didn't pay for sex, and Merry and Terry couldn't afford to give it away. They'd all made their positions clear within a day of his arrival. It didn't stop the twins from trying to change his mind.

"You got a wife back East, Jim?" Terry pouted. "She ain't gonna mind you giving me a little something on the side."

He didn't answer the question. He had a reporter's deep reticence about divulging anything about himself.

"Well." Merry spread one plump little paw against his chest. "My, oh, my! If'n you change your mind, sugar, it's Wednesday. I never work on Wednesdays . . . much." Her hands trailed away with unfeigned regret as she minced back into the saloon.

"I work"—Terry stopped in the doorway—"*real* hard." She winked and disappeared.

Jim stared after her.

"Well . . . uh." Mort's voice broke. He cleared his throat. "Well, uh . . . Say, Mr. Coyne, I wouldn't rile Tommy Baker if I were you. He's not much, but his uncle Ox is the biggest, orneriest—"

"God, Mort," Jim said. "You gotta help me."

Mort followed the direction of Jim's gaze. He pumped his head up and down in fervent understanding, digging his hand deep into his trouser pocket. "How much money you wanna borrow?"

"Huh? Oh. No, Mort."

The younger man flushed a brilliant red. "Well, I thought—Seeing how she—I just assumed—"

"And I appreciate your willingness to lend me cash," Jim assured him. "But I'm talking about helping me with a story. You heard Terry—or Merry. It's Wednesday. My editor is going to be expecting another 'Wild West' piece by tomorrow. I haven't got one. And I can't think of one. I did the 'Diamond in the Rough, Knights of the Prairie' thing. I did 'Lonesome Frontier.' I'd *do* the noble savage, except I haven't even seen an Indian and I have a few principles left. Not many, mind you, but a few. Help me, Mort."

In answer, Mort unfolded his newspaper and spread it on the railing. Emblazoned in bold typeface, its front-page headline read LIGHTNING STRIKES TWICE!

"You're kidding," Jim muttered, snatching the paper up and scanning the article.

"Nope."

"You need new typeface, Mort," Jim murmured. "I can barely read the *A*'s and *I*'s."

"I need new everything," Mort replied ruefully. "But I can't afford nothing."

"So where'd our girl show up this time?"

"She hit the Reynolds spread again," Mort said. "Bold as brass, she walks into the old man's office, holds a gun to his head, makes him open the ranch safe, and steals every dollar his foreman just brought back from Denver. Exact same thing she did last year. Once more and old George Reynolds is gonna be broke."

"Now that takes guts," Jim said admiringly. "And it's smart too. I mean, who'd expect she'd rob the same house twicc?" He folded the *Far Enough Guardian* back and studied the artist's—Mort's mother—rendition of Lightning Lil.

There wasn't much to study: a picture of a masked face, flat-brimmed hat pulled low over the brow, a phalanx of witchy hair hanging down either cheek.

Jim read beneath the illustration, *"Lightning Lil, as deadly accurate a gunfighter as the West has known, continued her sporadic five-year criminal career on Saturday night by once more robbing rancher George Reynolds in his home. This time, however, the price of Lil's audacity was her own blood. In fleeing the scene, shots fired by one of Reynold's employees wounded the female outlaw. The shootist claims to have seen her grab her leg. Blood stained an abandoned saddle found eight miles from the ranch. However, in spite of the quick formation of a posse dedicated to her arrest, the notorious woman has yet to be apprehended. Authorities are now offering a $1,000 reward for her capture.*

"Damn! I gotta get this woman's story. If I do, I can write my own ticket home," Jim muttered.

"Any luck on your ad?" Mort asked.

Jim shook his head and turned to the advertisement pages. There it was, double-lined box around it, two columns wide.

Would the lady known as Lightning Lil please contact J. C. Coyne regarding the possibility of a correspondence-based interview, for which the lady will be compensated in a most generous manner? Address replies to Mr. Coyne in the care of Mudruk's Mercantile, Far Enough, Texas.

A similar ad ran in every weekly newspaper within three hundred miles.

"Just a waste of good money," Jim muttered. "She probably can't even read."

He handed the paper back to Mort as a billow of dust heralded the arrival of the stagecoach. Standing here wasn't getting his story written, and if he didn't submit a story he couldn't submit his weekly demand that his publisher send him a return ticket to New York.

Of course, Jim thought, gazing longingly at the stagecoach, he could just jump on that coach and start traveling. He wouldn't have a job, but hell, it didn't feel like he had a job now. The carriage door opened and passengers began descending.

The first—a traveling salesman from the look of the leather sample case clutched beneath his arm—was followed by a somberly dressed white-haired man. Then the tip of a crutch appeared, delicately testing the stability of the crate stairs, followed by a small cream-colored leather boot and then another foot, this one hidden by a thick white plaster cast.

The older man held his hand out, and a slender

pink-gloved hand took it. A bonnet appeared—a confection of creamy feathers, damask-color silk roses, and golden-chipped straw—that hid its owner's face.

It had been a month since Jim had seen anything so exquisitely female. He'd always been susceptible to feminine beauty—if wary of it. He stared, aware that every other man within fifty yards was doing likewise.

She emerged fully, allowing the old man to lift her from the carriage and deposit her carefully on the ground. Not as small as the delicate ankle and slender hands would lead one to assume, she was, in fact, a shade above average height, slender, long-legged, and curved in an intoxicating fashion. She thanked the man, wobbling a little before balancing on her crutch and looking around.

Young. Very young. Her face was narrow and smooth, with refinement in the set of straight dark brows and coffee-color eyes, an aristocratic nose, and an unsettling determination about the small clipped jaw. Not strictly beautiful, but arresting.

Something about her dress jarred with that genteel face. It was cheap material, not what a lady would have worn. It was a bit tight in the bodice and loose in the waist, exposing a few too many inches of silky skin above the décolletage. He couldn't imagine what she was, or what she was doing here. Too elegant for a whore, too sporty for anything else.

Jim dismissed the notion. The Carmichael twins had pricked desires best left unserved, and this little crippled piece of baggage—just the look of her—was doing more to rouse them than Merry and

Terry's white plumpness could ever hope to achieve. He shook his head. He had a story to write.

He started down the raised walk, passing within a few inches of her—God, she even smelled clean—anticipating a date with a cold sponge bath when he heard his name. "Coyne! Jim Coyne!" He turned. Vance was standing at the entrance to the Cattleman's Saloon, looking petulant. "What about our drink?"

"Not today, Vance." From the corner of his eye he saw the leggy vision's eyes widen in surprise, and then she was pushing past her fellow passengers, coming fast, swinging along on her crutch, her skirts belling out with each purposeful stride. Her gaze fixed on his face in what appeared to be joyful recognition. Impossible. He would have remembered her, someone so—

"Jim! Darling!" He heard the crutch hit the dirt with a soft thud, felt her arms wrap around his neck and the fresh scent of expensive soap invade his nostrils. Her lithe, lusciously curved body pressed against his, warm and soft and . . . and . . . and with that, all conscious thoughts stuttered to a dead halt. Without another second's hesitation his over-tried body took control of his actions and he lifted her up into his arms. His mouth came down on hers with the hunger of a man who'd just realized he was starving.

It was pure chemical reaction. It had to be. There was no other way to account for a physical response so intense it ripped through him like lightning.

His body tightened. Hers softened. His mouth roved. Hers opened. It felt like welcome and passion, and God help him, he found her tongue and stroked it with his own.

She jerked away from the intimacy, and like a cad he followed her retreat, bending over her, demanding more, a part of him as shocked as she must look. . . .

He pulled back, realization arriving too late. God, she'd mistaken him for someone else, and he'd taken advantage of her!

No wonder she was staring at him in horrified fascination. He'd all but assaulted her.

"Dear Mother of Mercy," he gulped. "Lady, listen. I—" He backed from the alarm in her eyes.

"Please," she gasped, and he realized that having dropped her crutch she was in the position of having to rely on him for support. Her eyes—dark and luminous, like water-washed topaz—widened. Her hands tightened on his biceps as she steadied herself. He felt heat flood his cheeks. Mortified, he tried to think of some way to frame an apology. Amazingly, stunningly, the corners of her lush lips curved into a smile.

"So, Jim Coyne, you *do* remember you have a wife!"

2

He didn't look like a New York City reporter. He was bigger than she'd imagined he'd be, and even though he dressed like an Easterner—white shirt, crisp collar, and black stockinette tie—there was an awful lot of cloth covering his shoulders. Broad and flat-bellied, he wasn't lean. He was dense. He looked like a prizefighter five years past retirement.

His dark, rumpled hair was liberally peppered with silver, and fine laugh lines radiated from the corners of his pale pasqueflower-blue eyes. His nose would have been handsome, but an old break broadened the bridge. Further augmenting the Irish street brawler's look of him, a thin white scar started on the hard, uncompromising edge of his jaw and traveled across his lower lip, marring the lovely symmetry of his mouth.

A good-looking man. A formidable-looking man too, even though it was hard to look formidable when you were staring at someone in slack-jawed astonishment.

She hadn't known she was going to claim matrimony until she'd seen him, but once she'd clapped eyes on Jim Coyne there didn't seem to be any other relationship she *could* claim. He was too young to be her father, too old to be her brother. That left husband, and what would a wife do on seeing her husband? Embrace him.

She'd never expected him to kiss her. My God, how could anyone have expected something as stunning and eviscerating and—

She had to pull herself together. He was all but toeing the ground, like a student found in the faculty apartments. Any minute now he was going to blurt out a lengthy apology, followed by some questions, and ruin her plans.

"Jim, darlin'," she purred, snaking her arm through his and leaning heavily against him, "I can't wait to get you alone. I could just about . . ." She inhaled with a suggestive little hiss.

His blank confusion became black-visaged suspicion. He opened his mouth. She held her breath. And then those award-winning reporter's instincts of his took over, just as she'd hoped they would.

"Oh, and I can't wait to get you alone either, *darlin'*," he murmured meaningfully. He bent down to retrieve her crutch. "And I mean *now*."

He handed her the crutch and reached behind her for the trunk the porter had deposited on the walkway. One-handed, he hefted it onto his shoulder.

"Which way, darlin'?"

"Next street over." He motioned her forward, his fine blue eyes narrowing speculatively.

She swung lightly along, smiling at the curious onlookers who stood in the shop windows or wandered out of their businesses to catch a glimpse of her. A new woman was always a source of intense interest in a small western town. Especially one married to an exiled easterner. She knew it, and she played the role of Ruth to the hilt, casting lovesick sheep's eyes at the man beside her, batting her lashes. In response, a ruddy bronze blush had washed up his strong throat and tinted his ears, charming her.

He was adorable. Big and handsome and utterly nonplussed by her. And with manners that would have made any mother proud, because in spite of his size and the impediment of her cast and his obvious impatience to get her alone, he accommodated her limping progress.

He led the way to a dingy two-story clapboard house, a few scrawny hollyhocks leaning wearily on either side of the front door. He opened the door and she hobbled in. Directly inside, a steep flight of stairs marched upward at a sharp angle. A hall on the right gave entry to a hot, stuffy room, heavy curtains closed to keep the purple horsehair-covered furniture from fading. It was empty. She started in.

"Oh, no, *darlin'*. Someone might disturb us. Upstairs," Jim said. He had a deep, lovely voice, like the lichen-covered stones on the bottom of a creek— silky and gravelly at the same time. But the look he turned on her reminded her that just because a man blushes doesn't mean he's easily manipulated. She'd best remind herself of that often, because she didn't think she'd like having a man such as Jim Coyne mad at her.

She nodded and gamely started up the steep stairs.

She was halfway up when her crutch slipped out from under her. Her cast, too heavy and too big to fit on the narrow riser, slid off the step.

"Oh!" She heard the crutch clatter down, felt herself falling backward, waited for her head to crash into something hard and painful and . . . he caught her. He just plucked her from midair, scooped her up with a sound of impatience.

"You're okay," he said. "I've got you."

Her heartbeat thudded into double time. It had been years since she'd felt a man's arms around her, been touched so intimately and yet so innocently.

Long ago she'd forfeited romantic daydreams. She couldn't trust a relative stranger with her secrets, and she was too honest to encourage a relationship based on lies. But until this moment she'd never fully appreciated just what she'd given up.

Jim's body's heat had warmed the starched cotton of his shirt. Beneath the thin, crisp material his body was solid and muscular, his chest rising evenly with each breath as he strode up the stairs. She liked the feeling of his arms around her. Suddenly she was just a woman in the arms of a man. She was . . .

She was very stupid, that's what she was. A stupid spinster, yearning for a human touch. How her students would have snickered at her. She stiffened.

He nudged open the first door he came to and carried her into a tiny sitting room. A mismatched armchair and fainting couch, a scarred table, and a fringe-shaded floor lamp struggled for dominance. Papers, books, and lots of empty bottles covered every available surface. He searched around for a place to deposit her.

"Right here will do," she said.

He flushed again, but set her down and left, returning a moment later with her crutch and her trunk. He stared at her. Apparently something about her standing there didn't sit well with him, for he suddenly scooped her up and perched her on the edge of the chair.

He gave a sharp nod, as though manners had been satisfied. "Okay, lady. Who the hell are you? And don't give me any crap about being my wife. I don't drink that much. There's not *that* much liquor in the world."

"Of course I'm not your wife."

He released a gusty sigh of relief.

Her cheeks burned. She wasn't bad-looking, she had a nice figure, and she even had some money. The jackass! He could have done worse.

"Then who are you?"

She untied the bow beneath her chin and pulled the bonnet from her head. Her hair spilled out from under it. He stared at her. Oh, yes. She had very lovely blond hair too. She gave him her three-cornered smile. The cream smile, her mother called it.

"I've come in answer to your ad. I'm Lightning Lil."

Silky, glossy, the color of palest flax. Or honey swirled with cream. He wanted to touch her hair. He wanted to touch *her*. But he'd been wanting to touch her ever since he *had* touched her, and the minute he'd set her down he'd wanted to touch her again. Crazy. And damn it, what was her game with him anyway? Lightning Lil had dark hair.

"Lightning Lil has dark hair."

She crooked a brow at him. Exotic, the way her thick, darkish lashes and brows contrasted with the long flow of pale hair. "Lightning Lil has a wig."

She could be telling the truth. From what he'd found in researching Lil, no one had ever seen her with her hat off. He moved closer to her. The sunlight gleamed on her hair, burnished her skin, ruddied her lips . . . He halted the litany. He was a reporter, damn it, not a poet. "Why did you claim to be my wife? Why not just contact me through the mail?"

She leaned forward earnestly. "I need your help. I was shot." Her gaze fell to her ankle. "I found a doctor to patch me up, but I have to wear this cast for a while. I have nowhere to go. And an unattached woman in these parts is bound to attract attention. Particularly one with an injury to her leg. I want you to let me stay with you and heal up for a couple weeks. In return I'll give you the story of your career."

He thought. Since he was dealing with a woman he took his time thinking. She waited patiently while he ran through alternative explanations for her presence, but besides a rather elaborate hoax perpetrated by his little sisters, he couldn't think of one.

"Please, Mr. Coyne," she said quietly, gazing up at him with eyes the color of bittersweet chocolate.

"What happened to *darlin'*?"

She turned pink, but her gaze didn't fall beneath his sardonic regard. "Just think of what a story you could write. 'I lived with Lightning Lil.' "

Damn, she was right. It would make one helluva feature piece. It would all but guarantee that his publisher would bring him back to New York. And if he didn't? He could peddle a story like that to any newspaper in the city. "*Darlin'*, you have yourself a deal."

3

Long ago Jim had learned the value of studying what a man wore and how he wore it. He figured it wouldn't be any different with a woman. So he made Lightning Lil sit, looking awfully unhappy and guilty for a criminal, while he hung up her clothes.

Now the armoire was crowded with dresses and skirts and blouses and bright-colored . . . things. Jim, who'd had nearly two dozen years' observation of his sisters' "things," noted shiny elbows, double-stitched seams, turned hems. Apparently the outlaw business didn't pay that well.

In fact, the thought of the fresh-faced young woman blushing profusely as he produced an "un-mentionable" was so incongruous that he would have thrown her out as a charlatan if at the bottom of the trunk he hadn't found a neatly folded set of boy's clothes, a Smith & Wesson Pocket .32 tucked into a well-oiled leather holster, a battered Stetson with a black wig sewn into the sweatband, and a money clip with the name GEORGE E. REYNOLDS engraved on it.

He held up the pistol. "No guns allowed in this town. Sheriff's orders."

"Smart man," she said. "But what he doesn't know isn't going to hurt him."

He dropped the gun back into the trunk, closed the lid, and shoved it against the back wall. "You know," he said to her, "you sure have a lot of clothes for an outlaw."

"I'm only an outlaw part of the time."

"Oh, yeah?" He turned around. The bedroom was tiny, and she sat near the foot of the bed, occupying the one straight-back chair the room accommodated. He had a sudden image of her in that bed, hair spilled across the Irish-linen pillowcase, limbs loose and relaxed, all creamy smooth indolence. . . .

"What are you the rest of the time?"

"Schoolteacher?" she suggested brightly.

He snorted. "Play fair. The deal's only good if you fulfill your end of the bargain."

"Okay. I'm just a person the rest of the time." She dropped the scarf she'd been folding and it floated down between them, landing out of her reach. He knelt on one knee to retrieve it just as she bent forward to do the same. He lifted his head and found her a handbreadth away, so close to him that he smelled her. Lilac water. What sort of desperado used lilac water? He snapped upright, dropping the scarf into her lap.

"What does 'just a person' do?" he asked, ignoring her knowing smile.

"Oh . . . live in a house . . . and you better

believe it's a *real* nice house." She added with a hint of humor, "One doesn't go into outlawing for the sheer fun of it. I grow roses—"

"Roses?" he repeated in disbelief.

"Yes," she said. "Roses. A few *gallicas,* the damasks, *albas,* bourbons. Don't look so surprised. *Inest sua gratia parvis.* Even little things have their own grace."

Lightning Lil grew roses and spoke Latin. "What else?"

"I keep busy. Regular-person stuff: crochet doilies, put up jam, practice my fast draw . . ." She chuckled at his confounded expression.

She was teasing him. Didn't she realize the gravity of her situation? He could turn her in at any moment. One would think a hardened criminal would have learned a little mistrust along the way.

"Married?"

Her laughter trailed off. She glanced up. Little invisible currents seemed to arc from his skin to hers, galvanizing and stimulating him. He got up without waiting for her answer. He wished he hadn't asked that question. Particularly as he hadn't planned on it. Mostly, he didn't like her so close to that damn bed.

"I need paper and pencil if we're going to do this properly. We should go into the other room. Better light."

A slow, lingering smile. "Sure."

She rose, unaccountably graceful in spite of the awkward cast, and teetered her way crutchless into the sitting room, where she flopped into an armchair. "Okay. Ask what you will," she said. "I'm all yours."

Her lashes swept down, shadowing her dark eyes

and making him uncertain whether she knew how his body was interpreting her words. He was going as hard and taut in belly and thigh as blood and imagination can make a man. But as much as her career choice suggested a hard and calculating woman who'd use anything—her body as well as her wiles— to get what she wanted, there was too much joy in her to let him believe it. Her sass had softness; her bite lacked teeth.

Taking the opportunity to regain some composure, he found paper and pencil and returned. "Okay. Tell me about yourself. What's your name?"

"Gillian. Gilly for short, but I don't think you better call me that around here. Sounds too much like 'Lil.' Too many people could make the connection."

"What should I call you?"

"*Darlin'* was just fine." She chuckled at the color flooding his tanned skin.

He cleared his throat. "Okay, *darlin',* where were you born? Where did your parents come from? Start at the beginning."

"All right, Mr. Coyne." She straightened. "I was born in the gold fields of Colorado, in a shanty behind a bar."

He started to write.

"My father was a poor, wretched miner, and my mother was a dance-hall girl."

"Hold on." He held up his hand, waving her start of surprise away. "Hold on just a second there. If Dad was a miner and Mom was a saloon girl, how did you learn Latin?"

"Good question." Her brow furrowed in consternation before smoothing. "Daddy was a professor at

. . . at Harvard University before the gold bug bit him. One day a respected member of the academic community, the next a swill-guzzling shell of a man, scrabbling from slag heap to rock slide, ferreting like an animal into the bowels of the earth, searching, always searching for that vein of gold, the mother lode, El Dorado!" She gave a dramatic sigh. "Tragic, is it not?"

"Yeah," Jim answered sardonically. "I'm surprised Dad found time to bed Mom what with all that searching and scrabbling and ferreting."

She shot him a suspicious glare. "Mama was a stunner."

"I'll bet."

"You don't believe me?" she said, looking so affronted he nearly laughed.

"It doesn't matter what I believe. It matters what my readers believe. And this Harvard shi—" —he caught himself in the knick of time—"stuff isn't going to go down smooth. *Everyone* knows someone who went to Harvard. It would be too easy to check Daddy's credentials." He leaned back, cradling his head in one hand. "Try again."

She sniffed. "Well, if you don't want—"

"What I want is 'the story of my career.' Listen, lady, I'm risking more than a job here. I'm risking a nice little stay in a territorial prison for harboring a notorious thief."

"*Suspected* thief. I've never been convicted," she corrected haughtily.

"Yeah. Right. I'm not sure that isn't just a matter of time at this point. Unless you'd care to deny the allegations?"

"Would that make a better story?" she asked hopefully.

He shook his head. "Nah. Everyone denies allegations."

"Then I won't. I don't want to be hackneyed." She dimpled, looking incredibly young and appealing. He shook his head, trying to clear it. She must put off some sort of electricity that he acted as a giant conductor for. He'd read some amazing studies of electrical fields and the human body. He'd be willing to bet a year's paycheck that this woman put out one helluva charge.

"Shall I try again?" she asked ingenuously.

"Be my guest. Heck. Go for broke. Try the truth," he encouraged.

"The truth? But of course. I was born into a circus family. My father was an escape artist, which accounts for my gift with locks and fasteners. . . ."

He'd stopped writing anything down a half hour ago. He'd set the pencil firmly away and folded his hands behind his head, leaned back, and stared at her. He'd been staring at her ever since. Only the infinitesimal tightening and relaxing of his lovely scarred mouth changed his expression.

Since he hadn't said a word and she had no idea what this close scrutiny meant, she'd just babbled on, spinning through a fourth attempt at an "honest narrative of my youth" before her voice finally cracked and gave out altogether. She trailed off in mid-sentence and just sat too, meeting his blue-eyed gaze straight on. They sat like that for five minutes.

"Are you done?" he finally asked in a deceptively gentle tone.

She nodded.

"Good." He smiled. "We'll start again tomorrow." He rose, looked down at the pages he had scribbled, and gave what looked like a shudder.

"Is there anything to eat?" she croaked.

"Eat?"

"Yes." She snagged a whiskey bottle from the piecrust table beside her. It was empty. "You may prefer to drink your dinners. I eat."

"Lady, leave my bottle alone," he said with a touch of asperity, though what he had to be irritable about was beyond her. She'd given him a good start for his series on her—several good starts even if you discounted the Atlantis one—and managed to remain even-tempered.

Thank heaven for the school's summer thespian program. If she hadn't had to read through several hundred plays last year looking for one appropriate for sixteen-year-old girls to enact, she would never have had the grist this mill was demanding. In her five years as a thief no one had ever actually "talked" to Lightning Lil.

While she was aware of how very dangerous this was, she was also very tired and very near an end to it all, and so she did not deny herself the small crumbs of enjoyment teasing this big, tough-looking gentleman afforded. He stuck the bottle behind the fainting couch, glowering a bit.

"Besides, you're not exactly in any position to be moralizing to me," he said.

Gilly felt a wall come slamming down between them like the iron gates of a medieval castle. "You're right."

She'd been having such a fine time spinning him

tales that she'd almost forgotten who and what she was. An outlaw. A woman without morals.

Funny, she was usually much better at separating Gillian from Lil, knowing exactly what people thought of her outlaw side. The country's poor opinion of Lightning Lil had never before seemed too high a price to pay for the success of her masquerade. "I'm just hungry," she said. "I haven't had anything to eat since last evening."

He was immediately repentant. "Chrissake, why didn't you say something? I'm sorry. Listen, my rent doesn't include meals, but there's a couple bars that serve food in the evening. Let me help you up." He pulled her from the chair and balanced her against the wall as he retrieved her crutch and bonnet. Clumsily, beguilingly, he perched the chip-straw construction on her head and tied a bow beneath her chin.

She couldn't remember ever being the recipient of a man's tender touch. It was intoxicating. His strong, callused fingers brushed her throat, leaving her light-headed. He wet his lips. She stared. He dragged a deep breath through his nostrils, as though preparing for some physical endurance trial and, before she knew what he was about, picked her up, crutch and all.

"I can walk."

"Not down those stairs, you can't."

"I could try."

"You'd just break your other leg."

Lord, he felt so massive and safe and strong, and it had been so very long since she'd felt protected, let alone valued. He didn't argue further, but started out the door and down the stairs. She turned her head and closed her eyes so he couldn't see her give herself over to the guilty pleasure of being held. Beneath her ear, his heart beat strongly and his day-old beard rasped agreeably on her temple. He paused, bouncing her in his arms to readjust her weight, an inadvertent demonstration of his strength that sent her pulse racing.

"Mr. Coyne, who *is* that woman?" a strident voice from below demanded. "I'll have no sinful goings-on in my house, sir!"

Gilly's eyes snapped open and she found herself staring down into the upturned visage of a red-faced termagant of indeterminate age. It took Gilly a second to realize that they'd reached the bottom of the stairs and weren't still several steps above the woman she was that tiny. And angry. Her little face was puckered in on itself like a half-gnawed week-old apple. Little graying curls framed her face like mold on cheese.

"Ah, Mrs. Osby. This is . . . my wife."

Jim made no attempt to let her down.

"Wife?" the little woman exclaimed, all color leaching out of her face except for a thin crimson testimony to her use of lip salve. Obviously, Mrs. Osby didn't want Jim Coyne to have a wife. She stomped her foot. "You didn't . . . You never said nothing about no wife joining you!"

"Her arrival was unexpected."

The woman scowled. For a second, romantic disappointment contended with greed. Greed won. "That'll bring your room rate up two dollars more a week."

"Yes, ma'am."

"And there'll be no extra linens or towels."

"No, ma'am."

"No drinking."

"Of course not." Amazingly he managed to say this with a straight face. He started by the landlady.

But Mrs. Osby wasn't done with Jim yet. She put her little taloned hands on her hips, peering intently at Gilly. She sniffed. "You ought to be ashamed of yourself, Mr. Coyne. A man your age with such a young girl."

"I thought to give her the advantage of a mature man's guidance." Even though he flushed, Gilly saw the spark of humor in his eyes.

"Well," Mrs. Osby began, "I say an old goat and a y—"

Gilly had had enough. She linked her hands behind Jim's neck, combing her fingers through the crisp, clean curls. "Can Big Daddy Jimmums take Baby Pookums to eat now? Baby's hungry."

"How old are you, child?" Mrs. Osby demanded.

"Oh, I'm much older than I look," Gilly said sweetly, all the while fondling Jim's throat and the nape of his neck. "I'll be seventeen next month."

"Barely legal!" Mrs. Osby's one brown brow locked into a deep *V* above her nose. She stared purposefully at where Jim's hand lay so close to Gilly's breast. "Mind you, no noise past ten o'clock!"

Jim's nostrils flared, just a fraction. Then one side of his mouth suddenly crooked up in a devil's grin and by God if the man didn't have dimples—long, deep dimples. "Now, Mrs. Osby, don't tell me you expect to police *that*?"

Mrs. Osby's mouth dropped open and she gasped

for air like a beached fish. With a sharp snap of starched muslin, she fled down the narrow hallway.

Jim looked down into her bemused eyes and grinned again. She shivered. Dimples and a roguish sense of humor. She could be in real trouble here.

4

Why on earth would a rose-growing, Latin-spouting girl become a thief? He simply couldn't believe it was for the money. She didn't seem to *have* that much. For the thrills? He could imagine that of her, yet it still didn't quite fit. She looked too tired for a thrill seeker, and there was a certain wistfulness about her mouth in her few unguarded moments.

Jim hadn't pumped her for information during dinner. He simply enjoyed her conversation, and even though she carefully steered talk away from any personal information, he learned a lot more about her than she realized. Gilly wasn't the sort of woman to keep an opinion to herself.

She thought the Brooklyn Bridge currently under construction was a "monument to graft," an opinion with which he coincidentally agreed—ergo she kept herself apprised of New York newspapers. She thought that baseball was a fad, an opinion with which he definitely disagreed—ergo she was completely uninformed about sports. She thought that a person "had to accept whatever destination the path they walk leads them to," an opinion he didn't know whether he agreed with or not—ergo the essence of her still eluded him.

And finally, he knew that if nothing else, her mouth should be outlawed.

For the last twenty minutes he hadn't been able to concentrate, had barely touched his own plate of steak and eggs, simply because after every few bites she cleaned the corners of her mouth with the tip of her tongue. And because when her clean white teeth bit through a crisp apple peel, her bottom lip dragged provocatively up the smooth unmarked skin of the fruit. And because when she chewed, her mouth moved and he wanted it moving on him.

"Something wrong with your dinner?" she asked, pointing her fork at the half pound of steak remaining on his plate.

"No. It was fine. Just fine."

She took a sip of milk, leaving behind a narrow little white mustache above her upper lip, which she licked clean with a flourish of her pink tongue. He closed his eyes and begged for strength.

"It would be a shame to let it go to waste. Good meat. Mind if I . . ."

"No. No," he said, glad for the distraction. "Be my guest. Go right ahead."

Happily she speared the steak and began sawing into it. She ate with such enthusiasm that he wondered if maybe she wasn't a kid from the wrong side of the tracks, a kid who'd never gotten enough to eat. *Poor child.*

The thought blackened his mood. If she was sixteen, a child she assuredly was, and he was lusting after a girl young enough to be his daughter.

"Sixteen," he muttered.

"Sixteen what?" she asked, fork half-raised to her sinful-looking mouth.

Maybe she was real close to seventeen. . . . Nineteen years wasn't so very—Christ! What the hell was he thinking?

"When's your birthday?" he demanded. "You know, you don't look all that young to me. I would have put your age around twenty-one. For your own sake, when you're finally caught—and you will be— don't try pulling any 'shucks, I'm just a kid. I didn't know better' defense. It won't work. You look old enough to know better."

"Thank you for the advice, Mr. Coyne, but there are two minor points I'd like to make: One, I don't intend to get caught, and two, I'm not sixteen. I'm twenty-seven."

"Huh?"

She laughed. "I've always looked young for my years. Granted, not *that* young—and it isn't very gentlemanly of you to point it out even if it's true— but when that woman started in on you I just couldn't help myself."

He relaxed in relief, extraordinary and unaccountable. "You have a diabolical sense of humor."

She smiled, flattered.

Could she be twenty-seven, or was that just another in her string of endless lies? There was, for all her trust and vitality, a touch of weariness in her gaze, a tensile maturity in the set of her throat and shoulders, the brand of experience in her humor. She might be telling the truth.

"Jim!" The thunk between his shoulder blades announced Vance Calhoun's arrival. Jim offered up thanks that his mouth hadn't been full. He turned, looking straight up at the undercarriage of Margaret Calhoun's bosom. He stumbled to his feet.

Margaret gazed at him with cool amusement. She was a handsome, sharp-featured woman with a bosom worth noting and a possessive, nearly predatory air. He could see her in the role of Lightning Lil far more easily than he could the woman across from him.

"I heard your wife had arrived in town, Jim," Vance said, hauling out a chair next to Gilly's and dropping into it. "I told Margaret we had to come and meet her. Stuck way out here like this, Margaret gets starved for the company of women of her own class."

"Mrs. Calhoun, my wife . . . er, Mrs. Coyne," Jim said. "Mrs. Coyne, Mrs. Vance Calhoun."

"Come now, James," Margaret said. "I'm certain your bride and I shall become close friends. What do you call her?"

Jim swallowed. His brain seized up as he searched for a name, any name.

"Darling," said Gilly softly. "Jim calls me 'darling.' "

Margaret's head swiveled, like a snake watching a particularly colorful bird. The corners of her lips lifted. "How utterly charming," she murmured. "But I can hardly call you 'darling' too."

Gilly didn't respond; her attention turned to Vance who, having seized her hand, was patting it. "Pleased to meet you, Mrs. Coyne." No, the bastard was stroking it. "You'll certainly be a fine addition to the female population."

"Thank you," Gilly said in an odd, hushed voice. She made no move to retrieve her hand from Vance's clasp. "Won't you join us? We were just finishing dinner."

"Uh, *darlin'*," Jim said, "I don't think—"

"Isn't that sweet, dear?" Margaret cut in, studiously avoiding the sight of her husband playing with Gilly's hand. "James wants to be alone with his bride. Kind of Mrs. Coyne as it is to invite us, we mustn't impose on their reunion, Vance."

"Course not," Vance said, releasing Gilly's hand but continuing his slow perusal of her person.

"I'll tell you what," Margaret said to Gilly. "Come to our little soiree Saturday evening. Just a few of the best people this town has to offer. Though the best is hardly good enough. Eight o'clock, shall we say?"

"We'd be delighted," Gilly said before Jim could refuse.

"Come, Vance. Let's leave the lovebirds alone. Only look at how anxious James is to have us gone."

As soon as they'd left, Jim sat down. "Want to explain that?"

"What?" Gilly had already begun shoveling another fork of meat into her mouth and was chomping away in evident pleasure. She looked like a cat that had just been stroked. Which she had.

"You sure you didn't get hit in the head by that bullet? The less you and I are together in public, the better. It isn't going to take a real bright person to figure out that you and I are not man and wife. That was stupid, Gilly—"

"Hush!" she frowned. "I told you not to call me that in public."

"Okay, *darlin'*," he ground out. "But you better start penning your apologies to Mrs. Calhoun to-night."

"I'm going to that party," she said firmly, fright underlying the determination in her face. Why would missing a party frighten her? "I'm going with or without you. If you think I'm going to sit alone with you in that little two-by-four room for two weeks, clomping outside twice a day to eat, you are wrong. Dead wrong."

She held her breath, praying she wouldn't have to go to the Calhouns' alone, knowing she would if she must. She simply *had* to go to that party. She was so close to finishing things. Each year she seemed less a part of one world, but no more a part of the other. She wanted her identity back. She wanted an end to dusty trails, rifle reports, and the acrid scent of gunpowder. She wanted an end to leaving empty classrooms, coming home to an empty house and an empty life.

"Is that a threat?" Jim asked coldly.

His question stunned her. "What?"

"You're supposed to be pretty good with a pistol and more than a little ruthless. I'm asking you point-blank: Are you threatening me?" A tic had replaced his dimple, and his face had gone still and tense, his eyes and mouth, hard.

What did he think she was capable of doing?

The answer was obvious: anything. And why shouldn't he?

Once again she'd made the same mistake. For a short hour she'd tricked herself into believing she was simply a woman enjoying the company of a gentleman. But Jim wasn't her beau and she wasn't his lady, and he, at least, hadn't mistaken their dinner for anything more than the act of feeding the body. She was pathetic.

She stood up, her vision swimming in the sudden sting of tears. She refused to shed them. "I'm not going to answer that, Mr. Coyne. I'm going back to the boardinghouse now. You can stay here or come along to ensure I don't lay a trap for you." Her attempted mockery failed, sounded brittle.

Before he could answer she picked up her crutch and moved away, whacking her cast into the spring-loaded door and stepping out into the cold night air, leaving Jim and might-have-beens behind.

Outside, the main street teemed with lurid sound and motion. Men staggered and tripped on the boardwalk, hollered from the alleys, and raced their horses down the center of town. Bright, garish light spilling from the open doors of saloons mingled with the jangling of an off-key player piano and the cacophony of drunken singers. *This* was her world. Or, at least, Lil's.

Taking a deep breath, Gilly started the long, awkward walk back to the boardinghouse. Jim Coyne thought she could be violent. Good. That's what she wanted people to think. That's what had kept her safe: the perception that she was capable of any violence. But it *did* hurt, deep inside where she thought she'd killed every romantic notion. She'd thought for a short, wonderful hour that he saw her, *Gilly,* that in a deep instinctive way he knew her, knew she couldn't hurt anyone.

She lifted her chin. She'd known what she was

giving up a half decade earlier when she started this. But five years ago she'd been young, idealistic, ardent. Now . . . she saw her life racing away from her. And it was just too darn late to do anything about it except finish what she'd begun.

She was just passing the doors of one of the seedier saloons when a trio of boys sauntered out, blocking her way. She tried to get by them, but the shortest one—an ugly little tobacco chaw of a man—spied her and let out a little *whoop*. The blonde by his side gaped in wonderment.

"Boy, howdy! Lookee here, Tommy. A new soiled dove done flied into the coop!"

"Sorry, boys," she said tiredly. "You're mistaken. I'm not a dove. I'm a pigeon."

"Huh?" the squat boy said. "What she mean?"

She shook her head. "Just my attempt at humor, kid."

The word *kid* didn't seem to fit well with the ugly little troll. His face split in a sneer, and he swaggered within a few inches of Gilly. She recoiled from his whiskey-soaked breath. "Honey doll, the way you look you don't have to do nuthin' with that mouth of yours but—"

"Nuh-uh. Don't say it, Tommy," a soft voice behind her advised. *Jim*.

He moved in front of her, cutting off the young men's access, smiling pleasantly. "Don't even *think* it, Tommy."

Tommy snorted. "Think what, Pops? About this long-legged piece of high-priced tail opening up those lips and taking m—"

The troll keeled over, landing with a soft *thud* at

Gilly's feet. Gilly blinked and looked up. Jim was shaking his right hand.

"Did you . . . did you hit him?" she asked in disbelief.

"Well, he didn't fall over by himself, darlin'," Jim answered sarcastically. He looked down at the motionless form. Tommy's two companions took up positions on either side of him, staring down too. "Ah, shit—excuse my language—he's even younger than I thought," Jim said, sounding honestly upset.

"That's nearly two hundred pounds of 'boy,' Jim," she said. "And based on my admittedly short acquaintance with him, I'd guess he's been hit before. Often."

"I don't hit kids."

"You're gonna be sorry, m-mister," the blond youth stuttered, bending down and hoisting Tommy up under the arms. "Real sorry."

His other companion grabbed Tommy's feet and they started staggering sideways, muttering threats and imprecations until they found a saloon and disappeared inside, leaving Gilly and Jim alone.

"Thank you," Gilly said.

The light from the saloon window bathed her face with a buttery soft sheen and gilded her pale hair. Jim took a deep breath and made his hands stay at his side. They'd go back to the boardinghouse now. She'd let her hair down and gaze at him out of eyes the color of Creole coffee. She'd be feminine and vulnerable. Or worse, she'd speak intelligently and knowledgeably on any number of seemingly inconsequential matters, but with a flavor of experience that struck a note of accord with him.

He didn't want to be in accord with a criminal.

She was a story, a way out of here, and nothing else. Yet, when he'd asked her if she was threatening him and he'd seen the color bleed from her face as though he'd struck her, he'd felt ashamed, as though he'd backhanded a smiling child. Ashamed that he'd thought poorly of a self-confessed bandit. What a joke. She was probably laughing up her crooked sleeve at him. For God's sake, the woman came with a wanted poster, not a letter of introduction!

He looked up at the night sky, silently begging for direction. He couldn't remember ever feeling so frustrated, so confused.

Confused? She was a woman. What had he expected? But she *wasn't* like other women. There was a sense of purpose, a tempered quality of strength and regret, and yet an approachable gentleness about her. He felt comfortable with her, instinctively gauging the subtle shifts of her agile mind, anticipating her smile . . . ah, hell! "I'll take you back to the boardinghouse. Then I have to come back to town. I have some business to attend to."

"Of course."

She was quiet during the short walk home, making good time in spite of the crutch. It was getting late and the house was dark except for the flickering lantern lighting their window above. Not *their* window, Jim told himself. There was no *their*. Silently, Jim held open the front door, looking askance when she didn't enter. She stood, eyes lowered, head bowed.

"I've never killed anyone in my life," she finally said in a low, earnest voice. "I shot a man once. I hit him in the leg. I spent the next hour with my head over a basin, getting sick to my stomach. I have a reputation, and it's kept me and a lot of people from getting hurt. I'd appreciate it if you'd just leave that little bit of news out of your story. But I wanted you to know."

"Gilly, I never thought—" He stopped himself. He didn't know what the hell he thought.

"It's all right," she murmured, slipping by him into the house, the darkness masking her expression but unable to mask the hurt in her voice. He felt like a bully.

She might not be a killer, but before this charade was done he suspected she'd make him bleed. The despair and valiance with which she accepted his doubt made him want to comfort her. And more. Much more. He entered the house behind her, stopping at the bottom of the stairs.

He stepped near enough to feel the slight heat rise off her skin like an aura, to almost taste the flavor of her soft lips. Their eyes met. He didn't know a damn thing about her. She was more of a mystery than any he'd ever encountered in a career where mysteries were an everyday occurrence. He'd never wanted the answer to a puzzle more in his life.

He raised his arms and she walked into his embrace. No, he told himself sternly, she walked into an offer to be carried up the stairs. He lifted her easily, handed her the crutch, and started up.

It was exquisite torture. With each step her breasts bounced gently against him. Each movement translated into the push and drag of her body against his. Each breath she took stirred the air on his throat.

He made the landing and didn't want to put her down. As soon as he realized it, he made himself do it, made himself step away and touch his finger to the brim of his hat.

"Ma'am, if you would just set my toothbrush and the wash ewer in the sitting room, I'd be obliged."

Her dark, liquid eyes—tobacco-colored silk, deepening even as he watched—did not waver from his. She nodded.

"Thank you." He made himself turn, made himself take the long flight of steps down and out of the house, feeling her gaze on his back the entire time. With a firm stride he made the corner of the street. Once in the shadows he bent over, bracing his hands on his thighs. "I need a drink." He looked back.

The light was on in the upper room. He could see her, a lithe silhouette against the drawn curtain. She was brushing her hair. Each time she lifted her hand her breast rose, its ripe contours silhouetted against the glow of the globe lamp.

He'd return to that room later tonight, and he'd look at that cheap door and know that was all that separated them. All night. Every night. For a couple of weeks. Every morning he'd wake to the scent of her, the husky timbre of her voice, the sight of her. And, damn it all to hell, it was a good, practical business arrangement. She was getting a chance to heal up, and he was getting a ticket out of here. He glanced up again. Long, languid strokes of the brush.

"I *really* need a drink."

"Too bad, old man, 'cause I got a different plan fer you," Tommy said, and then the other two jumped him.

5

Gilly woke up to the sound of a masculine groan. Apparently, Jim's business last night had been with a liquor bottle. There was ample evidence that her Mr. Coyne was a hard-drinking Irishman. Not that he was *her* Mr. Coyne, she thought sadly, or her anything but a means to an end. The groan turned into a hiss of pain.

Worriedly, Gilly opened the door and peeked out. He wasn't sprawled in the disreputable heap she'd expected. He was sitting on the edge of the fainting couch, his back to her, pulling on a clean white shirt. He'd gotten one arm through a sleeve and was cautiously working on the other. The livid bruise marking the thick cable of muscle on top of his shoulders seemed to be giving him trouble. He lifted his arm, got it just high enough to slip in, and gave a muted groan.

"What happened to you?" Gilly asked.

His head snapped around, and she could see a

slight discoloration on his chin. Then his lovely pasqueflower-blue eyes narrowed and he jerked the shirt the rest of the way on, turning his back to do so.

A modest man. Who'd have imagined such a species existed? The thought made her smile.

"Chrissake, Gilly, get something on!"

He'd called her *Gilly*. Her smile broadened. She ignored his order, sashaying into the room as his hands made deft work of his shirt buttons. "I already have. I'm wearing what is commonly referred to as a 'morning gown.' Where'd you get those bruises?"

His mobile lips scrunched in disgust. "Tommy and his pals were waiting for me when I got back to the main street last night. They'll be okay," he assured her, although why he would think she cared about the welfare of Tommy and his nasty "pals" was an utter mystery. "I didn't hurt them. Much. Course, if their da had used a nice stout rod when the need arose, I doubt they'd be causing so much trouble now."

"Your dad use that stout rod much, Mr. Coyne?"

He grinned, that utterly charming Gaelic lopsided grin that crinkled the corners of his North Sea eyes and made that unnerving dimple appear. "When the need arose."

"Did it arise much?"

He shrugged and stood up. The movement made him grimace and he set his hands on his hips, arcing into the ache, working out the kinks. He looked sore and poorly used, she thought, a sense of empathy following her summation.

"I have some salve," she offered. "I always carry it in my saddlebag. A Cheyenne tracker gave it to me."

He turned his gorgeous eyes on her again, a touch of pity softening their brilliance. "I bet you need it, what with the life you lead. You must get pretty beat up out there on the range, huh?" he said sympathetically, finishing buttoning his shirt.

"Oh, it's not for me! My gelding is getting up there in years, and sometimes after a long day if I don't rub him down he's just no good for—"

"I am *not* old," he broke in through clenched teeth. "I am not a gelding, and I don't need any of your liniment, lady."

So, they were back to *lady*.

"I was just trying to help."

"The only thing I want from you is your story." He snatched his black silk tie off the table and crouched down so he could look in the little fish-eye mirror hung near the door. Deftly, he flipped the ends into a neat knot. That done, he picked up his brush and attacked his rich, glossy curls, sheer force making them lie flat. As soon as he turned from the mirror they sprang to life. She tried not to smile, and he eyed her suspiciously.

"You want breakfast first, or do you want to start in on the interview right away?"

"We can start to work right now if you'd like, Mr. Coyne."

"Not with you in that outfit, we can't." He made a disparaging gesture at her dressing gown, and to her chagrin she felt herself blush. Which was ridiculous. Her gown was demure in the extreme. The light muslin could hardly be said to cling; indeed, it dropped in soft folds to cover her feet. Besides, it was one of the few things she'd bought at that second-hand store that fit. Her real wardrobe was hardly suited to the role of adventuress she'd thought to be playing. Still, she didn't want to provoke him.

She emerged fifteen minutes later in a simple lilac-colored dress, only the deep keyhole neckline in the uncomfortably tight bodice worthy of comment. Jim didn't comment.

"Let's try a different tack today, shall we?" he said.

She nodded agreeably.

"Let's discuss opinions, not facts."

"Fine. What would you like to know?"

"Why do you do these things? What makes a pretty young woman become a common hoodlum, robbing people at the point of a gun rather than earning a living? Why do you risk physical harm to pursue such an infamous occupation? Money? Thrills? Are you simply crazy, or do you have reasons for your antisocial behavior?"

She squirmed on her seat. "That's putting it rather baldly."

He raked his hand through his hair, sending the last of the obedient waves into open riot.

"Is something wrong?" she asked.

"Look," he said, "I've interviewed plenty of criminals: labor bosses, union heads, gang leaders. I ask a question, and they respond with either a threat or an answer. But in all the years I've been doing this—and yeah, that's a lot of years—not one of them has ever complained that I didn't phrase a question delicately enough."

She gazed wide-eyed at him, and he gave a sound of exasperation. "I'm new at interviewing bandits with delicate sensibilities, but just spot me a few errors and I'm sure somehow we'll muddle through."

"Why are you here then?"

"Huh?"

"If you're normally interviewing gang and labor bosses, what are you doing in Far Enough, Texas, interviewing me?"

He plucked his paper and pencil from the table. "I'm asking the questions."

"Sorry."

He threw up his hands, capitulating to the hurt in her voice. "I was exiled here, okay? I wrote an article about a palm-oiling deal between a city councilman and a sewage contractor. It was a deal that made two men rich and left an entire section of the city—albeit a poor section—with a substandard sewage system."

"And they exiled you for that? That's just not fair!" she said incredulously, her ire—and her fanny—rising at such an injustice. He pushed her back down in her chair.

"Calm down, Gilly," he said with a hint of amusement. "I didn't get sent here for exposing wrongs. Papers love exposing wrongs. In fact, if we can't find wrong we're encouraged to invent it. No. I got sent here for getting my paper sued for libel."

"Oh."

"Satisfied?" His blue eyes danced.

"I was just curious."

"As am I. Now, Miss . . . it is Miss, isn't it?"

"It's Miss."

"You've never even been close to getting married?"

"Yes."

He held up both hands, waggling his fingers invitingly. "Could you elaborate?"

"I was engaged once."

"Yeah? What happened? Is he why you started rob—on your life of crime?"

"Oh, no. He was a fine, honest man. That was the problem. I just couldn't see explaining my, er, career choice to him. He was very ethical."

"Ethical men. God love 'em," Jim muttered with such commiseration that she concluded a few had interfered in his past. "Why didn't you just quit thieving?"

She was telling too much. Her desire to tell him the truth—to have another person know her, to discover if he'd recoil, sneer, or even accept what she was—fought with her need for safety. Not her own but her family's. The latter impulse won.

"He was poor. Poor as dirt," she said.

Jim immediately noted the change in her tone. A savvy, hard note had entered it. She's put on the Lightning Lil mask, he thought.

"Poor and honest," she continued flippantly. "Salt of the earth. A saint among men, but with no earthly possessions to call his own."

"Saints can be like that," Jim said sardonically, unhappily aware that somewhere in the last minutes he'd lost Gilly to the Lil role, and he strongly suspected Gilly was the real woman, the woman he wanted to . . . write about. Damn it.

"But by the time I met Francis—his name was Francis."

"As in Assisi."

"Yes." She gave him her three-cornered smile. "By the time I met Francis I was too far gone on the road to ruin. My hand was on the whip and I couldn't find the brakes. I had grown accustomed to

- the wicked ways of the flesh, the material prizes in Satan's carnival."

Some prizes, Jim thought. Her dress had to have been reworked at least three times.

"I didn't want to give them up."

"So that was that."

"Yup." She held out her hand, studied her nails, and peeped at him out of the corner of her eye. Was he buying any of this?

He tilted his head back and stared upward, as though petitioning the ceiling for patience. The light hit his jaw and illuminated the white line marking it. "Let's go on to another question."

"Sure. How'd you get that scar? The one on your chin."

"A fight."

"Fight?"

"Yeah. This Swede had a bruising right uppercut that—" He stopped suddenly and took the two broad steps separating them, looming over her, exasperation evident in every line of his big body. "Lady, will you please answer *my* questions?"

"Yes, Mr. Coyne." She folded her hands primly in her lap.

"Don't call me Mr. Coyne. It makes me feel older than I already am, and right now that's about as old as anyone in this territory."

She grinned. He was fine. Mature and seasoned and luscious, but she couldn't help teasing him. "That old . . . Jim?"

He almost smiled back. "I think there could be a sequoia out there that might have a few months on me."

She burst into laughter, and he responded with

that full, dazzling smile, leaning over her a little as he did so. She could feel his warm breath, taste it, flavored with some sort of minty tooth cleanser.

"You," he said softly, "are the prettiest outlaw I've ever met."

His low, intimate tone washed over her like a physical stroke. His eyes were so close she could see the little copper flecks that danced near the pupil of his blue eyes. It unbalanced her. Caught her off guard. "Pshaw," she responded breathlessly. "You haven't met any outlaws."

"I come from New York, darlin'. The last census listed outlaw as the second-most-common occupation in the city." He straightened with what appeared to be reluctance.

"And the first?"

"Politician."

She laughed again, and he watched her in obvious enjoyment until some sudden, unwelcome thought shuttered his expression, leaving formal pleasantness where there had been intimacy.

"I need to telegraph my editor in New York that I'm on a story," he said. "Let's go. On the way we can get something to eat."

What the hell were those women doing, Jim wondered. The Carmichael twins had practically run up the walkway, shouldered their way past Jim and Gilly, and were now lying in wait a few yards ahead. One of them slouched against the rail, panting, color splotching her chubby white cheeks. The other held up Mudruk's exterior wall, her breasts jostled around the framework of her bodice like poached eggs on toast.

"Hey!" one of them—Merry?—panted. "You . . . must be . . . Jim's . . . wife."

"Tall, ain't ya?" the other said, eyes insolently tracing each long inch of Gilly's form. Jim had the mental image of a spark touching off the fuse on a powder keg.

"Surprising Jim never mentioned he had a wife." Terry—it had to be Terry—said. "But maybe then it ain't so surprising." Her slow perusal noted and dismissed each one of Gilly's attributes.

The three women stared at one another for a dozen heartbeats.

"Well, Jim's a man," Gilly finally said. "What man that you know would acknowledge ties to an absent woman? 'Specially when there's two other pretty ones around?"

Whatever powder keg had been ignited was abruptly deffused. Merry and Terry giggled like ten-year-olds in pigtails, patting hair and adjusting their bodices. "True enough, honey. True enough."

Jim stared in open mystification. Another of those bizarre female alchemy things had happened. The women were grinning, all antipathy gone.

"Mr. Coyne!" Mort James came loping down the street, waving his hand. He got to the rail and easily vaulted over it, landing in front of the little gathering. Jim's mood soured. It had been a good decade since he'd vaulted anything through sheer enthusiasm. "Mr. Coyne, you gotta introduce me to your wife. I mean, you will, won't you, please?"

The boy snatched his hat off his head and slapped it against his thigh, raising a small cloud of dust. Gilly turned on her smile. The boy turned bright red.

They stared at each other, youth recognizing youth, and Jim felt every gray hair in his head.

"Ah, Gil—*darlin'*," he said, catching himself before he called her Gilly, "this is Mort James, editor of the local newspaper. Mort, my wife." The word *wife* came easily, too easily, bringing an unexpected swell of possessiveness with it.

"Pleased to meet you, ma'am."

Gilly sashayed up to the boy. Real close, much closer than a married woman approached a man, and laid her lace-clad fingers on his arm. Her expression was rapt and utterly feminine.

"I do so admire a man with a brain. So few of your gender ever take the time to think before they speak, let alone have the sense to write something down. But then, you men are such decisive creatures." Her playful tone robbed the words of sting, but Jim had the profound sense that they were meant for him.

"Thank you." Mort gulped.

"I'd love to read your work." She was practically purring.

"I'd like you to read me, er, my articles, ma'am." Mort's glance at Jim turned to a beet-red flush.

What the hell was the boy thinking about to make him blush like that? It better not be—

"Course, I'm not the journalist. Your husband is," Mort went on, and Jim relaxed slightly.

"Oh, no one's the man Jim is. In *any* way."

Heat raced like a grease fire up his neck and into his face. Now she had him doing it. Merry guffawed. Terry snorted in laughter, tears spilling out of her eyes. Jim grabbed Gilly's arm and spun her around. Pulling her close, he half-lifted, half-hauled her along the plank sidewalk, her cast making an erratic staccato as they went.

"See what I mean?" Gilly threw back over her shoulder at Mort, Merry, and Terry.

"Do I ever, honey!" Merry crowed.

"What the hell do you think you're doing?" Jim demanded when they were out of earshot.

The look she threw him could have iced hot ashes. "Repairing the damage you did."

"What damage?"

"You nearly called me Gilly in front of that boy. And he's a reporter! I saw him looking at my cast. He was working things out right there. I could practically see the thought forming. I just gave him something else to think about, is all."

She was truly upset. In spite of the sarcastic sting in her words, her eyes betrayed honest fear. It dawned on Jim, perhaps truly for the first time, that if she was caught they would be sending her to prison. For years. Her golden hair would turn gray, her whisper-soft skin would toughen into leather, the laughter in her eyes would die.

He gripped her shoulders. She felt agile and graceful beneath his touch. "I'm sorry I caused you anxiety. I'll be much more careful from now on. But the fact is, I didn't call you Gilly. And the subject matter you have that boy sweating over right now is going to probably occupy his thoughts not only for the next few days but the next few months."

"Do you think so?" She gazed up into his eyes, worry and something else—something intimate—shimmering in their depths.

He glanced over his shoulder at Mort, who was staring at him with a look of hot-blooded masculine envy.

"*Darlin'*, I'd bet the bank on it."

6

Jim held back the curtain in one fist and leaned his forehead against the window, exasperated and resigned. "So you decided to avenge your father's wrongful imprisonment by going after the business associates who'd framed him?"

"Yes." If he looked at her he'd see the way the sunlight brushed platinum gilding among her pale strands of hair, be forced to confront the unusual tension that had crept into her lovely face during the morning. So he didn't look. Because he already knew all about tension. For four days now he'd hauled her up and down those stairs. Each trip became a harsher lesson in self-control. Each climb lasted interminably long and not nearly long enough. Every time she clung to him he was more loath to let her go. Each time he glanced down he found her face tilted up toward his, an unreadable expression in her dark eyes.

They had a business arrangement. Nothing else.

He dug his fingers in on either side of the bridge of his nose, concentrating on the small pain. "And there's one man left out there who has yet to pay the wages of his sins?"

"That's right. One more and I can retire."

"Right." His mouth curled. "Say, you don't by any chance use all your stolen money to fund orphanages and old-folks' homes, do you?"

"Not *all* of it," she returned calmly. "I'm buying my father a ranch once he gets out of the penitentiary."

"And your saintly father isn't going to wonder where you got the money?"

"Investments." She smiled smugly. "I told him I've had the luck of the devil on the stock market."

Jim snorted. "Well, they're getting better, at any rate."

"Excuse me?"

He turned around, focused his gaze somewhere above her left shoulder. "Robin Hood with a twist. Just enough nobility to foment the country's popular concept of womanhood, just enough greed to suggest realism. If you don't come up with a better one, I'll use it."

"Oh, thank you," she said. Despite her mocking tone, he couldn't help notice disappointment cross her face. Did she think he was so gullible he'd buy anything as long as it was half-credible? "I'm so glad you finally approve of something I've said," she went on, and then brightened. "Does that mean we can stop for the day? I have to get ready for the Calhouns' party tonight."

All day there'd been an air of suppressed excitement about her. He thought he understood. She probably didn't get the opportunity to go to many parties. She certainly wasn't attending any galas during what he had come to think of as her "thief phase," and a spinster—even a lovely one—wouldn't be invited to many dinner parties.

"Go ahead and get ready," he said.

She didn't need further encouragement, but rose and hobbled into the bedroom. Jim looked over his interview notes. He couldn't discern much from among the weird concoctions she dreamed up. Almost impossible to tell what truth was buried in there. And discovering the truth about Gilly was becoming more and more important to him.

He had no idea why. He should be happy to cull the more dramatic and colorful bits in here and piece together one helluva good story. The readers would love it; his editor would love it; and, most important, he'd be chugging out of Far Enough inside a week of its submission.

But *Gilly* had become more important than leaving Far Enough. Or she'd been that important from the first. He drowned that impulsive thought in practicality. He wanted to know why she'd become a thief, what and who was important to her, what her future held.

The thought of the future pricked uncomfortably and made him shift his shoulders as though distributing an uneven burden. He needed to get out of here, he decided, while *he* still had a future.

Vance Calhoun owned the only brick house in Far Enough. Its brand-spanking-new Gothic Revivalist bulk splayed over half the length of a street, and its private stable yard took up the rest. In spite of the modern architecture and the white-gloved Negro man taking hats and coats in the doorway, there was no mistaking Far Enough for Chicago.

Close by, the lowing of thousands of cows—steers—set up a deep, melancholy counterpoint to the raucous sound of human voices spilling from the Calhouns' house. A dog started barking and a chicken squawked as women tittered and ranchers guffawed.

At the front door the servant bowed them in. "I'm really looking forward to this," Gilly whispered, turning from Jim and letting her shawl slide from her shoulders into his waiting hands.

"Well, at least one of us—" Jim stopped.

Apparently Gilly's dressmaker had used up all the sapphire-color fabric in the gown's voluminous skirt, because the damn thing didn't have a top. Or much of one. A ten-inch-wide swath of material acted as a bodice, and from his present position Jim could see a great deal of the lovely back that swath didn't do a damn thing to cover.

He'd never seen anything as provocative as Gilly's naked back.

Her shoulders, unfashionably straight and all too fashionably naked, spanned the delicate plumb line of her spine. Her skin was honey-tinted and silky and smooth, young muscle moving beneath its surface. She looked healthy and lithe and bewilderingly female.

"Mrs. Coyne! Jim." Vance Calhoun came striding down the hall, hand outstretched. Reluctantly, Jim raised his own. Vance ignored it, taking Gilly's elbow and turning her. At least the neckline didn't plunge like the back. "Let me show you the house. Jim, there's punch in the drawing room to your left."

"I'll just tag along if you don't mind."

"Suit yourself." The bastard didn't even bother turning his head. He took off with Gilly clomping along happily by his side, her face alight with admiration. Jim trailed behind like a stray dog. In spite of her claims of owning her own "very nice house," from the rapt expression Gilly wore, Jim had to wonder if she'd ever been in one as extravagant as the Calhouns'.

She acted like a tourist in a museum, exclaiming over the furniture and the drapes, admiring the oriental carpets and chandeliers, complimenting Calhoun on his objets d'art and paintings.

She was "charmed" by the billiards room. She "adored" the solarium. She thought the music room was "wonderful" and the drawing room "elegant." All the while Jim wondered where the hell Margaret Calhoun was while her husband leered over his wi— He stopped himself just in time. She was his ticket out of here. That's *all*. But he was having a harder time remembering that with each passing day. Hell, with each passing hour.

And it wasn't just her lovely body or siren's voice. He enjoyed her company, her nonsensical stories and glib wit, the fiery sense of outrage that any perceived injustice roused in her, an indignation so like his own.

"Look at all these books." Gilly's exclamation interrupted his thoughts. He looked over her shoulder into the library.

It was a big room crowded with hide-bound chairs and animal heads. One wall held a set of

French doors that led onto the house's wraparound porch; two others crawled with books.

"Have you read every one of these books, Mr. Calhoun?" Gilly asked.

"Vance, honey. And no, I haven't. They're for looks. What would I do with a book? I have work to do. My business doesn't run itself. A real man doesn't have time to read." He glanced at Jim. "No offense meant."

"Oh!" Gilly's hand flew with extreme—and therefore fake—chagrin to her mouth. "Of course not. I don't know what I was even thinking suggesting such a thing." She caught Jim's eye, and he saw the spark of amusement in her face. Evil creature. Wholly wondrous evil creature.

She wandered over to the bookshelves, running her fingertip along gold-embossed spines. She turned, smiling saucily, her hand on one leather-bound set. "These aren't even books, Mr. Calhoun." She waggled a fingertip at him. "They're glued together."

"Well, the rest of the books are real, honey." Jim fervently wished he'd stop calling Gilly "honey." "And those serve their purpose. They cover my safe."

"Oh!" Gilly's hand dropped as though scalded. Jim's heart thudded with sudden, awful certitude. "Should you be telling me that?" she asked.

Calhoun shrugged. "You're not going to rob me, are you?"

"You never know." Jesus. She didn't fidget a mite. Just smiled.

"Only a fool like George Reynolds gets robbed by a woman."

"Like who?"

"George Reynolds. Fellow up north. Got robbed twice by that Lightning Lil gal. Twice. I always said that he—"

"Vance!" Margaret Calhoun sailed into the library. "Ah. The Coynes. I see Vance is giving you a tour of *my* house." The emphasis on the pronoun was unmistakable.

"It's gorgeous, Mrs. Calhoun," Gilly enthused, releasing Vance's arm and stepping away.

"Thank you." Margaret thawed slightly. "It isn't furnished as I'd like yet. But as we'll be touring Europe, I expect I'll be able to pick up the few odds and ends there. Too tedious, all the travel, but worth the effort. Europe is so grandly . . . old. You've been there, of course."

Gilly shook her head, and Margaret smiled like a cat feeding on liver. "Oh, but my dear, you must induce James to take you. You'd love it."

"I'm sure I would. Are you going soon?" Gilly asked.

"In a few weeks," Margaret returned brightly. "Now, Vance, as delightful as it is to have cosmopolitan guests, we do have others. Don't neglect your duties as host." Her gaze found Gilly's cast. "It's too bad about your injury, Mrs. Coyne. We're to have dancing later. Or what passes as dancing in these parts. You might call it stomping. James, perhaps you would partner me that we might show the heathens how it's done?"

"My pleasure, Mrs. Calhoun."

"Good. Come along, Vance." She snagged her husband's arm and tugged him after her.

"How long has Mrs. Calhoun lived in Far Enough?" Gilly asked when they'd gone.

"All her life. She's the town barber's daughter."

Gilly burst into laughter. "You're teasing me."

"No. Vance met her when he moved here a few years back."

Her humor was infectious, and he grinned when she started laughing again. Until his eyes passed over the fake volumes of books.

"Gilly, you aren't going to rob Calhoun."

"No, Jim," she said thoughtfully. "I admit, I'd consider it under different circumstances, but this cast definitely hinders my style. It's difficult to be stealthy in one." She thumped the heel against the floor. "And impossible to fit one in a stirrup. Important when making a getaway." She grinned.

He smiled back. The sound of a fiddle and piano awoke in the interior of the house. He didn't quite feel up to dancing with Margaret Calhoun yet. He wanted to spend time with Gilly. Even after spending four days for all intents and purposes alone with her, he hadn't had enough of her company.

"Let's go outside for a few minutes," he suggested, opening the French doors to the porch and offering her his arm.

Outside the air was sweeter, cooler, and the moonlight brushed her skin with a faint blue glow.

Gilly hugged herself and rubbed her hands briskly over her upper arms. Jim shrugged out of his jacket and draped it over her, his hand brushing the velvet warmth of her shoulders and lingering.

"Thank you." Her eyes met his and held his gaze. Something as smooth and intoxicating and fiery as brandy flowed between them. She cleared her throat. "I wish Calhoun had shown us his trophy room. I would have liked to see his firearms."

"That's right. I almost forgot that you're 'one of the best shots in the territories.'"

She shook her head, smiling ruefully. She leaned on the railing, looking out over the darkness stretching endlessly away. "I'm an average shot at best," she said slowly. "Maybe a spot below average. What I am is fast. Very fast."

"Then how did you get a reputation for being a crack shot?"

"All right." She turned around, leaning on her elbows against the rails, as though she'd come to a decision and was relieved at having chosen it. "I'll tell you. On one of my first robberies I was cornered in a saloon by a couple of kids who'd lit out after me with their daddy's gun. They were scared. Almost as scared as I was. Heck, they caught me mostly by accident.

"So there we were. Two boys looking to save face and me looking to save my life. No one else in the saloon had a gun. Just me and these two kids. Now, behind the bar were shelves lined with liquor bottles. I figured I had one chance at bluffing my way out of there alive, so I said, 'Before you start something you can't finish, men, I want you to see this.' They stopped, more from surprise than anything else. I don't suppose anyone had called them 'men' before." She smiled, an utterly self-deprecating smile that charmed him more than any bravado could have, and he wondered if she knew and had gauged its effect.

"Yes?" he prompted.

"So with one hand I started pointing up at the shelves and saying, 'See that bottle? The one with the bright label—' *Boom!* Quicker than I've ever drawn before, I fired off a shot.

"Glass shattered. Liquor sprayed all over the place. I holstered my gun and, praying harder than a nun with her rosary, I looked those two kids in the face and said, 'Well, you don't see it anymore, do you?'

"It took maybe five seconds before the bartender, bless his nearsighted little hide, exclaimed, 'I never seen anythin' like that! She done hit that bottle square, boys! Save your lives and put up your guns!'

"The boys put up their guns. I don't know who was more relieved. And that's how I got my reputation. I pulled that stunt twice more, always making sure I was in a town with strict gun ordinances, at bars without too many customers, and always making sure that those customers who were there were surrounded by a whole lot of empty glasses. Voilà! I'm a sure shot."

He stared at her. One of her dark, elegant brows rose as if daring him to refute her. "I don't know what to believe about you," he admitted.

The smile drained from her face, leaving it vulnerable. "That's a problem, isn't it?" She took a deep breath and straightened up. "Let's go back inside, shall we?"

Though they stayed for only another forty minutes, it seemed like hours to Gilly. She'd told things to Jim Coyne she'd never told anyone else, but still he wanted more. Even though she realized that each fact she gave him could lead straight back to her real identity, she hadn't been able to stop herself. Heaven help her, she wanted to tell him everything.

She had no reason to trust him. He'd said himself that a good story was the most important thing to him. What she'd planned as a nice, even trade-off—a fistful of highly improbable exploits for the use of his name and room—had turned into something else. For the first time in years she was thinking of the future with a sense of longing, saw something she wanted for herself, and that was Jim Coyne. And that wasn't good.

She was courting heartbreak. In a few weeks, when he found out the truth about her, he'd never want to lay eyes on her again. She should be able to accept that.

But she hadn't expected to meet anyone like Jim. Funny that the very things that would ultimately keep them from having a future together—his outrage at injustice, his disregard for personal consequences in exposing that truth—were the very things that drew her to him.

But there were other qualities that drew her too. Worldly without being weary, knowing without being jaded. Big, strong, a little worn around the edges, with a sardonic, self-effacing wit and a shrewd intelligence. The least vain man she knew, he was also the most capable. Nothing she'd seen in her life was more appealing than his big, mature body, his rumpled silver-shot hair, the laugh lines radiating from blue eyes that had seen more than enough and yet still remained open, looking for more.

She knew better than to hope. Once she'd thought that after Lightning Lil had disappeared, Gillian Jones would live happily ever after. She'd given up on that notion years ago. But now . . . Jim Coyne had resurrected dreams she was better off without. Yet with every step she took, with every act she planned, she killed every potential that that dream could survive.

"You're slowing down," Jim said softly. "Are you tired? Do you want to stop and rest?"

"No. I'm fine. I just—"

"Jim Coyne!" A voice boomed from the door of the Cattleman's Saloon. A huge, neckless, bald-pated body stepped out of the smoky haze and marched stiff-legged down the walkway, directly toward them.

Jim pulled Gilly closer to him.

"Friend of yours?" Gilly asked.

"I've never seen that man in my life. I would re-member."

"I'm sure you would," she agreed.

"Jim Coyne, you are going to rue the day your sorry ass landed in Far Enough, Texas!" the gargan-tuan bellowed.

"I already do," Jim said over his shoulder, turning and shepherding Gilly down the steps onto the street.

They were almost to the center of the street when the hulking man called, "Stop right there, you lily-livered pantywaist!"

Jim didn't stop. Wise, wise, wonderful man, Gilly thought happily.

"Gutless wonder!"

He kept marching.

"Course, I might be running, too, if'n I had a wife like that. Maybe after I'm done with you, Coyne, I'll just comfort the widow. Nice piece of—"

Jim spun around. "Do *not* say it."

Gilly ground her teeth in frustration. "He didn't say anything."

The gargantuan, who'd followed them out onto the street, stopped and chuckled. Curiosity seekers, alerted to the possibility of entertainment by the bull-like man's shouts, began drifting out of various saloons and buildings and forming an impromptu circle around them. Among their number was Mort James, who, on seeing Jim, hastened forward.

"Who is that guy?" Jim asked him.

"Ox. I warned you about him, remember? Tommy's uncle?"

"Oh, yeah."

"Let's go, Jim," Gilly urged, tugging his arm.

"I'm gonna teach you to mess with my kin." Ox smiled. More of a baring of broken teeth than a real smile, but Gilly supposed it was as close an approximation as he could manage. She tugged harder.

"Listen, Ox," Jim said, "those kids jumped me. Whole thing was over in a few minutes."

"You broke my nephew's nose." Ox took off his shirt and threw it on the ground. Muscles bulged like knotty gourds beneath an oily layer of flesh.

"Oh, come on," Jim protested. "It wasn't anything special to begin with."

"I'm gonna tear you apart, New York City man."

Jim emitted a gusty sigh and peeled Gilly's fingers from his coat. The Carmichael twins appeared at the far side of the crowd, their little eyes gleaming with battle fever.

"Hey, Mrs. Coyne!" one of them shouted, waving her plumed headdress high above the crowd. "How you doin', sugar? I got me ten bucks says your husband there beats the hell outta old Ox!" She beamed like that bit of news was supposed to make Gilly feel better.

"Oh, no," Gilly said, yanking Jim's arm to get his attention. The din of the crowd had risen and Ox was flexing his muscles. Jim glanced down at her.

"Mort," he said sadly, "she doesn't want to see this."

Mort nodded. Ignoring her protests, he grabbed Gilly's arm and began dragging her away from the crowd. Jim let him do it, casting a look after her that said in no uncertain terms that he'd just as soon someone were hauling him away. That longing expression awoke her worst fears.

Even though they looked to be near the same age, Jim was probably some years older than Uncle Ox. Ox had lived like . . . well, an ox, and that tended to put years on a man's face. For all Gilly knew, Ox might be a decade younger than Jim. All too obviously he was also a savage, bare-knuckle grappler, who'd think nothing of gouging eyes—even Jim's glorious Irish blue eyes—and breaking bones and . . .

She twisted free of Mort's hold and started hopping one-footed toward the melee, the need to rescue Jim spurring her on.

"Stop it! Leave him alone!" she hollered, red-faced with her efforts to get back into the closed circle of loud, drunk, cheering spectators. She tried to push her way through them, but they were having none of it, repelling her most determined efforts to break in. Mort caught her hopping up and down on the outskirts of the crowd and grabbed her around the waist, hauling her backward, her cast leaving a deep groove in the dirt.

"Come on, Mrs. Coyne," he panted. "You heard Jim. He doesn't want you witnessing this." A deep, rough *uff* rose from the center of the crowd. "Just wait over here and—"

"Wait for what?" she panted as another cheer went up from the bloodthirsty crowd at the dull smack of flesh meeting flesh. "My husband to get torn apart? I have to stop this! Jim could get hurt!"

"Ma'am?" Mort blinked at her incredulously.

"You've got to help me stop this before Jim gets hurt!"

"*Jim* get hurt?"

"Yes! Are you deaf?"

"No, ma'am. But Ox'll be the one who gets hurt. I mean, Ox is nasty, but he's no champion like Jim. You didn't know that?" he asked, his brow furrowed in perplexity.

"Champion of what?" She broke free of Mort's grasp just as the wildly cheering crowd parted, and Jim Coyne, one sleeve ripped off, blood trickling from one corner of his mouth, hair curling riotously, walked calmly from their midst. Behind him she could just make out a prone figure lying in the dirt.

She noted Jim's rueful, apologetic expression, and tears started in her eyes.

"Let's go home, Jim," she said, securing his arm and leading him down the street.

Behind them, a thoughtful Mort James watched their departure.

"I made me twenty-seven bucks betting on Jim Coyne." Merry appeared at Mort's side, waving a handful of bills under the front of his nose. "What's wrong with you, Mortie James? You weren't fool enough to bet on Ox, were you?"

"No," Mort said, gaze fixed on the flash of plaster appearing and disappearing beneath the belling swing of Mrs. Coyne's skirts. "Miz Carmichael, wouldn't you think it's odd if a wife didn't know her husband was the 1880 New York State Middleweight Boxing Champion?"

"Huh?" Merry said, searching her person for a

place to stash her winnings, finally tucking it deep in her cleavage.

"Never mind," Mort said.

"Take your shirt off." Her tone brooked no argument and her eyes still flashed with unaccountable ire, so he did as he was told and stripped off his shirt while she went into the bedroom to get her dratted old horse liniment.

"Come in here."

Into the bedroom. He stood up. Okay, he could do that.

"I've spread a sheet on the bed. This stuff stains terribly and it stings at first. At least Juniper always twitches when I . . ." Her voice trailed off and her eyes darkened to ebony as they fell on his chest. "Sit down."

He sat. She approached cautiously, warily, as though he were a suddenly unknown quantity and not a man she'd shared five damnably blameless nights rooming with. The idea made his thoughts dance with notions he had no right entertaining, but the way she was gazing at his body didn't make him feel old at all.

She scooped out a little dollop of the oily-looking salve and placed the jar on the table before stepping between his splayed knees. The little edge of lace on her bodice lifted and dropped with each shallow breath she drew. The salve's pine-tar aroma mixed with her own soft lilac-water scent, making his head spin.

She swallowed, and his gaze fell on the movement with the intensity of a predator's on its prey. Her skirts brushed his inner thighs. In his present state of mind even the chaste touch of cloth on cloth had the power to arouse him.

Business. It was all business, he told himself sternly. She'd heal up and walk out of this room, this town, and his life. She didn't even trust him enough to tell the truth.

Gingerly, she spread the ointment on his left shoulder near the yellowing bruises that Tommy and his pals had given him a few days before. She was right. It did sting. But then the sting turned to a deep, penetrating heat that felt good. He rolled his shoulder into it, working the sore muscle.

"Stay still." Her voice sounded a little breathy, even to her own ears, but she didn't care. His chest was beautiful, dense, with long, sloping muscles tight beneath supple bronzed skin. She flattened her palm on his pectoral and smoothed the warming oil across the bulging muscle, working it in with the heel of her hand and her fingertips, kneading the resilient flesh deeply, finding little knots of tension and easing them out. "This speeds up healing all kinds of injuries," she murmured. "Cuts and scrapes and bruises."

Her fingertip brushed across his flat nipple and returned, moving across his broad chest, back and forth, soothing, rubbing, stroking him.

Lord in heaven.

Though he sat absolutely still beneath her touch, the heat rushing up from her palm swirled through her entire body, making it hard to breathe. He was smooth and hard and warm, and she wanted to fondle and stroke and urge his virility into expression, to make the male in him answer the female in her, to

touch her lips to his skin, test the heated temperature
of his body with her tongue, move—

"Gilly."

She struggled out of her sensuous torpor. Slowly,
her gaze refocused. He was regarding her strangely,
his head cocked to one side. The curls at the nape of
his neck hung in damp ringlets that she wanted to—

"*Darlin'.*"

"Hmm?"

"There aren't any cuts or bruises there."

"What?" Her voice was hazy, unfocused. She
could look into his eyes for hours, locked in their
blue embrace. . . .

"I wasn't injured there."

"Oh? Oh!" She broke eye contact with a jolt. She
glanced down. Her hand was on his left breast, fingers spread wide, barely denting the muscle beneath.
There wasn't a mark on him.

Embarrassment rippled in a molten current
through her, steaming her cheeks with color. She
wheeled.

"Gil!"

She stopped, counted to ten, and dared a glance
back over her shoulder. He sat where she'd left him,
hands clenched into fists on top of his knees, head
bowed slightly, lips parted, and eyes riveted on the
floorboards.

"We have a business arrangement." He looked up
at her, tension in his voice, in his hard face. "Don't
we? Isn't that what this is?"

She wanted to say no, to deny it. To deny the past
she hadn't asked for and the future she didn't want.
But that wouldn't be fair to him. She didn't want

him despising her more than he already would. "Yes. It's business."

"Then keep up your part of the bargain. Tell me."

"What?" she asked in confusion.

"Tell me the truth. Why are you a thief?" It was a demand, an urgent imperative.

He couldn't have made himself more clear. He had her heart, but he didn't want that. He wanted her story, and even that must be on his terms. She wouldn't give it to him. It was the one thing she had left. Her identity.

"Sure." Her voice was clipped and hard. She swung around. "Where should I begin?" She flopped down sideways in the upholstered chair, swinging her cast nonchalantly over the arm, petticoats playing peekaboo with him. "I suppose birth would be too early?" He didn't comment. Just sat watching her, his flesh rimed by the soft light, beautiful and unreachable. She pulled the tortoiseshell combs from her hair and shook her head, tilting it back so the unbound tresses fell to the ground. "Okay. I'm the daughter of an outlaw queen. I guess that makes me an outlaw princess, don't it?" She let loose a coarse chuckle.

"Outlaw princess."

"Yup. A hard-riding, hard-shooting woman who takes what she wants when she wants it. No questions asked, no answers given."

"Really?" His tone dripped doubt. "I suppose you're the James brothers' lost sister too."

"Sister? Hell, I hope not. You don't do with a sister the things me and the James boys have done. Shouldn't you be writing this down?"

"Had a lot of lovers, have you?" he asked calmly.

She tilted her head far back and kicked her loose leg toward the ceiling, laughing harshly. "Lovers? I've had more lovers than a Gatling has shells. But my chamber's empty now, and I'm lookin'—" She heard his chair clatter to the ground, his bootheels hard on the floor. She turned her head and found herself staring at his wool-clad thigh. She didn't look up any further.

"Yeah?" she sneered.

"Gilly"—his voice was low and hard—"you are full of shit."

His words acted like a prod. She lurched upright, furious and miserable. "Oh, yeah?"

"I've never heard such crap. Give me a little credit. Just a little. I do this for a living, ferret out the grain of honesty in the lies. You haven't given me anything *but* lies."

"How would you even know?" she demanded. "And so what anyway? So what if they're lies, each and every one of them? Who cares if Lightning Lil is a whore or a minister's daughter? Who cares what I am or what I do or why I do it, as long as you get your story and your readers believe it? Who gives a damn?"

He didn't touch her. He didn't have to. The look he gave her felt like a slap, it was so rife with disappointment and disgust. He shook his head.

"Maybe I do, Gilly. Maybe I do."

Before she could frame a retort, he was gone.

8

It was late afternoon. Bruised and battered clouds
piled up on the horizon, and a cutting wind skittered
along the streets, harrying most of the townspeople
inside. Jim stalked the abandoned plank walk, cursing himself. Gilly had touched more than his skin last
night. Her hand had moved over his flesh and he'd
been branded by an urge so powerful, he'd had to
clench his fists to keep from hauling her into his
arms and taking what she so sweetly offered.

He hadn't. Because as much as he'd wanted to
expose each creamy inch of her, he wanted even
more to expose the mute soul of her, to touch her as
deeply, as intimately as a man and a woman can. In
short, he'd wanted to make love to her . . . not to
have sex with the stranger she insisted on remaining.

He was falling in love with her.

The realization brought no surprise, only a frightening sensation of imminent loss that teased him

with terrible potential. He found the telegraph office and went inside. Behind the desk, the clerk grinned. "Whoa. I haven't had this many telegrams in one day never! First Mortie last night, back and forth to New York, and now you."

"Mortie's been pestering his New York friend again?"

"Yup. About you." The clerk waggled his brows. "Bein' very cagey about phrasing his questions too."

"You'd think the kid would have better ways of wasting his money," Jim muttered, picking up a pencil and scribbling a note.

"Oh, and I got a telegram from New York for you too," the clerk added.

Just what he needed, his ass hauled over the coals for failing to submit his exclusive interview with the "Outlaw Princess." He shook his head at the memory of Gilly's outrageous claim regarding lovers. How did she ever think she was going to pull that one off? He was thirty-six years old and he'd known more experienced women than she'd probably ever meet.

"Here you are," the clerk said, handing him the telegram. Sure enough, it was a terse demand for his story, the one he'd promised when he'd first arrived and come up with the great inspiration of how to get an exclusive interview with the notorious Lightning Lil. Maybe he shouldn't have all but guaranteed his editor that he'd find her. Too damn bad. His editor wasn't going to get an award-winning, circulation-doubling story from him. At least not one about Lightning Lil.

He quickly scribbled out message:

NO LIL. STOP. NO THRILLS. STOP. SORRY I
RAISED FALSE HOPES. STOP. PURSUING DIFFER-
ENT STORY. STOP. WILL SEND MORE WHEN I
HAVE IT. STOP. HAVING A GOOD TIME. STOP.
WISH YOU WERE HERE. STOP. JIM.

The one thing that had kept Gilly safe was her
anonymity. If he wrote that story it wouldn't take
the people in Far Enough ten minutes to realize who
he'd been calling Darlin for the past week. They'd
be the first eyewitnesses to the fact that Lightning Lil
had hair the color of polished ashwood, a luscious
smile, and a voice like sherbet—rich, cool, and
creamy. They'd know she looked twenty and
laughed easily, that her eyes sparkled like black diamonds, and that even wearing a cast she moved with
liquid grace. She'd be caught inside a week.

He finished writing his telegram and handed it to
the clerk.

"Boy, howdy," the man said, perusing the paper.
"This is a long one. Pretty near as long as young
Mort's. Not nearly so interesting though." He dan-
gled the invitation to query hopefully.

"Oh?" Jim prompted, more out of habit than anything else. After all, there was nothing for him to do
but go back to the room and stare at the door that
separated him from Gilly. He'd knocked once, just
before noon. She'd pled a headache.

"Fool boy sent for a federal marshal."

Jim stopped breathing.

"Yup. Old Mortie thinks he knows where Lightning Lil is."

His heart skipped a beat. "Really?" he said faintly.
"And where's that?"

"Oh, he wasn't tellin' me. Ain't gonna share the reward with no one, he says. Needs new typeface, he says. Pleased as a two-peckered dog, that boy is. I say he's full of crap. But hell, if a U.S. marshal wants to waste his time on Mortie James's wild-goose chase, fine."

"He's coming here?" Jim asked, his thoughts racing. Gilly had been right after all. The boy was more a reporter than Jim had given him credit for. Damn him.

"Yup. Be here day after tomorrow." He finished counting the lines on Jim's message. "That'll be two dollars twelve cents, Mr. Coyne."

"The stage leaves at five o'clock in the morning." Jim yanked the last of her dresses from the armoire and flung them on the bed. "We'll leave at four and head a few miles out of town. I'll wave the coach down and you'll get on it. I'll be back in town before anyone wakes up."

"They'll know." Her face was as pale as moonlight, and her eyes were black as a starless sky.

"No." He shook his head. "I'll just stay in my room for a couple of days. They'll think what they've been thinking all along. That you and I can't get enough of each other."

Now fire bloomed in her cheeks. He ignored it.

"When the marshal shows up in a few days, I'll tell him we had a spat and you went back to New York."

"Mort knows."

"Mort knows nothing," he ground out, clearing the toiletries, the ivory comb, the lilac water, and the old horse liniment from atop the walnut bureau.

"I don't even know this New York friend of his. As far as anyone knows we married just before I left there."

"Okay," she conceded. "What about the stage driver? They'll question him and find out where I went."

She was trying to be brave, but her lips gave her away, trembling delicately when she relaxed her guard. She was afraid for her life, and knowing she had every reason to be afraid pierced his guts with a thousand aching holes.

God. He'd give up everything to see that she was safe. He *was* giving up everything. He was giving up her.

"His route takes him up into Oklahoma. He won't be back in Far Enough for a couple weeks."

She nodded, hobbled over to the bed, and began folding her clothing. He watched her, slowly realizing what he was seeing. He'd forgotten. In his need to find her a sanctuary, he'd forgotten what had led her to him in the first place. Her cast. Where in all the country could she go where she wouldn't incite speculation with that type of injury? He raked his hair with his hands. "I don't know where I can send you."

She followed his stricken gaze to her cast and paled even further.

"I'll come with you," he suddenly said. "There's no other way. I'll leave a message saying that we've gone on a second honey—"

"No!" She shook her head in violent denial. "No. That'll just make it worse. When people see you've gone . . . we've gone . . . they'll start searching.

I . . . I have a friend I can trust. If I can just make it to Kansas City, I'll be fine."

"If?" he reiterated angrily. "What *if* you don't make it to Kansas City?"

She didn't back down from his desperation. "Then that's my problem, Jim. That's not part of our arrangement. Not part of the deal. You can't risk any more for the story—"

"Screw the story!"

Gilly bit down on her inner cheeks, welcoming the sharp pain. How could anything be so bittersweet? She couldn't meet his eyes, didn't dare for fear of what her own gaze would betray. She couldn't let him risk himself, or his career, or any part of himself, not after what she'd intended to do to him. Still intended to do.

"No," she swallowed, making herself do this. "It was a business arrangement from the beginning. I'll make it to Kansas City and that'll be it. I'll be out of your life forever."

"No."

"Yes." She blinked rapidly, forced herself to watch her hands mechanically folding a skirt. "What did you think, Jim? That after I'd gone, we'd stay pen pals? Just sort of keep up a correspondence? Toward what end?" Longing and disillusionment made her voice rough. "There's no future in it." She prayed for him to deny it. He didn't.

"It can't end here, like this," he said in a fierce, controlled shout. "There's too much unfinished between us."

"There is no 'us.' And insisting you come with me is only going to get me killed, Jim." *And you, darling.*

He snarled at the ceiling, a feral expression of frustration. "Damn it to hell. Damn it to hell! Gil—"

"Please. Don't make me run away," she pleaded, laying her hands on his forearm. He stared at the long fingers beseechingly plucking his sleeve before jerking away from her.

"You better finish packing the rest," he said, pacing from the bedroom. He caught the edge of the door in one big hand, squeezing until his knuckles were white and she thought the wood would splinter under the pressure. "Then get some sleep. You're going to need it."

A storm was waiting out there. Lightning tracery gleamed on the horizon, lighting the black caul of heaven. The air was charged with anticipation and urgency. A surging wind whipped the curtains at the open window into a lace froth, bringing with it the metallic smell of charged air. Gilly shivered, giving up the notion of sleep.

She wrapped the linen sheet around her shoulders and stood. In a few hours she'd be gone. If she was very lucky she'd never see him again. Never witness the scorn or hurt in his eyes.

Jim's eyes were made for laughing, not anger. They crinkled with the wit and the warmth and savvy only years of living can impart. Life. For a short week she'd tasted what life might have offered. A taste wasn't enough.

She lit the lantern, barely conscious of her own movement and, even less, of her intention. She entered the sitting room, overwhelmed by the desire to see him smiling, to steal just this one night from her destiny.

He lay spread across the fainting couch and the chair he'd placed at the end to add the extra length he needed to fit his body. His shirt was off, carefully draped over a chair, a light blanket twisted low on his hips.

Her gaze traveled deliberately over him, committing to memory the long cords of sinew in his outstretched arm, his broad chest moving gently with each deep, even breath, the subtle rippling contours in his forearm and belly. Underneath the sheet draped lightly over his thighs and legs, she could tell he was entirely naked. Lightning crackled outside the window, glazed him in a brilliance, limning his sculpted physique with silver gilt.

She moved closer, extended her hand, and trifled with the light furring on his chest. Perfect. Male. It took a few seconds for her to realize that the even cadence of his breathing had stopped. She raised her eyes to find his own gravely studying her.

"Smile," she whispered. "I've come to see you smile."

He complied slowly, the corners of his eyes crinkling with all an Irishman's inate charm and tragedy, a rueful, lopsided smile that turned up one corner of his beautiful scarred lips.

"Now it's your turn, Gilly. Smile for me, darlin'," he coaxed.

"I can't." She shook her head. Her hair snapped and crackled with electricity in the dry night air, sparking lights in the darkness around her face. She sank down by him, made awkward by her cast. "Make love to me, Jim."

In answer, he cupped her shoulders, his hands

warm through the linen sheet she wore. "Much as I want to, I can't do that."

She stared at him, betrayed and confused. It had never occurred to her that he would say no, that he would refuse her. "Is it the love or the making you can't do?" she asked bitterly.

Her bitterness didn't touch him. His smile just grew sadder. "I'm sorrier than you'll ever know."

"Dear Lord, Jim Coyne," she said on a sob of laughter, "you have our roles reversed. I'm supposed to be the one with maidenly blushes!"

"You're not a one-night pleasure, Gilly. Not for me. If we make love tonight, I'll never get over you. I may not even now. I'll want this for eternity. But you're going. 'No future.' Remember?"

"Jim—"

"You won't even tell me where you're going. Oh, yeah . . . Kansas City. Bullshit. You're planning something else, Gilly. Something you think might get you killed."

Or worse, she amended silently, stunned by his perceptiveness.

"And I'm supposed to spend the night making love to you? And then what? In a week or a month I read your obituary on the back page of some paper? No thanks, Gilly." The smile had left his beautiful eyes. He looked tired and weary. "I don't like the role you've cast me in, and I don't want the job."

"What do you want me to do?"

"Give yourself up. I'll find you a lawyer. The best."

She swallowed. "I can't surrender. I won't."

"Can't you?"

"You should understand. You would, if you knew—"

"But you won't tell me, will you?"

"I've worked for five years in order to get where I am—"

"And where the hell is that?" he demanded, heat entering his voice for the first time. "A trunk full of someone else's dresses? Running like a fox to ground, trying to find a little space, a little time to heal up from a gunshot wound? Begging to share the room of a stranger who, for all you knew, might rape you? Yeah, you've come a long way, Gilly." There was pity in his voice.

God, he'd seen so much. So much more than she'd realized. And yet there was more. Too much more. Too much to forgive.

"It's my choice."

"Just like this is mine," he returned, his hands dropping.

But it wasn't his choice. Or hers. It hadn't been since he'd kissed her on that boardwalk and rekindled warmth and passion in her life. "Just"—her head dipped low, her hair swung over his naked chest, slipping like cool satin across his hot skin— "kiss me good-bye."

The sheet fell unheeded from her shoulders. She was naked underneath, and he devoured the sight of her, rapacious with dreams barely realized and already being torn asunder. She raised her good leg over his hip, straddling him, and he couldn't have moved had the world been ending. She laid her forearms flat against his chest, bracing herself over him. The movement sent her unbound breasts swinging, soft and heavy, against him, nipples dragging slightly, marking his belly with electricity. His breath caught in a hiss, and her lips hovered near his.

He closed his eyes, arching his neck back, and felt the incredible sensation of her tongue delicately washing over the skin beneath his jaw, as she slowly settled on his lap.

"You're going to steal this too?" he managed to pant, experiencing each inch of the sensuous grace with which she flowed along his chest, lying fully on him now, molding her softness to his hardness, meeting his heat with her own fire.

"Just this night. It's all I'll ever have you. It will have to last me for eternity." She wriggled her hips, rubbing the soft core of her over his swollen manhood.

"Jim. Please," she implored. "*Give* to me. Don't make me steal." Her soft plea was his undoing.

He gripped her hips, pulling her tighter against him, trying desperately to accomodate her injured leg and cast. She gasped, arcing up, the movement exposing her breast to his mouth. He took as much of her as he could in his mouth, drawing deeply on her nipple, tonguing the silky areola.

Her breath pulsed in little gasps with each pull of his mouth, and her hips joined the rhythm, inciting him beyond thought to a place where desire held precedence. He let her go and she straightened, arching backward, golden hair streaming down past her hips, brushing his thighs. Her legs spread wide, riding his hips as intimately as a woman can, her cast lying alongside his thigh.

She reached between them and took him in her hand, stroking the stiff length of him, making him grit his teeth. He lifted her hips, holding her over him, waiting until he felt the velvet-slick lining of her across the swollen head of his shaft. Cushion and plush, she encased the tip of him. He groaned, pushing into her, thrusting past resistance. She gasped once, a little cry of pain, and he stopped. Her head fell forward, her hands splayed on his heaving chest.

Beneath her palm, his heart beat thick and violent. The little pain fled, leaving in its place the awareness of the size of him stretching inside her, the pulse of his blood heating his smooth satin skin, the strength and potency of his big body. She wanted it. She wanted more. She moved, a deliberate, experimental withdrawal that wrung a throat-strangled sound from him, then settled slowly back onto him again.

Sensation built on sensation, a coiling of needs, a tightening. She moved again, taking him deeper, and suddenly his hands clamped on her hips and he was moving her, lifting her and settling her, teaching her with the buck of his hips and the thrust of his loins, with hand and tongue, the synchronization of mating. She fell on his tutorial gratefully, straining to find release from the teasing spur of excitation, the lash of anticipation that drove her.

"Please!"

He laughed, a harsh sound, and released her hips. With one hand he fondled her breasts and throat, with the other he stroked her face and burnished her open mouth. Instinct made her catch his trailing finger between her lips and do to it what he'd done to her nipple, sucking and nipping its tip. On a growl he surged up, still joined to her, lifting her as he stood, his hands beneath her buttocks, his chest a furred wall of moisture-cloaked muscle, veins cording beneath its straining surface.

"Hold on to me," he said hoarsely. She clung to him, trying to lock her legs about his hips in spite of her cast. He drove into her, her arms wrapped tightly about his shoulders as he kissed her throat, buried his hands in her hair.

He pumped into her, friction making a sleek slide of body on body, all of his power concentrated in this act, this moment. His body was hard as rock, his arms like steel bands, his motion aggressive and male. She undulated, flowed about him, accepted it all, the power and virility, her female strength liquid in the taking, making his potency hers.

Together they strove toward completion, bodies wet with struggle. He murmured terse instruction, and she responded with a keening sound of exertion that nearly drove him to his knees. She strove, for a moment suspended on the cusp of climax, shuddering when it crashed in upon her, each muscle going rigid with excruciating pleasure, spurring him out of control.

His cry of completion was male, elemental, triumphant.

Long seconds passed until she could lift her damp face from where it had fallen against his throat. Slowly, he let her slide from his embrace and sag against him.

Her head dipped, the fall of her hair hiding her face from him. A shiver raised the flesh on her back.

"I—"

He stopped her with a stroke of his hand along the pert thrust of her buttocks. Her head flew up, eyes widened. He cupped the back of her head in his hand, his mouth coming down on hers in a soul-searing kiss, his tongue filling her mouth.

She pushed free, trying to read what was in his blue eyes. "Jim . . . ?"

He backed her up, feathering kisses along her lips, her nose, her eyelids. A tingling sensation, so lately appeased, sprang to life. She shivered again, this time not with the cold.

"Jim . . . ?"

"Hush," he murmured, his hand running with torturous lightness over her belly and between her thighs. "If all you're giving me is this night, 'forever' just started."

2

The blank sheets of paper stared accusingly at Jim. He ignored them, absently noting the mantel clock chime eight. It was getting dark outside.

He lifted a bottle from beside his chair and squinted at it. Empty. He scrubbed at the beard he'd neglected to shave for two days. If he tried much harder, he'd become a drunk. Not that it was doing any good. Even drunk, he saw her dark eyes shining, smelled the scent of her sun-heated skin, heard her husky laughter.

A knock on the door broke his reverie. Jim answered it, the whiskey bottle still swinging in his free hand. Mort James stood outside the door, Mrs. Osby's face a study in salacious interest behind him. Damn prizewinning reporter in the making. Damn kid.

"Yeah?"

"Mr. Coyne? I came because I—I gotta know,"

the boy stammered, his face the color of a broiled snapper.

Jim had never wanted to hit anyone as much as he did this boy. If it hadn't been for him, Gilly wouldn't have flown out of his life, ripping from him something that felt very like his soul. His lip lifted in a sneer. Mort didn't back away, but Mrs. Osby scuttled back a few paces.

"Can I come in?" Mort gulped.

Jim eyed the lad with bleary contempt. "Sure. Why the hell not? No one else here." Mrs. Osby gasped.

"Why don't you go tat an antimacassar, Mrs. Osby?"

"Well, I never!"

"I'm sorry, ma'am, but that's your problem," he said, hearing a whisper of his stepmother's scandalized reproach somewhere behind the haze of whiskey and for once not caring. Mrs. Osby fled in a whoosh of disapproving black cloth.

Mort skirted Jim, entering the room as though he were stepping around a dangerous animal and not simply a dangerous man. "She was Lightning Lil, wasn't she?" he asked. "The woman posing as your wife."

He sounded as excited as any reporter with a scoop. As Jim himself might have sounded in similar circumstances fifteen years ago. But fifteen years had taught him one thing: There was no story as important as Gilly's smile.

"No." Anger drained out of Jim, leaving only fatigue and emptiness. "It's just like I said, Mort. I met Gilly in New York just before I got sent here. Love at first sight. Her family didn't approve, so we mar-

ried in secret. She came out"—he shrugged, tipped
the whiskey bottle to his lips, and drained the final
drops—"and didn't like what she found. She left
me."

"Come on, you can tell me," the kid urged.
"She's made a clean getaway. The federal marshal
damn near broke my neck when he figured I'd called
him here on a wild-goose chase. The whole town is
laughing at me. It won't matter what I say now, or
what I write. No one will believe me. But *I* have to
know, for my sake. You're a reporter, you gotta understand what it's like, having to know."

He understood all too well. He wanted to know
everything about Gilly, but now he'd never have his
curiosity satisfied. He only knew he loved her. And
there'd never be anything more. She'd made that
clear without words, with tears in her eyes and a
smile trembling on her lips, as five miles out of town
he'd lifted her, passion-spent and wan, into that
damn stagecoach.

"She wasn't Lightning Lil, Mort," he said. "She
was laughter and wit and passion, but she wasn't
Lightning Lil. She's gone. That's all you or I or anyone has to know."

"Sure," the boy said in a truculent, unconvinced
voice. "Just remember, it was you who said a great
reporter should do anything for the story."

"Screw the story!" His anger, like all of his emotions over the past week, boiled to the surface. He
grabbed Mort's shirtfront and dangled him one foot
above the ground. "Screw the story, Mort. It's just a
story. *This is my life.*"

He dropped him, and the kid scrambled out of the
room, rubbing his neck, and ran down the stairs. Jim

turned away, cursing himself for being such an ass-hole. He wandered to the window and flung it wide, drinking in the cold, dank night air that so matched his mood.

Outside, indigo shadows absorbed the features of the town. It was early yet, so no one was carousing too loudly. Only a few cowboys on the street, gig-gling like the fifteen-year-old virgins they undoubt-edly were and counting their change in front of the Cattleman's Saloon. They soon tallied their funds, entering the bar and leaving the street empty.

Jim would never have seen it otherwise. Just a slender, dark figure detaching itself from the dark mouth of an alley and slipping noiselessly along the darkened shop windows in the mercantile end of town. The shape headed for the Calhouns' stable, moving cautiously. Alerted by the stealthy move-ment, Jim blew out the lantern and watched as the shape froze near the entrance gate to the estate.

There's nothing for it, mister, Jim thought humorlessly. *If you want to get to the Calhouns' house you're going to have to pass beneath that stable-yard light.*

The figure seemed to have drawn the same con-clusion. Moving fast, light as a cat on its feet and just as smooth, the figure darted across the yard. Jim's smile turned brittle, then savage. Long black hair sewn into that hatband, a gray-plaid flannel shirt, boy's jeans.

No cast.

He was out the back door heading down the alley that ran parallel to the main street, fury pounding in his temples.

From the way she'd moved, she'd never needed one.

★ ★ ★

Vance Calhoun was the last one. The last of the bastards who'd framed her father for stealing funds from the company he and his five "friends" had formed. The last who'd testified to her father's guilt, smiled remorsefully, and walked out of that courtroom to build a career and a life and a future on the one they'd stolen from her father. Left her father to pay for their crime. Gilly's mouth set with determination, the sick feeling of dread she always got just before committing herself to the actual act of robbery twisting her stomach into knots.

Get into the house, get into the safe, get out. And it would be over. Done. Her gaze was drawn once more, unwillingly, to Jim's window. Maybe . . . She stopped herself. *Not now.*

She ran across the stable yard and vaulted lightly over the porch railing, landing noiselessly on one side of the French doors leading into the library.

It wouldn't buy back her father's years in jail, but it would compensate. That's all she wanted now. She wasn't seeking justice anymore; she just wanted the future that had been stolen from her father, her family. And she was going to get it, even though, too late, she realized she'd traded her own in return.

Soundlessly, she slipped into the library and moved swiftly to the fake volumes of books. She tilted the casing out and sure enough, there was the safe handle, right next to a little dial. Good. She liked dials.

She stripped off her gloves and closed her eyes as her fingertips rested lightly on the outermost perimeter of the dial. She rotated it. Each little click translated a tiny shiver through the sensitive pads of her

index finger and thumb. Smooth, even clicks until
. . . there, the more decisive click of a tumbler falling into place. Eyes still closed, she spun the dial in
the other direction. It took less than a minute for her
to open the safe.

Her breath came out in a low, soundless whistle.
Apparently old Vance Calhoun had been planning to
invest heavily on his overseas trip, because inside,
neat as roosting hens, lay thick, banded stacks of Eu-
ropean bearer bonds. Several fortunes' worth. The
grin that started on her face died. As much money as
it was, it wasn't enough to purchase what she'd lost.

She withdrew the bag she had tucked in her waistband and opened it, filling it with every packet the
safe contained. She pulled the drawstring together
and was about to close the safe and replace the
dummy set of books when an impulse seized her.
Cocking her head to listen for sounds that the diners
were finished and preparing to leave the table, she
scribbled a quick note on a piece of paper.

> *Heard a U.S. marshal was here looking for
> me. Appears I was late for our date. A girl
> needs something to see her through her disap-
> pointment. Guess I'll have to make do with
> your money.*
> *Lightning Lil*

She stuck it in the safe, leaving the metal door
wide open. She swung the bag over her shoulder and
fled out the French doors, heading for the alley
across from Jim's boardinghouse, where she'd left her
horse. She'd caught a glimpse of Jim earlier as she
stood in the shadows staring up at his window like a

lovesick puppy, waiting for the sun to give up the last of its light. He'd looked rough, his silver-spackled curls tumbling over his forehead, his posture wearier than she'd remembered, as he looked out the upper window and studied the horizon. She'd wanted—

"Oh!"

A strong arm snatched her around the waist in an unbreakable grip as a hand clamped over her mouth.

"Going somewhere, Gilly?" His voice in her ear was as cold as a February midnight and twice as dark. He spun her around, releasing her abruptly, as though he couldn't stand to touch her any longer. "You set me up, didn't you? Right from the start. You never were hit by any bullet. The cast was just a prop, isn't that right?" he demanded.

She nodded. "Yes."

"I was the dupe, the patsy. It was all a setup, a way of getting you close enough to Calhoun to figure out where he kept his money, wasn't it?"

"Yes."

"You're smart as a whip, Gilly, I'll give you that. I don't know a man who could have planned it better."

"But that was before I knew—No!" He'd turned and was striding away, eating up distance at a killing pace. She'd known, she'd seen it in the future, she'd told herself a hundred times that when he found out what she'd done, he'd feel betrayed and used. He hated the sight of her.

But she couldn't let him go thinking it had all been planned. That everything had gone her way. That she hadn't suffered for her brilliant plan. She caught up with him at the mouth of the alley, grabbing his wrist and sinking her heels into the ground.

When he refused to turn, but just dragged her along, she pounded her fist against his back, tears flowing freely down her cheeks. "I'm sorry I used you."

He looked down at her slowly, eyes grave. "It isn't that you used me, Gilly, I can't damn you for something you started before we'd even met."

"You can't?" she echoed incredulously.

"I was using you too. Remember? I was using you as a way out of here. My big story." He shook his head. "But I let that notion go after I"—he broke off and then forced himself to meet her eyes—"realized I loved you."

"Jim!"

"No." He held her off with one arm. "You can't have it both ways, Gilly. You were willing to sacrifice what we had for your own purposes. I wasn't. That's the bottom line." Without a trace of discernible emotion he watched the tears stream from her eyes. "But then, if you were willing to sacrifice it, maybe it wasn't what I thought it was. It sure felt like it though." He turned.

She stared at his broad back, watching her life, her future, her love, step farther away with each second. And she couldn't do it. She ran after him, cutting in front, jamming her hands into his hard, flat belly.

"No! You listen, Jim Coyne. You've been hounding me for the truth for a week. Well, now, by God, you're going to listen!"

"Hush!" He hauled her into his arms, pulling her head close into his broad shoulder, his own raised to scan the dark alley. "Do you wanna get caught?"

"I don't care!"

"Coulda fooled me."

"Damn it, *listen* to me."

"I'm listening."

"I *am* a schoolteacher. I teach drama at a girls' school. And all the rest of it—the land speculation company, my gun reputation, and everything—it was the truth. Seven years ago Vance Calhoun and four others framed my father for their own scheme of embezzling funds from a land speculation company they were partners in up near Kansas City. My father didn't have anything to do with it, but the other men were all pillars of the community, with respected family names. My father was the outsider. No one believed him and he was convicted."

Though he still held her closely, it was with as much tenderness as a statue. His face was impassive. Doggedly she went on. "I'd visit my father in prison and watch first his spirit, then his health grow frail, and I'd go home and read in the paper about his old pals and their Midas touch with business.

"I didn't want justice, Jim. I'd been in that court. I knew there was no chance, not even with a hundred witnesses for the defense, of that happening. I wanted recompense."

She could see the interest kindle in his eyes, mistrustful but there. She gripped his arms, willing him to believe her.

"If my father was going to suffer for those men's crimes, at least they weren't going to feed on his corpse. If he was going to pay for the crime, he was going to at least enjoy the booty. I made my plans. I spent two years learning how to fire a gun, ride a horse. By the time I was ready to become Lightning Lil, the men who'd framed my father had spread out over the territory. I've spent half a decade finding them and making sure they don't enjoy the money they stole.

"Calhoun's the last one. I knew he lived here. I couldn't believe it when I got here and discovered he was the bank's *president*. Still, I didn't think he'd keep his cash in any bank . . . even his own. He never did trust banks. But I didn't know where he kept his money. I couldn't figure how to find out."

"Yeah?" His tone was flat, unemotional.

"I kept seeing your ads. I thought I could trade, give you a story in exchange for proximity to Calhoun. I didn't know . . . I didn't plan on claiming I was your wife."

"Why didn't you trust me?" His voice sounded as though it was wrenched unwillingly from deep within his chest.

"I wanted to, but you kept saying what we were doing was business. Even up to . . . that last night I didn't know how you felt about me, and then, when I did, I was afraid once you found what I intended to do you'd make me stop. And I couldn't. Not then. Not so close to the end. Don't tell me you'd feel different." She prayed, looking into the fine blue eyes that pinned her to the spot, studied her for what seemed an eternity. "I know you, Jim Coyne. You wouldn't quit, not when the finish was so close."

She was right, but his hurt was too great to ignore. "So why are you still standing here? You wanted to make us both feel better before you go? A little salve for your conscience, a *gratis* for the lover?" Who'd have thought his lovely voice could be so brittle, so cold.

"No. Because I was wrong. I can quit. I can turn away right now. I can just lay the money on Calhoun's doorstep and leave. Because I want you more than I want to finish this. That's why I'm still here."

His brows snapped together, his gaze pierced hers as he tried to understand the magnitude of her words. She was willing to give up the crusade for him. To give up this close to the end she'd set her sights on seven years ago.

"Because . . ." His voice was faint.

"Because I love you."

He hauled her into his arms, his hand cradling her head in one big palm as his mouth found hers.

"Don't ever leave me again, Gilly," he spoke against her open mouth, his voice raw with urgency. "I couldn't stand it."

"I promise I'll never leave you—"

The sudden report of a rifle blast rent the air, stunning them. Shouts arose from the direction of the Calhouns' house as a man's voice bellowed, "She can't be far gone. Five hundred dollars for the man who returns my money!"

She quivered, eyes like saucers. Behind Jim, the gelding danced nervously. The sound of running bootheels began beating the plank walk.

She clutched his shirtsleeve, looked straight in his eye without flinching. "Come with me."

"One horse."

"I'll surrender."

He didn't want a grand gesture. He wanted her. And now he was going to lose her again. There was no time to make plans, to devise a future. "Damn it all to hell!" The words erupted violently. He spun her around, shoving her toward her horse, and turned to face her pursuers. He didn't look back.

"Ride, Gilly! Ride like hell!"

10

"You are damn lucky you didn't get sent to prison on charges of obstructing justice."

"Someone would have had to be in pursuit of a criminal in order for me to have obstructed them. Lightning Lil has never been charged with, let alone convicted of, any crimes. And, besides, I don't know any Lightning Lil."

"You're taking up law, Jim?" his editor asked, rocking back on his heels.

"Nope." Jim opened up the bottom drawer of his desk and started emptying it. "Besides, I still maintain that those boys were after a ghost. I didn't see anyone in that alley, and I'd been there awhile."

"That's right." His editor, Jonas, nodded. "You were drunk. And, if I remember your testimony, feeling 'pugnacious.' At least that's the reason you gave for beating up on those poor men."

"Don't rub it in, Jonas. I feel very bad about my

actions that night," he said without much conviction.

"Sure you do. What really went on out there, Jim?"

Jim finished piling his belongings into cardboard boxes. He sat down on the edge of his desk and looked out the smoke-fogged window at New York. He'd miss the bustle. "Well," he said pensively, "the way I got it figured is, what with all the brouhaha that kid editor kicked up claiming my . . . er . . . uh . . . wife was Lightning Lil, the real thing just couldn't pass up the opportunity to take center stage. And it wasn't a bad idea either." He rubbed his jaw. "I mean, seeing how he'd just been there and left, the one place in the territory she could be pretty sure the U.S. marshal wouldn't be was Far Enough, Texas."

"About this wife . . ."

"Yeah." Heat burned the tips of Jim's ears, and for once he blessed the gift of his mother's telling complexion. "Hell, Jonas, I was bored, all right? So I sent for a . . . friend to come and visit me. I tried to be discreet, to consider the sensibilities of the local population, and where did my chivalry get me? A courtroom appearance."

"Would have been nice if your *friend* had shown up for your court appearance," Jonas muttered. "Might have substantiated your story and got you out of there faster. Your legal bill cost a pretty penny, I don't mind telling you."

"Yeah, and this paper got a damn good story out of it. Plus a fine series on graft and corruption in the land speculation offices too."

Jonas knew when he'd been outmaneuvered. He

picked up Jim's boxing trophy and polished it on his sleeve. "Jim," he said, "what the hell are you going to do out there in that big open nothingness?"

"Count cows, I imagine," Jim said.

"You don't sound too excited by the prospect."

"I wouldn't be going at all, Jonas, if I thought I could find what I'm looking for here. I love my job. I love this city."

"The paper needs another editor, Jim."

"Sorry."

"Can't you live without whatever it is you're looking for?"

"Maybe," Jim's smile was crooked. "But I don't want to."

"Well, if you change your mind . . ." He lifted his hand in a farewell salute and left Jim to his work.

It was an hour before Jim finished loading the last cardboard box. He looked around his "office": the unused storage closet he'd turned into his own corner. Here he'd written countless articles and chased down a thousand leads. He'd miss it. But he didn't have one misgiving about what he was doing.

Last week he'd read an article in a Chicago newspaper. It reported that a lady philanthropist, Miss Gillian Jones, had recently made a substantial endowment to the local orphanage.

He'd found her. And he wasn't ever going to lose her again.

"Jim?" Sherbet, rich and smooth.

His head snapped up. She stood framed by the doorway, her mouth curving, just a little, like she was remembering a smile. Her head tilted to the side, uncertainty in her expression.

"I bought that ranch. The one I told you about. I bought a bunch of steers and I hired a foreman."

He straightened, unable to find his breath.

"Last week my father got out. I deeded it all over to him." Her voice was hesitant, almost embarrassed.

He shook his head, unwilling to believe his eyes, unable to make himself blink for fear she'd disappear.

"And then I bought a one-way ticket here. Because this is where you were, and this is where you belong."

He took a step forward, cautiously, as one approaches a dream.

"I promised I'd never leave you, and I take those sorts of promises seriously."

"I know," he heard himself say.

Whatever she read in his face caused her mouth to bloom in a deep, rich smile.

He was across the room, catching her, crushing her in his embrace, savage joy exploding with the feel of her arms wrapping tightly around his neck. Laughter spilled from her lips as tears streamed down her face.

"Darlin'," he whispered.

Lady Desperado

❧

Cait Logan

1

Harp, Montana Territory, 1880

"If you wish to try me out, I'm more than willing," Grayson Sinjin Steele stated to Olympia Hutton, the woman he hoped would hire him—*and* the woman he suspected of robbing stagecoaches. As Olympia's clerk, and using his middle name as a disguise, Grayson would be able to track the luscious Miss Hutton, prove his theory, and retrieve "The Book."

"You *can* read?" she asked, her blue-black hair gleaming in the sunlight passing through the windows.

"I read very well." Grayson Steele, respected and sometimes feared cattleman, was not letting the entire West see his erotic artwork. Once he had that damn book—one that didn't need words—he was burning it.

"You'll find that I am a very particular employer, Mr. Sinjin. I approve of your neat appearance, by the way."

"Thank you, ma'am." Gray smoothed his hair; the top was oiled, parted, and pasted to his head. The padding he wore to make him appear flabby rustled. He glanced past the shop's window to Harp's busy street; he traced the trail-tired Texas drovers coming into town for their "toots."

There were miners down from Montana's gold fields, stocking up on supplies, and Chinese men and women dressed in conical straw hats, black tunics, and pants, marketing early vegetables and hurrying back to their crowded section of Harp. It was early morning, and the saloons were serving breakfast.

"Business is picking up now," Olympia noted. "I ask for a good day's work and no playing lie-a-bed."

It was early June, and Grayson *should* have been at his Wyoming ranch, checking on calving and rustlers, up at four o'clock in the morning, working until he dropped—with the occasional gun battle with thieves tossed into the day. Instead, he was chasing the elusive, exotic scent of a feather dropped at a stagecoach robbery.

"Don't let the clutter frighten you. If I hire you, you should be able to find your way around in a week or so," Olympia stated.

"I will try. I'm very good at finding things." As a mountain tracker, Gray had used his experience to find Olympia. She was the only woman in town who smelled like the feathers he'd found at the site of the last two robberies. Only an expert tracker could have picked through the gunpowder scent to find the erotic perfume left on a feather—slightly spicy, like cinnamon, mellowed by a delicate scent of lily and underlined with a wisp of a woman's headier fragrance. While one small feather was definitely goose down, like that used in a pillow or a feather-tick, the other was scarlet red and likely to have come from an elegant plume. The shoe and heel marks in the dust behind the Huttons' shop matched the ones Gray had found at previous stagecoach robbery sites and several other holdups.

"I see you sniffing. You're probably not used to the scent of gunpowder and oil." Olympia moved behind the gun counter; Grayson tried to imagine her slashing a big *R* for *Raven* on a stagecoach door. All he had to do was prove that Miss Olympia Hutton of Hutton Saddlery was the outlaw on the wanted poster.

He would trade that information for the return of The Book; the Code said he couldn't turn a woman in to the law. Gray ran a finger around his tight, starched collar. He needed to be on his Wyoming ranch for June calving instead of playing games with a lady desperado.

Olympia's blue eyes leveled on him. "You look very . . . intelligent. You do realize that we have rather seasoned customers at times?"

"I am prepared to face the Wild West elements and cowboys. I'm certain I can manage . . . if they don't hurt me," Grayson replied. A week of posing as a heavily bearded, long-haired, harmless drunk, running infrequent errands for the grocery store and cleaning the livery, had allowed him insights into the small town of Harp and its interesting citizens. The moment Olympia Hutton had swished hurriedly by him, looking down her nose with disdain at his sad-dle-tramp disguise, Gray caught the feathers' scent—the ones found at the stagecoach robberies—and knew he had found the Raven.

"No one will hurt you while you're my employee, if I hire you. You may be afraid to use a ladder to reach things on the top shelf." Olympia hauled a ladder from one side and propped it against the wall. She swung agilely onto it and took the rungs easily. "I've always been athletic and tall. I'll get them for you."

"Heights do frighten me," Gray murmured, and noted as she descended the rungs to the floor that Olympia's height could be added to by boots, bringing her to the Raven's six-foot-two-inch height. Her slender waist could be padded easily and the Raven's immense cape could produce the image of a thick-set, muscular, athletically moving man. The Raven's eye patch and huge hat with a scarlet plume would be easily added. The Raven always struck under the shield of night. A high collar prevented identification in moonlight. Yet the Raven's tracks had not sunk into the earth as would those of an appropriately heavy man. Gray noted Olympia's height and weight; he decided that her boots would sink into the dirt at the exact same depth as the Raven's footprints.

"I'll want the windows washed. If you have any reluctance to do cleaning, let me know now," Olympia said.

"I like cleaning. It is the best part," Gray returned, and thought that her low, feminine voice could be deepened into a man's whisper—the Raven whispered his orders while he robbed.

Olympia moved lightly around the counter and ran her oiled rag over the barrel of a Colt revolver. "We sometimes get ladies who are in need of protection. I would not want any of them—employed la-

dies of the saloon and of a house outside of town—
to be offended. I ask that they be serviced with absolute gallantry."

"I promise to service them well." In his youth
Grayson was known for his thorough servicing and
high regard for women. Though his "service" days
had waned, his respect for women remained. He
didn't want to see Olympia jailed or shamed—what
man would? All he wanted was The Book back in
his hands. Gray pressed his lips together; he remembered how his brother had sent his fiancée The Book
by stagecoach mail. The Raven had promptly stolen
The Book and left the other mail scattered upon the
ground.

After five stagecoach robberies the whole countryside was up in arms about the Raven. The outlaw
was a thorn in the law's backside. Gray didn't want
the law or bounty hunters catching the Raven—not
before he had The Book safely in his hands.

This woman with a gun-oil slick down her cheek
and a greasy rag tucked in her dirty shop-apron
pocket wore the scent. Her buttermilk mare, stabled
in the Smithson livery, wore a shoe with a chip that
exactly matched the prints found at the crime
scenes.

"You look sturdy enough. Boston, you said?
Now, I don't expect my clerk to enter any dangerous discussions, but rather to call me. The men in
this area can sometimes be bullies." Olympia's look
said she doubted that Grayson-in-disguise could hold
his own in a brawl.

"I've managed difficult situations, and I will call
you if danger arises." He shuddered deliberately.
"Physical debate terrifies me." If he ever wanted to

hold his head up as a Code of the West Westerner, he had to reclaim The Book—or simply kill Blue, his brother. Gray eased his neck in the stiffly starched high collar of his business shirt. He hadn't worn starch and suspenders since he'd returned to Wyoming. His legs and feet ached from wearing the flat-soled shoes rather than his western boots. His head ached from lack of sleep, and he wanted to kill his brother; the gentle tap on Blue's jaw that had sent him crashing through a thick door wasn't entirely satisfying.

The Book was Gray's first attempt at serious watercolor and ink; it had gotten him thrown out of his mother's favorite English school and out of her elegant house. An erotic monument to a young man's sensual dreams, the book clearly defined the ways to love a woman and for her to love him back, much of which he had only dreamed of at the time, but had since tried in real events. At eighteen he'd been expelled from class after the watercolor teacher had swooned—her distinguishing moles displayed clearly on rice paper.

The Book had served its purpose: His mother had promptly shipped him back to his father in Wyoming, where Gray could not damage her position in English society. At the time of his departure from England Gray was eighteen, a skillful lover—with a host of affairs in his past.

Years later Blue had discovered The Book hidden away in a chest. Blue, regretting his engagement to a Montana spinster and preacher's daughter, had sent his fiancée The Book by Grayson Steele, auto-graphed in big bold letters on every colorful, erotic, and steaming page.

"You'll need to wear an apron, much like mine," Olympia stated. Grayson looked at his suspect's delectable full bosom, shielded by the dirty apron. He realized that it had been almost a decade since he had truly been interested in chasing a woman and bedding her.

A symphony of gun-smoke-scented, graceful female, Miss Olympia Hutton glanced at Gray, dressed in a cheap brown suit, shoulders intentionally stooped, long hair confined at the base of his neck, and holding the HELP WANTED sign from her shop window. Olympia's long and proper blue dress ignited Gray's interest more than a low-cut satin gown on another woman. Olympia's slender hands were intuitive, strong, and graceful, caressing the Colt's barrel. Gray's body immediately went taut at the sight.

Her tall, elegantly posh body was meant to be loved, to be curled close to a man's body on cold winter nights. Yet she was a spinster, according to Harp's gossip.

She returned the revolver to its red velvet bed and closed the box; Gray let out the air he had been holding in feigned horror at the gun. Olympia moved, and from the corner of his eye Gray caught the sight of swishing petticoats and a slender, black-clad ankle. She bent slightly, replacing the box, and Gray caught the glint of the end of a gun barrel strapped to her calf.

Olympia looked appraisingly at him now, taking in his stooped shoulders, his center part, and his eyeglasses. Gray smiled hopefully, anxiously, perfecting his part as an applicant for the job of store clerk. In the filtered light her smoothly braided hair formed a gleaming raven coronet above her pale face. The angle of her jaw said she wasn't an easygoing woman, but one who knew what she wanted.

She shoved paper and pen at him. "I don't have all day. Please write your name."

After forcing a fearful look at her, Gray dipped the pen in ink and in his best script wrote *Grayson Sinjin*, using his middle name as his last. There were women in his past who called him simply "Sin," and since meeting Olympia he perhaps deserved the name—because before he departed with The Book in his keeping, he would have the six-foot-tall woman who called herself the Raven in his bed.

Her scent—the one lurking on the feathers—curled around him, and Gray damned his body for reacting instantly. Years of escaping a marriage noose had other disadvantages.

She glanced at his signature and nodded approvingly. "Can you do sums and make change?"

The impatience in her voice grated. Gray rose slowly, careful to keep his shoulders stooped. He laced his fingers in front of him and looked over his glasses at her. "Yes, ma'am. I was first in my class."

In some ways he was. At least the watercolor teacher, who posed for him in the nude, told him that he was excellent and the first student she had allowed into her bed.

Olympia Hutton stared at Gray, assessing him as an employee in her shop. Her slender, capable finger tapped a mouth he wanted to taste. He shifted, unused to being measured as a potential employee, especially one whose short suspenders were drawing his pants uncomfortably upward. In disguise, Gray peered hopefully at Olympia over his small, round glasses. With his shoulders stooped she was at his eye level as she said, "Do you know guns—not as a gun-smith, but enough to sell them?"

Gray thought of his matching set of Colt revolvers and the rifles lining his log home and promptly lied, "I don't like guns, but I can learn what is needed."

She patted his hand consolingly and Gray stifled his impulse to take it within his own, drawing it to his mouth. Instead, he shuddered under Olympia's sympathetic look.

"You won't have to worry about handling loaded guns. My father or I do the gunsmithing when needed." Olympia walked from the counter and thoughtfully circled him. "We can't pay much, but you'll have a room with us, upstairs. You can take your meals at Mildred's for free. I do not cook well, nor do I wash clothing. Su Linn collects it every Thursday and returns it on Friday."

There was a certain arrogance to Olympia's husky voice that challenged Gray on a sensual level. He decided to push his suspect and asked timidly, "I am worried about Harp, whether it is a safe community, Miss Hutton. I read in the local paper that there have been recent stagecoach robberies and several . . . uh . . . incidents here in which valuables have been found missing. The thief seems to know ex-actly the movements of the townspeople and strikes when they are absent from their abodes."

After one scent of Olympia, Gray had researched the Hutton family. After the accident her father, Pe-ter, had sixteen years ago, the Huttons left Harp. Olympia Hutton and her father returned from Gold Shaft six years ago. Before that it had been One Buf-falo and a series of towns while she was growing up.

Peter Hutton was a respected man when he wasn't
drinking, which was what the Smithsons said had
happened the day of his accident.

Gray studied the slow, even pulse hitting the oval
jet pin at Olympia's slender throat. He studied the
smudge of gun oil beneath her ear. He wondered
what her skin would taste like there . . . and other
places . . . how it would heat to the touch of his
lips. . . .

Olympia's brief, pleased smile intrigued Gray. She
patted his hand again and briskly stated, "Don't
worry, Mr. Sinjin. I'll protect you. I'm quite capable.
You're hired. Follow me and I'll introduce you to
my father. By the way, we're apt to stir about at
night, so please don't let that disturb your rest."

Peter Hutton was a man plagued by the past; Gray
had seen the look before and sensed instantly that
Olympia's actions were tied to her father's bitter expression. He wondered if Peter Hutton knew of his
daughter's other occupation.

All the pieces were fitting together, Gray thought,
as she led him to his room, next to hers. The upstairs
apartment was worn and comfortable, a blend of
practical elegance, with a scrolled gilt-and-black
sewing machine occupying the light from the windows. Gray enjoyed the elegant sway of Olympia's
hips, and her enticing fragrance curled around him.
There were certain preferences he had retained since
his artistic efforts, and one of them was women with
full breasts. Olympia's would settle quite nicely into
his waiting hands. All he had to do was wait for the
Raven to make her move, and then he had her—and
The Book.

He wanted to make love to her to their mutual

satisfaction, not to marry her. One look at Olympia
in front of the small iron bed in his new bedroom
and Gray wanted to toss her upon it. He managed a
tight smile as she sailed from the room, closing the
door behind her.

Gray decided not to search her room at the moment. He'd wait until the shop was empty. He inhaled her fragrance. He would make love to her, and
she would love it. But Grayson Sinjin Steele would
never offer true love, nor would he ever offer marriage.

The middle of June was perfect for robbing the
Smithsons. Olympia slathered bluing onto the Colt's
barrel and watched Grayson Sinjin tend the front of
the shop.

She'd watched him carefully, rifling through his
room and finding nothing. In his first week she'd
discovered that he wasn't particularly alert, almost
getting run over by a wagon on the street as he went
to get his cooking supplies. She'd had to rescue him,
and he shivered as she'd dusted off his clothing,
down his chest and legs and his backside.

There was just the slightest hesitation when she
gave him an order. His head went back and his eyes
narrowed at her briefly, as though he were debating
something. Once she'd caught a dark flush moving
up his cheeks and he'd glanced at her through his
glasses. It was a sharp glance, too keen and with a
flash of something that irritated her. But Henry
Smithson irritated her far more as he walked into her
shop just then. "Do not wait on him, Mr. Sinjin. I
will take care of him personally."

"Olympia. I'd like to place this poster in your

front window." Henry slapped the wanted poster on her counter and glanced at Grayson, who was wearing his cooking apron. "New man, isn't he? I hear he's been here a week, cooking and cleaning and shopkeeping."

Olympia did not like Henry Smithson at all, and she didn't like his arrogant sneer at Grayson. She placed herself in front of her slightly flabby clerk, protecting him as she studied the poster. "That's a lovely drawing of the Raven. Of course you may, Henry. My, doesn't he have that outlaw look?"

"He's a big one. Strong as an ox. We'll have him swinging before long. That, or a bullet between his eyes."

Olympia frowned and noted the new diamond ring Henry was wearing. It would go nicely with the other jewels she would ship to San Francisco when the time was right to leave Harp. "Ah . . . are you certain that one hundred dollars is enough for the capture of the Raven?"

Her father had come to lean against the doorway, and Henry glanced at him. "I can't just go giving money away, Olympia. That is bad business."

She smiled, disguising her instant anger. She remembered him saying the same thing when her father came to ask for a loan. She toyed with the revolver and enjoyed the thought of Henry missing his big toe. The loss would stop his bull-of-the-woods walk. "You may have to raise the price before the Raven is finished, Henry. I understand that one of your stage doors alone costs more than that. You may leave now."

After Henry had gone, Olympia sniffed the delicious aromas of tonight's dinner, coming from upstairs. Grayson had prepared the meal between waiting on customers. To keep such a jewel, Olympia had taken care to mind her manners. She'd patted him on top of the head to let him know he was doing a good job. Grayson held very still, a pulse beating heavily beneath his left muttonchop sideburn. She'd been very careful to watch her movements while he was around, and now she knew he could be trusted to be sweet, obedient, and not that alert. He'd run at the first sight of a mouse, much less danger. Gun smoke terrified him. Grayson was a perfect shield for the Raven's activities.

Now Grayson ran a feather duster across the shelves. He delicately lifted the tip of a revolver barrel between his thumb and forefinger and gingerly placed it upon the velvet pad used for display, swishing the feather duster across the counter.

Olympia smiled as she noted that Grayson's tight suspenders pulled his pants too high and left his stockings showing at the ankle. He seemed oddly off balance as he moved, unlike most of the Westerners, who strode into the shop wearing heeled boots. He was a quiet, shy man, just her height, who loved to putter around the kitchen. The luscious scent of stew bubbling upstairs and freshly brewed morning coffee filled the shop. With another smile, she decided to help him get over his fear of guns. Her father, once a top ranch foreman and then a stagecoach driver before his leg was crushed, meticulously avoided Grayson and called him "that damn high-pants sissy."

Olympia quickly rubbed the bluing from another revolver, polishing it, as she thought about her father's crushed leg and the way the Smithson Stage Company had given him a pittance and relieved him of his duties. Sixteen years ago she'd been just ten and terrified that her father's drinking would kill him. To escape pity they'd moved from Harp. To survive she'd become a thief and managed to keep her father busy repairing saddles and tack. She narrowed her eyes as a Smithson stage rolled by her workroom window. Priscilla Smithson, a member of Olympia's ladies' circle and wife of Henry Smithson, the stagecoach line's owner, had chattered about business freely—today's stagecoach was a decoy, carrying a cheap-rate bounty hunter after the Raven. Tomorrow night's evening run would carry money for the bank, tucked away into a compartment beneath the floor of the stage.

In the week that Grayson had worked for her, Olympia was able to catch up on her gunsmithing and attend the ladies' circle final planning session for the Founders' Day Ball in June. The grand finale would be held next Saturday night after days of festivities, including horse racing.

The Harp Ladies of Distinction accepted working-class Olympia only because they had to—Olympia was the only good gunsmith for miles. She'd made it plain that if she was not good enough to be a member of the Distinction, she was not good enough to work on their husband's firearms. Eventually the husbands protested and Olympia waltzed into the Distinction. Once in the circle she'd made it her business to pilfer through Harp's secrets. The Borgsens really shouldn't leave their bedroom windows open, even on the second floor—a rose trellis led Olympia neatly upward and she learned that perfect-wife Sissy Mae entertained when Joseph Borgsen wasn't home. Joseph, on the other hand, was often busy with the local painted ladies. The madam, Charity Jones, and her girls were frequent customers in the Hutton Saddlery, which also gave Olympia all the information she needed.

She hummed as she neatened her work area. Everything was fitting into place, and soon the Smithsons would be hovering at financial ruin. While the Smithsons and their snobby friends were dancing the quadrille next Saturday night at yet another ball, Olympia would relieve their homes of excess jewelry. She glanced at her small smelting pot, used for making musket balls. On the work shelf used by her alone, the lead-covered gold balls—formerly gold coins—rested in neat, profitable rows. The gold bricks had been more difficult to fashion, but they were safely fitted into the foundation of the old building behind the shop and layered with adobe mud. Upstairs in Olympia's room, beneath a loose board in her huge walnut wardrobe, a small sack of pillaged jewels nestled with that awful book.

That book. Men and women couldn't possibly contort themselves into so many positions. The deranged artist had actually portrayed women riding men, straddling them, delight pasted on both participants' faces. No righteous woman would grab a man and try to devour his mouth. No righteous man would suckle at a woman's breast. No woman would allow a man to cup both of her breasts and press his face into them. What sort of man would allow a big red bow to be tied to his . . . his anatomy?

Olympia shuddered and swallowed, turning her mind back to business. While she thought of ruining the Smithsons, who practically owned Harp, Olympia unintentionally scowled at Grayson, whose rather

thin eyebrows shot upward in alarm. Amid the
shelves of balls and knives and guns, Grayson seemed
to shiver in terror, his feather duster quivering.

Since that was her effect on most men Olympia
was not concerned. She had always been a powerful,
dynamic woman and unafraid to speak her mind,
which most men she'd met had considered a worthless attribute in a woman. However, because Grayson was too good at his job to lose, Olympia forced
herself to smile, to reassure the timid man, who
promptly swallowed and straightened his bow tie.
Olympia allowed her smile to warm. She had nothing to fear from Grayson Sinjin; he was a truly nice
man. Her father, however, had stated quite crudely
what Grayson lacked as a man. The word *gelded* had
been used.

Olympia closed her eyes and shivered. Thanks to
the vivid watercolor pictures in the small book, she
knew exactly what a man looked like . . . everywhere. She did not believe for one moment that
anyone would partake of such activities. The positions could cause permanent injury.

Still, the book was an oddity that satisfied her curiosity about physical mechanics. She touched her
hot cheek. She'd been too busy tending her father
and surviving to know much about men. She had
never thought to marry, nor to love. She dealt with
realities, and the uppermost priority was making the
Smithsons pay for discarding her father. Although
they had provided good customer service, the
Smithsons had scrimped on safety and repairs, leaving the employees on a tight schedule with poor
equipment.

She frowned; her father had *not* been drunk the

day of the accident. Olympia intended that they would pay well for the rusted bolt that snapped. The stage's axel had slipped, a wheel had broken, and her father, who was nearby, unloading trunks, had been pinned beneath the stage's weight, his leg had been crushed.

Tomorrow night, Olympia decided as she lightly caressed the lead-covered gold balls, she would relieve the Smithsons of the bank's gold coins. She smiled at Grayson. With him tending the store she would have more time to plan.

She hummed lightly, excited about the Raven's next robbery. It was her skill, her entertainment, something she did best of all. If there was anything Olympia had discovered she loved, it was the sheer challenge of the game.

Her new clerk stared at the balls she was rolling and caressing in her palm and swallowed heavily. His muttonchop sideburns moved along his jaw as though he was grinding his teeth.

"Are you feeling all right, Mr. Sinjin?" she asked, noting the drops of perspiration on his furrowed, pale brow.

"Why do you have to teach me about guns?" he asked fearfully. "Can't we just ignore them?"

"Nonsense. You need to appreciate the value of a good mechanism." Olympia picked up a revolver, cradled it in her hands, and ran her cloth up and down the barrel. She kissed the tip, a signature blessing of every weapon she repaired or customized. Grayson looked shocked; he flushed and recoiled a step. "Come along, Mr. Sinjin," Olympia said. "It's time for your lesson. We'll close up early and shoot in the back room."

Minutes later Olympia positioned her clerk's body in a firing stance. The back room she used for sighting and testing guns was a perfect place to teach. She stuffed cotton in her ears and in his. Since Grayson was left-handed and she used her right hand, the task was not easy. She had to lean her cheek on his upper arm and sight down the barrel. She had to place her cheek against his and lean closely against him. He was firmer than she suspected, except for the soft cushioning of fat across his belly. She moved around to the front of Grayson and bent down to his ankles, easing them apart. Grayson peered down at her backside. "Uh . . . excuse me, Miss Hutton, but you've got a feather on your uh . . . uh . . . lower anatomy."

"What?" she yelled, then looked around to where he was pointing.

She impatiently dusted the feather away and stepped behind him, enclosing him with her arms to aim the revolver. He was only her height and stoop-shouldered, and his eyes closed as he fired, his head turned away from the target. She patted his head and yelled, "A miss. Do not be discouraged, Mr. Sinjin. I have abundant patience."

She lost her patience within the hour. Grayson could not hold a pose long enough to fire properly, and she had to constantly place her arms around him to prop up the revolver. She had to place her cheek along his to help him sight the target. She had to place her fingers over his to hold the gun. She had to step inside his arms and aim the gun herself. . . . She took the cotton from her ears. "We'll try some other time, when I'm not so tired," she muttered, running the back of her hand across her cheek.

"I believe my rump roast is almost ready for potatoes and carrots," Grayson said very tightly, his
glasses slightly awry because she had bumped his
chin. He jerked the cotton from his ears. "Did you
serve in the army, Miss Hutton?"

The question startled her. "No, of course not.
Why do you ask?"

"You know how to give orders like a sergeant I
once knew," he replied evenly, and then walked
stiffly away.

Her father, who had just entered the shooting
room, snickered. "You won't run him off, will you,
honey? I'm looking forward to his fried chicken."

Before the shop opened on Monday morning,
Olympia picked her way across Harp's main street.
She glanced back at her clerk, who followed her
carrying her shopping basket. Grayson was a wonderful cook, and she wanted him to have everything
he needed in the kitchen. Olympia had never cared
for kitchen utensils, but if her clerk needed them to
cook her meals, he would have them. He'd prepared
a neat list of vegetables, eggs, and a proper pan in
which to wash dishes, which he did quickly and me-
thodically, a fascinating process. Her father scowled,
looking up from his dime novel as Grayson
hummed, steam frothing around him as he washed
dishes. Though Grayson wasn't manly in her father's
eyes, Olympia's feelings ran to gratitude. Grayson
had her protection. "Come along, Mr. Sinjin.
Hurry. We have work to do and can't spend all day
shopping. We have a glorious week ahead of us.
There will be horse racing every day and shooting

contests, and then the ball on Saturday night. Do you dance, Mr. Sinjin?"

She frowned when he almost stepped over his own brogans, and she decided not to mention more about dancing. He eased carefully around a horse and stepped up on the board sidewalk. "Look at that."

Olympia looked at the wanted poster once and then again. The Raven's sketched image looked back at her. The Smithsons had posted a bounty.

"It's too small. An insignificant drop in the bucket. I'm worth more than that," she muttered.

"What did you say?" Grayson asked at her side, peering at the poster closely.

"I said we probably need a new mopping bucket if you are going to scrub the floors."

Gray watched the slender shadow carrying a huge bundle slide from the shop's back porch. He listened to Peter Hutton snoring softly in the next room and decided that Olympia's father knew nothing of his daughter's outlaw activities.

Olympia was a very sensual woman, given to caressing what she loved. Her father's shoulder, a tintype of her mother, and various weapons, including an evil-looking short, light saber. When he'd inspected the scabbard it bore a minute trace of red enamel at the tip—the same color as the Smithsons' stage door in which the Raven had artistically etched a big *R*.

Gray frowned, rubbing the shaved place between his eyebrows. For a solid week she'd had him fetching and carrying, treating him like a . . . utensil, an insignificant piece of do-this, do-that equipment.

Bent over her beloved revolvers and rifles, she barely noticed when he brought her coffee. Her actions grated. As a man he wanted her attention—all of it. He wanted to be caressed.

If the sheriff or the bounty hunters caught her first, they'd—Gray pushed that ugly thought away as she eased through a patch of moonlight and into the shadows.

"She's damn good at it," Gray murmured, slipping on his pants and buttoning them. Now that Olympia wasn't snooping through his things, he'd brought in his saddlebags and western clothing. He grabbed his boots and the rest of his clothing on his way to search her room. He looked down at the western boots fitting his feet comfortably and sighed with relief.

He dressed and followed Olympia—a graceful shadow carrying a bundle—across the quiet street; she paused at the Raven's wanted poster and then slid down an alley leading to the livery. Minutes later Gray paused at the poster to find the words *Not Enough* written across the poster with an *R* beneath them. Olympia was pushing, taking chances, and it was only a matter of time before someone caught her.

The livery boy sleeping in the stables didn't stir as Olympia and Gray took their horses. The buttermilk's light hide showed clearly in the moonlight as it crossed the rolling hills, and Gray's Appaloosa mare, accustomed to midnight rides, wanted to run.

A wisp of white shimmered and rolled on the moonlit road, and without stopping, Gray expertly held his mare's mane, swung down, and plucked a goose-down feather from the earth. Gray slid it be-

neath his nose; it smelled faintly like Olympia, feminine and exotic with just that tiny bite of gun oil and
gun smoke.

An hour and a half later and ten miles from Harp,
Olympia's horse eased into the shadows and Gray
tied his mare to a stand of aspens a safe distance away.
An experienced tracker, he moved through the
brush and over the slight knoll to look down on the
road. Moonlight outlined the Raven, on foot and
poised at a bend in the road. Within minutes the
stage surged around a corner and a commanding
shot rang out into the night sky. The Raven stepped
onto the road, dressed in a huge cape and a hat with
a plume. Twin revolvers gleamed in the moonlight,
fixed straight at the driver.

Gray eased closer. He wanted to be very certain
about Olympia's identity.

Olympia crouched, removed the stone from the
foundation, and slid the heavy sack inside. She
glanced at her father's and her clerk's darkened windows and smiled; they were still sleeping.

She felt wonderful, too excited to enter the house
and go to her bed. She decided instead to check on
the town, to drift across the rooftops to the sheriff's
office. There the stagecoach driver was certain to be
explaining why he had allowed the Raven to take
the Smithsons' payroll. X. Jones, the stagecoach
driver, could have helped prevent the accident to her
father, but instead he used it to his advantage with
the Smithsons. Olympia stuffed her pillow and cape
into the cloth sack and exchanged her high-heeled
boots for moccasins; in the next moment she was
moving swiftly across the rooftops of Harp.

Within minutes she lay on the roof overlooking the street. Henry Smithson's outraged yells boiled up to her: "That was my payroll on the stagecoach! You sit around all day, eating donuts and drinking coffee, and the Raven is out there helping himself to *my* money!"

While Smithson ran his hands through his hair, paced back and forth on the street, and raged, the sheriff spoke too low for Olympia to hear. Smithson clarified the discussion. " 'We'll catch him,' you say. Hell's bells, man, I'm running a business! I've got to deliver a payroll! Now, if you can't catch the Raven then maybe we'd better get a sheriff who can protect this city's good citizens. Get a posse together now! Ventilate the villain and *get me my money*!"

Supremely happy with Smithson's outrage, Olympia eased into her house minutes later. She tossed her bundle of the Raven's cape, boots, and hat onto the floor and kicked it under her bed. She danced around the room, hugged herself, then undressed in the moonlight coming from the window. She slid her arms into her long nightgown, loosening her hair and running her fingers through it, reveling in her success. She pivoted neatly on one foot, sighed happily, smiled, and reached for her quilt to turn down her bed. Everything was going as planned.

2

Her hand found a man's hard thigh as her clerk glared up at her from her bed. His big hand wrapped firmly around her wrist, and he jerked. She sprawled across him and he flipped her easily to her back, lying over her. "Watch it."

"How dare you, Mr. Sinjin! You are fired!" Olympia found her wrists pinned beside her head, her body trapped by his heavy one. He was more solid than she had expected, with not a drop of clerk's fat on him.

In the moonlight he looked nothing like the man she'd hired. With his hair waving deeply and rumpled about his shoulders and a heavy stubble covering his jaw—which didn't look kind at the moment—her mild Mr. Sinjin looked hard and menacing.

His deep scowl changed to a slow, shockingly sensuous smile. His hips pressed downward upon hers. Olympia shivered when she realized she was the object, the reason, for the gleam in his eye. Gray stared at her lips and spoke in a hushed, low drawl. "The name is Grayson Sinjin Steele, Olympia. But you may call me Gray."

She blinked, trying to recover. "I won't call you anything. Gct off me."

He was stronger than he had looked as Mr. Sinjin; he held her wrists easily.

His smile widened and his teeth gleamed in the shadows. "Always have been a cad, according to my dear sainted mother and other ladies. But then, you're not a lady, are you?"

She squirmed, bucked against his weight, and found herself securely pinned. Olympia blew a long, sleek strand of hair from her cheek and glared up at him. "What do you want?"

His hips eased down firmly upon hers, impressing her with a hard male outline. He wiggled his bare toes against her insole and asked in a deep, sensual tone, "Right now?"

She flushed, knowing that at the moment she hated Gray Steele more than she hated the Smithsons. "I will shoot you myself. Or run a saber through your damnable guts. I'm capable, you know."

He easily moved her wrists into the grasp of one hand, and a long finger prowled across her cheek, tracing a path to her lips. "Why do you do it?" he asked softly.

She scowled up at him. "Do what?"

"I followed you tonight, dear heart," Gray said slowly, watching her. "Or should I say Raven?"

Olympia clamped her lips closed. She sent him a glare that wilted most men, but found Gray grinning down at her, clearly enjoying himself. She tried to remember why the name Grayson Steele seemed oddly familiar to her. She moved her bare foot from his large, caressing one. "You are wicked and obviously mad."

"You're in trouble. We'll settle the rest at another time, but right now you're putting the Smithson payroll back in their hands. It's only one o'clock. You've got hours before daylight. There are two scrub bounty hunters in town now, and the Smithsons are certain to offer a better reward for your neck. They'll be on your trail at first light."

She smiled sweetly up at him. "I don't know what you're talking about."

"Don't you?" Then Gray held a musket ball in front of her nose. He scratched the lead coating with his thumbnail, and a line of gold sparkled in the moonlight. "Come on, Oly, be a good girl. Just put on your black pants and shirt and moccasins, and get the bag from the stone foundation of the building in back. We'll deal with the fake bricks later."

Olympia studied his face in the shadows. He seemed amused, waiting for her to respond, just as a mountain cat would do, playing with his prey.

"If there was a . . . a take, I suppose you'd want a portion of it," she said warily, hoping that she could buy him off or temporarily distract him. He watched her as he slowly released her wrists, and while she forced a smile Olympia slid her hand beneath her pillow. No one would blame her for stopping a thief—

"Looking for that?" he asked, nodding at the sawed-off shotgun standing against her bedroom wall.

"There are plenty more where that came from," Olympia said sweetly, and frowned as he chuckled.

"I know where every one of them is, neatly tucked away. You had some interesting hiding places." Gray rolled to his feet, bringing her easily with him. He patted her backside beneath the voluminous gown and grinned. "Be a nice girl. Return the money. I'm expecting to be fired, so you can tell everyone that Mr. Sinjin had to return to his ailing mother. Sinjin with his muttonchop sideburns will be replaced by me, your well-warmed groom-to-be."

Olympia swatted away his hand and found hers instantly trapped within his larger one. She'd missed the calluses and the strength, but there was no dismissing his hard look. In the shadows Gray's eyes had narrowed and glinted like the edge of a raised sword. "What do you want?" Olympia asked very softly.

"You," Gray stated simply, and knew it was the truth. Olympia excited his instincts as no other woman had done; he wanted to take her, here, now, on the tumbled bed. He wanted to hear her cry out his name.

His instinct told him that making love to Olympia Hutton one time would not be enough.

She smiled coolly and crossed her arms. "You can't have me."

Gray ran his finger down her cheek, down her throat, and across her chest, toying with the pearl buttons of her nightgown. He studied the shadow of her nipple and damned himself for being so hungry for her. "Can't I? Just what would you do to protect your father and this shop? How far would you go to do that, Miss Hutton?"

She lifted her chin. "Only a man without honor would suggest such a cowardly, low–down–as–a–snake's–belly thing."

Gray eased his fingers beneath the buttons on the front of her nightgown. Her skin was silky, fragrant. . . . Reluctantly Gray admitted to himself that he admired her—her back to the wall, Olympia had just attacked him. "A fate worse than death?"

"You are not acceptable, Mr. . . . Mr. Steele. I reject you."

He chuckled outright at that. "May I remind you of your options? Here you are, caught with the goods—"

"I'll say that I found them in your possession, that I saw you hide them," Olympia shot back.

He placed his hand on her throat, her pulse racing against his palm like the fluttering wings of a small, trapped bird. Gray's body tightened; he didn't want the sheriff or the bounty hunters to catch Olympia. Her pride wouldn't save her. The image of her fighting valiantly and being roughly used flicked across his mind. He shouldn't care. . . . "Get dressed," he ordered finally, wary of her—wary of himself getting snared in the softness he'd always avoided.

A toss upon the bed was one thing, but the protective feelings she had aroused in him were unfamiliar and unwanted.

Minutes later Olympia leapt from one rooftop to another, then paused to glance behind her. In one long leap Gray easily breached the distance. Dressed in black, her hair in one long neat braid, Olympia glared at him. "You are now a good two inches taller than Mr. Sinjin. You've hunched your shoulders to no avail, and you've suspected the wrong person. There is no evidence that I might be the Raven."

He took the feathers from his pocket and held them up to the moonlight. "Evidence."

"Ordinary feathers. Not something you could show a judge."

"Your buttermilk mare, Josie, has a notch on one shoe that leaves a good trail—"

"Someone borrowed her. Teddy Smithson tried once and she's hated him ever since."

"Your boots match the tracks." Gray brushed the feathers across her nose. He couldn't resist—he wrapped her thick braid in his fist and bent to kiss her lightly. She tasted of moonlight and dreams and dark, stormy hungers. She tasted of sunshine and tomorrow's something he wanted desperately—and he regretted ever finding her.

Her hand touched his flat stomach, and Olympia glared up at him. "You're not fat at all."

"Wonderful what a pillow will do, or a money roll and papers, isn't it?" he asked blandly.

Their stares locked. He should let her break her neck. He liked his life—without the interference of women—and here he was, trying to save one. "I am a prince among men," he declared in a tone as dark as his mood. "I should let you hang. It's only a matter of time before someone breaks your neck anyway. There's already a price on your head."

"Beast." Olympia swung the heavy bag of gold coins at him, missed, and leapt to another rooftop. She stopped to look back at him. "You could carry this. A gentleman would."

Gray chuckled; Olympia simply delighted him. She acted as if he owed her tribute. "What? And get caught with the goods? No, thank you. I've been fetching and carrying for you this past week, and as of now we're changing that. You'll be cooking my breakfast in no time. You'll be running to do my every wish. Why, you might even want to fondle me as you do your beloved Colts. I suggest you do not run your fingers up and down the barrels of revolvers in front of men—nor kiss the ends of the barrels. The action is provocative. Are you a siren, luring men with one look, Miss Hutton?"

She paused, her shocked expression caught in the silvery moonlight. Then she turned, grabbed a brick chimney, and hoisted herself upward. "That is for good luck; I kiss the barrels to bless them. It's a signature, a blessing, like all good gunsmiths do to a good piece of equipment. There is no way that any man would think I was . . . leading him on."

"Really?" he asked, taunting her. Her flash of anger pleased him, small payment for all the times she'd rapped out an order to him. Gray followed his prey, admiring the neat curve of her bottom as she moved up and over the crest of a rooftop. She stood, her breasts silhouetted against the dying night sky, and he knew he wanted more than her body.

Moments later Olympia dropped to the ground, releasing her grip on the trellis. She caught a branch, swung, and allowed it to swing back at Gray. Gray ducked instantly—the mark of a man used to hunting—caught the branch, and swung down to her. Olympia brushed her dusty clothing briskly and frowned up at him. "There. You didn't break your neck as I had hoped. The money is returned. Satisfied?"

"Not quite," Gray stated grimly, and pulled her

into his arms. He fused his mouth with Olympia's before she could protest, deepening the kiss as he dived into her sweet, untutored flavor. He gathered her closer against him, fitting her softness exactly, perfectly into the line of his body as if he'd been waiting for her all his lifetime.

Her soft sigh caressed his cheek, circled his brain, and slid into the tiny part of it that was still capable of thinking. Olympia was just enough of a disaster to keep his life interesting. She tasted like mystery and happiness and—Gray slanted his mouth carefully to one side, aware that Olympia was standing absolutely still as if she'd been stunned.

He'd caught her, Gray decided as he smoothed his open hand up her back, easing it carefully to her side. Olympia Hutton was his—permanently. The humming inside his head told him that there could be no other women; she enchanted him. His thumb caressed the soft side of her breast, and his body told him that Olympia could make him very, very happy.

Gray glanced at Olympia's drowsy eyes before refastening his lips to her soft, parted ones. There wouldn't be other men tasting her lips, drawing her body so close that her heart raced against his. No other man would experience that soft purr at the back of her throat. She was perfect and just what he needed to complete his life. A woman like Olympia needed children—oh, yes, Gray's body told him that he was more than ready to respond.

The thought of children usually brought warning bells clanging inside his brain; they had changed to wedding bells. He saw himself holding a baby in one arm and Olympia in the other.

Gray trusted his gut instincts. Slowly removing his

lips from hers, Gray held Olympia's bemused face between his hands and resisted the urge to kiss her again. "Olympia?"

"Mmm?" She sounded as if she were floating, and Gray wanted all of her attention. He wanted no mistakes in his claiming of Olympia. He eased one hand slowly down and over her breast; it filled his hand gloriously, softly.

Gray inhaled and realized that his body felt like red-hot steel, throbbing with need. He groaned, the sound echoing his hunger. He fought to keep his mind on making his vision clear to his future wife. "Olympia, I'm a man of action. Once I see something that suits me, I take it. You suit me, Olympia. I want to marry you and let you give me a son."

A son. The dream echoed in Gray's mind. He smiled tenderly at the woman he intended to marry.

She blinked rapidly, her eyes widening. "The days are gone when a man marries because he has kissed a lady. You are certainly no prude."

"That I am not, as you will find out." Gray leaned down to brush a kiss across her lips before she pushed him away. "You've had enough excitement for one day, my lovely. We'll discuss our plans in the morning."

He ducked the fist that came flying at his head and sidestepped the kick at his shins. "You'll be more reasonable in the morning, dear heart."

"What do you mean, you've decided to let me marry you and have your son?" Olympia asked on Tuesday morning when Gray brought a mug of coffee to her workbench. She'd had all night to think about his ghastly proposal and his hard, demanding kiss. She glanced at the closed door to her father's workshop and then at Gray. There was nothing foppish about him this morning. Her mild-mannered clerk had departed and Gray stood, dressed in western garb and looking as if he'd been born to the West. He looked at her with those cool gray, assessing eyes, his newly shaved jaw too firm, a muscle tensing as he watched her. Without his muttonchop sideburns, Gray looked like a tough westerner. He looked well-rested, vibrant, and ready for challenges. Olympia hadn't slept, had circles under her eyes, and her nerves ran screaming throughout her body.

She couldn't trust him, of course, not a man who could play an intelligent bookish clerk, who could cook and mend, and who attracted children like flowers drew butterflies. She'd changed that image. Gray was a wolf, a cactus, a low-down . . . womanizer, she decided as his gaze slid across her lips and downward to her bosom.

Gray lifted one of her lead-covered gold musket balls from its case and tossed it lightly in the air. She caught it and replaced it. "No. I won't consider marrying you. No marriage. No children."

Gray reached for a brick weighting a stack of paper, and Olympia shivered and ordered, "Stop."

"You'll have to return that." Gray tapped the red coating on the gold brick. "And the others, covered with adobe in the old foundation. I'll help you. Make a list of what goes to whom, and I'll see that it is done. I've got just the person for the job. And then you'll be my willing bride. Because if you won't, dear Olympia, your father will be left alone to fend for himself while you—never mind what they would do to you."

When Olympia paled, Gray ran on with his plan, pushing her. "It's a simple matter of me wanting you and wanting a son. I didn't plan this, Olympia, but now that the idea is on the hot platter, so to speak, I like the feel of it and I'm very good at taking and keeping what is good for me. We can explain a hasty marriage easily. We'll say you answered an ad for a wife and that we've been corresponding for a year. Now I've come to collect you. It's a common arrangement. I've never wanted to marry, Olympia dear heart, but marriage vows would keep my son from being called a bastard. I wouldn't like that at all, and a child would be a natural consequence of our time in bed, which will very likely be quite frequent judging from your response last night."

Olympia fought the urge to hit him; his grin said he'd enjoy a tussle with her. She would deal with his outrageous ideas coolly. She studied Gray's broad-brimmed hat tipped back on his head, the western shirt fitting across his wide shoulders and chest, and his long legs down to his worn western boots. Last night he'd worn moccasins just as she had, and he'd been just as agile, despite his greater weight. She glanced at the hair on his chest escaping the V of his open collar and the red scarf tied around his muscled neck. He was a hunter, a predator, and now she was the hunted.

"You are demented. You bore me," she murmured in an attempt at bravado and faked a yawn, while her heart pounded wildly. "And I've never trusted men who shave their eyebrows. It isn't natural. And you are left-handed."

Gray's finger ran across her lips, his eyes darkening to smoke. His voice was too low, dark, and filled with meaning she didn't understand. "Do I really bore you? Is that why your heart leaps at my touch?"

He bent to give her one of those light, earth-shattering kisses that promised softness and something darker, headier, as she'd discovered with his kiss last night. He'd kissed her as if he'd take her soul if she'd let him.

When Gray eased away he was grinning. Olympia blinked, swaying toward the warmth of his body. She forced her fingertips to release his shoulders and realized that they were stiff from digging into his hard muscles.

"You kiss like a child, sweetheart," Gray said, irritating her. "And you smell like oil and gun smoke."

Olympia patted her mussed hair. When Gray took her in his arms, his hand bracing the back of her head, his fingers had caressed her scalp, oddly stilling her. "I think I would rather duel with you. Pistols or blades?"

He laughed outright and strolled out of her shop, all long legs and narrow hips. Olympia studied the Colt tied low on his left thigh. She'd never trusted a man with an agile left hand.

Beauregard Steele, Gray's brother, sprawled upon his hotel bed. Blue was dusty and tired after the fast ride from his Wyoming ranch adjacent to Gray's. "Olympia's too good for you, female thief or not. I knew that when you telegraphed me last week and said you were staying a bit. I saw her. She's as innocent as a child and tasty as a peach. Maybe I'll give up the fiancée business and poach a bit on my brother's good fortune. She has no idea what kissing the barrel of a gun can do to a man."

When Gray sent him an ominous look, Blue grinned. "So you took one look at Miss Thief and decided you wanted to save her pretty neck. I could get shot, returning the gold she's stolen. I wouldn't want my face on a wanted poster. What would my beloved say?"

Gray picked up a chair, twirled it, and sat, straddling it. He placed his arms across the back. "How many beloveds is that, Blue? You had too much to drink when you asked Mary Lou to marry you. She was only being kind when she held your head up out of that watering trough. You called her an angel and thanked her with a marriage invitation. Since then you've been trying to get out of it."

He leveled a stare at Blue. "And may I remind you that you owe me? There's a certain matter of The Book, which is in the possession of the Raven, thanks to you. You sent it to Mary Lou only because she is a preacher's daughter and a spinster and you thought you'd shock her enough to break the engagement."

"Gray, you're acting like a man in love. Don't tell me after all these years of starving all the women in the West—holing up on your ranch and avoiding their invitations—you've decided to claim a woman who will never let you have a moment's peace. She's a woman who likes adventure and trouble—"

"I intend to give her what she wants and needs," Gray said grimly.

"She's not a delicate little flower, Gray. I'd hate to see you get ventilated—a most likely event from the way she handles revolvers. I have no doubt she is also very effective with the sabers she hones to perfec-

tion. And I don't want to be a part of your black-
mailing her into bed."

Gray studied his hands, remembering the smooth
movement of Olympia's body. "I'll make her happy.
She'll have everything she needs."

Blue hooted and laughed outright. "Mother said
you'd meet your end shot through the heart by a
jealous husband or an outraged mother. Instead it
may be the bride herself."

Gray stared at his brother. "I've changed."

"You've got a mile-wide cold spot in your heart.
Thanks to our dear mother and her lovers. Only Dad
and I know why you act like a lobo wolf sometimes—getting up for midnight rides and frightening
women with one cold look," Blue returned in a
quiet tone. "There's more to a woman than what
she needs. You'll have to give a bit of your cold
heart, and be glad of it. I'll return the gold to its
owners, but if you hurt the girl and break her heart,
I'll be back. I adore the delicate species and make it
my business to protect them from villains like yourself."

"You won't have far to look. I'm taking her back
to my ranch. I'm marrying her."

For a moment Blue stared at him. His eyes were
almost the shade of a Montana sky, while Gray's
were cool as steel. "Marriage isn't a game, Gray. I
may have been drunk, and wanting a warm nest to
settle into when I proposed to Mary Lou, but I
wouldn't ruin her life, or mine, just for the sake
of—"

"From the moment I saw Olympia Hutton, I
knew she was mine," Gray stated carefully, then
frowned. He sounded like the hero in a stage drama;

all he needed was one hand upon his chest and the
other flung wide to the audience. He'd shocked
himself—for just a moment he'd been jealous.

Blue sighed wearily. "I always knew it would happen. Some sweet filly would knock you sideways and
you'd be even more disgusting than you are. She's
got The Book, Gray. It's only a matter of time before she realizes what a snake you are and puts a
bullet in you."

"I'll have to work fast then, won't I? I'll have to
make her like me."

Blue stared at his brother and then began to grin.
"Oh, hell, Gray, I knew it would happen someday.
You're in love. The Lone Wolf of Wyoming, who
declared he'd never love or marry, has been shot
down." In seconds Blue was guffawing so hard that
he held his aching sides. He paused when Gray
calmly ripped the blanket from beneath him, flipping
him to the floor.

Olympia sighted the empty revolver at Gray as he
walked toward her workbench, carrying a huge bouquet of mid-June wildflowers mixed with lilies of the
valley in one hand and a picnic basket in the other. It
was only Wednesday, and he was losing no time in
displaying his intentions to the whole town. How
dare he discover her weakness for the tiny, bell-
shaped white flowers? There was only one woman in
town who had them, and that was Miss Ellie
McDougal, a spinster who knew that men were lust-
ful beasts; she preferred to live with cats. Olympia
scowled at the flowers. "Did you kill Miss Ellie, or
did you just steal them?"

"Why, Olympia. I'm shocked. We had a proper

cup of morning tea. I explained how you had answered my ad and we had corresponded for a good year and that I desperately needed to further my suit with her delightful flowers. She was only too happy to help me pursue my sweetheart." Gray placed the basket on the floor, took the revolver away from her with one hand, and shoved the bouquet under her nose. "Let's go for a picnic. You can sample my best fried chicken—cooked it myself in the hotel kitchen—and after that, I'll let you kiss me."

"I've got work to do," she returned sweetly and began filing the trigger on her favorite Colt. She ignored the wonderful fragrances of the flowers and the delicious aromas coming from the basket, picking through them to find Gray's oddly exciting soap-and-male scent. She fought the blush rising up her cheek; she'd never been courted or kissed or given a bouquet. The combination had sent her off balance.

She'd ignore him—as she had the previous men who tried to catch her eye. Gray would get bored and move on to more willing women. If her sharp tongue didn't send him away, she'd find other ways. She would find a way to distract Gray—perhaps kidnap him, tie him securely in a remote cabin while she and her father disappeared.

Gray's lips eased aside the lace collar at the back of her neck, and he whispered something husky, dark, and sensuous in another language. She turned to him, shivering with something she didn't understand. "What did you say?"

He tucked a tiny stalk of lily of the valley into her hair and studied the effect of the tiny bell-shaped flowers against the gleaming black silk. "That I want you very much—in French. Come with me, Oly. Let's play awhile.''

She noted that Gray's eyebrows were oddly thicker than she remembered and that he was looking at her almost wistfully. For just a heartbeat she recognized something alone and wary within him, some tiny, shadowy part of him she wanted to comfort. But he was too dangerous, and she knew him for what he was—a seasoned Westerner, a hunter, and a taker. She blamed her momentary weakness on the delicate flowers, her secret passions.

Sonny Parker, a mischievous three-year-old boy, ran in the open door of the shop and straight for Gray. Olympia watched, fascinated as Gray grinned, chuckled, and shoved the bouquet at her. He hoisted the boy high into his arms, bounced him until he laughed, and asked, "Where is your mother, young man?"

When Gray had moved from the Huttons' to the hotel, he'd apparently made a friend—Sonny's mother was the evening cook at the hotel. A chubby hand foraged inside Gray's jacket and pulled out a tiny bag. "Good cookies for Sonny. Mommy coming."

Olympia went light-headed as Gray turned to her, the child fitted perfectly in his arms. Gray was meant to be a father, chuckling while the boy munched on the cookie, sending crumbs down his immaculate jacket. Sonny's mother appeared and, after a distracted thank-you, hurried out of the store with her son.

"I would like a duel," Olympia stated very carefully, discarding the need to smooth Gray's cheek, to touch him. It was difficult threatening a man while she held his bouquet in a death grip—it was her first genuine courting bouquet, after all. "Not to the death, but rather as a bet. If I win, you leave and I promise not to . . . uh . . ."

"Partake of other persons' fortunes?" he offered, amused.

She nodded slowly and knew that somehow she would have her revenge.

Gray tugged her from her high stool and placed her bonnet on her head. He adjusted it as though experienced and neatly tied the big bow to one side, just brushing her jawline. He looked down at her like an artist studying his handiwork and then nodded curtly. "Come along, Oly, let us proceed to the dueling fields."

She grabbed the workbench counter as an anchor. When Gray looked at her like that, some infinite part of her shifted and warmed. "What is your wager?"

"That I have you, of course," he answered slowly. "I'll tell your father that we're leaving." Gray reached out to touch her cheek with his fingertips. "Don't worry, Oly, I know how much you love your father. Our courtship will look very normal to him, and he'll never know that you once carved big *R*s on pretty red stagecoach doors. He'll never know that I was Mr. Sinjin, and that my disguise was used to trap you. He'll be welcome at my ranch, to live with us."

"We're alone. Shoot me," Gray stated, tossing a revolver to her. One spin of the cylinder told Olympia that bullets rested in the chambers. One brush of his lips on hers, a smoky flash of his eyes, told her that he wanted her.

The Montana glade surrounded by pine trees echoed with her heartbeat, louder than the birds, the chattering squirrels, or the rippling stream. She looked at the gun in her hand and knew that she could kill him; she could put a small, deadly hole in him and his blood would flow. The thought sickened her. He stood there, his legs spead wide as he watched her, waiting for her to shoot him. Olympia tossed the revolver to the blanket he had spread upon the lush grass. "Why do you want me?"

He bent to pluck a wildflower, giving it to her. He moved gracefully, like a man accustomed to moving through forests and over rugged mountains to take what he wanted. "I want a son, a tiny part of me to live on. It's an ordinary desire, of an ordinary man."

Olympia remembered how Gray had held Sonny, close and protective. She smoothed the petals of the wildflower and knew that behind Gray's quiet stare lurked pain. "Why me? Surely there are other women, more interesting women."

The tip of Gray's finger lifted her chin and their eyes met. "I do not think life with you, sweetheart, even for a long time, would bore me. But I think that for now, this is the best reason of all." Then he bent to place his lips on hers and lifted her up, high into his arms. "I like this," he whispered softly. "Holding you in my arms. You fit perfectly. Not one of those delicate little flowers that might snap in the wind."

He stared at her breasts, and a dark red tint began to move up his tanned cheeks.

"I could kill you in your sleep. I could tie you to the bed and make my escape," Olympia whispered, uneasy with the shivering tension in her body, the tight bond enclosing her heart as Gray looked at her tenderly. She held very still, dealing with the novelty of being handled as lightly as a child—and desired as a woman.

He lowered her to the blanket and lay beside her. He slowly began pulling the tortoiseshell hairpins from her hair, despite her swatting hands. Gray locked her wrists in one hand and continued to smooth her hair with his other. "You'll have to give up your favorite hobby, of course. I couldn't have my wife and the future mother of my son running around robbing people. You'll have to cook for me and try to entice me. I'll let you do my washing—not too much starch on my collars—and I'll be available anytime you wish to practice your womanly charms."

"How wonderful. I get to wash your clothes and cook your meals," she repeated hollowly.

Gray laughed outright. "Don't look so disgusted. I'm told I can be quite entertaining when I try. Marriage won't be that bad, Oly. I'll bake those apple pies you like."

Olympia shot him a dark look and sat up. He tugged on her shoulder, pressed her back to the blanket, and grabbed the foot that had just kicked his shin. "What's wrong, Oly? Don't I fit the picture of your prince as well as young Teddy Smithson?"

Her heart stopped as Gray's fingers caressed her black-stockinged leg, sliding upward. He'd discovered her damnable secret. She pushed his hand away and straightened her skirts. "You're disgusting, Gray.

A typical man, certain that I'm dying to cook your food, clean your house, and have your child. Just how do you know you would produce a son anyway? I suppose you already have had experience?"

Gray lifted a strand of her hair, studied the soft, gleaming texture. "I want you where I can protect you, Oly. That would be at my ranch and in my bed. A son would be a natural consequence of me loving you, of you taking me to bed. I've asked your father if I could court you in short order and declared my intentions. He understands that I need to get back to my ranch soon, taking my bride with me. I told him I would be faithful and that you'd never want for anything and that you'd have the biggest bed of lilies of the valley and bleeding hearts in all of Wyoming."

Bleeding hearts, her second-favorite flowers. Olympia's determination wobbled, crushed by the image of the perfect little drooping heart-shaped flowers. Instead, she bit her lip and fought the tears she'd kept locked inside her for years. They began to fall slowly to her cheeks.

"Come here, Oly. Let me take care of you," Gray murmured softly and drew her down to him, her head upon his shoulder.

There in the sunshine and the scents of flowers and grass, Olympia pressed her face against the comfort of Gray's shoulder and began to cry. She couldn't forgive him for that or for his next words. He whispered against her forehead, "I won't leave you waiting at the church like Teddy Smithson."

Olympia tore herself out of Gray's arms and struggled to her feet. "How did you discover that? We were running away together—"

"You thought you had him, didn't you, Oly? You

Lady Desperado

thought you'd make him pay that day five years ago. There Teddy was, an eighteen-year-old boy, prime for the plucking and blind with desire. As Mrs. Smithson you could ruin the family honestly, couldn't you?"

There was nothing kind in Gray's dark look; he caught her skirts, jerking her down to straddle him. His hands caught her face. "I'm not a boy, Oly, but a man who knows what he wants."

Then Gray's hand roamed downward and locked to the pistol strapped to her thigh, covered by layers of her clothing. "I'd really appreciate your discarding this, Oly. I could get shot in the process of loving you."

"I don't think that will be an event," she returned uneasily and rose gingerly to her feet.

With his arms behind his head, Gray looked up at her. "Won't it?" he drawled.

3

Everything happened so quickly. Later that afternoon Gray had won a horse race and had plucked Olympia from the crowd, lifting her easily into the saddle in front of him. With his arm around her, Gray had given an interview to the local paper, saying he was thrilled to be visiting Harp. Grayson Steele of the Wyoming Steeles was a respected cattleman, a seasoned Westerner, who knew how to rope and ride and shoot. Morris Steele was rumored to have a blue-blood English wife, though he lived in Wyoming near his two sons, Beauregard and Grayson, who were much sought-after gentlemen bachelors.

It was now Thursday before the Saturday ball, and Olympia slapped the morning extra-edition newspaper on the counter. She tapped the article: Famed Cattleman Comes to Harp. Grayson Steele. The name sounded oddly familiar, and yet she had just met him. The article praised Gray lavishly and, since he had mentioned politics, predicted that he would be a senator. Olympia frowned; she detested politicians.

RAVEN REPENTS, RETURNS PICKFORD JEWELS. Olympia read quickly: The Raven had left a note, explaining that he'd stolen for his poor, sick, dying mother, but now that she was gone he had repented and would never thieve again. He was taking religion and preaching to save others of his ilk.

Olympia intended to save something, but it wasn't souls.

She turned the newspaper page, checked to see if they printed the Hutton Saddlery advertisement, and moved on to the social news of Harp.

WYOMING RANCHER CLAIMS HARP MISS AS BRIDE. The announcement in the newspaper declared that Grayson Steele had come to claim his bride, one Miss Olympia Hutton. Her father and Miss Hutton would be leaving Harp immediately to reside at the Steele ranch in Wyoming.

Olympia watched a Smithson stage roll by her window, the door freshly painted to conceal the Raven's best *R*. Five prime cows and a huge bull followed, herded by Grayson Steele. His hat tipped back on his head, Gray rode easily, his red bandanna tied around his throat and flying in the wind. He was clearly a Westerner, at home in the expensive tooled leather saddle he'd just purchased from her father. Gray shot a look directly at her shop, found her in the window, and lifted his hat in a flourish.

Olympia inhaled sharply and walked out onto the sidewalk. She motioned Gray to her, but he didn't budge. When he sat on his horse in the middle of the street, resting his arms across the saddle, she understood—Gray wanted her to come to him. The bull stopped and one cow went into a store, yet despite the commotion Gray sat on his Appaloosa mare and stared at her, his gaze shadowed by his hat.

Olympia would not be treated like one of the cows being herded down the street. She wouldn't be forced into anything; once he saw how determined and evil she could be, he wouldn't want her. She ran into the shop, picked up the nearest revolver, and shot his hat from his head. It tumbled onto the dusty street, the crowd chasing the cows came to watch, and still Gray didn't move.

On the sidewalks of Harp, betting began, and the professional gamblers came from the saloon.

"I did not agree to marry you, Grayson Steele!" she yelled at him. "You had no right to announce it to the world."

"So you decided to come out of your shop after holing up last night. You should have come to the hotel and helped Blue and me bake cookies." Gray glanced at the bull, who had leapt up onto the board sidewalk. The cattleman immediately twirled his rope, swung a loop that settled around the bull's neck, and tied the rope to his saddlehorn. He nudged his horse, tightening the rope, and the bull came off the sidewalk. Gray looked at Olympia. "You're scaring my new stock, Oly. I need that bull to better my herd. You keep yelling like that, and he won't sire any calves."

Olympia heard Martha Bates's hushed comment: "That giantess should be glad anyone wants her. She's a spinster and ill-mannered. He's quite a catch—wealthy and headed into politics. She'll ruin his chances for sure. He'll need a lady at his side. He has English manners, you know."

Red Ear Jones spat a stream of tobacco onto the street. "I hear Steele told the sheriff that the Raven was shot down in the canyon. He said he buried the body with the Raven's Bible on top of him. The flies and the heat weren't for leaving a body lying about. Guess that's why the Smithsons aren't worried about the next stage. At least the Raven repented and delivered back the goods before he met his Maker."

Gray eased his horse nearer Olympia, and for the first time Olympia understood fully what he wanted. His eyes locked with hers, narrowed, and his jaw clenched rhythmically. He wanted her to come to him, to choose him over anything she'd known and the safety she had created. A trickle of fear ran through her, but also an odd excitement. She decided to exit the field of honor, hurrying into her shop and closing the door.

Gray's bootsteps echoed closer on the board floors. He opened the door and slapped his ruined hat against his thigh. "You're not exactly sweet, Oly," he said grimly. "But you are a good shot. That will come in handy on the ranch. I've always admired a woman who can take care of herself and call it. Now, come kiss me with that fire I saw in your eyes a minute ago."

"Gray, you are purely thick-headed. I have no need of a thick-headed husband. I prefer a solitary life and am accustomed to this one."

"Our son won't want his mama leading a solitary life," he returned reasonably, tossing his ruined hat at a peg on the wall.

"I hate politics. Politicians are no more than legalized thieves."

He locked his boots to the floor and hooked his thumbs into his gunbelt. "I won't be. I'll do my best, and I'm honest. Just what don't you like about me, Oly?"

Olympia decided to retreat to the back of her shop, back to her workbench so recently emptied of her lead-covered gold balls. Gray had also removed the gold bricks she'd disguised, replacing the discarded old ones in the foundation. In a matter of one day he'd found her treasures, including the gold blade of the old saber and the jewels resting within the leather-bound handle.

"Am I going to get that damn kiss or not, Oly?" Gray demanded, his hands going on either side of her head, effectively corralling her, her back to the wall. "What don't you like about me, Oly?" he repeated softly, and again she sensed the deep pain moving within him.

She decided in favor of the kiss and flung her arms around his neck, pasting her mouth to his and watching his reaction with open eyes. His eyes crinkled at the sides, his lips gently pushed against hers. The tip of his tongue lightly prowled across her lips, the sensation causing her stomach to flutter. He moved his lips to the corner of her mouth and whispered, "You're delectable, sweetheart. Quite tasty."

Olympia shivered. His chest was warm and hard against her soft breasts. Because she needed to taste him, she smoothed the taut muscles at the back of his neck and slowly placed her lips on his again. She traced the hard contour of his mouth and rested her cheek against his.

Gray held very still. Tenderness lurked in him, and it needed tending. She met his gray eyes, seeking—

Gray slowly looked downward to where their bodies touched and her heart beat wildly, just above her bodice. Finally he looked back up into her eyes. "You'll have to marry me to have me, Miss Hutton," he whispered huskily.

He dropped a new wedding band between her breasts, fitted his lips to hers, and when the steamy kiss was done, bit her lip gently. He patted her bottom and whistled as he strolled out of her store. He chuckled when Sonny ran at him and began crawling his way up Gray's tall body. Sonny found his cookie, and Gray lifted the boy high on his shoulders, walking back to the hotel kitchen.

Olympia touched her lips, flicking her tongue to find the spot he had bitten. "I think you are in for a surprise, Mr. Cookie-Baking Steele," she whispered softly.

"You're handling this all wrong, brother. You're pushing her too hard. I saw that when she shot the hat off your head this morning. She could have plugged you right then, put a slug in the righteous male part of you," Blue stated as he braced his boot on the board sidewalk. They had just herded more new stock into a small corral outside of town. "Though after meeting your sweetheart I can see why you want her for a bride. She'll stand the weather, and she's not an eyesore either. I'm glad to help keep her pretty neck in one piece. It's only a matter of time before they find her. That shoe her buttermilk is wearing leaves an easily tracked trail."

"I didn't ask your opinion about Oly, but you're

right about tracking her. That's why you and I are going to reshoe her horse," Gray shot back and swung up on his horse, waiting for Blue to mount. "Do you want to look at those new horses with me or not? We may as well load up on stock while I'm on the marrying trail."

Blue tipped back his hat and placed his hands on his hips, locking his eyes with Gray's. "You skunk. You're acting rangy because you're missing her and you're wanting her to look at you the way every other female does. She won't. She's toughed it through with her father, and here you come, ruining her life. If you really wanted The Book you'd have it, but instead you just like her having a part of you with her. You can't just push the woman into marrying you. Yes, I'll be there."

"I'll give her a good life." Gray looked down the street to Olympia, who was striding toward him, her long legs causing her skirts to whip around her ankles. She wore an indigo-blue cotton dress and a gun belt low on her waist. Gray noted that the holstered Colt was placed slightly to the center, allowing for the neat curve of her hip. Her expression wasn't that of a loving bride to be. She hefted a small package in one hand, tossing it lightly up and down as she walked purposefully toward him.

Gray admired the fine sway of her hips, the proud line of her breasts, and the lift of her chin. She was perfect.

"Hello, Blue," she murmured pleasantly. "How nice to see you. I understand you've been doing some errands for your brother."

" 'Morning, Olympia. I was most pleased to help in his pursuit of you. However, should you want a better man, I'd be happy to oblige. You look prettier than the dew on the daisies." Blue swept off his hat in a gallant bow, and Gray scowled at him.

Olympia smiled briefly at Gray. He didn't like her look as she continued to heft the small package. She glanced out into the street, smiling at the gathering crowd, who were curious about their unlikely spinster and the man who had come to claim her. "I understand the Raven is dead, Gray," she tossed at him.

"Truly dead. Gray buried the galoot himself," Blue offered, with laughter in his tone. "Gray returned with the hat, the cape, and the eye patch. The scarlet feather must have gotten lost somewhere."

"How wonderful. We are all safe at last." Olympia's tone lacked sincerity. She tossed away the brown paper wrapper and held up a small book. "I am on my way to the newspaper to tell them that I cannot possibly marry Gray. This book is why. I did not know when I answered his ad that he was such an artist, and he did not indicate his interests during our yearlong correspondence."

Gray recognized the cover he'd had specially made for The Book. In Olympia's hands his book looked like a weapon.

When Gray swung down from his horse she rested her hand on the butt of her gun. "Or Grayson Steele can remove himself from my life. I have never wanted to ventilate anyone, but you are now a likely candidate."

Blue's hoot of laughter shot into the morning sunlight.

Gray braced one boot on the sidewalk and studied

Olympia. This was the woman he wanted, the one who would stick by him in the bad times, facing life with him.

She smiled coldly. "You'd be a laughingstock, Gray. You'd never make it in politics without someone bringing up your . . . uh . . . artwork."

"Gray has always been talented," Blue murmured after a chuckle.

Olympia's eyebrows rose, her blush rising slowly from her throat. "He appears to be quite knowledgeable."

"It's been a while, Oly. Maybe we could study The Book together. It could come back to me." He wanted her to know that he didn't try to collect women every day and that she was special. It surprised him, how much he wanted her to know that she would be prized and not added to a list of conquests. "I was a boy when I made that book. I'm not tasting every ready wildflower now. I've got a good eye for what I want, and it happens to be an ill-mannered, bossy woman. You have ruined me for a good woman."

Her expression rigid and defiant, Olympia tapped the small book against her palm. "I'd say we're at a standoff, Gray. For I do not intend to be blackmailed into an association with a snake who takes advantage of innocent women."

Gray stared at her, locked in his thoughts. Olympia was likely to be a virgin, and the thought terrified him—he didn't want to hurt her. He intended to be very careful with her; he'd lead her slowly, surely into pleasure. He wondered if he touched the white lace at her throat, bent to kiss her there, what she would do. Gray hooked his thumbs into his belt and leaned against the wall, staring at her. If he hadn't gripped his gun belt he would have reached for her, kissed her silly, and taken her to a place where he could love her as he wanted.

He wondered then if he could wait until marriage gave him rights to Olympia's ripe body. Olympia glared at him, and he knew it was more than her body that fascinated and delighted him. She raised an excitement in him that he hadn't known could exist. She made him slightly light-headed with desire, and yet . . . there was more. There was a quietness within him, a certain calm that told him Olympia suited him, that she was right. He decided to share his thought with her. "Oly, I know a good she-cow when I see one. One that will make it through bad winters and drought and will not be stampeded with the first foul weather or sign of coyotes."

Blue snickered while Olympia gaped. "Are you saying that I am a piece of livestock, Grayson Sinjin Steele?"

He tipped his hat back on his head and crossed his arms. When she looked at him with those narrowed blue-fire eyes, he just had to grin. "You'll do."

Not even the cattleman who had just dismounted could distract Gray. "When your dander is up, heart of my heart, your eyes turn a magnificent blue," he drawled and enjoyed the heat moving into her cheeks. "Is that your final word, Miss Hutton? That you are reluctant to be my beloved bride?"

"I do believe it is my final word," she returned firmly, not giving an inch.

The older man leaned against the store wall, one boot braced back against it. Gray flicked him an impatient glance, and the man, his hair touched with gray, nodded just once.

Gray didn't like the amusement crinkling the sides of the man's tanned face. "Dad, may I present my future wife, the charming and mule-headed Olympia Hutton. I call her Oly. Oly, this is Morris Steele, my father. He's been helping Blue with a little repayment chore."

Olympia smiled tightly. "Mr. Steele, I am not marrying Gray."

"She adores me. It's just a matter of time," Gray stated coolly.

"He's scared her, Dad," Blue offered, grinning at Gray. "He's been pushing her around, just like he does when he wants something badly. She doesn't like it. We'll never get a woman between us at this rate. My fiancée has just dropped me by telegraph, and I'm in the market again."

"Oly, dear heart. My life is in your hands. The Book is yours to do with what you will," Gray said, meaning it. "My fate is yours."

Olympia continued to slap The Book against her palm, her eyes narrowed at him. "I do not wish to be pursued," she stated evenly.

"I am afraid I cannot grant your wish," Gray returned, allowing his gaze to travel slowly down her body and back up to her flushed face. Their eyes locked and held.

She tapped The Book with one finger. "You'll be sorry, Gray."

"I await your pleasure, ma'am. Truly I do." Gray allowed his slow drawl to indicate which pleasure he awaited.

"Well, at least she's not running after him like half

the women in the West. I had a notion this would happen one day." The elder Steele moved gracefully away from the wall and lifted his hat from his head. "Miss Hutton, I'd be honored if you'd have dinner with me. Boys, I'll see you later," he said as Olympia nodded and took his arm.

She shot a dark look at Gray over her shoulder.

"I'm afraid Gray is determined to have you, Olympia," Morris Steele said as he pushed back his empty plate. "It might help if you understood a bit more about him."

Shadows stirred in Morris's gray eyes as he continued, "No matter how much I tried, my English wife never liked the West. When Gray was only six she took him to England with her, and left Blue, just four years old, with me. I didn't see Gray again until he was almost twenty. He came back to Wyoming with a coat of ice around his heart. He didn't trust women by then, and I learned that she'd locked my boy in closets. My wife—we're still married—is a cold woman."

Olympia remembered her mother—a tall woman, always ready with a laugh, a hug, and a kiss. When Olympia was eight pneumonia had taken her mother, and her father had almost died of heartbreak.

"She hurt him," Morris continued as the waitress poured another cup of coffee. "I was afraid that he'd never trust a woman again—but now it seems he trusts you, or he wouldn't want to marry you."

Olympia thought of how she wanted to use The Book to blackmail Gray into freeing her.

"Gray has a good chance in politics. He'd be good

for the country." Morris sipped his coffee. "I'd like
to see my boy make a difference. There's not a thing
that can stop him now."

If Olympia exposed Gray as the artist of The
Book, she could destroy him. She had tasted a
mother's love and was confident with it, while
Gray's life had lacked that warmth. Olympia
wouldn't prove that all women had hearts of brass
and coal, and she wouldn't hurt him more. She
would return The Book to Gray.

"Nothing can stop Gray now," she repeated with
a smile.

At midnight Olympia eased around a chimney,
leapt over a roof, and stepped out onto a ledge. She
paused to watch Teddy Smithson, Tom Davidson,
and George Blue Hair ride into the moonlit, quiet
street. Teddy had been keeping his friendship with
the two rough men very quiet.

She'd barricaded herself in her room after dinner.
At midnight the Steeles were still in the Red Dog
Saloon with other cattlemen, discussing the first cattle rustling event in years. Her father was asleep, and
the perfect time to return The Book spread before
her. She liked to move in the light rain and the
night, on a mission to protect Gray from further
harm.

She did not want Gray in on her plan to ruin the
Smithsons, nor did she want to ruin Gray's chances
at politics.

Olympia eased Gray's hotel window open and
stepped into the darkened room. She understood
now why a part of Gray seemed to be missing, and
she mourned for the child that had not been shown

love. According to Morris, the teenage Gray had looked for attention and love in older women; The Book was a monument to the hours spent loving. Olympia swallowed and pushed away the memory of Gray's experienced lips, his hands stroking her until she melted. She inhaled; she would not damage him further. A few short steps took her to his neatly made bed, where she placed The Book upon his pillow.

She glanced around the room again. It wasn't neat—it was cold, as cold as Gray's life had been.

His new cattle had been stolen, the Raven had robbed and slashed another *R* on the Smithsons' stage door, and Olympia had just said, "Yes, Gray, I will marry you" in the same tone she used when completing a sale. "All we have to do is work out the terms."

Terms. He remembered his mother bargaining with his father. Elizabeth Steele had been cold, calculating, but ingenious about getting her freedom and a healthy American allowance. She'd left her son no illusions about his father, and Gray had always been angry with his father. As Gray grew older that anger softened, and now he remembered his father crying late one night. Gray had promised himself that no woman would do that to him. He now understood how much power a woman had over a man. He did not like it.

"Why are you making this so easy—marriage to me?" he asked flatly, disliking the ease with which Olympia could put him off balance and rattle his control.

Olympia stopped fitting a rosewood handle onto

the butt of a Colt revolver. She leveled a look at him before delicately selecting the right screws from a box. "You've gotten yourself out on a limb, Gray. You've told the whole territory that we're getting married. We barely know each other, and by now the news is spreading like wildfire. In short, I can either look like an idiot, a spinster, trying to escape a big strong man—the idea! I wouldn't try to escape, I'd just shoot you in a very important place. Or I can help you out of your predicament, save your questionable honor, and marry you. It's a favor, nothing more. I just want to lay out the terms before the ceremony, so there will be no confusion later. If you meet my terms I do not see where we have a problem. You would have the option at any time, of course, to withdraw."

Her eyes suddenly shifted, and Gray traced the fine color rising up her cheeks. He spoke carefully. "Let me get this straight. You are rescuing me and my pride. I've made a fool out of myself, and only you can clean up the cowpile, right?"

She squinted one eye, lifting the revolver to look down the sights. "Mmm, something like that. You are mule-headed and probably too old to change. They are saying you lied, Gray, when you said that the Raven is dead and that you buried him."

Gray propped his boot on a scarred wooden chair and his forearms rested on his knee. Olympia's keen mind had carefully dissected the facts. He was furious that he couldn't trust her, that the instant he was too busy to watch her she'd managed to steal his herd, waylay the stage, and carve another damn *R*. "You look very rested for someone who spent the night robbing the countryside. Priscilla Smithson is missing her best jewels."

When he dropped that tidbit she inhaled sharply, her hand going to her throat. He didn't like the fine anger only this woman could raise within him. He didn't like the pain of betrayal tearing wildly through him. "You were not in your room last night. I climbed up the tree by your window. I'd had a little to drink and brought you a bouquet. Your father does not like my singing," he added stiffly. "He called it bellowing."

She looked at him, her eyes wide in her pale face. "Gray, I did not steal one thing last night. . . . Well, except a small stalk of lily of the valley from Miss Ellie's garden. It was raining slightly, and the moonlight caught the drops on the tiny white bells. They looked like diamonds and I—"

"You've never lied to me, Olympia. Don't start now. Your mare's prints are all over the cattle tracks and where the stagecoach was held up. The *R* wasn't your usual flourish, but it served the purpose. We're getting married now, and I'm getting you out of here. Two of us will stay to clean up the mess and then bring your father to you. You can have your pick of who takes you back to Wyoming—Dad, Blue, or me."

Gray waited while Olympia's lips parted then closed several times. It was insane, he knew—she'd betrayed his trust, made him look like a fool, and threatened him. She wanted marriage terms, and yet he desperately wanted her to choose him. "Which one—Dad, Blue, or me?"

His heart began to beat again only when Olympia

placed her hand on his chest, looked at him with huge, soft, misting eyes, and whispered, "You."

"We'll get married at noon today," Gray said before he turned and walked away without a backward look. He felt as if he were in pieces.

His new bride sat on her camp bedding, her arms circling her legs, her chin resting on her knees. She was dressed in her best blue Sunday dress, still holding the bouquet of wildflowers and lilies of the valley that Blue had given her. Gray crouched by the campfire, mulling over his guilt. He'd promised he'd give her what she needed, and that wasn't a bedroll on their wedding night.

He was right about one thing: It was only a matter of time before someone discovered the Raven's identity. He had to get Olympia to safety—where she couldn't steal anything.

She should have complained about the rough camp; brides should spend their wedding night in fine hotels. At the church Olympia did not blink when she saw the saddled horses, but said, "You won't like my cooking. It's worse on the trail."

The townspeople understood why Gray, a cattleman, wanted to rush the wedding, why he had to return to tending his sprawling ranch. Others said that he'd been caught in a lie, that the Raven was still thieving, and that Gray wanted to get to safety. At the church his father had been too quiet, taking Olympia in his arms and holding her. He had whispered something to her, and Olympia had glanced at Gray with a small, timid smile. Blue had offered to teach Gray manners when needed and kissed Olympia long and hard, bending her over his arm.

To Gray's disgust, Olympia had flung her arms around Blue and held tight. When Gray had tugged her away, she staggered, sighed, and swooned in his arms. "Blue kisses wonderfully," Olympia had murmured, smiling hopefully at Gray.

"There will be no more of that, and I'm better," he had said curtly.

"Mmm, that remains to be seen, doesn't it?" she asked, setting him off balance once again with a slanted look and a flick of her tongue across her lips.

Her father sat, holding his hat, and staring at the church floor. Gray took one look at Olympia's silent plea and took her hand. "Sir, we'd be pleased if you'd live with us. Oly is good at her trade and so are you. You'd be a welcome addition to Wyoming."

Olympia had inhaled sharply, and Gray glanced down to find her eyes bright with tears and her expression adoring him. He felt like a giant and powerful enough to fly.

Still . . . he'd forced her to marry him. He was a snake.

Now the firelight flickered over Olympia's face and Gray glanced at her. Coyotes howled on the mountain as she met his look. "I did not rustle those cattle and I did not steal the Smithson jewels. Nor did I carve an *R* on the stage, as much as I would have liked to."

"You married me. That confirms your guilt." Disturbed by his uncertainty, Gray didn't welcome the tenderness Olympia dragged from him. She should have a wedding night in a roadhouse or a fine hotel, not a rugged campsite along a rocky mountain trail.

Olympia looked at the new gold band on her finger, toyed with it. "I married you because I wanted you, Gray. Nothing else could have made me."

At the wedding, she'd looked at him as though she adored him, her expression glowing. "You've got that backward, haven't you, dear heart? I wanted you and the son you could give me, and now I have you." Gray ripped The Book from his saddlebags. "I'm going to get rid of this."

4

"Stop! Don't you dare!" Olympia moved suddenly. She grabbed Gray's hand as he began to rip a page from The Book. Gray acted instinctively; he caught her in one arm and fell backward into the bedding he had spread.

She rested upon him and trailed a fingertip across his lips. "I have you now, Gray. Admit it. Admit that I wanted you, and now I have you. You said I couldn't have you unless I married you, and because I'm a sensible woman and know a good bargain, I did claim you. I intend to have you tonight, Gray, in all the positions described in the book."

At the wedding Olympia had looked at him as though she wanted to taste him. Her gaze had run from the top of his head to his boots, as though she was deciding where to start. . . .

While Gray's mind dealt with Olympia's statement, his body responded immediately.

She lowered her lips to his and kissed him lightly.

Experimenting with his taste, she opened her lips, the tip of her tongue delicately flicking at him. "I noticed in your watercolors the most delicate shade of pink as the couple progressed—as though they were getting very warm. Does that really happen? The heat that I saw in your drawings? Do you think a woman can actually—"

Olympia swallowed and closed her eyes. She pushed her tongue into Gray's mouth; he realized her fingers were fumbling downward and her hand sought him intimately.

"Oly, what are you doing?" he demanded, stilling her hand with his own over his hardness.

She lifted from him, gathered her skirts around her, and sat, looking into the fire. "You see? Men do not want to be touched there. You told me to open my lips and I just did. And what did you do? You acted frightened. You actually shivered and groaned with fear. You are a hoax, Gray, and an innocent. You cannot even kiss as well as Blue. There were times I had hopes for you, when I saw the beauty of your work and the heavenly look upon the woman's face. It was all your imagination. You probably don't know a thing more than I do. Blue and your father say that you haven't been interested in a woman in years. How can I—who has never experienced the summit of desire, and Edna Watkins told me there is one if the woman can participate—actually teach you anything if I don't have the book?"

"Edna Watkins?"

"A woman who has had several affairs and has her gun cleaned regularly. She told me when she read that we were getting married." Olympia's face flushed in the firelight. "She thought that you . . .

uh . . . might be able to raise my interest and said that you had the look of a man who enjoyed a woman's . . . uh . . . contribution."

Gray lay very still as an owl hooted and the moonlight skipped through the pine trees over him. Olympia's tone had shocked him. She let out a long wail of frustration that frightened the horses, tethered to the trees. "Why do I always have to do everything by myself?"

Gray struggled to recover and shook his head to clear it. "Oly, dear heart. Do I understand that you are well warmed and ready for me?"

She continued to look at the fire, shrugged, and then threw up her hands. "Just how would I know? It's a fairy tale then, your drawings in the book. I am a bride, you know," she stated, pointing out her new status.

Gray struggled with his frustration and the fact that Olympia was still delectable despite her thieving ways. "Well, it isn't quite a fairy tale. But it might be a nice bedtime story to read tonight."

Olympia shrugged carelessly, her illusions shattered. She looked so forlorn and desirable, continuing to shake her head at the myth he had just destroyed.

"I think I could manage something," Gray offered, smoothing the long line of her back. He began to unbutton her dress.

She looked over her shoulder. "I still care for you, whether you can . . . uh . . . perform or not. You've been wonderful with my father and quite the picture of a man on a horse. You are a good cook and you can mend. You don't seem intimidated when I yell at you, and it is important to me that you recognize my craftsmanship, and you're not at all bothered that I am a woman in business. Oh, look at that!" she exclaimed as Gray opened The Book.

The firelight flickered over the naked images on the paper. It was an exotic pose, the bodies spooned together, both on their knees.

He captured her pointing finger and drew it to his lips for a kiss. "Oly, this is a working-up matter. That is, there is a start and a middle and a finish. Or so I understand."

Olympia studied him as he sucked one finger, then the rest, slowly. When he opened her hand to kiss her palm, she inhaled. "I trust you, Gray. In some ways you are still Mr. Sinjin, a sweet innocent. You have always handled me very gently, and I find that . . . endearing. I have not always wanted to handle you gently." She peered down at the first picture in the book. "The women are all so . . . round. He's kissing her bosom. She looks . . . she looks as if she's just had a revelation of joy. He looks almost pained—"

"I'll try, Oly." Gray eased Olympia's dress from her shoulders, kissing the smooth skin and lightly flicking it with his tongue. He tugged a bit when she resisted and shivered when he saw the rise of her breasts in the moonlight.

She inhaled deeply and bent over to study the picture. Gray nuzzled her softness and prayed that he could go slowly. He gently cradled one lovely breast in his hand and eased the camisole straps away, leaving her in her tight corset. Olympia hurriedly opened the corset, stood, and wiggled free of it and her dress and petticoats, leaving her standing in her drawers. She sank gracefully down next to him on the blanket. "What's next?"

Gray listened to the roar of desire pounding at his head and other places. He forced himself to say evenly, "I believe I put my lips just there."

Her flesh was smooth and fragrant and flushed. Mine, and made for me, Gray thought wildly, his desire singing through him. He kissed the tip of one breast and Olympia cried out with surprise, her body shivering. "Do it again, Gray."

This time he suckled gently and Olympia stiffened, her body flowing rhythmically against his mouth. "Oh, Gray, even if you can't do more than this . . . this is delightful."

She beamed at him and slowly unbuttoned his shirt, running her fingers through the hair on his chest. "Let me do that to you."

She peeled back the shirt, hesitated, and trailed her fingers down the line of hair leading to his belt buckle; she began to unbuckle it. Gray gripped her hands. Another minute of her fumbling and he'd— "What are you doing, dear heart?"

"Why I'd like to see you, of course. I've never seen a man in the altogether, and after all I did marry you to have you. I'm not like most women, I suppose. As a gunsmith I like and respect fine equipment, and I've always been a good judge of horses. That, and I like you and you don't bore me." She looked into Gray's eyes and smiled softly. "I will respect you, dear heart. You won't regret letting me look at you. I know that it is a lot to ask of you."

Gray groaned and released her hands. "If you must."

"Thank you, Gray. I do appreciate your satisfying

my curiosity." She bent to kiss him and her soft, bare breast gently dragged his chest.

He groaned, raging with the need to bury himself in his new bride, to let the soft, fragrant folds—he settled for placing his hand on her thigh. "Go ahead. Look," he whispered when he could manage to breathe. He hoped he was up to Olympia's standards for fine equipment.

"Won't be a minute," Olympia whispered back, fumbling more with his pants.

The cool night air helped restore some of Gray's control—until Olympia's fingers touched him lightly, exploring him. "Goodness," was all she said in a rush of breath. "It won't work. I've judged enough guns to know about suitable holsters. You were wrong, Gray. It is a fairy tale." And then she began to cry.

Gray, his shirt undone, his anatomy standing proud beneath the night sky, stared up at the stars and shook his head. He took her hand and placed it on his chest. Olympia turned to look at him, her fingers smoothing his skin. "Your heart is racing, Gray. Is it so awful? Have I frightened you so much?"

"You have beautiful breasts," he whispered finally, urging her closer to him and kissing the smooth sweep of her jaw, her throat, and then suckling her breast gently.

Her fingertips latched on to his arms and she gasped, writhing against him with each tug. "At least that part is true."

He nibbled gently, flicking her with his tongue. "You are delicious."

"I am? Oh, Gray, this is so wonderful. What's the next drawing?"

"Uh . . . Oly, I think she has her hands on him. Smoothing his shoulders."

"Oh, yes!" Olympia stiffened suddenly as Gray's fingers found her inner thigh, pushing gently against the cloth covering her. He almost groaned when the dampness rushed to meet his fingers. She looked down at the book and traced the exact position of the man's hand. "Yes, you are right. That is—"

She stood up and jerked down her drawers; she sat quickly to take off her stockings and shoes. "They aren't wearing a stitch," she explained to Gray as she resettled, sitting back against him, arranging his hands on her as they were before.

The scent of her mixed with the flowers and the night almost caused him to grab her. A bare leash of control tethered him—Olympia deserved to be handled gently.

"They are reclining, dear heart—see?" Gray waited for her to examine the book. She flipped several pages to the back and said, "Let's do this, Gray. It looks a lot more active. I can do that. She is sitting astride—do you really think women do that?"

He was all too ready, but the woman he wanted to claim gently, carefully, was not. "I feel the need to do this by The Book, step by step."

"Yes, of course," Olympia returned thoughtfully after a moment. "You are a very methodical man, I've noticed. As a gunsmith I respect your precision. Perhaps it would make you feel better to proceed at your own slow pace. Why are you groaning? Are you dreading the event? Are you in pain? Tell me everything." She placed his hand over the nest of

curls between her legs. "I feel very . . . very warm
and damp."

"I am not always methodical. Maybe we can
hurry through the pages at a pace that pleases you."
This time, it was Gray who stood up and ripped off
his clothes, discarding them. He sank back to the
blanket, pleased that Olympia seemed delighted with
him. "What's next?"

She patted his bare knee and her fingers slowly
wandered up his thigh, squeezing gently. "You're
not that stiff and unyielding. You're considerate in
spite of yourself, and if you can just manage to make
it through a few more pages, I'll let you sleep."

Gray's body was truly stiff and unyielding, and he
realized that he had never cared so deeply for a
woman, never enough to indulge her whims or to
treasure her.

Olympia shot an assessing look at his body. "Look
at that page. See how he's lying on top of her. You
don't look that heavy. Let's do that one."

Gray settled on top of her and Olympia wiggled
beneath him, getting comfortable. "You're very
hard, dear one," she whispered as Gray nudged her
legs apart.

He looked at her beneath him, her hands smoothing him, her expression one of trust and of softness.

He treasured her. She had put herself in his hands,
trusting him despite his rustling of her life. She responded to his every touch, pleasing him.

"Oly . . ." He wanted to give her something
tender to cling to, to know that he cared for her at
this moment.

She lifted suddenly, barely catching him in the

soft, damp folds of her body. "Kiss me. Open your lips and kiss me, Gray."

Stormed by his emotions, those of tenderness and desire and the need to open his heart to her, Gray lowered his head.

He'd hurt her, Olympia realized distantly, her body clenching with pain. Something had just torn within her, rendered apart by Gray, by the man she had chosen to love.

He was a part of her now, unfamiliar and strong where she was soft, his mouth fusing with hers, taking her higher. His hands were strong upon her, smoothing, gentle, easing her hips away and then closer as he went deeper and away and deeper yet, and she held him tightly.

She would not release him to his cold life, to his disillusions about ties of the heart.

He was hers to tend, moving swiftly over her, delighting her, as the center of the storm grew hot and focused. The pleasure came rushing at her as he let out a shout and thrust deeply within her.

Waves of heat and ultimate pleasure crashed upon her, sucked her slowly into a warm cushion as her body throbbed, clenched around him. Circles of pleasure washed through her, replacing the fierce desperation to reach the height of her desire.

She floated, easing downward, like a feather floating from a soaring bird that had tossed itself against a tropical storm. Gray lay wasted upon her, no longer fierce and demanding and meeting her desperation, but a gentle, sharing companion. His head rested on her breasts, kissing them gently as she surfaced, smoothing his hair. He eased the pins from her hair, stroking her scalp in the way that sent her arching slowly against his hand. Then Gray gathered her closer, tugged the heavy quilt up and around them, and held her tight.

She was where she wanted to be, held close to Gray's heart, listening to the heavy thudding of it as it slowed beneath her cheek.

Twice in the night she awoke to Gray's lips upon hers, upon her breasts; she awoke to delight that rose into waves of pleasure, each more beautiful than before.

In the predawn light a fully dressed Gray sipped his morning coffee and watched Olympia sleep. They would soon be in his bed at the ranch. A fine mist layered the glade, settling on the sumac and dripping steadily to the ground. Strands of Olympia's hair flowed across the bedding they had shared, gleaming in the firelight. Her face seemed too pale, shadows beneath her black lashes. A bare shoulder escaped the blanket, and Gray quietly covered her.

Her breath warmed his skin, and Gray's heart leapt. He eased back to sit near her, unwilling to leave her side and yet certain that if he lay with her, he would once again make love to her. *Who was she, this woman he'd caught, forced to marry him?*

He rubbed the stubble on his jaw and counted the few minutes he'd had to sleep after each sizzling encounter. Something was wrong—he wasn't certain if he'd taken his bride, or if she'd claimed him. He intended to lay down the rules for their marriage last night and had instead been caught by her innocence and enthusiasm. She'd frightened him, Gray realized slowly, darkly—he who had fought desperadoes, Indian wars, killed bears with only his knife, and who knew how to handle himself in the most vicious of elegant-parlor tongue fights.

He, who had never worried about the consequences of loving, was in awe of his stirring, tender emotions.

Olympia delighted him; she frightened him.

Her lashes fluttered and she arched slowly, a long line of curves, a creamy breast escaping the blanket. Gray forced himself to swallow the sip he had just taken as Olympia wiggled her bottom, getting more comfortable. He smiled when she sniffed delicately, her eyes closed, catching the aroma of coffee and sizzling bacon.

When she finally opened her eyes after moments of squirming and yawning and stretching, Gray was astonished by his need—he who had promised never to need any woman so desperately.

"You're looking dark and evil this morning," Olympia stated pleasantly and squirmed again, gathering the quilt up to her breasts and wrapping it around her shoulders. "In a bad mood, Gray?"

She should have had clean sheets and a morning bath waiting for her. He should have given a wedding gift to his bride. He'd set out to demonstrate his power over her so that she would obey him and he in turn would spare her no luxuries, or his time, or his heart. She intrigued him, fascinated him, and what he had planned—his rules for their marriage—was slowly crumbling beneath his feet.

After just one night of his bride, he wanted the best for her, including a proper husband. He wasn't certain of the cold spot in his heart, or how much he could give his wife.

Olympia watched him, her hair gleaming, web-
bing around her pale shoulders, slashes of raven
against her pale skin. He frowned at the small patches
beside her mouth and marring her throat, and he
knew that his new beard had scratched her. He
should have taken time to shave, but she'd taken him
into desire, fascinated him until he was careless.

She flushed and pushed her hair back, glaring at
him. "I know. You don't have to sit there glaring at
me. I'm a mess. I should have braided my hair. But I
won't take all the blame. You certainly had your way
with it."

Gray fought the smile growing in him. He'd rev-
eled in the rich scents and silky texture flowing
around him—she needed blue ribbons to bring out
the sky color of her eyes.

Daft, he thought darkly. *I'm half-drunk just looking
at her.*

He asked the question that had bothered him.
"Why did you steal, Olympia?"

She began to braid her hair loosely and sniffed
delicately. "I'm starved. One of the things that I like
about you, Gray, is your cooking. You always add a
little something special, and you do it with such a
flourish."

She glanced at a covered skillet propped on a rock
and reached for the lid. She plucked a biscuit, and
because it was hot, tossed it from one hand to another. "Mmm, biscuits. I just knew you'd cook
something special."

"Trail biscuits, nothing more," he muttered, dis-
armed at her pleasure. She acted as though he were
serving her crepes in a Parisian bedroom.

"Mmm." The butter she had slathered on his biscuits ran down her hand, and when she sucked her fingers a sharp pain of desire shot through Gray.

She glanced at him as she munched on the biscuit. "Revenge was one reason that I entered the grand state of outlawing. You know how the Smithsons discarded my father." Olympia hesitated and looked at him, the mist and smoke swirling around their camp. "I have not stolen anything, including cattle, since your discovery of my . . . hobby. I was returning The Book when you came singing at my window."

"Outlawing wasn't always a hobby, was it?" he asked, and already knew the answer.

Olympia's expression turned bleak and hard as she looked into the fire. "No. We had to eat, and my father was having a bad time. Later, when I managed to buy the shop and stock a few . . . uh . . . remodeled firearms, and when we had food on the table, I knew I had to ruin the Smithsons. Teddy never kissed me, by the way. I didn't like how he handled guns, and I'm certain he couldn't cook. So you're a better bargain. I heard once that he had hurt a child, bullied a woman, and you would never do that. You love children—I've seen you follow them with your eyes and know that you would treat them well. If you want a son I will do my best to give you one. I will do my best to fight roaming at night when the restlessness comes upon me."

Brilliant with defiance, her gaze swung to him. "You had a right to the truth. I don't regret anything. In fact, I enjoyed it. I mean it when I say that there's a certain restlessness that comes over me at night—"

"There is that," Gray said firmly, his body recall-
ing instantly the lovemaking between them.

"You consider me to be indelicate, don't you? A
woman eager for a man's body?" She looked at him,
appraisingly. "You are a fine mechanism, Gray. A
rather quick trigger fitting well in the hand. You
were there when I needed you, supplying—well,
never mind what you supplied. You seemed well
primed, and I've always appreciated—"

He remembered her patting his bottom as he lay
over her and murmuring drowsily about his "fine
equipment." He had the gravest suspicion that
Olympia had married him for himself and not for his
money or his blackmail. Gray dragged Olympia,
blanket and all, onto his lap. "Who are you?" he
asked, more uncertain of himself and his tender
emotions for Olympia. "Why did you give back The
Book?"

Olympia curled up in his arms, smoothing his
cheek with her hand. "Dear heart, I could not bear
for you to be hurt again. Aren't I heavy?"

Gray sat very still, uneasy with the emotions tan-
gling within him. He refused to be distracted. "You
sacrificed yourself for me, is that it?" he asked
tightly, disgusted that Olympia had seen his weak-
nesses: his desire for her and his tenderness. He
checked his outrage and found it seething. "You felt
sorry for me?"

Gray stood up and Olympia rolled to the ground,
tangled in the blanket. Gray braced his legs apart,
placed his hands on his hips, and looked down at her
as if he didn't know what to do with her. "Do you
have any more revelations you might want to share
with me?"

★ ★ ★

Back in Harp in her upstairs apartment over the gun shop, Olympia brooded. It was only hours since Gray had dumped her from his lap and one hour until the Founder's Day Ball would begin. In the hours between, she'd been pushed and prodded and tortured.

She shouldn't have gotten angry, just after the beauty of making love to Gray. But he'd dumped her on the ground after holding her so beautifully. She shouldn't have said she'd never danced and that if he wasn't such an uppity, mean-tempered jackass, she would be going to the Harp Founders' Day Ball that night. She shouldn't have said that she'd counted on sweet Mr. Sinjin to take her to her first dance and now her chances were gone.

It was too late now, for Gray had his determined look and was set upon torturing her, making her attend the ball. He'd dragged her back to her bedroom and had set upon her as if fashioning a lump of clay into Venus, all within a day. He was relentless, shampooing her hair and smearing a concoction of oatmeal, honey, and raw egg on her face. Then he slapped a warm towel on her face while he oiled her body. He'd touched her in such a businesslike way that Olympia fought crying.

"What's wrong, Oly?" Gray had asked gently, peering down at her.

Tears burned at her lids, spilling over onto her cheeks. "It's all over, isn't it, Gray? You've had your—our pleasure and now it will never happen again."

"Won't it?" he'd asked with enough leering in his tone to lift her spirits. He'd held her breasts within his hands and caressed them, then licked the scented oil from her skin. He'd spoken unevenly, his deep voice caressing her in French, and Olympia knew that she would have him again. She'd picked through the phrases surrounding *adore* and *ma belle* and *chérie,* and hoped he meant her.

Now, only an hour before the ball, she closed her eyes and held on to the bedpost while Gray grimly pulled the corset laces tighter. She glanced at the array of evening gowns, fans, petticoats, and shoes strewn across their bedroom over the shop. She gasped as he jerked the corset tighter. "Go ahead, torture me. I will not do it. You cannot force me to."

Gray dropped a gown over her head, tugging it down around her. "Think of it as a masquerade. You've done that before, haven't you? Placed a pillow around you, draped yourself in a cloak and a hat and an eye patch, and gone out for your revenge. This is just the same thing."

Olympia kicked at the brilliant blue gown while Gray adjusted the cloth over her bustle. "I really don't like being fussed over, and I don't know how to act at a ball."

"This morning you said you'd never been to a ball and you didn't know how to dance. You said you were counting on your first experience with Sinjin. Well, you're about to have it." Gray began buttoning the tiny buttons at her back. "You're going to the ball and you're dancing. I want everyone to know exactly where you are and that you belong to me and that you couldn't be happier."

"I don't like having Blue and your father waiting on me hand and foot—" Olympia stopped to look at her new husband. With his shirt unbuttoned and his tanned chest exposed, he was tempting. A wave of heat washed over her as she studied him closely. Gray wore suspenders, but not like Mr. Sinjin's. They emphasized his shoulders and his narrow waist. She reached out to touch his chest, to place her splayed fingers exactly on the tanned wedge of his bare skin that was exposed by his open shirt. She wiggled her fingers in the crisp hair. Gray was much better-looking than the man in his drawings.

He hadn't said a word about the missing herd or the robbery. Did he trust her? Did he believe her?

His mother had given Gray no reason to trust any woman.

But Olympia promised that she would never hurt him.

From the front, Gray snorted, and reached around her to expertly adjust her bustle. "My brother and father like decking you out. Blue owes me, and my father hasn't had a daughter. He's enjoying himself."

"He didn't have to press this gown and haul buckets of water upstairs for my bath. Blue didn't have to telegraph dress shops all over the territory and hire riders to bring these gowns." Olympia placed her hands on her waist as Gray moved around her, dressed in an elegant frilled shirt and trim black pants. He studied his creation like an artist, and she knew that she would let him down. "I don't have the slightest idea about making delicate female conversation. You know how blunt-spoken I am—Gray, do you believe I stole your herd and robbed the stagecoach?"

She needed to understand how he could make

exquisite love to her and then believe she was guilty. Her heart stopped as she waited for him to answer.

Gray leaned close to steal a kiss. His fingertip roamed across her breasts, which leapt to his touch. His eyes, a smoky gray, darkened with a look that made her shiver. She'd never forget him rising above her, firelight flickering on his taut expression as he claimed her.

She bit his lip, gently, not enough to hurt him. "Right now I could kill you. You've been in an evil mood ever since this morning. You've barely said a word to me, except to order me to do this or that or to take a nap. I could tell you didn't want to discuss any more sessions with The Book."

"I'm taking care of my well-primed machinery, dear heart."

"Gray?" Olympia stood in her finery, her new husband busily adjusting silk and satin around her. She knew she'd fail him. She had offended him somehow, and he wasn't making things easy. "Go ahead, torture me. I'm taller than any woman in Harp, and I'll be looking down at any man who dances with me. They'll be looking right into my bosom. Make me go to the ball and dance until my feet fall off. These slippers aren't comfortable at all."

"I intend to do just that, Oly."

"So you don't mind then, that men will be ogling my bosom."

"It's a fine bosom," Gray stated firmly, and for a moment the softness was in his deep voice, and the lover of her wedding night returned to her. She fell into the tenderness of his eyes.

"Is she decent?" Blue knocked at the door.

Blue came into the room, dressed in a frilled shirt, dress pants, and suspenders like Gray's. Blue's big hands and his pockets were filled with ribbons of every color. "Which one—"

He stopped and blinked when he saw Olympia scowling at him. "Dad, come up here," Gray called.

Morris and Olympia's father came into the room and stared blankly at Olympia, who was not far from tears. She stood there, looking delicious and petulant—and like a sheep about to be led to slaughter.

Gray would teach her to sacrifice herself for him. He'd teach her to challenge the artist of The Book.

When her bottom lip trembled and she looked uncertainly at him, Gray relented. "I think you are the best thing that has ever happened to me, dear heart," he said, meaning it.

"You villain," she muttered.

"My wife, Mrs. Olympia Hutton Steele," Gray announced grandly, and took her hand to twirl her around. Blue took her hand, twirled her again, and then Morris gave her a kiss on the cheek.

"I'll get all of you," Olympia threatened when she could talk. But the tears in her father's eyes told her that he was happy, and that was something she hadn't seen in years. "You'll dance with me, won't you, Dad?" she asked, desperate for his safety, for the arms that had comforted her when she was a child.

For just a heartbeat she saw Gray's concealed expression—she'd hurt him again.

How could Gray do this to her? How could he bring her to the ball and then not dance with her, leaving her to the other males of the party? As they waltzed, Olympia smiled at Morris Steele and for-

gave him for being Gray's father. "You're a wonderful teacher, Morris. I don't know why Gray is
making so much of this. He's been evil-tempered
and on edge, glaring at me." She decided not to tell
Gray's father what she had tried, following the ex-
amples of The Book.

She studied Gray as he talked with Libby Wash-
ington, his head tilted intimately toward her blond
curled one. Libby knew how to slant her face, flutter
her lashes, and flirt, skills that Olympia did not possess. At the moment Gray seemed enchanted with
Libby, but no more than he did most of the women
at the ball—everyone but his wife.

"He's protecting you," Morris stated as they
swirled around the room. "The Smithsons have
hired a top gunhand with a nose like a blood-
hound's. He's been checking the horses at the livery,
looking at their shoes. That's why we reshod your
buttermilk mare ourselves and buried the shoes.
Gray wants to dig out the real outlaw and save your
pretty neck. Meanwhile, he wants you in plain sight
during a moment when the Raven might strike."

Gray shot Olympia a hard, moody look, as if re-
senting their marriage. "He said I'd have to marry
him to get him," she muttered to Morris.

"Did he?" Morris grinned and reminded her of
Gray.

"I don't understand why he hasn't danced with
me."

"Maybe you'll have to go after him and remove
the burr from under his saddle."

"Men ask women to dance, everyone knows that.
There he goes, laughing and dancing with China

Frankson, and she's—" Olympia glared at Gray, who seemed not to notice that China was pressing her overflowing bosom against his chest. "Excuse me, Morris."

Olympia edged around dancing couples and ran into Teddy Smithson's arms. She stood absolutely still. Teddy had grown from a boy to a man in five short years. She hadn't seen him at close range and the change shocked her. He was heavier, taller, and his mouth had grown cruel. She began to move away from him, and he caught her close. "Aren't you the blushing bride?" he drawled, and his eyes locked on to her bodice.

He was stronger now, and Olympia, not wanting to make a scene and embarrass Gray, allowed Teddy to lead her around the floor. "He's dancing with every woman here and not you, Olympia. Why is that? Would that be because he's discovered you have a nasty temper?"

Olympia lifted her chin and met Teddy's sneer. "He adores me."

Teddy laughed. "He's wondering how he can get China into bed. It shouldn't be that difficult. I had her years ago. She likes it rough. Do you?"

Olympia stopped, took one look at Gray talking to China, and pushed Teddy away. He jerked her back and whispered sharply, "Don't you ever do that to me. I know who you are, Olympia, who you really are, and it won't be long before One Shot knows too. He's a bounty hunter, the best."

She pulled away and went toward Gray, every step infuriating her because he was looking at her over the top of China's head. Olympia tapped China's shoulder with her fan. "I haven't been able to dance with my husband all evening. Would you mind?"

"Feeling sorry for me again, Oly?" Gray asked as they began to waltz. He seemed pleased with her and jerked her closer than the other men had. Olympia rested her hand on his arm, liking the steely muscles moving beneath the cloth. Her husband was a handsome man—clothed. But she preferred him unclothed and pressed against him. He intently surveyed the softness of her breasts swelling above the cut of her gown. There was no denying the hunger in his look as it flickered to her lips. "Did you come to rescue me?"

"She was crushing you, and you were enjoying yourself. What is this about a top bounty hunter after the Raven?"

Gray's expression hardened. "They call him One Shot, because that's all he takes, even if he can bring in the outlaws alive. You wouldn't want to know what he does to women on the wrong side of the law."

Olympia swallowed, realizing from Gray's dark look that she didn't want to know more about One Shot and the women he captured. She didn't want Gray anywhere near One Shot. "Let's go to Wyoming, Gray. Let's go tonight."

"We're cleaning up this mess first. There's someone out there who is leaving a trail right to your door. I heard that One Shot called me a liar. I hear that again and—" Gray stopped talking, his expression hardening as he looked at a man leaning casually against the wall.

The man blended with the shadows, looking tall and deadly. He was dressed in a black suit, like an undertaker. His thin mustache drooped on either side of his mouth. His eyes shifted, side to side, flicking at details, never stopping. "One Shot," Gray stated in a flat tone.

Olympia, who had struggled to survive, to keep her father alive, to build a business, had never really been frightened. She realized that now. She'd always been loved and confident that she could take care of her own. But now Gray was studying One Shot—

She grabbed Gray's chin and turned his face to her. "You're no good to me dead, Grayson Steele. So help me, if you call One Shot out, I'll . . . I'll see that The Book gets into the hands of the newspaper. Then, as a matter of pride, I'll have to drill One Shot dead. In fact, I might do that before he kills you. I like your biscuits too much."

Gray expertly whirled her under his arm and then jerked her against his body, keeping her close. "You'd do it, wouldn't you? Strap on a Colt and call him out to defend what you considered yours. You'd ruin my good name and let people think I was a coward, would you? After trying to protect me from gossip, saving me from the cowpile I've created, and—"

Olympia did not want Gray calling out One Shot. She fluttered her eyelashes at him, because according to Edna Watkins, it stopped men from thinking.

She pressed close to Gray, wanting to keep him safe. As they waltzed around the room Gray studied her as if deciding how to handle her. "Kiss me, Oly. You're my bride, remember?"

He was sulking, bending his pride for her, and she loved him.

"Kiss and dance at the same time?" Olympia closed her eyes as Gray's lips touched hers, slanted to fit exactly upon hers, and the flick of his tongue entered her mouth.

5

"Come on, Oly. Get dressed. We've got work to do." Gray's big hand patted Olympia's bare bottom and stayed to caress her.

She struggled to lift her head from his chest, holding on tight to him amid their tangled clothing. She managed to lift an eyelid. "The dance wasn't even over. You dragged me off from the ball, carried me all the way to the shop, and had me on my workbench the first time—just scraped the tools away with a sweep of your hand and lifted me to sit on the table. You hoisted my skirts and you . . . I barely recovered and you herded me up here and tossed me on the bed. I'm staying here."

"Grump." Gray smoothed her hair, bringing a strand to his lips. "You can't just kiss a man blind on a dance floor and not expect his machinery to get primed, sweetheart," he murmured with a smile in his tone.

"You were there, you were mine, and I took you," she reasoned drowsily.

Gray lifted her chin with a gentle touch of his finger and kissed her. "Oly, if we're going to catch whoever is playing your part as the Raven, we'd better be on our way."

"What do you mean?" She sat up. Gray peeled away the camisole that had flopped onto his face. He took the slightly crushed stalk of lily of the valley from her hair and smelled it; stolen from Miss Ellie's garden on their way home from the ball, the delicate flowers suited his bride.

"I'm a cattleman and I can't have my cattle stolen, nor can I have my wife's good name tarnished. Someone has copied the notch in your mare's shoe and held up a farmer's wagon. Whoever it is he is smart, and according to Dad, he's a big man and his weight matches his footprints. He's not working alone. Once I was able to think clearly—a thing I don't do well these days with you around—I saw that the three events were impossible for one person. One man couldn't have herded those cattle, robbed a stagecoach, and taken Priscilla's best jewels, all in one night. There wasn't enough time. Now, just exactly what do you think someone posing as the Raven would be doing tonight, Oly?"

"I had planned to—" Olympia almost tossed her plans for robbery upon the sheets around them. She closed her mouth and decided that for now she wouldn't admit anything. She looked down at Gray, his hair rumpled and his lips slightly swollen from their kisses. She tugged his shirt across his manhood to allow her to think more clearly. "You're right, Gray. The Raven would be—"

"That's right, my outlaw bride," he said as if reading her mind. "That is exactly what he would be doing." He stood in one of those quick, lithe movements that always surprised her.

Gray stretched, and pleasure rushed through Olympia's already sated body. "You're doing this—hunting the real thief—to save face, aren't you? It wouldn't do for your wife to be an outlaw."

"I'm a selfish man, Oly. Never doubt that I intend to keep what is mine safe, or that I know what is good for me." He stood, a tall man draped in shadows and moonlight, and looked down at her. He took her hands, studying her long pale fingers with his darker ones. "I'm sorry that you had a hard time growing up, dear heart. I'm sorry I wasn't here for you, to help feed and clothe and keep you warm and send you off to school. Your father told me how you always tended him first and then hurried off to school and stayed up late nights studying after you'd helped him with the odd jobs he could find."

"It wasn't so bad. He loved me. I always had his love and what I remembered of my mother. It just hurt so to see the Smithsons move on with their selfish lives, discarding him."

Gray ran his thumb across her knuckles, then tugged her from the bed to hold her against him. He pressed her head to his shoulder and rubbed his cheek against hers as though he enjoyed the fit of her in his arms. "Yes. Well, I don't suppose they will be too happy with a competing stage line, but that's just what the Steeles are prepared to do."

Passion leapt and skimmed around them, then softened into gentleness. Olympia wrapped her arms around Gray, keeping the shadows from him. He wasn't ready to talk to her about his past and perhaps he never would be, but he wasn't alone anymore. "You have me, you know. More than I wanted to give," he said.

"I will take very good care of what you gave me," Olympia promised softly and kissed the hand he had placed against her cheek.

"Reach for the sky," a man's deep voice purred behind Gray. Gray had been enjoying the view from the ground of Olympia's pants-clad bottom moving up the trellis. She hadn't stayed put as he'd ordered, but instead had been leaping across rooftops. She'd just blown him a kiss, a defiant one, and he was wondering how he could step into danger with her at his side. Gray had been too intent upon her, on the emotions she caused within him. The sound of music coming from the ball had covered the man's approach. Gray had been off guard for just one moment, and it could cost Olympia her life, or worse.

"Up, pilgrim," the man behind him ordered, pressing the gun barrel deeper into his ribs. Gray raised his hands and knew that if anything happened to Olympia, a part of him would die.

He turned slowly, Miss Ellie's stolen lily of the valley tucked in his hair and in every pocket Olympia could find before he left their room. Gray found One Shot's cold, deadly stare. A deputy's badge gleamed in the moonlight. One Shot wouldn't hesitate to shoot a woman.

"Drop it," One Shot ordered, and Gray slowly began to unbuckle his gun belt. He tried not to look up at the church belfry, at Olympia's tall, curved body outlined in the silvery moonlight. He prayed that she would run, willed her to return to the ball where she would be safe with her father, his dad, and Blue. Blue had always been fast with a gun.

Gray had to keep One Shot busy, to keep him from looking up at Olympia, who hadn't moved. She had to be able to see One Shot holding the gun on him, and yet she stood in the moonlight, an easy shot. He decided grimly, that she needed a houseful of babies to keep her busy. She wanted adventure— he'd give her plenty of it. When he got his hands on her, her outlaw days would be over. But now he had to keep One Shot's attention. "I see you're wearing a badge, One Shot."

"The Smithsons thought I could help. Their local law is a silly old man. I didn't see much use in coming after this outlaw for the small bounty, but now they're mad enough to up the ante to a right nice sum—" One Shot turned, his face hard in the moonlight as he looked up. The church bell had just rung through the night, carrying over the sound of the ball.

"I'm up here, you half-brain," Olympia yelled, her hands on her hips.

One Shot pivoted, ready to shoot, and Gray put his full weight into his fist. One Shot had a delicate jaw and crumbled easily. Gray dragged him into the shadows, tying his wrists together and tethering them to his ankles. He gagged One Shot and turned just as Miss Ellie bumped into him.

"That is the impolite man who tromped all over my flower beds," she stated indignantly. "Olympia and you are always very careful of my garden, and I don't mind a bit sharing my lovely blossoms with you. But I do so hate rude and uncaring people who tromp on beautiful plants. You can always tell a person by the way they treat plants."

Sensing that Miss Ellie was just getting warmed up on her tirade, Gray handed her One Shot's revolver. "Would you mind entertaining him for a while?"

"Not at all. But would you mind fetching my teapot? I've just made a fresh pot, and I'd love to have some while I guard the culprit."

Gray inhaled slowly and glanced to the rooftops. Olympia was out of sight now, on her way to the richest house in Harp, property of Maximilian Fearson, Esquire.

He hesitated. In the time he took to get Miss Ellie's tea and chair, Olympia could be caught or worse. He looked down at the elderly spinster's face and knew that Olympia would want him to tend to Miss Ellie first.

"I'd be delighted to get your tea and chair, Miss Ellie. Sugar or lemon?" He tapped One Shot on the jaw again and listened to directions about placing the tea cozy over the pot. Gray hurried to bring her tea and chair, the tea cozy in place. Every heartbeat told him that at any moment a shot could take Olympia's life. He realized he was sweating, though the night was cool. He was shaking too. Though only minutes had passed, Gray realized his fear for Olympia had devoured him.

He waited while Miss Ellie settled daintily into her chair. He handed her the china cup from his pocket. She beamed at him. Gray forced a tight smile. Women would be the ruin of him. Olympia would have his hair turned white before his time. "Give me twenty minutes and then fire two shots. That should bring the sheriff running."

Gray hurried through the alleys to catch up with his wife. He rounded a corner and bumped into a familiar, curved backside. Olympia turned and hurled herself at him. She wrapped her arms around his neck and peppered his face with tiny soft kisses. "I adore you. Only you would take time to please Miss Ellie. I saw it all," she whispered unevenly, before pushing him away.

While Gray felt himself become one big smile, she turned and pointed to an upstairs window. "He's up there. He's wearing a shoddy cape that drags the ground, a white plume instead of a scarlet one, and he makes enough noise to wake all the dogs. I was a much better outlaw. At least I had skill. There is absolutely no beauty at all in the way he banged a ladder against the upstairs window. *I* would have swung down that—"

Gray put his hand over her mouth. "Yes, dear. But your outlawing days are over."

Olympia frowned at him. "Gray, you know the Raven's scarlet plume has never turned up. What do you suppose happened to it?"

"It's probably tucked away somewhere. The next time you pull a stunt like yelling to distract a killer, I'll make you pay."

"Mmm. I like the sound of that," Olympia purred sensuously.

Gray blinked at the mischievous smile curling around her lips. "I told you I could handle this alone, but oh, no, you had to come dancing across the rooftops, scaring the hell out of me."

"If you think for one minute that you're having all the fun—"

A sound caused Gray to turn. He watched the

caped outlaw making his way down the ladder. Gray slid through the shadows with Olympia's hand lodged firmly on his belt. Somehow the tether was endearing and pleased him. Gray pushed her back from harm as he flipped the cape over the outlaw's head and wrapped rope around the length of his body, trapping him with a bundle of the Fearsons' stolen goods.

When the thief swung, trussed and alive, from the rope tossed over a small porch roof, Olympia studied Gray's work. "Not bad. He's alive. He's in costume, and he's trapped with the take. Not bad at all. He sounds enraged—that's Tom Davidson."

"Go home, dear heart," Gray ordered, moving toward the livery. He knew she wouldn't, her hand was already latched to the back of his belt.

Gray allowed himself a tight, pleased smile. Olympia would likely cause him an early death from worrying over her, but she wasn't deserting him when times were rough. Their marriage was practical; she suited him.

He stopped abruptly and Olympia collided softly with his back. Instantly her arms encircled him, she hugged him fiercely, and for just a moment Gray allowed himself to wallow in the tenderness washing over him.

"Gray! Look at that!" Olympia turned and bumped Gray's chin. They were hiding in the bushes overlooking the stagecoach robbery outside of Harp. He rubbed the slight injury and grabbed her arm before she could run toward the two outlaws who had stopped the stage. One moved in the shadows, while the other—dressed in a cape and a hat with a plume—swung down from his horse.

Olympia jerked her arm, freeing herself from Gray's protective grasp. "They have Josie. I'd know her markings anywhere. She wasn't at the livery."

He gripped the back of her black shirt, and she didn't notice. If she made one move toward the robbery Gray would haul her back to safety. "The other horse is wearing the imitation notch. They're making certain that your horse is seen this time, not hidden in the bushes. The gold on that stage is a king's ransom, and once you're found guilty they won't have to worry about spending it."

"But Gray, how do you suppose they knew it was me in the first place?" Olympia placed her hands on her waist. "Now, who would want to ride Josie in that close and expose her to gunfire?"

But Gray was intent on the big man wearing the cape and issuing orders to whoever was in the stagecoach. Gray turned to Olympia and kissed her hard, dragging her against his body. "Now, listen, Miss Outlaw, you stay put. I don't want you anywhere near this. If anyone sees you and these no-goods point the finger at you—"

She batted her lashes. "Yes, dear."

He stared at her a moment, wondering just how much he could trust her to obey and keep safe. Gray began to move toward the man in the shadows. The man crumpled immediately, and Gray tied and gagged him. He glanced to where he had left Olympia and found the spot empty. "Hell."

The caped bandit jerked open the stagecoach door. "Get out, now, before I start shooting."

"I wouldn't do that," Gray stated, moving out

into the moonlight, his revolver drawn. He shot the
large hat, and when it tumbled to the ground Teddy
Smithson screamed, fell to his knees, and clutched
his chest. "I'm shot! I'm shot!"

"I'll let you know when you will be. And if you
don't stop yelling, I'll ventilate you sooner." Gray
looked down at Teddy, disgusted by the man's grov-
eling. Gray jerked him up, lashing his wrists behind
him. "Teddy, didn't anyone ever tell you about the
Code of the West?"

Ray Morales, the driver, leapt to the ground and
eyed Teddy. "You polecat, lower than a snake's belly,
stealing from your pa."

"He won't miss it. I am due more than the pittance he gives me."

The stagecoach door opened, and a woman
stepped down to the ground, an elegant movement
that spoke of money and breeding. "Grayson. After
all these years. How like you to be in the middle of a
criminal event."

Gray recognized the English accent and the distaste in the voice immediately. Olympia had moved
silently to his side. He felt old suddenly, weighted by
the past. "Hello, Mother. May I present my bride?
Mrs. Grayson Steele. Olympia, this is my mother,
Elizabeth."

"How dare you!" Elizabeth Steele whispered,
glaring at Olympia. People were coming home from
church, strolling on Harp's streets below the hotel.
The midday light in the parlor did not hide the vivid
anger contorting the older woman's face. "I am
merely checking on my beloved sons and my dear
husband. You have no right to tell me that they are

yours now, that they are under your protection. The idea of a woman protecting grown men against their own mother."

"You must grow up. Go back to England until you do." Olympia studied Gray's mother. The woman wore a heavy scent, and though Elizabeth was beautiful, she wore a hard, cold expression.

"Grow up?" Elizabeth shot back in high, quivering, outraged tones. Her beautiful face contorted with rage, she leaned threateningly toward Olympia, and yelled, "I? Grow up? How dare you! How dare you order me back to England!"

Olympia straightened her shoulders. She refused to yell back and spoke quietly. "I dare. You have been far too selfish. Morris Steele is a lovely man, and women want him. He adores you and you treat him poorly, yet he remains faithful to you. I call that remarkable, because I did not see one glimpse of love and tenderness on your part. You simply demanded that Morris and your sons sell their 'rough American land' to buy the English estate that you wish. They love their land. Only a selfish woman would want them to sell it for her benefit. I want you to go back to England and think about how you once loved him. You are to write him a very nice letter. You are to either release Morris or come back to him. If you come back to him you are to make his life—and your sons' lives—pleasant."

"You will not order me about. You are not a suitable wife for my son," Elizabeth stated in a low hissing tone.

Olympia fought the icy fear skittering up the nape of her neck. She was no match for Gray's education and wealth, but she loved him. "Perhaps I am not, but that is for him and for me to decide. You will not bring him more pain. I won't let you."

"Pain? I'm his mother. I have that right. He may think you'll bring him happiness, but you won't. You couldn't possibly." Elizabeth's hand swept out. "Look at you. Big as a man—six feet tall, if you're an inch. You're a gunsmith, with . . . with work hands."

"I know what I am. For the moment I am Gray's wife, and no one will hurt him, not even you. Gray wants a son from me. I believe the proper event has occurred to ensure a child. You may visit us. But that child and Gray and his father and Blue will have every bit of love I can give."

Elizabeth sneered. "What can you give him? Money? A heritage? Good taste? Why, I saw you kiss him in public after the criminals were in jail and he announced that new idiotic stage line owned by the Steeles. He asked your father—a man with only one good leg—to be in charge. This morning at the sheriff's you actually leapt upon Grayson, led him down into the street, and kissed him silly. Grayson looked like he was drunk when you finished mauling him. Now, that's a fine way for an up-and-coming politician to act, isn't it?"

Olympia tapped her finger on the fringed lamp-shade. "Nothing I could do could damage the respect that Gray deserves. I believe I please him. But you should know that to protect him, I am prepared to send The Book to English newspapers."

"The Book?" Elizabeth's stunned expression slid into horror. "To English newspapers? You wouldn't. It would ruin me in society."

"Gray's reputation would recover, and he and

Blue and Morris are my concern. Morris likes me. I will also suggest that he cut your funds and invest more in his properties. With grandchildren on his lap he may see his life differently."

"I can manage Morris. I always have. What can you possibly give or bring to Gray?" Elizabeth demanded.

"Only love," Olympia returned softly, meaning it. She turned to a sound and found Gray watching her with shadowed eyes and a grim expression. A tear went skimming down her cheek, and she dashed the others away. She walked past Gray, pasting her pride together.

He didn't touch her or follow her, and each step away from him, Olympia knew, was a step away from the momentary happiness she had found.

"Mother, since you're here, perhaps it is time we talked," Gray murmured softly.

Olympia swallowed the emotion wadding her throat. She closed the door and leaned against the hotel wall, allowing her tears to flow freely. Gray would explain to his mother how he would divorce Olympia and get a suitable wife—one not prone to leaping from rooftops. The pain tearing through her was worse than an outlaw's bullet.

"Oly?" Twenty minutes later Gray entered Olympia's bedroom, where she lay sprawled, stomach down, on her bed. His weight dipped the bed, rolling her toward him, and when she scrambled away, Gray's weight covered her backside and he tugged away the pillow concealing her tears.

"Get off me. You weigh a ton," she muttered and tried not to sob.

"I think you're magnificent," Gray whispered,

kissing her damp cheek. "A regular warrior goddess. The queen of my heart."

"Get your hands out from under me." Olympia sniffed as Gray's large hands claimed her breasts. "Don't ask me to take back one word that I said to your mother. Sweet talk won't change my mind— you've just popped one of my buttons, Gray."

"Turn over so I can unbutton you better, my dear, and I would never ask you to take back something so grand."

"Stop blowing in my ear." Olympia turned slowly, and Gray settled back on top of her.

He smoothed back a damp strand from her cheek and tenderly looked down at her. "I love you, Oly."

"Why?" Olympia held her breath as Gray's thumb stroked the line of her jaw.

"Because you take care of those you love—you'll fight for them and care little for your own needs. And that is only one reason. You were right about my mother. I could never see you locking your child in a closet. You're loyal and brave, Oly."

"Rubbish." Olympia returned the soft, fleeting kiss Gray gave her and smiled tremulously. "You're not mad at me?"

"My mother deserved those truths a long time ago. I was proud of you, and suddenly I saw how really selfish she is. After you left I told her that I supported any decision you made as the woman of my heart. Dad and Blue will too. So we're yours, dear Oly."

"Mine," Olympia said, promising herself to Gray and his family. She stroked her fingers through Gray's hair.

He smiled tenderly. "Tell me you love me. I like the sound of it."

"You're blushing, sweetheart," she whispered. "I love you. Your turn."

"Exactly. My turn. I love you, Oly."

~❦❀❦~

Epilogue

"How did you know it was Teddy, Gray?" Olympia stretched upon the blanket beneath their tangled bodies, her skirt and petticoat bunched up around her waist and her drawers down at her ankles. While the residents of Harp were gossiping over their Sunday dinner, she was on her way to her new home. Once they were deep into the trees on the outskirts of Harp, she had been hungrily waylaid by her new husband.

Gray nuzzled her breasts, exposed by the torn camisole laces. He ran his hand over her hip and slowly down her thigh, squeezing gently. "Mmm. Wait until I come back into this world, Oly."

She stroked the back of his head, luxuriating in his weight sprawled upon her. "You didn't have to toss me onto the ground as soon as we got into the first stand of pines. It was enough you hurried me away like that, leaving your brother and father to herd the cattle and bring my things to your ranch."

With a slow movement, mixed with caresses and kisses, Gray eased to her side. He wrapped an arm around her and brought her close to him. "Teddy had just enough brains to recognize the notch on

Josie's shoe when the stable boy pointed out that she needed to be shod. He was generous with the boy, asking him to keep track of the times Josie was missing during the night. As Mr. Sinjin it was easy to gather that the Smithsons hadn't treated your father right, and in all the instances of the Raven's thefts, someone had a link to you. You would have been caught sooner or later. The boy wasn't asleep at all. Josie was missing the nights that the Raven struck. Teddy decided to step out on his own, and he wanted to pin it all on you. His friends stole our herd, he robbed the stagecoach. His tracks sank deeper into the dirt than yours, which meant he didn't need to wear a pillow, scattering proof to the wind and all over the ground."

Olympia eased to sit upon Gray, primly arranging her skirts around them. She enjoyed his delighted chuckle. "Why, Mrs. Steele, what are you doing?"

"I believe that from now on, you will be my adventure, my love," she returned as Gray's hand smoothed her thigh. "You know, if anyone comes along they'll think I'm terrible, a perfect outlaw, sitting upon you."

He tucked a stalk of lily of the valley into the buttonhole of her opened bodice. He caught her hands, which were smoothing his chest, and brought them to his lips. "You are perfect, dear heart. I will cherish you forever—and that is what I told my mother when she said you were an outrageous, bold Amazon, who would surely give me a huge gang of untamed outlaw children."

Gray's tender expression told her that there would be more, when he was ready to share his heart. "You don't mind marrying a reformed outlaw?" She took him slowly, carefully into her, as carefully as she would tend him all the days of their lives, long past the heat that now devoured them.

"Dear heart, you have stolen more than my body—we both know that. You have stolen my heart and soul." Then Gray smiled, a careless, happy smile that took away lines and years. "Mmm. I believe we are in the midst of a certain holdup right now."

"I am truly glad your mother didn't force me to mail The Book to England. It has become very dear to me. Now I can see if this really works."

Gray chuckled, a deep, rich, pleased sound that Olympia hoped she'd hear many times through the years.

Wishing for More

❧

Stephanie Mittman

THE MONTANA SENTINEL
JUNE 17, 1892

Yesterday afternoon just after 2:00 P.M. the Butte National Bank became the latest victim in a string of robberies perpetrated by Moreland and Lesley Rivers, who are making themselves well known around these parts as the Rivers Brothers. As with the four previous robberies attributed to the once well-liked men, there was a female hostage taken against her will, preventing apprehension by the bank guard who was unable to get a clear shot at the two men. This time the unfortunate lady, identified by the clerk at the Butte Grand Hotel, where she had registered only two days before, was the widow of one Geoffrey Briggs of County Cork, Ireland. Mrs. Briggs was bound and gagged by one of the brothers as three horrified tellers, the bank's vice president, and two customers were held at gunpoint by the remaining brother.

Once again the brothers demanded the sum of $1,704.85 to be removed from the account of the Columbia Copper Mine, as they have in the previous robberies. The five robberies have now netted the

brothers nearly $10,000.00 and the
admiration of hundreds of workers
dissatisfied with the company's pol-
icy of lowering workers' wages while
raising dividends to investors (back
in their comfortable mansions on
Fifth Avenue in New York City,
New York).

But any admiration must be tempered by distaste for the uncivilized
behavior of the men in regard to decent law-abiding women taken
against their will for the simple
crime of being in the wrong place at
the wrong time. Add to that the fact
that, to this paper's knowledge, none
of the hostages has been seen since
their abductions. One can only guess
at their ultimate fate. Knowing that a
civilization is measured by the way it
treats its weakest citizens, and ac-
knowledging that our fairer sex is
surely our weaker sex, the Montana
Sentinel, in the interest of justice and
with concern for our women,
hereby offers a reward for the apprehension of Moreland and Lesley
Rivers of $500 each. *Dead or Alive.*

1

"Okay now, ladies and gentlemen, you can make this nice and easy or you can make it mean and bloody. I ain't a great fan of breakin' my manners, but it's really up to y'all," Lesley Rivers said, sounding to Moreland like one of those dang Beadle's Dime Library novels that his brother was always reading. If the man was so partial to hearing himself talk, maybe he should have taken up performing on the gosh-darn stage instead of robbing banks.

Moreland pointed his gun at Mr. Barone, who, More had taken the trouble to learn on one of his earlier trips to Granite, was president of the bank. More knew it all in every town they hit: the name of the president of the bank, the routes in and out, which day the sheriff visited the widow on the far side of town.

"Unless you got the same philosophy that Crazy Horse had about it bein' a good day to die," he told Barone, "I'd open the safe and fill up the bags right quick." Heck, he was no better than his brother. He supposed there was just something about having an audience that gave a normally taciturn man a real dramatic turn.

"You men ought to be ashamed of yourselves," Barone said, disgust written all over his face. "Robbing is one thing, Rivers, and I can't say a lot of us don't have our own gripe with the Columbia Mine, but the women . . . I demand to know what you've done with those women."

More looked up at the clock. Two minutes until two o'clock. This one better not be late.

"He worried about those women?" Lesley shouted the question over his shoulder while he kept his two fancy six-guns trained on the remaining tellers and the three customers who'd been fool enough to want to conduct their bank business smack dab at two o'clock.

"He's fillin' up bags with bills," More answered. "Unless he's wanting to see this floor covered with his own blood and the bank's ceiling for his last earthly sight."

That lit a fire under Barone's feet, and the man hurried to the safe, opened it, and began counting the money into the sacks stacked beside it, grumbling all the while about decent women wrenched from their families.

More let a low chuckle escape him, quieting when Barone sent him a scowl, his bushy eyebrows raised in contempt. The women were Lesley's idea. Women were always Lesley's idea, robbery or not. To More, a woman was usually a pound of trouble for an ounce of flesh, but Lesley just couldn't seem to resist.

He checked the time again. This one better not talk her mouth off or they'd have to gag her too, just like Curly Cyla. He knew what they said about birds of a feather, but between Lesley's tongue wagging and the woman's lips jabbering, he didn't know where they found time to play "hide the dynamite stick and watch it explode!"

At 2:01 P.M. she stepped through the door, and the breath caught in his throat. The long-barreled Colt in his hand took aim at the slick maple floor, and it took him a couple of seconds to right it.

For the first time in More's memory, Lesley hadn't exaggerated. It was like seeing a goddamn angel come down from the sky and land smack in their path, all decked out in a fine green dress whose stripes zigged here and zagged there. And jeez, it wasn't just him. Even the other women in the bank gasped at the sight of her. Mr. Barone's eyes bugged so, More thought they might just fall out of his head.

"What's going on here?" she demanded, halting in the middle of pulling off one incredibly spotless white glove. Whatever it was she charged, More would lay nuggets to nails she was worth it. The woman sure did clean up good.

"About time," More said under his breath, grabbing the sacks of money from Barone and sliding them across the highly polished wood floor toward Lesley. If he ever owned a bank, the first thing he'd do would be to put bumps in the floor to slow down men like himself and Lesley.

He pointed at the woman in green as if his brother couldn't figure out the plan himself—hadn't *made* the plan himself. "Take that one and let's go," he added.

His brother sunk the hooks they'd devised into the bags of money and threw them over his shoulder, leaving his hands free for their new lady friend. Easily, with a smile on his face that went from hell to Sunday, Lesley slipped his arm around her waist.

"What do you think you're doing?" The lady pushed at his hand, and when that failed she stamped one awfully small foot back onto his instep—damn hard if the look on Les's face was for real.

More couldn't tell which of them was more surprised. So she wasn't just beautiful, but a first-class actress too. She fought off Lesley as if she meant to kill him, shouting while she squirmed.

"My brother's going to come after both of you if you don't let go of me right this minute. He won't eat or sleep until he's got you looking down the barrel of his gun and pleading for mercy. And I'm gonna watch him pull that trigger. Let me go, you idiot. You don't know who—"

More pulled the extra kerchief out of his back pocket and had it around the woman's mouth before she could get out another word. Lord only knew what she'd say next. Franny had certainly messed up her exit—dropping her accent and calling Les by name—and More wasn't taking any chances with this new one.

While Lesley saw to the onlookers, More quickly bound the angel's hands behind her back, using the ribbon that encircled her waist. It was smooth and soft, and he fumbled with it more that he ought to have. He reminded her that she'd asked for it, his voice cracking as he did.

Whoa, he was lucky those gray eyes weren't loaded, or he'd be dead where he stood.

"Come on," he yelled at Lesley, who was sure taking enough time binding up the teller and his customers.

"Uh, More?" Lesley said. "There's something . . ." He was looking at the woman as if this was the first time he'd ever seen one with clothes on.

"Now!" More said, secure in the knowledge that his brother was one hell of a knot-maker and that their witnesses weren't going anywhere anytime soon. He tipped his hat at the ladies and gentlemen sprawled on the floor. One lady's ankle had somehow revealed itself in her squirming, and More bent and covered it with her dress. He then thanked them all for their cooperation.

"And don't you worry none about the little lady," Lesley said as he turned the sign in the window to announce that the bank was closed and would open at eight the next morning. "It'll be just like with all the others." He paused and smiled, and More knew just what was coming next. He'd heard it often enough that it shouldn't ride his neck the way it did. "I'm gonna have the pleasure of being the little lady's last."

The twisting and fidgeting on the floor stopped cold. The little filly who was pulled against More's side, however, began kicking and elbowing him as if she hadn't known all along that would be part of the deal.

Anyone who knew Lesley knew he'd want that particular bonus thrown in for his trouble.

And trouble this one was, pulling against More all the way to the horses, nearly tripping him twice until it was easier to simply pick her up in his arms and carry her there. It wasn't as if she weighed as much

as his rifle, anyway. "Take her until I get up." He
threw her into Lesley's arms, mounted up, and then
took her by whatever part was convenient, tossing
her over the saddle in front of him.

"Hell of a time to change your mind, honey," he
said once he'd pushed himself halfway up the cantle
to settle her between himself and the saddle horn.
"You'll wind up getting us all killed."

Down the street he could see people going about
their business. There was a man riding north up
Main Street on a lame horse. There was a woman
headed their way in a deep-green satin dress.

"Uh, More?" Lesley said, clearing his throat and
pointing at the angel's rounded bottom, which stared
up at him like a full moon on a dark night.

"Later," More said, shaking his head at his
brother. If he let Les take the woman on his horse,
there was a good chance they'd never even make it
out of town alive. He raised his head and listened to
the normal goings-on of Granite, Montana, then exchanged a glance with his brother.

A moment. Another. Then a small *pop*, followed
by a chain of *bang*s and *boom*s, as the fireworks he'd
left in the one-holer behind the saloon exploded.

A man might not be able to count on the Northern Pacific coming through on time or paying its
workers a decent wage. He might not be able to set
his watch by the sheriff's rounds or rely on his protection. But he sure as hell could count on a kid
needing to take a leak after four free sarsaparillas.
And he could lay odds on that kid setting a match to
the string of crackers he'd found and then tossing
them back into the old half-moon when it was oc-
cupied next.

More nodded and gave Magic a good solid kick to the flanks with his boot. He headed out of Granite with a broad smile on his face and a woman bouncing against his thighs before the good people of Granite could have had any idea what had hit them.

More's first indication that things weren't going as smoothly as planned came from Lesley, who shouted over the commotion for him to "move it." The second was a bit less subtle, as a bullet whizzed past his ear.

"Shit!" he muttered, leaning low over the woman, who squirmed in front of him. "Lie still," he told her, slapping the fanny she kept waving against his cheek as he crouched over her.

He didn't bother looking back, nor did he have to. Just from the sound of it he knew the gun was a small one, probably a .22-caliber Defender. A few more feet and they'd be well out of its range. He heard the second shot, the third, and then Magic's hooves drowned out any that might have followed.

Lesley was a dust cloud ahead of him, riding hard. The woman had stopped her damn thrashing, and he prayed his bulk hadn't suffocated the thing. But then he reminded himself that no matter how delicate and pure she might appear, she'd worked at Chicago Joe's and had had enough men on top of her to bear the weight of one more.

"The canyon," Lesley shouted over his shoulder. More leaned over the woman and told her to keep still, just the way she was doing, and he'd get her untied and upright as soon as they were safe.

Dust was flying, but still her scent filled his nostrils, clean and sweet, like the house his family had lived in on Maple Street all those years ago, before life had soured and their mama had died. He wondered what his mama would think of her boys—outlaws now—and whether she'd understand that someone had to stand up for these people, that he and Les figured there weren't many who had more raw skill and less to lose than the two of them.

Lesley threw him a look over his shoulder and raised his gaze above More's head to the town behind them. With a quick tug on the reins he stopped and waited for More to catch up to him.

"Slower with the extra weight," More said, gently touching the rounded bottom between his splayed legs and foolishly wishing he'd been the first to do so. He and his brother had little in common when it came to women. Les took his pleasure in being last: He'd share a woman's joy at the passing of a way of life she hated, then he'd drop her in a new town with enough for a fresh start. But More . . . More wanted to share the wonder of some sweet lady's first time and maybe all the times after that as well. To own something as simple and as wonderful as someone's heart.

"Hear that?" Les asked him, tipping his black hat back off his forehead and wiping the sweat from his brow.

The train whistle pierced the prairie, prouder than it had any right to be. The Northern Pacific didn't even have the decency to be ashamed of itself for stealing food from children, warmth from wives, and pride from men. Hungry for work, they'd all let the railroad get away with it, standing on lines and watching as the railroad cut wages, refused widow's pensions, and fired hard-working men to hire greener, cheaper labor that couldn't speak the language well enough to understand what they were doing to the men they replaced.

They'd all rolled over and taken jobs in the mines, risking their lives to keep their families fed and their women clothed. And again wages were cut as the fat cats in New York and Boston wanted more profits than they could ever spend. Legacies for their children's children, while the miner's children wore hand-me-down shoes and dreamed hand-me-down dreams.

Until Jerry Lucas's daughter died. The doc had sworn an operation would save her, but who could afford the trip back East? Who could even afford to make her last days on earth comfortable, warm, satisfying?

The Columbia Copper Mine could, and Moreland and Lesley Rivers were just the ones to see to it that they did. They weren't greedy men, nor were they reckless or evil. But they weren't anybody's fools, and they weren't ones to stand aside while good people dug themselves deeper and deeper into debt.

As they wound their way into the canyon, where the chances of being followed were next to nil, More watched the sunlight play on the woman's hair. What was her name? Louise? Yes, that was what Les had told him. Louise from Chicago, who had thought to find herself a husband and instead wound up working at Chicago Joe's in Helena. She wanted out, wanted to open a small shop in a town where no one knew the hard times she'd fallen upon and what she'd become.

And Les had offered her his share of the take—and More's too—if she'd show up at the bank in Granite at two o'clock in a green dress and present herself as a woman of worth. The town would care if this woman had been abducted—even if they didn't know just who she was.

Spun gold. That's what her hair reminded him of every time a ray of sunshine penetrated the leaves to find her head.

"Think it's safe to stop a minute?" he asked Les, figuring that the woman had to be pretty damn tired of belly riding.

Less nodded, and they came to a stop near a copse of trees, where the lady might freshen herself with a bit of privacy if she was of a mind to. More untied the gag—which he would have done a long time ago if that idiot back in Granite hadn't pulled his useless little Defender and started shooting—and tried to get a response from the woman.

"Miss Louise?" he asked, trying to right her with no cooperation on her part. "Miss?" He rolled her over onto his lap, one arm supporting her back and the other under her knees as if he were carrying her. Her head fell back against him at the same moment that he saw the blood soaking through the hem of her dress.

"Easy now. Damn it, watch her head," she heard a man's voice say, and felt herself jostled this way and that. She blinked up at the bright sunlight and quickly slammed her eyes shut, pressing her face against something rock-hard that smelled faintly pungent and felt damp against her cheek. She burrowed deeper, pain searing through her leg with every movement. A hammering near her ear increased to double-time.

"It hurts," she whimpered, arching her back against the sharp throbbing of her calf.

"It's all right, Louise," the man said softly, his words brushing her forehead. "Spread the damn blanket," he said, and she could hear quick movements and feel the breeze rush behind her. "I'm gonna put you down and take a look, honey," the man said, staring at her with concern.

He put her down on the blanket and tore his shirt off, rolled it in a ball, and lifted her head gently to tuck it beneath her neck. Then he lifted her skirts way up over her knees.

"No!" she said, fighting him rather feebly. "You can't just—"

"Heck of a time to be playing Miss Modesty, honey," the man said to her. "Just pretend I'm one of the paying customers and I'm working my way up slow."

She was going to ask him just what he meant by that when a pain—as bad as the one she'd felt moments after she'd been thrown over the horse in Granite—ripped through her legs. She screamed out and found that there were two men: one inflicting the agony to her leg, and the other now covering her mouth with one hand and stroking her hair with the other. She tried to jerk her head away, but his hand remained clamped over her mouth.

"Why didn't you tell me you were hit?" the man by her leg demanded. "I'da never—"

At his probing, she screamed against the hand quieting her and tried to squirm away. From behind her the second man somehow managed to pin her shoulders to the blanket.

"She's cryin', More," the man near her head said,

his voice cracking and his hand massaging her shoulder gently. "Can't ya hurry?"

"I gotta make sure the bullet ain't in there," he said. "Looks to have just grazed her. I told you I didn't like this part of the plan, didn't I? Even if Louise here was willing to risk it."

"Uh, More?" the man by her head said, tentatively taking his hand from her mouth with a look that asked if she meant to scream again.

She clenched her teeth and grasped the blankets in her fists. *More*. So she was in the clutches of the Rivers Boys. And her brother insisted they weren't dangerous! Robin Hoods, he'd called them. Just wait until he got back to Granite and found that they'd taken off with her. And wait until he saw that she'd been shot!

"Okay," the one called More said. "I think it's safe to wrap it up good. When we get her to Kirkville she can get a doctor to look at it. You still think it was worth it, Louise?"

Before she could answer him, the one by her head—he'd have to be Les—interrupted. "Uh, More?"

"Lesley, you practicin' your French? *Amour, amour, amour?*" He was on his feet and moving toward the horses. No doubt it was just the angle, but he appeared to be the biggest, strongest man she'd ever seen. In a matter of two strides he was at the horse and back with a canteen. "I'm gonna wash that wound out as best as I can, Louise," he said. "Before I do, you ought to drink some. Bleeding can lead to a powerful thirst."

"I'm not—" she said as he lifted her head and

pressed the canteen to her lips, cradling her against him, one of his huge thighs supporting her back.

"You don't have to be thirsty to drink," he said, brushing the hair off her face and pulling a strand from between her lips and the neck of the canteen. "But I suppose you've never done what's good for you, have you?"

"Uh, More?"

With an exasperated sigh, Moreland Rivers turned to his brother. "Will you spit it out, Les?" he said as he continued to stroke her hair. "What is it?"

"She ain't Louise."

The stroking stopped. Moreland took the canteen from her lips and eased her back down onto the blanket, backing slightly away from her. "What do you mean *she ain't Louise*?" he asked, his gaze darting between her face and his brother's, slipping down to her leg and then racing back to her face. "Who is she?"

Samantha couldn't help looking at Lesley Rivers for his answer, despite the fact that she obviously already knew who she was. In fact, she knew a lot better than they did.

Lesley Rivers shrugged, biting at the edge of his lip. "Don't know."

"Don't know?" Moreland grew larger still with a mammoth intake of breath that swelled his chest and nearly burst his shirt buttons.

Lesley shook his head. "Don't know."

Slowly, as if he didn't really want to, Moreland returned his gaze to Samantha's face. He backed up a good foot, his hands behind him as if to deny he'd ever even touched her.

She smiled weakly. Gosh, but her leg hurt like

blazes. Still, she couldn't remember so much excitement ever happening to her. This beat the Fourth of July and Christmas by a mile. Hadn't she complained just last week to her brother that her life was dull, dull, dull? And hadn't he promised to keep it that way?

"Samantha Maddigan," she said, offering her hand.

Moreland mouthed her name, but no sound came out. Finally he just whispered. "No. Oh, no, no, no."

She nodded almost apologetically. "Yes."

"Not Carson Maddigan's sister," he said, shaking his head and looking down at her wounded leg.

"It really hurts, you know," she said, raising herself up onto her elbows. "Are you going to tie it up?"

"I'm not going to touch you," he said, bending forward to pick up the hem of her dress with the very tips of two fingers. He dropped it down over her exposed leg.

"I don't think Carson would like that," she warned.

"If I touched you?" he asked. The color had drained from his face.

"If you let me bleed to death," she answered, pulling at her skirt and raising the hem an inch at a time.

"That's far enough!" he shouted at her when she revealed her knee. "Not another inch."

Moreland Rivers was probably right. The good Lord only knew what Carson would do if he thought the man had seen more than he needed to. Hadn't Billy Sellars spent two months with his ribs taped after he'd kissed Samantha behind the Thompsons' barn?

"Okay," he said, repositioning himself down near her foot. "I'm washin' this out, I'm wrappin' it up, and I'm takin' you back to Granite soon as I'm done." He lifted her leg, gulped, and gently lowered it again. "Might be easier if you kinda rolled over onto your stomach," he suggested. She noticed there was a thin sheen of sweat on his chest and that his breathing was ragged.

Berris Forbes said that she had just that effect on Johnny Phelps. Wilma Yates said that Jesse Martin could hardly breathe when she was within two feet of him. But no one ever got within two feet of Samantha Maddigan.

Until now.

And if Moreland Rivers, with those moss-green eyes and those rippling muscles, thought he could just dump her back in Granite . . .

She rolled over gingerly while More kept talking, his voice low and rough. "This is gonna hurt some, hon—Miss Maddigan," he said. "And we ain't looking to bring the law down on us, so my brother here's gonna have to—"

Lesley Rivers put his hand gently over her mouth. "He wouldn't hurt a flea, Missy," he whispered. "Don't even like to swat at gnats. Why once there was a—"

Samantha gripped the blankets, bit down on Lesley's finger, and tried with all her might to pull her leg from Moreland Rivers's grasp as her calf seemed to catch fire.

Les jerked his hand away, but Sam just gasped for air and choked on a mouthful of it.

"She bit me," Les whined, putting his finger in his mouth.

"It's done," More said softly. "I'll just wrap it up." He ripped her petticoat without asking, and with his leg keeping hers at the right angle, quickly wrapped the fabric around her calf and tied it off.

His hand rested on the back of her knee for a moment, and then he jerked it away.

"Do you think you can ride? I wanna get you back home before dark."

"We can't take her back, More," Lesley said, getting to his feet and stretching out his tall but lanky form. "Maddigan'll kill us on sight."

"So what do you suggest?" More asked, loosening the strings of her boot and easing it off her foot before it started to swell, his head turned as if he didn't want to see her bare toes.

"We took her as a hostage," Les said. "Now I think she is one."

More shook his head. "We don't take unwilling hostages." So Sam was right. Louise, whoever she was, was in on the abduction. She should have known a man with eyes the color of soft moss could never be a hardened criminal. "And I'm not gonna start with Carson Maddigan's sister. When I hang I'd prefer it was for something I meant to do, not for a mistake."

"I hear horses." Her ear was to the ground, and the faint vibrations were getting stronger by the moment.

"We can't take her back."

"We can't keep her."

"We're being followed," she said more loudly. "At least two horses."

More turned to stare at her. "What?"

She put her palms to the ground. The horses weren't even a mile away. "There are two horses, at least, following us."

"What's this *us*?" he asked, squinting his eyes down the trail and seeing nothing. "I don't hear anything. You, Les?"

"Carson and I learned it as kids. Put your ear to the ground and you'll hear them," she said, trying to rise to her feet and gasping at the pain.

"Oh, jeez," More said, whisking her up almost as if she were five years old and he was merely playing with her. She half-expected him to toss her up in the air and yell "whee!" the way her father might have in another lifetime. But one look at his drawn face and she knew he was in no mood to play.

"Come on," Les said, already up on his own horse. "Give her to me and let's go."

More shook his head. Beneath the arm she had wrapped about his shoulder, he felt warm, and the scent of sweat and bay rum rose off his body like heat waves rising from the rocks on the horizon. His skin was tanned from the sun. Up close she could see the whiteness of each crack by his eyes and the slight burn on the tip of his nose, which somehow hadn't escaped the sun even under the shade of his wide-brimmed hat.

She chose to ignore the fact that he held her away from his body as if cradling her would commit him to some course of action he didn't have any desire to pursue, and she allowed herself to feel welcome in his arms. But the feeling was short-lived.

"I'm not taking her. The posse can find her and take her back. I'd feel better if a doctor looked at that leg anyways, and then they can take her home where she belongs."

He looked around as if she were a sack of potatoes and he was trying to decide where to store her. Apparently he'd decided that her adventure was over.

Well, she'd just see about that. She unfastened the top two buttons on her dress and then yanked the rest open, buttons flying this way and that.

"Leave me here," she warned as he stood with his mouth open, staring at the lacy camisole that still covered her chest, "and I'll swear you had your way with me."

2

Well, his mother'd always warned him to be careful what he wished for 'cause he just might get it. And sure as manure follows in a horse's wake, here More was, a beautiful woman between his legs, just like he'd been wishing for, and who was she but Carson Maddigan's sister. Now, there was sweet justice!

He had her crosswise in front of him, her legs thrown over his thigh to keep the bleeding of her calf in check. With the job she'd done on her dress, he had a perfect view of the top of two creamy breasts and the shadowed hollow between them where a locket swung wildly as they rode.

Two more turns and they would be at Hell's Gate, where Les could shin up the rocky cliff and release the rope that held back enough rocks to close the passageway behind them. More had heard tales of men who could enjoy a woman in the heat of danger, but he'd always sworn there was no way he could be one of them. He didn't like risks, didn't relish death, and wasn't so in need of a woman that his want would overcome his fear.

So it surprised him that with men in hot pursuit, his eyes kept returning to watch her locket dance in its hold. And it shocked him to feel himself responding to her nearness in the most basic way a man could. And to have no control over it. And to be thinking about touching her, tasting her, taking her, when behind him the gap was closing between them and disaster.

He kicked Magic's flanks harder, and Samantha Maddigan's hands lost their tenuous hold around him. She settled for gripping at his shirt for dear life. He shot a quick glance at her and caught the brightness of her gray eyes, the flash of smile she raised to him.

Stupid woman! Didn't she know she ought to be scared to death?

He was scared enough for both of them now. After all, the idiots behind them could miss him entirely and hit her, just as the fool back in town had done. Did they think she was some goddamn target, shooting so carelessly? If he ever got out of his present mess, he was going right back to Granite and putting a bullet in that hero-seeking idiot's own calf. Let him see how he liked it!

He curled his body around hers as best he could. They took the second bend in the path quickly, rocks and sand sputtering down the cliff. Once, and then again, Magic came within a hair of losing his footing. Not used to the second rider, the horse was having trouble balancing on the narrow strip, and More had no choice but to let him slow down some.

It was hard to believe that such a tiny bit of a woman could even be noticed by the massive animal, but then More, too, was having trouble keeping his own center as she bounced within the confines of his lap.

Why the heck hadn't he just let Les take the lady with him? He looked down at Samantha Maddigan and felt a clutch in his chest, just like he had in the bank. Damn woman. Just the kind that could get a man killed.

Les was already climbing the rocks on foot, slipping and sliding on the slick stones.

"Where's he going?" Samantha Maddigan twisted in his arms, her elbow coming in contact with his manhood and jabbing it unmercifully. Though he groaned, her blank look indicated that she had no idea what she'd done. "Why is he climbing up there?"

"You see that rope?" More asked, pointing up the mountainside about fifty yards or so. "He's going to cut it and close off the pass with a rockslide."

Samantha's light brows came down hard over pure gray eyes. "Why does he have to climb up there?" she asked, shifting again in his arms until he could hardly remember her question.

"Because if the rope was all the way down here, anyone could reach it," he explained as patiently as he could. Women like Samantha Maddigan just didn't have the slightest inkling how these sorts of things worked. They were used to pulling a cord and having a servant appear with whatever it was they desired. Some things had to be worked at. They had to take time.

Precious time, which they didn't have.

"Oh, for heaven's sake," she said, her hand run-

ning down his back in sweet agony. When he felt
her hand run down his past his waist and realized
what she was about, there was only time for a moment's panic before it was too late to do anything
about it.

She was holding his rifle.

But rather than pointing it at him, she was aiming
up at the top of the mountain.

"No," he warned her. "If you hit the rocks it'll
ricochet and you could get us all killed."

"Don't move a muscle," she warned him, then
proceeded to put a knee in his groin, a breast against
his chin, and take aim, while he tried not to breathe.

The small body in his arms jerked with the recoil,
her breast brushing his lips both up and down and
grazing slowly against his chin, leaving his mouth
open and his jaw hanging wide enough to catch a
sparrow.

The rocks tumbling down the mountain weren't
nearly as loud as his own swallow when she eased
back down into his lap and gave him a smile that was
half victory and half pain.

"My leg hurts like hell," she said, leaning her full
weight against him and letting out a ragged sigh.
"Do you think we could rest a bit?"

She didn't see why he was so angry. The rocks
had fallen just the way they were supposed to, hadn't
they? Why did he have to keep saying that he should
have stopped her? Of course, he could have just
taken the Winchester from her, overpowered her.
Hell, he could have broken her in two.

He'd taken the rifle from her and idly threatened
to use it if she tried anything so foolish again. He'd

reminded her that she was his prisoner and nothing more. Then, despite the harsh tone he'd taken, he'd handed her down to his brother as if she were a butterfly with a broken wing. After dismounting himself, he'd taken her back into his own arms with the softest of sighs and set her down gently on the grassiest patch he could find. Settling himself as far away from her as he could, he crouched on some hard rocks Sam was quite sure couldn't be comfortable at all.

She smiled to herself while she watched him scowl. He liked her. Berris Forbes was right. You *could* tell when a man fancied you. And Moreland Rivers fancied her. Craved her, lusted after her! Wait until she told Berris!

"What's the matter with you?" Lesley Rivers asked the enormous man who'd tried to shelter her with his body as they rode. "What are you sulking about? The path's closed, ain't it?"

More grunted. It was a very manly sound. Better than her brother's grunts, which were much more like growls. "*Me?* What's the matter with *me?* It's her," he said, pointing at Sam. "That woman doesn't have a lick of sense in that whole lusciou—stupid, foolish, mindless little body! She coulda got killed. She coulda killed you or me. She coulda—"

She crossed her arms over her chest. Why didn't she have a needle and thread on her like a woman was supposed to? Berris would have a needle, thread, some pomade for her lips, and some Garfield's Headache Powder to boot, which Sam could certainly use around now. For all his good looks and gentle ways, the man could be as irritating as her brother. Did he really think she couldn't handle something as easy to shoot as a Winchester?

"Who," she asked as haughtily as she could, "do you think taught Carson Maddigan how to shoot?" She batted her eyes and smiled.

More's eyes widened, and then he threw his head back and laughed. "Way I heard it, Earp did, but then I guess it wouldn't be so all-fired intimidatin' for a bounty hunter's sister to have taught him everything he knows. Can't wait till that little bit of news gets around."

Sam counted her fingernails, a habit that Carson had endeavored to instill in her in an effort to check her impetuousness. Well, she still had ten fingers, but not a lick of brains. "It was Earp," she allowed, smiling. "But he taught me first."

"Tell her it was a good shot and get it over with," Les said, taking a last swig of water and rising to his feet. "Time to make tracks, if she's okay."

For some reason Les had apparently decided that only More would talk to Samantha. Not one of his comments had been directed to her, though almost all of them had concerned her. He'd complimented her, fussed over her, and worried about her, all through his brother, who didn't seem to enjoy talking to her either.

But here again Berris was right. Women were so much better at communicating. Women knew how they felt and weren't afraid of it.

More was afraid. Sam knew it from the way he trembled when he carried her, from the way his hand shook when he lifted her skirt to check on her leg. From the way his voice cracked when he asked if she was ready.

But he liked her, all right. Why else would he insist that she go on his horse rather than Les's? All right, so maybe his black horse was a little bigger than Les's gray one. Still, he was the one who now carried her to the horse, handed her to Les for only a second or two while he mounted, and then took her in his own arms again and cradled her against him.

After she'd settled her fanny against him, he pushed her slightly away and removed his shirt. Rolling it into a ball, he backed up slightly in the saddle and made a pillow of it between his thighs. "You'll be more comfortable like this," he assured her, and then let go such a big sigh that her hair danced in the breeze of it.

"I was fine before," she assured him, wondering what she'd hold on to now that his chest was bare.

"Yeah, well, I wasn't," he said gruffly, looking around as if he, too, didn't know what she'd find to grasp. "Aw, hell." He pulled the shirt out from between them and shoved his arms back into it angrily. Again she adjusted herself against him. He was rock-hard and it wasn't easy getting comfortable. Then she realized why.

And felt herself turn six shades of red.

"Oh!" was all she could manage.

"Yeah, *oh*," he repeated.

She shifted around, trying to put some distance between her body and his. "I could just—"

Gritting his teeth, he closed his eyes.

"Or—" She put her hands on his thigh and lifted herself an inch or two.

"Could you just stay put?" The words came out through a clenched jaw. His eyes were still closed.

"I just want to—" she explained, trying to

straighten herself, as the hand on his thigh slid toward the seam in his well-worn blue Levi Strauss jeans.

"And believe me, I want you to," he said, covering her hand and removing it. Glistening green eyes stared at her own, moved slowly down to her lips, and returned to meet hers once again. "But Miss Maddigan, while you may like to play with matches, I ain't looking to get burned. I like to think that I'll at least have all my parts on me when your brother brings me in for the reward on my head."

"My brother isn't going to touch a hair on your head," she said, fingering a few strands by his temple and delighting in their surprising softness.

"It ain't my head I think your brother will be after, ma'am," he said, twisting her so that her back was against him and both her legs were over one of his. He clicked at his horse. "Now that's the last on that subject, far as I'm concerned."

"But—"

"I take it that shot before was no accident," he said. "You're quite a marksman, for a lady."

"Carson and I practiced a lot, and we were good competition for each other." She had rebuttoned the top two buttons of her dress, but there still was an awful gap where she had lost the next several ones.

Les, traveling ahead, stopped and waited for them. "Should be just over the next ridge. What do you want to do about our share?"

"Well, Louise sure as heck didn't earn it. Guess we could just give it all over to Gerz to split up with the other miners."

Sam let out a pitiful sigh. "My leg is throbbing," she complained. "Don't you think I ought to get

Louise's share? I did her job, after all." Well, no doubt about it. Samantha Maddigan was a pistol. Les covered his mouth to hide his smile, but More's chuckle bounced her head against his chest. How did a woman get her hair to smell so good? He was already beginning to miss her and he hadn't even turned her over to Gerz to bring her back to Granite. Surely the man would see her safely home if he ever wanted to see another penny of the Columbia's money by way of the Rivers Brothers.

"You can have Louise's share," More told her, "if you tell your brother this was all a mistake—which it was. And that we didn't do you any harm—which we didn't. And we aren't worth catching—which we ain't."

"Who gets the rest of it?" she asked just as Gerz, Beattie, and Sessa came riding around the bend, each of them looking around suspiciously, their horses nudging each other and nipping when they got too close.

Gerz rode up, his eyes clamped on Samantha Maddigan as if she were some kind of snake and if he looked away she'd bite him. More peeled his shirt from his body once again and put it around the woman's shoulders, encouraging her to cover that lacy bit of a thing that didn't cover what a man's imagination couldn't forget.

"Rivers," Gerz said by way of a greeting. "It go all right?" His eyes were still on Samantha, and More had the urge to cover her with a blanket as well as his shirt. Hell, he wanted to hide her behind a goddamn barn. He snapped his mind back to the business at hand. The sooner they turned over the money, the sooner he could figure out how to get Samantha back to Granite. Without losing any of his parts.

"Slight hitch," Les said, maneuvering his horse between Gerz's and More's and placing himself smack dab in the way of the miner's view.

"Hitch?" The man was drooling now, so high in the saddle in an effort to see Samantha that a woman could have fit beneath him and he'd have never even noticed.

In More's arms, Samantha swiped at her forehead. Her breathing became heavier and her little hands were curled in fists.

"Hurting?" he asked her quietly. Stubbornly she swatted away a tear and shook her head.

"I'm fine."

"The hell you are," he snapped. He'd been winged himself, more than once, and knew how the pain could set in when you least expected it, when you thought the worst of it was over. He was down off the horse and had her in his arms in one movement. "You got some whiskey?" he shouted over at Sessa.

"Got a whole damn feast," Sessa answered him. "The missus thought it was the least she could do what with you helping everyone out."

"Never mind the food," he said, *or the praise*. Samantha Maddigan knew too much already. If she knew where the money was going she could be a real danger to the miners who were depending on him. Receiving stolen money was a crime, and her brother was damn close to being the law. "The lady got grazed in the leg and it's seizing up. You got something strong?"

Sessa was off his horse and beside More as quick as

a man of his size could be. In his huge hands the whiskey bottle looked like a toy as he opened it and offered it to More. "Ain't got a glass or nothing," he said by way of apology.

More waved him off. How was the woman supposed to breathe with all these men hovering over her? He raised her head, her neck, her shoulders, slowly, carefully, afraid of breaking her, hurting her, and offered her the bottle. "Try to drink a little," he said, putting the rim to her lips.

She shook her head at him, raised herself to her elbows, took the bottle in her own hand, and took the goddamn biggest swig he'd ever seen a woman—even in a whorehouse—manage. A good third of the bottle was gone when she handed it back to him and wiped her mouth with the back of her hand.

"I suppose Carson taught you to guzzle too," More said, disgusted with himself for falling into her trap again.

Her eyes widened and she blinked furiously, tears coming from nowhere to pour down her face. She coughed until her whole body shook and she grabbed at her leg in pain. Taking great gasps of air, she fanned at her mouth, tried to talk, and coughed some more.

"Then again," More said, his smile wide and satisfied, "maybe he didn't."

She shook her head vehemently, still unable to get her breath, and tried to rap herself on the back. Stifling his laugh, he rubbed between her shoulder blades with his hand, telling her she'd be all right.

"It's hot," she said, pointing to her belly. "Burning!"

"Leg hurt anymore?" he asked.

"What leg?" she answered, raising her skirt to see which one was bandaged.

It would have been funny if he hadn't caught the hunger in Gerz's eyes as she flashed her little ankles and that bare right foot.

"You sure are the prettiest woman west of the Mississippi," Gerz told her, squatting by her side.

Miss Maddigan stretched, a very satisfied look on her face. She stuck her nose in the air as if it was about time someone told her how beautiful she was, then turned her pretty smile on More and hiccupped.

So far he'd robbed a bank, kidnapped Carson Maddigan's sister, gotten her shot, and gotten her drunk. And it wasn't even dark yet. He had no intention of thinking about the trouble he could get in with her once the sun had set and the stars fanned out overhead.

In fact, he had no intention of still being with her when the moon rose up.

"Sessa, you think you and Beattie can take this young lady back to Granite tonight? There was a little mistake made and—"

"She ain't a hurdy-gurdy girl?" Beattie asked as he set about opening the baskets of food his wife too, had sent along and offering up chicken legs and slices of buffalo dripping with sweet-smelling sauce.

"A hurdy-gurdy girl?" Samantha asked, twisting around to look at More. "You mean a dancing girl? Why, I've never even been kissed." She looked up at him, all dewy from the liquor, her lip trembling. "Not thoroughly, anyway."

"I can take her back," Gerz said, the edges of his mouth turning up in what More took to be a sneer.

"Beattie's girl is ailing and he wants to get some medicine with his share, and Sessa's gotta give out the rest of the cuts."

Samantha leaned forward toward Beattie, the gap in her dress revealing more than the man had a right to see. More reached over her and closed his shirt around her, glaring at each of them in turn. "Your little girl is sick?" she asked, holding the shirt closed and backing up slightly.

Beattie nodded. "I'm hoping she'll be okay now that I can pay for the doc and the medicine," he said, looking past her at More and Lesley. "Without those two men . . . well, I don't know."

"Think your mama made a mistake when it come to naming you," Sessa said, saluting Les with a drumstick. "Shoulda called you More, too."

"Heck," More said, coughing as some buffalo caught in his throat. "Mama liked me so much she said 'More, more!' Took one look at my brother and she shouted 'Less, less!' "

"Ain't true," Les said, wiping his nose the same way he did when he was just a kid. Wasn't right, his ma and pa saddling their kids with names like More and Les. Pa thought better of it too—when he was sober—but the times never lasted long enough to do anything about it.

"Moreland was my mama's people," More said, then added the lie he'd told so many times he'd almost forgotten it wasn't true. Damn his pa and the man's sense of humor. "And Lesley was her papa's name. Guess being first I was luckier."

"Mustn't have been easy growing up with the kind of name kids make fun of," Samantha said. Her shoulders jerked up with a silent hiccup, and she quickly covered the sweetest little mouth More had ever been forbidden.

"Name's something you learn to rise above," Les said thoughtfully. "Don't matter what name they give you, long as you do right by it. Les Rivers stands for something." He thumped his chest proudly. "More does too."

More shrugged. "Yeah, more or less." He ducked as Les swatted at him with his hat. A name meant nothing. Just the same, he'd give his eyeteeth to have been named John.

"So then, you're all bank robbers?" Samantha asked. He could see the teeth marks she'd left in her knuckle and knew she was aching something fierce.

"I think you'd best lie down," he said, trying to ease her back onto the blanket one of the men had spread out.

"You ought to pour some of that whiskey on her leg while she's feelin' no pain," Les suggested.

"They can clean it when they get her back home," More said. Another look at that leg and his hand was gonna find its own way up her thigh. He just knew it. "Beattie?"

Beattie shook his head. I'm late now," he explained. "Got Aaron to agree to come back and open the apothecary at eight. I'm not there, I won't get that medicine until tomorrow. Gerz's your man."

Gerz rose and stretched out his formidable bulk. Each of these men was bigger than the one beside him. But then, miners had to have that kind of weight behind their picks. Samantha looked even smaller as Sessa leaned over her and told her to take good care of his friends.

"Wait! How are they helping you?" she asked.

More wasn't about to listen to his praises being sung one more time. He'd heard it all over Montana. Les swore they were even the subject of some song the miners' kids were singing. They were becoming legends. And More knew what happened to legends. He wondered why the hell he ever thought it might be nice to be one.

Because he and Les had agreed that if they died tomorrow it would be a comfort to know they'd be remembered. But as he headed for a cluster of trees where he could take care of some private business, More was beginning to think that, rather than being remembered, it might be nice if he was still alive tomorrow.

By the time he returned, the group had thinned considerably. Sessa and Beattie had taken off, and Samantha was hanging on each of Gerz's words, which he drawled out between drools and praises of her beauty.

"Bet that hair shines in the moonlight," he was saying when More sat down and took Samantha's hand in his own as if he owned her.

"Bet you don't get to find out," More said. He studied the woman's face, trying to decide if she was drunk enough for him to clean the wound with whiskey. She smiled at him, tried to rise up on her elbows, and missed. He decided she'd be about as steady on her feet as a newborn calf, and told Les to bring the whiskey over. "You think you can roll over and put your head down for a bit?" he asked her softly.

Fear flashed in her eyes, but she nodded. He

helped her turn, watching her wince as he moved her leg.

"Might be best if you took off," More told Gerz, who seemed just a little too interested in helping touch and tug and look.

"Thought he was taking her back," Les asked, handing More the bottle while he lifted her skirts just far enough to see that the bandage was now too tight and the blood was still seeping through the layers of cotton. "Best for us all if he did," he added.

More untied the cloth that bound her calf and felt her low moan rise in his own throat as if he'd been the one to utter it. He'd seen better-looking wounds on dead coyotes, and he swallowed convulsively at the sight of the puckered sore marring her creamy skin.

"It's gonna hurt some," he warned her. Les and Gerz had both turned away, so More reached out and held the lady's hand tightly with his left and poured the whiskey over her wound with his right.

Her nails bit into his skin. Her cry cut him deeper still. With tears in her eyes she reached behind her and took the bottle from him, tipped her head back and gulped.

This time there wasn't a cough, a sputter—nothing but a shuddering breath.

"It really hurts, More," she said, her face screwed up to stop her tears. *More.* He'd hated his name for all of his twenty-eight years. Now he blessed his mother and her ancestors for giving it to him.

"It's all right, Samantha," he told her, stroking the golden strands of hair off her cheek and wiping the tears. "You'll be fine."

"I could take her to a doctor in Granite," Gerz

said when More had wrapped the leg back up and she had finished her crying. "And then take her back to wherever she wants."

He should let her go. She needed medical attention, and there was a chance, however slight, that she could talk her brother out of coming after them. After all, they hadn't harmed her.

"Don't send me back," she begged him, the liquor no doubt talking. No woman in her right mind wanted to hole up with two outlaws who could take advantage of her at any moment. One of whom was lusting after her so badly that he wasn't sure he'd ever be able to straighten up to his full height again if she didn't leave in minutes.

"It's best," he said, sizing up Gerz and praying the man could be trusted.

"Oh." She rolled over gingerly and sat up. "Well, then, I guess you'll be needing your shirt back." She unbuttoned it slowly, taking her tantalizing time as if she'd been a stripper for years. It fell from her shoulders, taking enough of her dress with it to show off the top of that damn lacy thing she was wearing, which was next to worthless. "You're gonna have to carry me," she said to Gerz, batting lashes that More could have sworn were growing while he watched.

"My pleasure, ma'am," Gerz managed to get out before falling to his knees in front of her and attempting to gather her into his arms. She smiled at More as she put her arms around Gerz's too-wide neck.

"Course, Maddigan's bound to kill us if we don't have her with us to explain," More found himself saying, as her breasts pressed against each other in Gerz's arms.

"Oh, he'll kill you if I'm not there," she agreed readily. Then, all smiles, she beamed up at Gerz. "I don't think we've been properly introduced. I'm Samantha Maddigan. Carson's sister."

Lord, but the pain had been unbearable when that Gerz fellow had lost hold of her and she'd gone tumbling to the ground. If Moreland Rivers thought a half bottle of watered-down scotch could deaden a Maddigan's pain, he obviously had no Irish blood.

Oh, but he wanted her to be a little lady just like Carson did. What a look he gave her when she downed those first few gulps!

Berris was right. Men didn't know what they wanted. If they really wanted those demure little ladies who spoke so softly and so sweetly that they'd choke on a sugar cube before it melted, she'd like to know how come they spent every spare dollar they had at Chicago Joe's Pleasure Palace.

Beattie's story had moved her nearly to tears, as had the one that Sessa had told her. She could see the embarrassment written on the men's faces when they told how without More and Lesley they couldn't provide the simplest of necessities for their families.

It was as if bells and whistles and rockets had gone off for her then, and she understood what she was put on the planet for after all.

She was there for Moreland Rivers. To be his strength, his softness, and his safety.

Whether he wanted her to be or not.

Berris was right. Some men didn't know what was best for them, and it was a woman's job to make them understand.

She closed her eyes and snuggled against the

warmth of More's chest, listening to the steady beat of his heart as Magic wandered in the hills. Her leg throbbed, she had no idea where they were headed, and she had no doubt that Carson was going to come after the Rivers Brothers to kill them.

All right—there were a few things that needed working out. Still, all in all, it had been the best day of Samantha Maddigan's life.

Thus far.

3

Could a man die of want, of desire? More felt the weight of Samantha Maddigan pressed to him, her head lolling against his chest, one of her breasts brushing his forearm, her bottom seated on his thighs and then some, rubbing, rubbing, rubbing. She'd fallen asleep twice now, and each time he'd woken her up, more comfortable with the stiff primness of her consciousness than the yielding softness of her slumber.

Again he prodded her. If he had to be damn uncomfortable—and that wasn't the half of it—then so did she. "Come on now," he said, jostling her. "Don't you know you're in the arms of a dangerous man?"

"Oh, and I'm shaking," she said sleepily, stretching like he supposed a wife did, with no thought to what she looked like or what she was doing to his insides. He'd seen his share of women stretch—it wasn't as if he were a priest or anything—but they all did it for effect, or for the effect it had on him. Miss Maddigan's breasts rose up in that goddamn tiny little lacy thing and then, before he'd gotten a good-enough look, disappeared again to form that dark hollow, now empty.

"Where's that heart you were wearing before?" he asked, but got only a shrug for an answer. "You lose it?"

"She gave it to Beattie," Les said, picking at a nub on his pants leg as they rode slowly against the side of the mountain that had become their home since they'd had to take to the hills to hide. "For his daughter."

He tried not to be touched, tried to ignore that lump in his throat that made it hard to swallow. "He'll probably just trade the thing for food," he said, feeling her slacken in his arms again.

"She told him to," Les said. "Told him not to settle for less than ten dollars' worth, and to be sure there was some treat in there for Becky Sue."

"Did she also tell him to stay the hell out of the saloon and not to drink up the damn ten dollars?" he asked. Her breast pressed against his hand, harder than he would have thought, firmer. If he tipped his wrist, gave his horse a bit more head, it would be resting in his hand.

"Yup." Les smiled. "Told him if he drank more than two bits' worth, she'd know and come after him with a loaded Colt."

The trail turned sharply to the left. Magic knew it, but still More guided him, and with the shift Samantha Maddigan's breast slid solidly into his reining hand. In response he nudged her quite unintentionally from beneath, unable to stop his natural response. He'd told the woman not to fall asleep—not to trust him. He'd told her he was a desperate man.

And the truth was he was getting more desperate by the minute.

"I can't go on like this," he said, and started at the sound of the words when they finally passed his lips. He'd been thinking them for weeks now, as each robbery was a greater risk, as each posse came closer to catching them and collecting the reward that rested on the two of their heads, dead or alive.

"I'll take her," Les said, sidling up against Magic's flanks and reaching out for the woman, apparently assuming that More was talking of a much smaller matter than his life as a whole. Les's eyes landed on More's full left hand. "Enjoying yourself with Carson Maddigan's sister? Why, you're braver than the legends say!"

"It's not easy to hold on to her," More lied. In truth, she fit like sun-warmed boots on a cold morning. There was a welcoming snugness that kept trying to tell him he was home. "How long you think before she can put weight on that leg?" he asked Les, who had been winged more often than a choir boy at a Christmas pageant.

"Week at most," Les said, his eyes looking everywhere but at More and his burden. "Before we hit Kirkville, anyways."

A week. A week of carrying her in his arms, helping her see to her needs, hearing her voice, and seeing her smile. He'd be bursting by Tuesday. By Thursday he'd be dead, with his tombstone rising up through the fly of his almost-new Levi Strauss blue jeans.

In the event that he wasn't, a plan was forming in his head.

Easy enough, provided he could make it through the week.

"Home, sweet home," Les said, waving at the ugliest, most dilapidated cabin More had ever had the misfortune of appropriating. Sagging four ways from square, its door held on by only one hinge, the run-down shack clawed at the ground with only a half-hearted hope of not sliding down the side of the mountain. On the roof lay a jumble of antlers some previous tenant must have found appealing. To More it looked as if death had found the cabin and tried to bury it.

Coming to a halt, he looked down at the golden-haired beauty in his arms and felt a wave of embarrassment wash over him, drowning him when he dragged his eyes from her to the pile of boards and promises he had the nerve to carry her into.

Off his horse already, Les tied up Magic, rubbed his hands on his jeans in an effort to clean them, and reached up for Samantha Maddigan.

More didn't want to hand her down. Oh, he was well aware that there was little chance they'd wind up in one piece if he tried to get down while holding her, but knowing that didn't seem to convince his arms to release her into his brother's care. It didn't warm the cold spot on his chest where her head had been resting or fill the emptiness he felt when she woke and blinked questioningly at him as he transferred her into Les's waiting arms.

All it did was get him out of that saddle faster than a coyote would jump on a jackrabbit in a blizzard. And then she was back in his arms, against his chest, her arms around his neck before she was even fully awake.

"I need to get down," she said shyly, her face coloring at her predicament. "To visit the privy."

Oh, hell. No one who'd holed up at the wreck of a cabin had ever bothered with something as frivolous as an outhouse. The bushes had been more than adequate, until now. He stood, holding her, looking for the most private place, and finally carried her to the far side of the densest of the scraggly bushes.

There he stopped and let her legs down gingerly, keeping her upright with the length of his body. Her thighs brushed his as he pressed her against him. He was searching for the words to apologize for his hardness, which nestled against her belly, when a hardness of her own pressed back.

He was, despite his lack of interest in dancing girls and palaces of pleasure, no monk. Granted, Les's experience was far more vast. Still, he knew how a woman was made, every soft inch of her. With eager hands and moist lips he'd examined more than one of them, from the tips of their feet to the hair buns he'd uncoiled and back again. He'd taken every detour there was to take, and a woman just didn't have a length of hardness to poke back with.

But Samantha Maddigan was poking back, every bit as hard as he was. And looking guilty as a fox with the feathers still in her mouth.

More insinuated his hand between them, his fingers tracing her waist and moving down her belly while she struggled to squirm away from him without letting go of his shoulders, which she needed for support. He could feel the junction where legs met body and woman was made to meet man. Still something pressed against his thigh, and reluctantly his hand moved on until he found the hardness he sought.

"What the hell?" he asked, but knew before he'd finished the question that their sweet, innocent victim was packing a derringer. And he suspected, from the way she shook in his arms, that it was loaded. "Well, sweetheart, I guess you missed your chance," he said, reaching into her deep pocket and pulling out the small but deadly weapon. He was going to tell her that she should have used it when she had the opportunity, but it occurred to him that she was all too aware of that.

"I still need some privacy," she said, raising her eyes slowly from the small gun, which sat innocently in the palm of his hand.

"Why didn't you use it?" he asked, looking for something for her to hold on to besides his arm. He transferred her hand to the fattest of the branches on the puny bush.

"Why didn't you use *that*?" she said, pointing her chin at the Colt on his hip.

Samantha tipped her face up at him, and More looked into gray eyes that read his soul like a wanted poster she'd decided to collect the reward on. "I figured you'd be worth more to me alive than dead," he said. Then he turned away and walked toward the house.

"I'll do my best."

The words followed him into the shack, where he raced around like some sort of burrowing animal, digging here and there, burying that mess and clearing this piece of furniture. Les looked on, not even trying to hide his smile and laughing so damn loud that More could hardly hear Samantha when she called out his name.

4

For two days after he'd picked her up from the
ground and carried her to the house, Samantha had
been treated like a princess who'd wandered away
from the castle and been stuck in the poorest hovel
her kingdom had to offer. Despite the deference,
there was never a moment when she didn't feel like
an unwelcome guest. Whenever Les was in the
house he spent his time staring at More, as if waiting
for him to come to some decision, no doubt about
her. And More spent his time staring at her when he
thought she wasn't looking.

Like now, when he thought she was asleep.

She fooled him all the time, or at least as often as
she wanted to. Berris was right. Men only thought
they had the upper hand. It was women who held all
the cards. And no one bluffed better than Sam.

"Maybe you ought to think about riding out to
Silver Ethel's," Les said.

Through nearly closed eyes she could see More

lean his head against the back of his chair. He studied the ceiling and sighed hopelessly. *Oh, Berris, you could really give lessons!*

"You could close your eyes over at Ethel's and pretend," Les said. "Christ, you don't gotta look to know where to put it, More."

"Don't take the Lord's name in vain, Lesley. Ma wouldn't like it."

"Ma wouldn't like a lotta things. S'pose she'd like us robbing banks? Or you keeping that girl here, dreaming about her and wanting her so bad you can't hardly think straight?"

It took everything Sam had not to make a sound, not to gasp, or sigh, or shout *hallelujah*! from the rooftop.

"You telling me she don't turn your insides upside down?" More snapped. "You telling me she don't make you wanna hang curtains on the window like when Ma was alive and wash up good and watch your mouth like we ain't done in a good two years of fighting the railroads and the mines and all the other sons of bitches that've come out here and tried to take the food out of the mouths of hard-working men?"

Sam fought to keep the smile from her lips. If they were really singing songs about the Rivers Brothers as Les said, she'd sure like to add a verse or two about her hero.

"Sons of guns," Les corrected. "She might hear you even in her sleep and think less of you than she already does, what with you kidnappin' her and all. And you can bet if she turned *my* insides over the way she does *yours*, I'd be doing something about it, instead of mooning over her like a bull with no balls."

"Go fuck a tree," More said, and Samantha turned on the cot, covering her mouth with her arm so they wouldn't know from her smile that she was awake and hearing their every word. They'd be shocked to know she even knew what that word meant. Carson would wash her mouth out with soap if he so much as thought she'd ever said it. But Berris said that a woman needed to know things to protect herself in this world, and a word never turned a virgin into a scarlet woman, but a lack of knowledge might.

"I was gonna recommend you do just that," Les said. "You think she can cook any? I'm getting damn sick of your rabbit stew."

"How much you think she hates me?" More asked.

Well, Berris was right. Men were idiots. Sam didn't hate him even the tiniest bit.

He was standing over her, inches from the cot on which she lay. She held her breath while he brushed her hair off her forehead, then gently covered her with the blanket he'd aired out all day.

"How much? What's the biggest number you know?" Les asked. Then he laughed and shook his head. "Did she sew those buttons back onto that dress yet? Has she told you not to help her out to the bushes? Has she stopped watching your every move like you was one of them actors on the stage in Virginia City? If I didn't know better, I'd swear she was sweet on you."

Okay, so maybe they weren't all idiots. Still, none of them was half as bright as she or Berris.

"Her leg's healin' good," More said, turning the end of the blanket down so that her neck was exposed. "You ever see anything so white in your life?"

"Nice of her to give that necklace to Beattie, huh?" Les said.

"She's a good woman." He put the blanket back up, tucking it under her chin.

"I figure she thinks you're a good man."

"Then she don't know what I'm thinkin' right now," More said, and crossed the room in just a few steps.

"Where are you going?" The door opened and a cool breeze filled the room, sweeping strands of Sam's hair across her face.

"Thought I'd take a cool dip in the creek," More answered. "Damn hot in the cabin."

"A bath. Hey, that's a good idea. How often you think a woman like Miss Maddigan takes one?" Les asked.

More stopped in the doorway. He didn't turn, didn't answer, didn't move.

"Yeah," Les said softly. "I was thinking the same thing."

"You want to go down to the creek first?" More asked. He still hadn't turned around in the doorway.

"Me?" Les reached for his hat and his guns. "Think I'll take a ride down the hill and see if Silver Ethel's free. I could tell her to expect you later. . . ."

"So by the end of the week?" More asked. "She'll be walking by the Kirkville job?"

"Thought you wanted to hold off on that," Les said. "What's the hurry now?"

"We'll bring her to Kirkville and leave her there,"

More said, slamming his fist on the door frame. "Then, I don't know about you, but I'm heading north and I'm done with it."

He was still talking as he walked farther from the house, but if Les heard him any better than Sam, he didn't answer.

"Who'd think such a little bit of a thing would be a match for the great Moreland Rivers?" Les stood in the doorway looking at her, she supposed, for now her eyes were shut tight to hold back the tears. "Sleep tight, Miss Maddigan," he said softly, then left and shut the door quietly behind him.

"Leave me in Kirkville," she said under her breath, flexing her foot to test the pain in her calf. She winced, and more tears filled her eyes. Her leg hurt, but it was her heart that was beginning to worry her.

He couldn't believe it was the same cabin. As if the dish towels she'd hung in the windows as curtains weren't enough, she'd swept the floors, had him rearrange the furniture, and now he could smell supper from the creek. He was the cleanest desperado in Montana. If he could only wash his mind there'd be some hope for him.

He checked his watch. He had to live through only twenty-seven more hours of torture and he'd be rid of her. She'd be out of his life forever. And there'd be no reason for Carson Maddigan to come after him once she explained that he'd made a mistake and that he'd treated her well and hadn't taken advantage of her, no matter how it had killed him.

He took one more plunge into the icy waters of Flint Creek in a futile attempt to cool feelings that threatened to overwhelm his better judgment. Things had gone from bad to worse when he'd realized that his desire for her wasn't confined to a swift trip beneath her skirts.

He couldn't help remembering a conversation that he'd overheard between his mother and father when they'd fallen on hard times and were all living in a small set of rooms with paper-thin walls.

"I love you," his father had said, *"because you always make me brave enough to do the right thing."*

"And I love you," his mama had answered, *"because you make me brave enough to ask it of you."*

Wasn't it just his luck that when he finally fell for someone, doing the right thing meant giving her up? Not that he was in love or anything. He just wasn't only interested in touching her body anymore. He wanted to touch more—her heart maybe. Her soul.

He wanted to know what made her so brave that being captured by the Rivers Brothers seemed to delight her. What made her so caring that she'd give her locket to buy food for a stranger? And more than knowing all of the secrets in her heart, he wanted to know that he was the only one who knew them.

In short, he was an ass.

At least that was how he felt when he came back into the cabin and found her sitting on the table stirring a pot on the stove in his shirt and little else.

"Smell good?" she asked. "I hope you like onions. Can't have Irish stew without onions."

For such a little woman, her legs stretched beyond her tattered petticoat for miles.

"I thought if it wasn't too much trouble you

might help me down to that creek you keep going to."

Her hair was loose, hanging halfway down her back like liquid gold.

"Since you're planning on taking me back to civilization tomorrow . . ."

Onions. Why hadn't they thought to put onions in their stew? It smelled heavenly. But then, an angel was stirring the pot.

"And I looked around, but I couldn't find a needle and thread to fix my dress with. Have you any?"

She turned her full face to him, one cheek dusted with flour, a strand of her hair teasing her lips, and waited for his answer.

Unable to speak, he reached into a drawer, pulled out a small sewing kit someone had left in the cabin at some unknown point in time, and set it on the table.

"Thanks. I'll sew it after my bath." She blew gently on the ladle and stuck a tiny pink tongue into the broth. More felt his backbone melt into jelly and eased himself into a chair. At eye level was her bare knee. He couldn't breathe. He couldn't swallow.

"Is now a good time?" she asked. "For a dip in the creek?"

He nodded, stood, took her in his arms, and walked toward the door. Juggling her on a knee, he managed to open the door and step through it with her in his arms.

"Good time for me to head into town and make the arrangements with Velvet Joan?" Les drawled, leaning against a railing that was leaning back against him.

More nodded.

"Ain't no hurry up, so don't expect me before morning." Les tipped his hat at Sam and picked up his saddle, heading for his gelding, Gray.

Halfway down to the creek he could still hear Les's chuckle and wished he'd taken the time to wipe the smile off his brother's face. In his arms Sam fussed with her buttons, and More kept his eyes on the Flint Creek current.

Near the creek's banks he set her down gently. "You ain't got the brains of a goddamn toad," he said, sitting down on a rock with his back to her and the creek.

"I don't?" she asked innocently. He could hear her limping toward the water and hoped to God she still had his shirt on. He fought the urge to tell her to be careful on the slippery rocks.

"I'm an outlaw. There's a price on my head. A damn respectable one. I've enough muscle to have my way with you and—" Even as he said it, he knew that it was an empty, idle threat, and he didn't blame her for being sure that he wouldn't do it, no matter what he said.

"You're a robber who gives away every cent he steals. Why, you even pay your hostages. No matter what happens, I want you to know that I think you're a hero."

When was it that he'd lost the ability to swallow? He stroked at his throat, trying to make it work.

"Ooh! The water's really cold." Her voice came out high, a squeak that was a mixture of shock and pleasure. "It feels wonderful on my leg. We should have done this sooner."

"A pissant!" he shouted, spinning around and looking at her as she fought to keep her balance against the current in the shoulder-deep water. She tipped her head back to wet her hair, and the sun set it on fire. "You don't have the goddamn brains of a pissant. I'm a man, Samantha. And a man can only be so good."

She shrugged, enough for him to realize that she'd left his shirt on. He found that he could breathe, a little.

"I think I'm in love with you." She said it so softly that he had to take several steps into the water and ask her to repeat it. "I think I love you." Her eyes were wide with all the fear he felt himself.

For the first time since he'd thrown her over his horse, the ache in his loins subsided.

And moved into his heart.

She'd sewn new buttons onto her dress; More had donated them from a shirt he pulled from one of the drawers. She'd brushed her hair until it shone and dished up the finest Irish stew this side of the Atlantic. But if she had started the day with any hope of changing his mind about leaving her in Kirkville, she was losing it rapidly.

He'd whisked her out of the water, charged back to the cabin, dumped her on her cot, and disappeared for an hour. He'd come back soaked to the skin and taken a seat at the table as if it were the most normal thing in the world to make a puddle beneath one's seat and send droplets flying with every shake of one's head.

He'd said two words up to this point. *Let's eat.*

And then he'd eaten. And eaten.

"I suppose you cook for your brother," he said after he'd mopped up every thread of gravy on his plate with the biscuits she'd managed to scrape together from whatever she could find around the cabin. They weren't Irish soda bread, but she had to admit they were pretty tasty.

"When he's home," she said. "Mostly he's away hunting . . ." She let her voice trail off. Pretty soon Carson would be hunting More. He knew it and she knew it, and the room was silent enough to hear a bug crawling down the wall.

"So who do you live with?" he asked. He was savoring her meal despite himself. He was savoring her too. She could tell from the way his eyes scoured her face, lingered on her neck, checked the sewing job she'd done on her buttons. Supper had been a good idea. She just prayed that Berris was right about the way to a man's heart being through his stomach.

"I live alone."

"Alone?" His eyes widened and the muscles in his jaw tensed. "Ain't you got some aunt or something?"

He knew about her parents then. Of course he did. Everyone in Montana knew that Carson Maddigan's parents had been killed in a stagecoach holdup that netted the men less than a hundred dollars in silver and the undying enmity of a young man left to raise his little sister alone.

"It ain't safe for a woman to live alone."

"Well, I do."

"You got a beau though, coming courting, who's looking out for you, I hope."

"And who, besides you, would mess with Carson Maddigan's sister?" *A beau coming courting*. That was a laugh. She felt her blood boil and let it spill over.

"Who would even talk to her, beside Sheriff Forbes's daughter? Who would risk saying the wrong thing, doing the wrong thing, and having Carson Maddigan mad at them?"

"You're exaggerating." The corners of his mouth were twitching and heading south.

She unbuttoned the cuff of her sleeve and rolled it back once, revealing the scar on her wrist. " 'Don't let Miss Maddigan help with the cooking. She might burn herself again, and Carson will have our heads!' " She tried to sound like Mavis Carter, speaking through her nose like the old biddy herself. Unbuttoning the other sleeve to reveal her other scar, she continued. " 'Don't let Miss Maddigan help with the serving. She might cut herself again, and Lord knows, poor Miss Pruitt is still shaking from the dressing down she got from Carson. Don't even talk to Miss Maddigan. Carson might think you told her to do one of those silly things she's always doing. And if we tell her not to, she might get mad and tell Carson on us. Yes, let's not talk to Miss Maddigan at all. That's the safest thing. But be polite, Milly dear. Oh, yes. *Politely* don't talk to her, of course!' "

He humphed at her, folding his arms across his chest.

"Do you think I could have given that locket to Mr. Beattie if he'd known who I was? Do you think he'd have taken it, or thought better of it, knowing it was Carson's sister's jewelry? Maybe it was a gift from him. What if Carson didn't like that? *Best not to,* he'd think. It wouldn't pay to have Carson Maddigan mad at him. Better not to allow me even that small kindness."

More balled up the dish towel she'd given him as a

napkin—because there surely wasn't anything *that* refined to be found in the cabin—and threw it onto his plate. "That's the stupidest, dumbest, all-fired . . . well, I don't even have a word for it!"

She studied the hands in her lap then lifted her gaze until it met his. "Lonely. The word is *lonely*. These past few days have been the most exciting, warmest days of my life. I've talked and been talked to more than with anyone but Berris Forbes, who doesn't let me get a word in edgewise. Here I wasn't Carson's sister—"

More pushed away from the table and stood, looking down at her as if she'd lost her mind. "You've been nothing *but* Carson Maddigan's sister! Do you think that if you were anyone else you'd still be in the same condition you were when we started out? Do you think that I'da kept my distance? Do you think that I wouldn'ta—"

"Yes."

He pushed the chair out of his way and went to the sink, where he gulped air from the open window. "You're crazy."

"Maybe. I don't have much experience with people."

"You telling the truth about never being kissed?" He was facing the window, his back to her, and he didn't turn to speak.

"I said I was kissed once. A peck. Carson caught us."

"Jeez."

"He recovered. But he still crosses the street when he sees me coming. And so does every other man in Granite."

"Well, that's good," he said, his shoulders sagging. "No one ought to be trifling with you."

"Is that what you're doing? Trifling?"

"I never trifled," he said, finally turning and looking at her. "And I never mean to."

"Am I that ugly? That awful? Is there something so terribly wrong with me that the thought of taking me in your arms is so . . . so—"

"You mean besides the fact that your brother would kill me?" Grimacing more than smiling as he intended, he came back to the table and took his seat again. He looked thoroughly disgusted as he shook his head at her. "I was right about you. You don't have the brains of a pissant."

Now it was her turn to rise from the table, to limp over to the sink and look out at the setting sun. Tomorrow it would all be over. He'd drop her off in Kirkville and be done with her. Her life would go back to rattling around her house with an occasional visit from Berris. "Maybe I could get a cat," she mumbled.

"I'm on the run, for Christ's sake!" He stayed at the table, his hands clenched in fists. "I'm an outlaw. A bank robber. They're going to catch me and hang me. And that's only if I'm lucky. If I'm not, your brother will get me first."

"What if you'd met me before?"

He uttered the saddest sigh she'd ever heard. It reached the rafters of the cabin, sought out the cobwebs in the corner, ran down her spine, caught in her throat.

"This is a dangerous game to play, Miss Maddigan," he warned. "Maybe more dangerous than the one we've been playin'."

Twisting around, she steadied herself against the sink, as open as she could be, her hands against the counter edge, her weight on her good leg, and let his gaze roam over her.

"If you were just some cowboy or a clerk in a store? If you were a miner, or a railroad man, what then?"

"Then you wouldn't be over there while I'm over here," he answered. His voice was low and ragged, and he rubbed his hands down his thighs.

"Where would I be?" Her voice came out as a squeak, but he didn't seem to notice. He was looking straight at her, but she guessed he was seeing some other time and place.

"In a house with lace curtains on the windows," he said softly. "That smells of biscuits every morning and peach tart at noon. You'd have a baby in the cradle and another beneath your heart, and a smile on your face instead of that tear running down your cheek." He gestured with his chin at her face. "But life ain't wishes and dreams, Samantha. It's choices and consequences, and I made mine and I gotta live with the results."

"But you're a good man," she said, letting the tears fall where they would. "You didn't keep the money; you didn't really kidnap the girls."

" 'Cept you," he said, the smile going no farther than his lips. "And I got you shot. And Lord knows what I've done to your reputation, though I can guess."

"If I didn't go back it wouldn't matter." She swallowed hard, the sound filling her ears against the silence.

"I'm taking you to Kirkville tomorrow," he said

finally, after taking a moment to clear his throat. "That's the plan, and I'm sticking to it. I've done enough damage to your life already. I'll be damned if I'll do any more."

"Then there's only tonight," she said, reaching out her hand to him so that he could help her over to the narrow cot that waited.

"What's that supposed to mean?" He looked at her warily, reluctantly taking her hand and guiding her over to the bed.

How was she supposed to tell him that she wanted to cram a lifetime into this one night, that she'd been waiting for him forever, wishing for him, and that now all the rest of her days would be spent just remembering?

There was no way to tell him, and so she shrugged and mumbled, "Nothing."

"Oh." Was that disappointment or relief? She couldn't tell.

She opened the top two buttons on her dress and fanned at her neck with her hand. She supposed it was all the cooking that had made the cabin so warm. Sweat beaded on More's upper lip and trickled at his temples.

"You want to sit outside?" he offered. "It'll be cooler."

He rose as if the decision had been made and put out his hand to her much the way a gentleman requests a dance of a lady at some church social. She slipped her hand into his and, putting her weight on her good leg, came to her feet. She reached for him to carry her.

"Might be a good idea if you tested out that leg,"

he said, offering his arm rather than reaching to lift her.

His muscles were tight, and holding his arm was like embracing a tree limb baking in the sun. She took a deep breath and her breast brushed his upper arm. She pressed herself closer, in the guise of needing his support, and swallowed hard as the need to get even closer urged her on.

God help her, it felt like heaven to press her breast against him, and hell when he eased her softly from him and took her elbow to guide her out the door.

"No chairs," he said, his voice a plaintive whisper. "It woulda been nice to sit on a porch with chairs, don't you think?"

"Bring out the kitchen chairs and we'll pretend," she said, releasing his arm and testing her ability to stand without him beside her. It didn't mean she wanted to, just because she could.

He put the chairs side by side, so close that their thighs had to touch. His hands rested in his lap, and she reached out boldly and joined a hand with his.

"You always hold hands when you pretend," she said. "And when you make a wish."

She tilted her head back and looked up to find the first star. There were a million blinking down at them, but she only had one wish.

"I can't make 'em come true, Samantha," he said, his thumb making circle after circle on the back of her hand.

"You could make just one come true." She held her breath, knowing he was fighting hard not to ask, knowing that she could never make her request unless he did.

She watched him close his eyes, saw him swallow

hard. He ceased the rubbing of her hand and his shoulders fell in defeat.

"Which one?"

"I want to be kissed once. Just once if that's all you want, but for real. Not some peck on the cheek to prove you're brave enough to kiss Carson Maddigan's sister. I want to know what it's all about, be part of it, even if it's just for a moment."

"No." He choked the word out. It would have been easier if she'd offered up her whole body and he'd had to say no—but to just kiss her? To taste the sweetness of those small pink lips that she was biting on furiously to hold back her tears? And to stop there? "For God's sake, Samantha. I'm just a man!"

"Isn't that what a man does?" she asked, ending her question with a sniff. "Isn't it what he wants to do, conspires to do, steals if he isn't granted permission?"

She pulled her hand from his, and he was slow to let it go. "He does that, yes," he admitted. "But he does a whole lot more. You must know some of the basics between a man and a woman. Someone must have told you. . . ."

How many times had he wished for an innocent? For a woman who could learn with him the mysteries of the heart and mind and soul that the body had hidden in the sweetest recesses? Now here he was, praying that very woman knew more about lovemaking than she could have seen in a barnyard.

"You don't mean to tell me that every time you've ever kissed a woman, you've . . . you've . . . you've . . . that!" In the darkness her eyes glistened black with unspilled tears.

"Of course not. A kiss is kind of like a ticket for a

train ride. Now, maybe you're getting off at the next stop. And maybe you're going across the whole state. More often than not, when I buy a ticket I stay on to the end of the line."

"Well, couldn't we just get off at the first stop?" Did she have to put that little hand of hers against his chest like that when she asked? Just the rhythm of his heart ought to tell her this train was moving too fast—and it hadn't even left the station.

"You wouldn't get on a train without knowing where it was going, now, would you?" he asked.

"If you were on it." Her words came out low and strangled.

He sighed. She was wearing him down. All the strength he had was no match for her soft, pliant, willing body. "I don't know that I can get off at that first stop, honey. So it's best if I don't board the train at all."

"Are you afraid of me?" She'd moved even closer to him, and he could feel her trembling from his boots to his brain. He put his arm around her to share his warmth, and nothing more. He ran his big meaty hand up and down her thin arm to rid her of her chills—not because his knuckles brushed against her breast, taking his breath away. "Are you?"

He nodded, his head against hers, breathing in the clean scent of her hair, the silken strands sticking to his lips. Without his permission, his mouth played against her temple.

"Don't be," she said, stretching until his lips were tracing her high cheekbones and her soft lashes were fluttering against his nose. "I'm scared enough for both of us."

Her honesty undid him.

He scooped her onto his lap and took her tiny head between his two big paws and tilted it to just the right angle. He teased her mouth with his breath, touched her lips, and pulled back, then came at them again and let his tongue taste the passion that had been waiting there forever for him to awaken it.

He told himself that was enough, that it was time to stop. But then her lips parted in invitation, and his tongue, so quick to say no before, betrayed him and slipped between them to delve into the warmth of her sweet mouth. And his hand, the very same hand that had held her away from him, made its way down from her cheek to caress her neck, her shoulder, and finally one small breast, which fit neatly into his palm as though the one had been made for the other.

Beneath her breast he could feel the rapid beating of her heart—a heart she was willing to give to a bastard like himself who could love her tonight and leave her tomorrow. It was even harder than he'd anticipated, pulling himself back from her mouth, sliding his hand from her breast, and then rising with her in his arms.

"I'll bring you inside," he said, and she nodded against him, her arms trying to reach around his back, her love trying to wrap around his heart. She was heavy in his arms now, a burden, and he laid her down on the cot and stood over her, while her arms reached out to him, inviting him to take what he so desperately wanted.

From somewhere deep inside his chest, words rumbled out. "You get a good night's sleep," he said, kissing his finger and placing the kiss on her forehead. "You've a big day tomorrow."

Even in the dim lamplight he could see the pain in her face, just as he had seen every other emotion she'd had from the moment he'd met her. But it was nothing compared to the pain he felt himself. She'd go on to love again, he was sure. And she'd have no regrets. Someday she'd thank him for just walking away.

"Then you're going ahead with your plan?" she asked when he picked up the lantern from the table and headed for the door. Maybe outside he'd be able to settle his breathing down and maybe, if he was lucky, get a little sleep.

"This train only goes as far as Kirkville," he said softly. "That's where you get off."

"I had hoped for a longer ride," she answered. "My own plan was to go to the end of the line."

Someday that honesty would be her undoing. Already, it was his.

He didn't bother to tell her again to get some sleep. He knew they'd both be watching the sunrise and wishing the night could last a little longer.

5

Kirkville was a hell of a town. More saw it through different eyes as he rode into the heart of town with Samantha on his lap. He'd wanted her to ride astride behind him, hoping not to have to look at her sad little face. But it required hiking her dress up to kingdom come, and he'd be damned if some other man was going to look at her ankles when he couldn't see them himself.

Instead, she sat crosswise on his thighs, where he could feel the weight of her against his manhood. He'd been honorable. All night he'd tossed and turned and cursed his honorable hide. She'd as much as offered herself to him the night before. He'd been sorry to decline the offer then, but now he knew himself for the fool he was.

Did he really think that, just because he hadn't tasted the nipples that strained through her dress toward him, he could convince himself that she wouldn't have tasted sweeter than a peach ripe for the plucking? Did he really imagine that, just because he hadn't lain down beside her in that narrow little bed, he wouldn't feel her absence beside him each and every time he lay down for however long he had left in life?

The smell of mining filled his nostrils—coal and wood fires going day and night, stench belching from the twin chimneys of the enormous mine, which crushed the ore in beds of mercury and spit tailings down the ponds.

"Kirkville isn't what I'd expected," Samantha told him, lifting her chin proudly. "But then, I hadn't expected to stop at Kirkville."

The woman just loved pouring salt in his wounds. And she did it so very well.

He grunted. There was no way to tell her that he, too, was sorry he'd brought her only as far as Kirkville, that he'd give his soul to be able to take her to the end of the line.

If only he knew where this line ended. He'd told Les that he was done with it all. This would be his last job. And he'd meant it. Before. But now, looking at it from another side, he questioned his decision.

Maybe going out in a blaze of glory would be a damn sight better than playing out his days in some godforsaken wilderness, with no better reason to go on than to see the sun rise again in the morning and the moon come up at night.

He clicked at Magic, who was sure taking his time making his way past the Bi-Metallic Mill, through the seedier side of town, on his way toward the right side of the tracks.

"Is that what I think it is?" Samantha asked him, pointing toward the Golden Palace of Pleasure.

"Yeah, it is," he said, pulling on Magic's reins so that she could look her fill. "And if you so much as walk on the sidewalk in front of it, count on your brother being the least of your worries."

"Do you suppose I'll die childless?" she asked, tracing a green stripe as it danced across her skirts.

Why didn't she just take a knife, jab it between his ribs, and twist it some? Why didn't she just take out the little derringer he'd returned to her earlier and shoot him every few inches starting with his knees? Why didn't she just put poison in those eggs and biscuits she'd served him before the sun was even flirting with the sky?

"No," he said, clicking at Magic and continuing on toward the more reputable side of town. "I think you'll wind up in that house with the lace curtains, just like I saw you."

"I already have a house with lace curtains. And it already smells of biscuits and peach tart. I want to smell bay rum and cigars"—she paused, then plunged ahead—"and diapers that need changing."

He'd have been happy to loan her either of his Colts—both, in fact—if she wanted to just finish him off quickly instead of stretching out the job.

"Well," he said, pushing her forward so that she was no longer against his chest, "I hope you find someone willing to oblige."

"I doubt anyone is brave enough."

Magic picked his way across the railroad tracks, Samantha twisting to look as far as she could see down the tracks.

"I suppose I'll never know where it goes," she

said, stiffening in his arms as she checked her buttons and puffed out her sleeves. Her elbows dug at his ribs, her words jabbed at his heart. "Guess it's time, isn't it?" she asked, looking around at the busy comings and goings in the town and making ready to get down from Magic's broad back.

"I'll take you by the telegraph office," he said. "You can wire your brother to come and get you from there. You got the money I gave you?"

She nodded. Glints of gold shot from her hair, temporarily blinding him. He closed his eyes, but saw her still.

"Remember, you're to stay at the Golden Grand Hotel, not the Silver Dollar. That's for trash like me."

He stopped Magic just outside the wire office. "You'll be careful?" she asked. "And you'll tell Les I said good-bye?"

"You be easy on that leg," he said, laying a hand on her thigh. His heart was pounding so loudly he wasn't sure she could hear him over it. "And don't you settle for less than you deserve."

"No," she agreed, letting him hand her down, then getting her footing. "I won't."

"Don't you go falling for someone like me," he couldn't resist warning her.

"Think I'd do that twice?" she asked, a bright smile dimmed by her glistening eyes.

"I never guessed you'd do it once," he said softly, a frog lodged in his throat.

Her hand rested against his leg as he looked down at her from Magic's back. "You'd better go," she said.

He'd have liked the house, the lace, the tarts. But

more than anything he'd have liked to wake up next to her in the morning and know what it was he was living for.

Since he couldn't, he nodded at her and yanked harder than necessary on Magic's reins, steering him down the street without ever looking back.

And that man actually expected her to go into the Western Union office and wire her brother to come and get her! Berris was right. A man's head was bigger than a woman's so that there'd be more room for the padding that was needed to protect so small and fragile a kernel of a brain.

Her only worry was allayed by the first person she passed on the street, who assured her there was only one bank in Kirkville and that it was two blocks up on the left. She gave the brothers two minutes, sauntering slowly up the block favoring her badly throbbing left leg, and gave them another three minutes after she had the bank in sight.

Les's gray gelding was tied out to the left of the Kirkville National Bank and Trust in the alleyway. Beyond it, Magic's black coat shone in the sun. Both horses were without their riders, and Samantha took up her position on the corner, hazarding a glance into the bank's window to make sure she wasn't too late.

A sparkle of green danced in the bank's shiny window, and she looked up to see that it was the reflection of a pretty woman who was hurrying toward the bank. Sam shifted, placing herself directly in the woman's path.

"You Velvet Joan?" Samantha asked. With the

woman's deep-chestnut hair shining in the sun, Sam had little doubt.

"Never heard of her," the woman answered, still headed for the bank, her hair so soft-looking even Samantha was tempted to touch it.

"Les told me to meet you here," she called out, and the woman stopped. Samantha once again positioned herself between Velvet Joan and the bank's massive double doors.

"I'm late," the dark beauty said. "I know. But I'm here now." She tried to get past Samantha, but Sam just sidestepped with her, blocking her once again.

"He told me to give you this," she said, pulling out the money that More had given her for the hotel, meals, and any emergency that might come up. "And tell you that the deal is off."

"Lady, you and the whole state of Montana couldn't keep me out of that bank. So move the hell out of my way and let me hear it from Les himself." Despite the words, she took the money from Sam and tucked it into the bodice of her dress.

She tried again to pass, and this time Samantha grabbed her arm, nearly tipping over as the pain shot up from her bad leg like a hot iron branding her calf. "You can't go in there," she said, locking gazes with Joan.

Eyes the color of dark emeralds stared back into hers. Full lips grimaced. More would avail himself of this woman's services and pay her well for her time, Sam was sure. He'd bury his regrets within her womanhood while Sam was left to wait for Carson to come and get her.

Velvet Joan pulled free of Sam's grasp, leaving her no choice. As discreetly as she could, Sam pulled the derringer from her pocket and pushed it against the woman's ribs. "It makes a clean little hole," she said against Joan's ear. "You could still be buried in this dress."

"Let go of me," the dancing girl shouted, causing two passersby to turn their heads in Sam's direction.

"Keep your voice down," Sam warned, trying to push her further from the bank's double doors.

This time when Velvet Joan grabbed at her, Sam yanked her hand away. Pain shot through her leg and she lost her balance. Flailing wildly for one of the posts that flanked the bank's doors, her hand came down. The little gun made a small popping sound.

In horror, she watched as the woman clutched at her arm, blood flowing between her fingers and running down her sleeve.

"You shot me!" the woman shouted just as Les opened the door and looked outside.

"We're taking the women out here," he shouted over his shoulder. "Don't come after us, I warn you, or you'll never see these women again."

"She shot me," Velvet Joan said again, pointing at Sam as More pushed through the door and stood, both guns drawn, staring at her.

"She's one of them!" someone shouted.

"She's in on it!"

"Who is she?"

"The Rivers have a woman!"

More made his way toward her slowly, as if the world were made of pea soup, and he had to wade through it to get to her. He looked at the gun in her hand and the blood seeping through Velvet Joan's sleeve and groaned.

"I think you'd better take me with you," she said,

handing him the little gun and leaning heavily against him. "I've really done it now, haven't I?"

"Take her too," More said to Les, gesturing toward Joan. "And let's get out of here."

He scooped Sam up in his arms and hurried to Magic. On the street in back of them, people had begun to hurry in the direction of the bank. One of them looked more than a little familiar, and Sam's jaw dropped at the sight.

"Put me behind you," Samantha demanded when he tried to pull her up onto Magic's back.

"Not on your life," he said, pulling on her arm and nearly yanking it out of her socket.

She crawled around his hip and he fought her, trying to settle her in his lap and ride at the same time.

"No!" she shouted over his shoulder, and flung herself beneath his arm. "Don't!" He pulled at her dress, an arm, or a leg—he wasn't even sure—and tried to force her into the shelter of his body, but she wouldn't relent. He grabbed at her while she slithered behind him like some mad bobcat bent on riding his back.

"Get in front of me or I will turn this damn horse around and head right back into town," he threatened her with as much control as he could muster.

"You can't!" she yelled back at him. "I'm an outlaw too. A murderess. I'm worse than you!"

He could feel her hands reaching around his waist, or trying to and settling for his belt loops. Remarkably, they'd somehow managed to pass the outskirts of town, and all he could do now was hope they'd put enough distance between themselves and their pursuers. He didn't dare look back.

"You didn't kill her," More corrected, watching Velvet Joan bounce wildly on Les's horse a good thirty yards in front of them. "Now get the hell in front of me!"

"I can't," she said, looping a hand around his neck. "Just go faster."

He was lost in Les's dust and hoped that anyone following him was having as much trouble seeing as he was. Still, he couldn't—wouldn't—risk a stray bullet hitting Samantha. Choking at her hold, he took Magic's reins between his teeth, and with both hands over his head he yanked her with all his might up and over him. Angrier than he could ever remember being, he slammed her into place in front of him, an arm on either side of her, the reins in one hand and growled in her ear. "Try to slip behind me again, and I'll knock you out and throw you over the damn horse's neck."

Despite his threat, he could still feel her slinking lower and lower in his arms until she ducked her head and tried to slip behind him. He jerked her back by the hair.

"Carson teach you how to ride too? We survive this, you could get a job with Wild Bill's show."

"We won't survive this if you don't let me get behind you," she insisted.

A chill raced through him despite the hot sun and the fast ride. "Oh, shit." He crossed himself and tucked his arms around her tighter. "It's him back there, isn't it?"

He felt her nod against his chest, and he kicked Magic all the harder.

"Get up there, you stupid animal!" He urged the gelding on, his heels pounding the horse's flanks until he closed the gap between himself and Les.

"She's losing a lot of blood," Les shouted to him above the furor of the horses' hooves. "We're going to have to stop."

"Let's go for height," More said. He wanted to be sure the women were safe before—well, before anything.

They aimed for the rocks, pushing the horses hard. Gray stumbled, but got his footing. Magic followed close on the first horse's heels.

And all the while it was quiet behind them. When they were hidden, Les slid down and dragged Velvet Joan with him. "Think we lost them?" he asked More.

"No." Carson Maddigan wouldn't give up. Hell, if it was More thinking that Sam was in danger—and surely that's what Carson thought—he'd ride to hell on a three-legged horse to get her back. And nothing and no one would get in the way of seeing her safe. "He'll be here. Sooner or later, but he'll be here."

Pale as the winter sky, Samantha was leaning against a rock, no doubt listening for the sound of her brother's horse. And thinking. He could tell now when she was hatching a plan, and he kicked himself for not figuring that was just what she was doing when she quietly agreed to be dropped off in Kirkville.

"I don't hear anything," she said. She shrugged, but kept her ear against the rock, listening, thinking, planning.

"So then we lost him?" Les asked, crouching next

to Velvet Joan and ripping the sleeve of her dress to get a better look at her wound. It looked to More as if the woman was getting a bit woozy, and he bent to help his brother.

Samantha came over as well, wincing at the sight of the torn flesh on Joan's arm. She might talk a good game, but there were still some departments where a woman was just a woman, or at least this one was. And he liked those parts. And surprisingly, he liked the others as well.

"Not necessarily. It means he's either alone or he's got some control over the posse," Samantha said, ripping strips from her own already torn petticoat and handing them to Les. "You never hear Carson coming. He's just there."

"I didn't know you had a girl working for you," Velvet Joan said, hurt marring what More grudgingly admitted were attractive features. "If you'da told me, Les, I'da been prepared. It was just that you said . . . you made those promises. I shoulda known, huh?"

"She ain't workin' for us," More was quick to say. If he ever got them all out of this mess, he didn't want a smear on Samantha's reputation. Not when he'd taken such pains to protect her honor. "She's a bona fide hostage. A real one."

"Oh, you can't expect her to believe that," his golden-haired girl said with a wave of her hand. "I had a gun."

"I know a lookout when I see one," Joan said, leaning back against the boulder and fighting to keep her eyes open. "I just don't get why she shot me. I ain't after her man, after all."

"Because the woman don't have the brains of—"

More started. Then he turned to her, saw that soft face smiling tentatively at him, and knew the real reason. "Your brother's taking you back, Miss Maddigan. You ain't settling for this life. It ain't happening. You understand me?"

"Well, I didn't get off the train at Kirkville, anyway, did I? Maybe you could think about taking me with you to the end of the line?"

"What train?" Les asked as he fashioned a sling out of two bandannas.

For all her brazenness, Samantha Maddigan's cheeks turned to two red apples.

"You guys taking a train?" Les had taken Velvet Joan's head into his lap and was stroking her cheek and murmuring to her that she'd be fine.

Samantha waited for More to answer. "No," he said, more to her than to his brother. "At least not together. Joannie gonna be all right?"

"Looks like," Les said. "But I figure it'll cost us a little extra." He winked at Velvet Joan.

"Double," Joannie said, and flashed a look at Samantha, who opened her mouth and then merely closed it again.

Maybe More could get Joannie to reason with the woman. Sam sure didn't seem to hear what he was saying to her.

"You're damn lucky this was an accident," Les told Sam while he rubbed Joan's good arm, every now and then making a slight detour. to her left breast. Each time he'd catch himself and return his hand to her arm as if he had no idea how it had gone astray in the first place.

"So was she," Samantha answered. "If I'd tried to

hit her, that bullet wouldn't have just grazed her arm."

They all let the comment hang in the air for a while as they listened for bullets aimed at them. All that seemed to be out there was silence.

"Are we gonna head back home?" Samantha asked More.

"It ain't home," he said to her through closed teeth. "I ain't got a home. And if I did, it wouldn't be yours. You got a home of your own, with that brother of yours." *Where you're goddamn lonely, Samantha Maddigan, but at least you're safe.*

"I see," she said softly, that voice of hers a mixture of butter and determination. "So the way you see it, Carson kills you and then I go home with him to live the same life I had before you yanked me out of it."

"That was an accident."

"So was shooting that woman," Samantha said, pointing at Joannie. "But I think I'll have to pay for it, don't you?"

"Double," Joan said. Les was surprisingly quiet and More took a half second to study him. His brother had taken it upon himself to make Joannie comfortable, rifling through his saddlebags and stuffing a spare shirt under her head. More would have laughed if it wasn't all so damn sad. He and Les had sure picked one helluva time to start softening to the idea of settling down with a good woman.

Not that he was thinking that, as he clung to the side of a mountain, leaning against a boulder for safety. If there was anything he understood it was that actions had consequences, and deeds came with price tags on them. And there was a big one on his head.

"Several people saw me shoot her," Samantha said. "I'm probably just as wanted as you."

"Well, I'll say this," More conceded. "I'm sure your brother wants you even more than he wants me." And it was likely he'd stop at nothing to get her back. More could count on Carson Maddigan to find a way to get Sam out of any difficulties arising from the shooting.

After all, Joannie was about to disappear, and without a victim there wouldn't be much of a case against a woman who would make a jury trip over itself to set her free.

"It's awfully quiet," Velvet Joan said. "Ain't it?"

"I'd say we lost 'em," Les answered. "Want to head back?"

A piece of More was wishing that Carson Maddigan would simply come around the boulder he was leaning against, claim his sister, and get it all over with. Knowing Samantha was safe would be compensation enough for what would be facing him. More couldn't count on a posse being careful enough. He shuddered at the thought and pulled Samantha against him, finally giving in to the need to feel her breath against his neck, her warmth pressed to the length of him.

"You're thinking of leaving me here," she said into his chest before the idea had even fully formed in his head. "Thinking Carson will find me and take me back."

He clutched her tighter, smelled her hair, tasted her forehead with his lips.

"Someone else could find me, More. What then?

And what if no one finds me at all? Would I starve first, or freeze to death at night? What if a cougar or a bear—"

He sighed heavily. "You can stop anytime you want. You made your point with the first question."

She snuggled against him, and when she spoke, her lips and breath did crazy things to his neck and his insides. "Face it, More. If I ever get to ride that train, you know you'll have to be there. I'm yours, and I think maybe you're glad."

Well, little by little, that honesty of hers was killing him, just the way he knew it would.

"Your brother is out there waiting to kill me. A half dozen other bounty hunters will follow him if he can't get the job done fast enough. And you want me to be glad I kidnapped you?"

She tilted her head back, shot him that smile that melted his insides, and said, "Look at it this way. Could you have better insurance? Is Carson likely to take even one wild shot? Is he going to set your cabin on fire with me in it? Is he going to—"

"Is he gonna cut off my privates and stake me out for the crows?"

"The real question," Samantha said, placing an actual kiss on his jaw and stopping his heart, "is will he listen to reason?"

6

He took the answer to be a resounding *no* as a shot rang out in the air. More grabbed at Samantha, pushed her behind him, and pulled his Colts despite the fact that there was nowhere to take aim.

"Don't be an idiot," Sam said, coming around from behind him and trying to commandeer one of his guns. "He isn't going to hurt me." He pushed her back behind him, imprisoning her between himself and the boulder. It was as safe as he could make her.

"Give it up, Rivers, or say your prayers."

"That him?" More asked her.

"Yes, but—" was all he let her get out.

"Maddigan," he shouted out. "Hold your fire."

"Carson! Don't shoot!" Samantha added. "Or he'll kill me!"

He reeled around and stared, his mouth open, his head spinning.

"What was I supposed to tell him?" she asked.

"Do you suppose he'd care if I told him about how the green of your eyes sets my heart pounding? That when you touch me, my insides go—"

"Stop it!" He didn't want to know about her insides, didn't want to know everything that might have been. Not now that all the dreams were over. His train was going straight to hell, no doubt in a matter of minutes. And hers . . . His stomach turned over at the thought of someone else taking her even so far as the very next stop.

"You all right?" Carson Maddigan's voice was as chilling as his reputation. It had a kind of echo to it that made him sound like a chorus of lawmen instead of just one lone bounty hunter.

"Carson, go away," Sam pleaded. "Please."

"Nothing to be scared of Sammy, honey." The voice rumbled over the buttes and mesas, and More detected a softness he supposed was reserved just for the woman who squirmed behind him trying to protect his body with her own. "I'm not going to let anything happen to you. Now, you and the other woman just start walking west into the sun, nice and slow."

"I can't walk," she said. "I hurt my leg. And the other lady's out cold. Just go away, Carson. Please."

More glanced over toward Les and his woman. Joannie lay motionless, Les crouching by her, his guns drawn.

"What do you mean you hurt your leg?" Maddigan's voice thundered with indignation. "You're dead, Rivers," he added. "The coyotes are tearing your flesh as we speak."

"Then they're tearing mine too," Sam said, her voice choked with tears.

"Maddigan?" The quiver in his voice embarrassed him, and More cleared his throat before continuing. In all his life he'd never let his emotions betray him, and now was not the time to start. "Give me a minute to reason with her and then I'll carry her and Joannie wherever you want them."

"I'd use that minute for my prayers," Maddigan shouted back. "It's all you got left."

Sam painted herself against him, nearly climbing him like a tree. With a sigh, he plucked her off and set her aside.

"Listen to me," More shouted. "Your sister's safe. We forced her into that robbery, and I want your word that you'll give me a chance to say my piece in court or on paper before you send me to my Maker. You gotta let me clear her, Maddigan."

"Nobody made me do anything," Sam yelled out to her brother. There was no answer. Only silence. More strained to pick up the sound of a boot compacting the earth beneath it. "I was the lookout, Carson. If you're gonna take them in, you're gonna have to take me."

The cocking of the hammer of Carson Maddigan's gun was deafening. More threw himself over Samantha, both of them eating dirt. The explosion was louder still.

Les cried out and grabbed at his leg, blood spurting from the fresh wound and soaking his pants leg before More could crawl to him, dragging Sam along beneath him.

"Oh, jeez." The words whistled through his lips as he pressed his hand against the steady flow of blood. This was how a bank robber met his end. This was how a man who flaunted the law, no matter what his cause, left this world. He looked at Sam, her face a mess of dirt and tears, her hands busy trying to rip off still more of her already shredded petticoats.

"Get the hell away from us," More shouted at her, steeling himself against the trembling of her lip. Better to hurt her with words than to even let himself imagine that the blood staining her dress was her own. "You and your stinking brother will pay for what you've done."

He left the Colt where she could reach it. If she could find the nerve to pull the trigger, so be it. And he set to tending his brother while Carson Maddigan, he had no doubt, moved in closer.

He knew her every move, even with his back turned to her. Knew when she reached out for the gun, knew when she scooted back away from him. Knew, too, when she took her stance and aimed. Knew, though his eyes were closed and his lips were offering a silent prayer, that she would be able to go on with her life. That she would bake those tarts and change the diapers of a dozen children.

"Is it as bad as it feels?" Les asked him.

More swallowed the bile that rose in his throat and tied his bandanna tight around his brother's thigh. "Flesh wound," he lied. What difference did it make, after all? A few more minutes and the Rivers Brothers would be the legend that Les always wanted them to be.

"Don't move a muscle," the deep voice warned, and for the second time More heard the cocking of Carson Maddigan's gun. This time it wasn't more than ten feet away.

He raised his hands slowly, keeping his movements slow and in plain sight. He hoped to God that Samantha's eyes were closed. She would be long enough putting the memory behind her. "For the love of God," he said quietly. "Shoot!"

There was no bright white light as he expected. No chorus of angels or cackling of the devil. Nothing accompanied the sound of the shot but a small, short gasp, which he prayed wasn't his.

Epilogue

THE MONTANA SENTINEL
JULY 14, 1892
extra

It was with a mixture of sadness and relief that the $1,000 reward for the killing of Moreland and Lesley Rivers was claimed today. The Rivers Brothers robbed a total of six banks, each of which carried accounts for the Columbia Mining Company. During the course of each robbery the Rivers Brothers always took a woman hostage, but the boys made a fatal mistake in Granite when they took off with Miss Samantha Maddigan, sister of the renowned bounty hunter Carson Maddigan.

Maddigan tracked the pair, who

still had his sister and another female hostage in tow, to Cathedral
Pass in the Bitterroot Mountains.
There, according to Maddigan, the
Rivers Brothers begged for their
lives, crawling on the ground like
cowards and at one point even hiding behind the women.

Below is the picture of the dead
Rivers Brothers that was offered as
proof, along with their boots, hats,
and holsters, for the reward. Sadly,
both women were caught in the
melee and killed by the cowards,
though one wonders what kind of
life they could have lived after suf-
fering through such an ordeal.

Services . . .

"Crawled on their bellies?" More snorted, throwing the newspaper from the bed in which he and
Samantha were snuggling. "He could have said we
were brave and dedicated until the end."

Samantha played with the hairs on her new husband's chest and agreed. "He should have said you
threw yourself in front of me and begged him to kill
you."

"I would have too," More said with his bottom
lip sticking out far enough to fry eggs on. "If you
hadn't done it first."

"Well, it was easier for me," she said, running her
finger against the warm, moist inside of that petulant
bottom lip. "I knew he'd never shoot me. You could
hardly expect the same."

"I don't know why you were so sure. Not after you'd just missed his head by an inch."

Samantha giggled. "He sure was mad about that hat!"

"He wasn't exactly happy when you told him you were in love with me either." More lifted her onto his chest, every inch of her nakedness against his.

"You didn't look so happy yourself," she said softly. In fact, he'd looked as if he'd have preferred a bullet from Carson's gun to her confession. "Are you sorry he let us go?"

More's eyebrows arched at her question, and she realized how stupid it was. Les was alive and mending nicely, his blood loss having served them well when it came time to prove them dead. Just a few pictures taken with Carson's new box camera and their old lives were laid to rest.

"I mean, are you sorry about him making you marry me?" She studied his chest, making little circles with her finger, knowing she was tantalizing him with the view of her breasts as she raised herself slightly against him. It was Berris's opinion that a wife couldn't be a hussy, but Sam feared she might be crossing the line.

His Adam's apple bobbed wildly before he spoke. "I wanted better for you," he finally said.

He'd offered his life for hers every moment they'd been together. He'd sheltered her with his body, honored her innocence with his restraint.

"I wanted a man who could give you his own name, not something that was made up so that no one would know who you were really marrying."

"I married the man, not the name," she said,

squirming up his body until her lips were a hair-breadth from his.

He wasn't sorry to have given up his name. Not that he much liked his new last name—*Carson*. His new brother-in-law had said he wanted to be sure that More would never forget who'd be looking over his shoulder for the rest of his life, making sure that Samantha got everything she was entitled to.

How she'd ever talked her brother into letting him and Les go was one of life's mysteries, right up there along with whatever it was that a beautiful, educated, fine woman like Sam could see in a big dumb ox like him. Carson Maddigan had claimed that seeing them fight over who would take the first bullet convinced him that they had half a chance at making a go of it.

More supposed Maddigan didn't have too many choices. If he'd brought Sam back, everyone would suppose . . . He grimaced. He didn't want to think about what people would have thought of his precious Sam. He especially didn't want to think about her having gone back to Granite without him. He didn't want to think about her separate from him at all.

In fact, he didn't want to think about anything. Not when there was a naked woman with her thigh quivering against his privates. And not when that woman was Samantha.

And not when, if he just shifted slightly, he might be able to convince her to let him take his love home. Again.

He shifted.

She raised herself against him and gave him access to all he could ever want.

Later—after—in the great darkness that fell over their new Canadian wilderness, when the cool winds began to blow over their damp bodies and he pulled the covers up over his love, she whispered something he couldn't quite hear.

"Hmm?" he asked, putting his ear close to her warm mouth. "What?"

"Guess I got to go to the end of the line after all," she murmured, stretching above him like a she-cat that caught her prey.

His laughter filled the cabin, echoed off the walls and out into the valley. It competed with the distant sound of a train whistle, which made them both smile in the darkness and remember what it was they were about.

"All aboard!" he called loudly, his breath sending her hair flying around them. "Watch your step there, madam. This train's going clear around the world!"

"Oh," she said coyly. "My husband has my ticket. He's taking me clear to the end of the line."

And then, just as the last strains of the train whistle faded away, he rolled over, tucking his wife beneath him, and headed for home.

Did You Find
HEAVEN
WITH A GUN
Heavenly?

Read all of Connie Brockway's
other breathtaking
novels.

AS YOU DESIRE

Desdemona Carlisle has loved the dashing Harry Braxton since the day their
eyes first met. But Harry acts as if they are the best of friends, and nothing more.
When Desdemona is kidnapped by a desert gang looking for a fortune in
ransom, Harry comes to her rescue on horseback—saving Desdemona's life
and bringing new sparks to their friendship . . .

A DANGEROUS MAN

The beautiful, red-haired American had seen the distant, sophisticated aristocrat
Hart Moreland before. Mercy Coltrane remembered him from his Texas gunsling-
ing days, and had traveled all the way to England to find him. He was a
dangerous man, the kind who could help her find her missing brother . . . and
pull her into his arms to unleash sudden, blinding desire.

```
___ 22199-4   AS YOU DESIRE          $5.99
___ 22198-6   A DANGEROUS MAN        $5.99
```

Available wherever books are sold or use this handy page for ordering:

DELL READERS SERVICE, DEPT. DCB
2451 South Wolf Road, Des Plaines, IL. 60018
Please send me the above title(s). I am enclosing $_____.
(Please add $2.50 per order to cover shipping and handling).
Send check or money order - no cash or C.O.D.s please.

Ms./Mrs./Mr._____

Address_____

City/State_____ Zip_____

Prices and availability subject to change without notice.
Please allow four to six weeks for delivery.   DCB-5/97